FOR THE LOVE OF MY NAME

AUTHOR'S NOTE

This novel is based on the voices of the victims of tyranny, as well as those of its silent supporters, observers and bystanders. I wish to acknowledge the debt I owe to the many who recalled their past to me. In the circumstances I have withheld their names. Many have since died. I would also like to thank Neal Ascherson for allowing the young Pottaro to narrate an incident he described in his article 'Greater privilege hath no man...' (*The Observer*, 21.6.87). Selected extracts from the Memorial of the Notables are drawn from the actual petition they made to the Secretary of State as well as the correspondence in 1903 between the Secretary of State and the Governor of the colony of British Guiana. Other correspondence in the latter half of the nineteenth century to the Governor of that colony also contributed to the writing of the 'extracts' as they appear in this book. I wish to acknowledge Fritz Stern's essay: 'Freedom and Its Discontents' (Foriegn Affairs, Sept/Oct. 1993) for the term *Lebenslüge* and all that it carries.

FOR THE LOVE OF MY NAME

LAKSHMI PERSAUD

PEEPAL TREE

First published in Great Britain in 2000
Peepal Tree Press Ltd
17 King's Avenue
Leeds LS6 1QS
England

ISBN 1 900715 42 2

A field
After battle utters its own sound
Which is like nothing on earth, but is earth.

from 'Funeral Music' by Geoffrey Hill

Somewhere in the heaven
Of lost futures
The lives we might have led

from 'Leaves' by Derek Mahon

In memory of those who died

For Vishnu

And all the children of Maya

PART ONE: THE MASK

1   THE LIBRARY OF MYSTERIES

I stood before the colossal door embossed like a shield. Her words reverberated in my head:

"The wearer becomes the mask."

Brilliant crotons, growing with martial uprightness – custodians to *The Library of Mysteries* – had absorbed the vibrant hues of a younger sun. The pebbled steps curved like a taut bow. There was neither bell nor knocker. I pushed – nothing.

The voice that sent me to this ancient door returned: "You're sure to find something on masks in *The Library of Mysteries*," Dr Ann Ward had said. "It's on Independence Square." She had grown old graciously, this scholar of Greek literature and of the ancient world, her eyes warm, quizzical, ever questioning. The clarity of her thoughts, the simplicity of her manner, had long held a deep attraction for me. I was embarrassed to say I had not heard of the Library of Mysteries. So I turned my attention to what was disturbing me. *"Purple masks bonded to the human skin.* How strange, Dr Ward!"

"Masks," she replied smiling, "are as you well know – disguises, covers, cloaks, a form of concealment."

What manner of mask? A concealment of what could have resulted in this bonding with human flesh? Why had Mayans worn such masks? These questions were troubling. But what further alerted me was the way Dr Ward bypassed my curiosity.

It was not her way.

"A concealment of the psyche – the wearer's," she continued, "but in this instance – the psychic fear of the entire community and that is deadly." Her voice dropped. "Its energy – bottomless. Grotesque masks caught by fishermen, entangled in their nets, that much is known."

"Grotesque? Did the salt water distort them?"

The curvature of her beady eyes, focusing on something in the distant past, intensified. "Civilisation and Barbarism are Siamese twins," she whispered, as in a reverie. "Twins – bound together. A time comes when the one leads the other."

A changed expression came to her face and a silence. It seemed to direct her thoughts to some hidden profundity.

She was a fine tutor of Greek literature, and I was happy to have met her again by chance, in that quaint coffee shop in this ancient metropolis. "More likely than not it was the wearer's unbridled passion... primeval... a feeling unrestrained, kept within the gut," she said, "rose like sweat, imprinting itself upon the mask, adhering to it. Purple masks were swallowed up, whipped into the ocean's gigantic stomach by its mighty waving tongues. This much we know." Her cup was now empty. "A cool resting place... Fitting." She had spoken softly, and on regaining a conscious presence said, "Fitting don't you think, that this be returned to the primeval ooze?"

"The sea walls collapsed, Dr Ward," I reminded her, "and the island submerged."

On taking her coat, she said, "Try that number." Then turning around, as if pivoted, her eyes alight, I heard her say, *"The wearer becomes the mask... It is inevitable... the mask is chosen by the wearer. With time wearer and mask are one."*

And here I was before this iron gateway, when quite by chance a gust of wind that would have toppled prams and trolleys and carts forced me to hold on to a projecting knob.

I found myself in a clinically clean room; an arrow pointing to a polished desk. The space was neat, cool; it had an enquiring hush as in an archive of rare documents, an unfrequented enclosure. I began to search above and around the many closed cabinets for the service button.

On the desk of rosewood were documents and reports, Royal Commissions and other Commissions of Enquiry, audio and video tapes, official letters, personal letters – their broken envelopes resealed, diaries, paper cuttings in files, photographs and photocopies of documents.

Standing upright, encased in glass, was a grand purple mask, intricately designed, a mix of time past and a time to come. I marvelled at its construction – simple, sophisticated, awesome. I must have been staring at it too intensely, for I began to feel light and distinctly dizzy. I moved away, walked behind it. Seeing its open vacuous form like an ocean's shell, I regained my composure. Was something there alive? A captured time? A loss? Another's eye? Had I absorbed something?

To the left of this collection was the Mayan exhibit room. Costumes once worn by pepper reapers and their supervisors were displayed in secure glass cases. A photograph of a white mare – 'Abundance' – hung on the wall, beside it a grand purple mask, not unlike the one I had just seen – worn by the privileged few, according to the caption.

To the right of the mask were two poems, carefully mounted.

POEMS OF REMEMBRANCE

Falling Leaves

Falling leaves
Rain
Running streams
Crumbling earth
Tumbling rocks
Cover the pogrom's cries
Cover the pogrom.
Begrudge me not this song
For when my voice leaves,
this truth
will fall
as petals to the wind
Beyond recall.

Three Mounds of Earth

She sits besides three mounds of earth
Her husband, daughter, son.

A stately carriage halts,
The horses stand.
He coughs:
Forget the past, the pain of yesteryear.
This she cannot hear.

Through films of falling dew
Her husband, daughter, son, she sees.
From cushioned carriage high,
Again he coughs –
I say hello,
Hello I say
Begin anew
Reconciliation I prescribe for you.

Good morning, Sir,
Your carriage like your voice is grand.
My embraces are all these mounds of earth
have had.
And when my memory goes its way
alas, too soon it will,
These truths will Justice Shade
not know.
So, grudge them not
these mounds of earth,
My shadow's shade.
Nor me –
Life's breath,
Life's light,
Lives three.

Rena

From where I stood I could see through a partially parted
curtain. I thought I saw a dike or a sea wall. It could have been an
embankment, a rampart. I wanted to know. Beside it, a yellow poui
in full bloom – shards of dawn caught on branches. Drawn to it, I

thought of micro-climates, of how a tropical flowering shrub could be here on a Mediterranean hilltop, when from behind, a firm, tutored voice held me: "What may I do for you, Madam?"

I explained.

"The purple masks? We were lucky, Madam. One of our scholars from our Open University made a fine film about these masks and the consequences of a 'Culture of Masks'. She recorded voices, even the President's and his sister's, Miss Marguerite Devonish, who was of invaluable help to our researcher. Very well spoken I believe they both were. Like twins in some ways... yet so unlike in others. The report tells of desolation – rice fields left abandoned. There was a public lecture on these masks. The rapid debasement of the island was one of the consequences of the culture of masks. Yet you must decide for yourself, Madam. Did you know that it was Mr Robert Augustus Devonish, the President of Maya himself, who created the purple mask, and as far as I can make out, whose artfulness led to its demise? A circle completed."

He handed me a programme.

"This way, Madam."

He stopped. "The island seemed to have lost its grip, Madam, and sank." He lowered his voice and faced me. "We were fortunate, our researcher was amongst the last to leave. I distinctly recall her saying that one Maude Cummings, a nurse who lived on the island, had said to her that its submergence would come to pass and with it the fulfilment of a prophesy – *Revelation*, chapter sixteen, verse twenty." I was puzzled. "Do not trouble yourself, Madam, what the visitor wishes is part of the service we provide. *And every island fled away and the mountains were not found.*"

He lifted his eyebrows. As we approached the door, I wanted to verify what I had heard. "Not found?" I said. "You mean no more?"

"Yes, Madam. The island of Maya is no more. Whether it will one day rise again to the surface I am unable to say. I take my leave."

I found myself in a small lecture theatre and opened the programme – *The Purple Masked Mayans*:

There are religious, mystic, tectonic and economic explanations as to why the island of Maya sank. And though I was there and did feel a pending catastrophe, I offer a rational reason and leave viewers to make up their own minds:

The sea walls were collapsing; drains had silted, rising level with the roads. After days of torrential rain the inland dams containing the waters from the interior highlands were severely damaged in places. Skilled men had long emigrated. Makeshift earthen dams softened and gave way, unable to cope with the renewed energies of an awe-inspiring Spring tide.

The reclaimed, rich, coastal plain of alluvium, abandoned by the flight of farmers, was swamped. Then the rapidly rising water covered the settlements, the once intensively cultivated vegetable plots, the rice lands and the sugar-cane lands. Soon houses were beneath the stagnant stillness. Men and beasts were drowned. Those in the hinterland hadn't a chance. Screaming, fleeing winged birds sought refuge in the open sky.

There was no Noah's ark.

The surrounding ocean opened its gigantic mouth and from reports given by passing aircraft, within six hours the island of Maya was swallowed. Of its last moments this much is known: A passing fisherman with a priest on board picked up a solitary figure standing on the only remaining part of the sea wall which, for reasons no one can explain, had broken off and miraculously drifted from the island, kept afloat by a school of dolphins, in the main shipping lanes.

When interviewed on the island of Santa Maria, the priest recalled, 'The ocean's gurgle was uncanny, yet it was unable to drown a loud, prolonged agony, a disturbed presence coming from the land as it sank. We are here by the grace of God and give thanks.'

At the back of the programme I read:

Maya was one of a group of islands forming an archipelago. In the fifteenth and sixteenth centuries, this crescent shaped group was called the Maritime Region by sailors and adventurers. Today the islands are collectively referred to, as 'the Region'. Politically they are held together in a loose confederation, supporting each other against outside interference. Their island economies are broadly similar, and so from time to time, the Region's political economists, philosophers and intellectuals, referred collectively as Assorted University Luminaries (AUL), come together as a Maritime Regional Community to consider their common interests.

I folded the programme. The soft overhead light lowered; dusk entered. On the screen, moving images came and went. I saw and heard lost Mayan voices – chords of varying pitch, each recalling a truth of life within the 'Culture of Purple Masks'. These various voices were Maya's last songs.

Coming from some faraway place were incoherent voices, locked together; the choking utterances of two young girls. I strained, bending forward to catch the sound of the tormented. Two children, as if in a container closing in upon them, unable to lift their hands to stay it. I strained again to listen. Thankfully it ceased... Yet, to this day, I carry these cries within me.

On the island, the wind raged, the ocean's waves rose and fell as if there was no land, and there came another voice – clear, musical, sadly moving, telling of the coming and going of humanity as if it were but one wave of life's ocean. Then came yet another – with snippets of unaccompanied song: *Where are the clowns, ... there ought to be clowns... well... maybe next year.*

2 HOPE BRIDGE

A heavy mist clings to the land. Four o'clock. Dawn is far. Through the broken shutters Kamelia's lips move.

"It is dark, so dark."

"You hardly eat," her mother says, covering the plate.

"I'm worried, Ma. Even now men are leaving Bon Aire to break the strike."

"From Town? Town people travelling miles, crossing the river to sweat in mud, do hard donkey work?"

"They come to break the strike, Ma, not to work for long."

"The management from the estate hired them, na?... Ahhhhh... Working people against working people. What to do."

"The estate doesn't want to recognise us – the new union. They prefer the old union – empty men, hollow like calabash. But we can't go on like that, Ma."

"They surrounding you, Kamelia. From all sides they coming. Look how they circling you – banding together, coming down from Bon Aire, na? Scabs from over there. The estate managers over here. You're like Abhimanyu on the battlefield, Kamelia... Do not go. Let me take your place. Don't go, Kamelia. Stay home today with the children."

The old lady seeks reassurance that the carriers of just causes and the disadvantaged can win wars. She unties the clean, bright orange cotton cloth that protects the sacred text and reads to her daughter in Hindi one of her many well-loved passages from the *Mahabharata*:

"Then throwing away all sense of shame and chivalry, a large number of veteran warriors spurred on by their past glories and the need for a conquest that day, made a combined and simultaneous attack on the young Abhimanyu – inexperienced, untried in battle.

But even as on all sides a rock receives the rising tide of the sea, Arjuna's son withstood this united onslaught."

Tears came, but the end of her ornhi suppressed them.

Kamelia closed the text and replaced it on the shelf. "Look at our condition, Ma. Today we must show courage. We work hard and yet nothing. Look. Nothing. And nothing more to come. How long, Ma? How long like this?"

In his official residence, the Prime Minister of Maya, Robert Augustus Devonish, paces, his thoughts flowing with the rhythm of his stride: "Those Country Mayans, descendants from another continent, still loyal to other shores, are merely agricultural workers. They have been in our way too long. Even as early as the turn of the century, our forefathers, the Notables, understood this. They perceived a Maya without them and tried to bring this about. The Region's intellectuals too, our Assorted University Luminaries have long shared these ambitions in private."

The path to independence from colonial rule, the path to becoming the first Prime Minister of an independent Maya had been cleared for Robert Augustus Devonish by two powerful wealthy democracies, so that he might rule the island of Maya for as long as he pleased. They understood him and his leaping ambition. "A rascal, a racist, and more," they said amongst themselves. Why then did they enable him to capture power in a society of diverse men, who covered their heads in varying ways depending upon the routes they took on their long journeys to Maya? But all this in good time.

Meanwhile Country Mayans journey to Hope Bridge in support of the strike.

Everyone knows, and this is why Kamelia's mother is sick with worry, that the strike is not merely about an old unrepresentative union that had supped with the bosses, not wanting to give way to a new union more representative of the workers. It is also about two struggles for dignity and power: the later arrivals offering their labour to make a living, hoping to improve the lives of their children; the earlier arrivals wishing to keep the power they have gained and add to it so that they, and they alone, decide for all times who are the 'Chiefs' and who the 'Indians'.

Time passes and something has happened. It may be an excess of electrical charges in the atmosphere, or it may be pulses of anxiety from somewhere. The workers of Hope sugar estate have become wary, their apprehension growing as they gather and sit around Hope Bridge, the main entrance to the estate. Their thoughts scan the starkness of what is before them, perceiving ever more clearly the incredible alliance they face.

Devonish's new socialist government and the estate managers and owners are at one on the need to defeat the strike. This, the workers understand, explains the obduracy of management, and its unwillingness to recognise the new union.

Robert Augustus Devonish would like to outlaw strikes. The shadow of the strike he organised to destroy the last government, the government of Emmanuel Pottaro, walks with him.

He is only too aware that to nip in the bud this first strike of Country Mayans, who form the main opposition, will send an important message to all, including his own supporters. He is a master planner, shrewd, astute. "Only a fool loses power," he says and means it.

He chuckles to himself. Successful strategies have greatly increased his confidence, Prime Ministerial power has steadily enlarged his stature. Fear, cunning, and craft. These will see him through, for they are foolproof. Smacking his lips, savouring his thoughts, his compositions subscribe to a formula: "Comrades…" He stands before the mirror. Effortlessly, his thoughts find his voice, "We are all in this together. This is *your* elected Government. Today, for the first time, government and governed are one. This historical milestone you have created, do not dismantle it. Think what you will be allowing to come to pass if we don't keep together. The enemy is within. When things get rough, as they will, for there is much to do, we must hold together. For better or worse, we are one. You, our people, are in power." He stops. It is easy to rouse a people when their grievances are large. He has reawakened past hurts that were fading, were losing their resonance. He knows that much progress has been made in their lives, since the days the Notables sent a masterly Memorial to the Secretary of State for the Colonies.

But it is in fierce anger, hurt and dissatisfaction that the flames of energy burn. This he well understands.

The cadences of his voice flow naturally. He is a man for the stage. And what better stage is there? Maya? The Third World? The United Nations?

On that celebratory night of Independence, he reminded his supporters of what they and their forebears had suffered under colonialism – the relentless discrimination, perpetual servitude.

"Massa day done." His voice zoomed. They were enthused. Many danced. From others tears flowed, a release that a saviour was here, a prophet had come. Standing before them was one of their very own – half saviour, half man. Freedom at last! Praise God! Independence! To be in charge of the growth, and direction of oneself. Thank God! The day had come. That historic day was here at last. Give praise! Give thanks!

Again he reminded them of what had been endured under Imperialism; again they relived the pain, the inner anguish of the powerless. "Our forefathers have known the whiplash, our foremothers aborted under the kicks of the estate overseer. We were always alone. But no more. Whatsoever was done to one of us, was done to us all. We are brothers one and all – inseparable. You are with me and I with you."

He moves from the mirror and contemplates. This strike is a godsend. It will send the message that the first Government of Independent Maya intends to be tough and strong. Economically weak countries need strong governments to move swiftly, to put the engines of production in place. There can be no room for a destructive opposition – an indulgence. No room on the rostrum of government for division. He will not tolerate interruptions in the production of goods or services. He will not have strikes.

What an opportunity now presents itself at his door, to use the opposition as a scapegoat, to get across a valuable first lesson to the working man, who must be bridled to do his bidding. They must all see that he holds the reins of power and will use them.

Kamelia sees her poverty in the tattered curtains, her clothes washed out of colour and texture, daily beaten and rubbed away from the threads of things. She sees the broken sandals, chipped

enamel cups and aluminium pots, old and twisted as worn,
labouring hands. Her knees fold as she breaks down before her
mother, who wipes her tears, embraces her. Their shared silences
comfort. Her pain lifts.

"I manning Hope Bridge – the main entrance to the fields. Is
our only hope. I can't let you go there, Ma. It go be too rough.
I can't let you go. The strike breakers go make the six o'clock
ferry crossing and get to Hope Estate by half past seven, but I
will be on that bridge by six. We making a formation before the
gate. This is our last stand."

"The pumpkin, have a little more, Kamelia; it sweet. The
morning mist hanging still. The air too damp. The wind growing
worse. Have a little more, Kamelia. Good quality pumpkin. The
paratha rotie hot."

"It good, Ma. I like it. Why you think everybody wants you in
their kitchen whenever they have a katha or puja? You are the best
cook in these parts." Her mother is silent. Kamelia's compliments
cannot ease the pain within her. She knows it is her daughter's way
of coping with her own fear and pain, searching for a place of
comfort for them both to rest.

"Take my big shawl. Let me wrap you. It was your aggie's, you
know. The night so cold. The dew so heavy. All night you hear it
fall on the old tin roof, travelling... travelling to end... Go kiss
Rupa and Leila."

"They sleeping, Ma."

"Never mind. Is nice to be kissed when you're sleeping,
Kamelia. It keeps you company till you get up."

When Kamelia returns from the bedroom, she finds her
mother in tears. "I wish you didn't have to go, Kamelia. My
stomach paining me so bad. Not a good sign. Not a good sign
at all, at all. Don't go, Kamelia. Not today. Let me go today."

"I won't be alone like Abhimanyu. It have seven women
manning Hope Bridge. This is war, Ma. How can I send you?
I am your daughter. I must stand before you in war."

"Don't be in the front, right up to the front when the scabs from
town come . Think of the children. I am old, Kamelia. Think of your
children. At a time like this, if Ramesh was here. He would know
where to stand, where to let you stand."

"I don't feel hungry, Ma. But when I come back I will make up for this. Don't cry. Look at it this way. We sugar workers are at the bottom of the pile. How to climb out like ants. This we have to do. Soon Rupa and Leila will need schools. And when you hear people from overseas talk, you know life here is poverty – no water, no electricity, no good schools. No roads. Nothing here, Ma."

"No hospitals. Everything in town. Here we have malaria and that sickness – gastro-enteritis. Everyday we put small coffins in the earth and we cover them with our own short lives. Even when mothers boil the water, is not enough. Their babies wouldn't stay... Take your lunch."

"Bless me, Ma. I ready to go."

The old lady places both her hands on her daughter's bowed head: "May God never leave your side. I bless you and ask His blessings to sit with you before the gate. Take care, my daughter, take care. God be with you and keep you."

The parting is silent.

Two corbeaux slowly circle the early morning sky. As the sun steadily rises the numbers of scavenger birds increase. Groups of sugar workers approach the estate. Their numbers are growing with the rising sun. Today they are not entering the sugar-cane fields, their slender swinging arms swiftly slicing the sweet stems. Today they are not all backs bending – grasshoppers cutting, cutting, hidden by the tall stems – heads pivoted, arms and legs in motion. Today they are upright. Men and women seeking wages more akin to the value of their tasks. It is a simple way and all they have – the withdrawal of their energies – like a power cut. They know they must stay together, or their weave will unravel.

Over the bridge, the corbeaux continue to hover; not yet descending. They sense their time will come.

On her way to Hope Bridge, Kamelia's feet have taken wings. "By six I will be there. If only Ramesh was here. O God that morning... why didn't I stop him? Why didn't I say, Don't go....? I knew when it happened. A sudden darkness. A slipping and sliding down, down, down. Stillness. I was struggling to breathe, to see. A good husband, a father who play and laugh with his children, who know how to care even with empty hands. He was trying so hard, all his short life, to manage. He had health and willingness and skill, and yet this place offered him nothing. Only twenty-eight years he lived... Nothing. How to get out with the children. I must. I must. But how? How to get out? That morning Ramesh told me the drainage on Dhanraj land was bad. Not ready for ploughing. The land not maintained, and the best time for planting just passed. He said all that. But there was Dhanraj pleading with him, flattering him. Ahhhh, the risks poor men will grasp. And for what? When you come back to the empty house after the cremation, you see what your husband turned into ashes for. You die. Each night you die over and over again. Is this life? O God is this life? They found him pressed down in the soft mud – the tractor like an upside down beetle on top of him. The mud too soft, the tractor slipped, just as he said it would, just as I felt it. Dhanraj say, "Only you can manage it, Ramesh. You the best.".... He was so healthy, so good with the tractor... His skin glowed like an East Indian mango. It was worth living just to be covered by him... Dhanraj told me he couldn't believe when he heard. I was waiting for him to say he shouldn't have asked. I waited. The best ploughman in this polder, he sent to his grave, ploughing his land. Ma says Dhanraj was ashamed. What use is that to me? To Rupa? To Leila ?"

Even now her throat is on fire. She opens her mouth to protect her throat.

"I waited and waited, but he said nothing. Never... I expect too much, the villagers say. Expect less and keep whole. Will knowing the truth burden us? Will it prevent us from running? From keeping whole? Keep all in our stomachs? A silence that kills justice? And if we open our mouths? Be condemned for that? Is this life – to carry a light pack to live? So light that we forget ourselves, become nothing, float away without a sound? Is this life – to endure as the mud the bullock tramples on? NO! NO! If it is so, I hope the sea will mine the sea-wall and swallow us."

Meanwhile at Hope Bridge the crowd is growing. The formation is being put together on the bridge, their rampart against the strike breakers from Bon Aire. The women will stand on the bridge, the men at the gates to the fields, the sugar-cane factory, the administration – the nerve centre of the estate.

"Those scabs will be violent. They'll bring the police and them fellas from the army. That position before the bridge is for men."

"We can't have women facing those thugs."

"Where is Kamelia?"

"She coming from the deep polder. A good two hour walk in the dry season, but when it rains, even mules can't make it."

"I say let the men man the bridge."

"If they break us today, we finish for good."

"We might as well be dead."

"Kamelia hear of railway workers in India who lie down on the railway track to prevent the train driver from moving."

"You mean on the track self?"

"Where else? So the driver can't move."

"Well how can he?"

"That is what I mean. How can he move?"

"So we put ourselves on the line then?"

"What else we have?"

"What else to put?"

"We women must stay right on the front line. Kamelia say so yesterday. That is the formation."

"They will find it harder to crush the women."

"Where is Kamelia?"

"Is not like she to be late."

"I wonder what could be wrong?"

"She's never late."

"I think something, something is wrong. I feel it. I didn't want to say. But something is not right today."

"I'm going to say this now. I'm not happy at all with women on the front line. That is wrong. Remember Ica?"

"Remember Ica? What they did to the women there? If you were there, you would never forget."

"The Prime Minister have them Bon Aire people in the palm of his hand."

"He didn't even have to call them; they jumping up to get a place there."

"He knows we wouldn't. So he will use another tactic with us."

"Listen! Listen! The tassa drums. Dem fellas warning us."

"The scabs just crossed with the ferry. They have landed."

"Where is Kamelia? Oh my God, she going to be late."

Kamelia's stomach hurts, a darkness, a dizziness envelops her. She falls. Coming to, she sees her left foot has slipped into a hole. Her ankle is badly twisted and swelling rapidly. It is too painful to move. She is a few yards from the road junction. If she drags herself there she can see the end of the road. Carts and trucks are passing, but fields of tall sugar-cane bar her from being seen.

The swelling and the pain increase. Her ankle is badly swollen and the foot has become very hot. With her cloth bag round her neck she creeps on all fours towards the junction. Her knees and her palms are cut by the newly strewn quartz and sandstone. With the help of a piece of bamboo, she stands at the junction. After a while, a Morris Oxford approaches. She hails it and finds it is Vasu Nath on his way to Hope Bridge.

At the bridge the large crowd silently waits. Vasu Nath is an independent member of parliament. He absorbs the vulnerability of this gathering, their restraint, their quiet dignity. The justice of their cause holds them together. A quiet contemplation rests here. There is little to say. For too long they suffered the lowest wages, their heads bowed to the land. Too long a bending. What is there to say? Cultivators all. Not warriors.

Sensing the ankle may be broken, Vasu Nath takes Kamelia as close to the bridge as he can and asks her to wait. Two women run to the car. "My God! Look at your foot. You cannot sit here with us."

"What about the Estate clinic? Take her there. This is an emergency!" a woman cries.

"Only one ankle twisted," Kamelia says smiling, despite the throbbing pain. "We must not knock at their door. It will weaken us. One thing at a time. The scabs from Bon Aire will be here any minute now. It will ease once I rest it." The women listen, but nevertheless they begin moving her away from the bridge.

"To the bridge, the bridge, to the bridge," she cries so fiercely that they do her bidding.

As Vasu parks his car, he is thinking that this is a test case of the Government's attitude to agriculture. Will they be encouraged by this Government to give themselves to the land, to let cultivation prosper and so keep the cost of fresh foods within the reach of all?

Vasu has come for he wants to see for himself, get the feel, the sense of the thinking, the mood of the Government towards these workers. The men acknowledge his presence with the time-old salutation – hands together in prayer, heads bowed to honour. He returns the greeting with the grace of a peacemaker.

The drums again. They stir the air. This time there is a powerful vibrancy in the beat. The drummers are anxious. The temperature is rising even in the shade.

"Listen," the women cry, "they have only a mile to go. Everybody back into line. Let us have a good formation." Kamelia asks to be placed in the centre of the women's front line and declares her wish to speak:

"Fellow workers," she cries, straining her voice, "mothers, fathers, sisters, brothers – time has come and now we are making a stand for our children's future. So do not have a heavy heart. Let your spirit rise, for it is a day to be proud, a day to feel close to those too young to understand. Whatever the outcome, do not cry. I tell you, our spirits will roam this land and will not rest until justice comes. But let me say now, if we are denied this, you will see our shadows near trees and riverbanks for we will not desert you. We will always be with you. And this, remember. If today we are brought low, it will be the beginning of the end for all those responsible. They will move and not know they're moving towards their end. They will sing and dance all the way, not understand where their feet are going. Their eyes will not see, for their eyes will show them whatever they wish to carry in their heads. This, my fellow workers, I promise you."

Another stands up and speaks: "Look, the scabs coming round the fields, they will soon be here, but we must not answer back, even under provocation. Think why we are here. Brothers and sisters, let we keep it cool. Let those who have to speak, speak bravely. Remember, no answering back. No insults. Keep our sights high."

Coming straight towards them at full speed are four lorries – two of urban workers and two of armed soldiers who lift their rifles high over the unarmed gathering. They are led by a BMW carrying three high-ranking police officers. All stop abruptly beside the bridge. Neither the soldiers nor the scabs dismount. They remain standing, awaiting orders. The vehicles form a military column parallel to the bridge.

The superintendent and his two senior officers slam the car doors and stride briskly in new boots to the gates at the end of the bridge. They are armed. The superintendent addresses the women sitting across the gate: "You women, listen to me carefully. We are here to do a job and we're going to do it, whatever the consequences. I am warning you. I repeat. Whatever the consequences, we will do what is necessary to open those gates. We represent the law. You are obstructing the freedom of others to work. These men are here to do the work you don't want to do. I have been instructed by the Commander of our forces – the Prime Minister himself. These men on the truck have travelled far and wish to start their work. I am giving you five minutes to leave the gates."

The senior police officers return to their car. They talk in low voices. There seems to be no other way that the armed and the unarmed can communicate save to watch each other.

A child cries, then another and another and the crowd is stirred. A low buzz. At the gate the women are whispering. Suddenly they stop and stare. A tractor with its blade raised is approaching the bridge. Children point. Adults become sculptured pieces. A masked man is on the tractor. The mask is purple.

Five minutes pass.

The masked driver lifts the blade high and descends from the tractor. The superintendent and the two officers surround him. They speak, he listens. The driver's face is covered by the mask. Two narrow vents provide a window. He is the lever to open the gates. The superintendent and his officers walk back to the bridge.

"We are ordering you women to CLEAR OUT. CLEAR THE BRIDGE! WE ARE COMING THROUGH. COMRADE, GET THE TRACTOR MOVING!"

The masked driver wears an ordinary pair of brown cotton trousers and a short-sleeved shirt. Yesterday, he was working on a building site, cutting the earth with this tractor's razor-sharp broad blade. This morning its silver cutting edge gleams.

He climbs high into the driver's seat. He will not need a handkerchief to wipe his brow, though the sun is hot, for his mask will absorb the moisture. He starts the engine; the tractor throbs, moves forward.

His face cannot feel the pulsating life-beat of the women which the air currents are taking to him. He cannot feel their trembling warmth, the emptiness in their stomachs, their shaking hands, nor the moisture on their brows. His purple mask protects him from their strivings.

A young man stands up and the superintendent is hopeful. "Give us a hearing before you bring the tractor on the bridge," he says. A murmuring like buzzing bees comes from the gathering.

The superintendent indicates to the driver to hold.

"We'll never leave this hell hole if you break this strike," the young man says. "Could you live as we? We drink the water strained from boiled rice to give us the energy we need to cut and load the canes, to dig the trenches, to maintain the land. Look at your boots. We can never afford those, working here. Is we bare feet face the sharp blades of canes, snakes in deep grass, alligators in trenches. We quick with our cutlass most of the time.... Most of the time."

The superintendent says nothing, but a senior officer, who has so far been silent, walks to the young man and says, "Stop wasting our time. Those are your concerns. Not ours. We're here to do a job. This is a free country. If you don't like it, leave. Who is stopping you? CLEAR THE BRIDGE , You hear me? Answer me. I am your superior. We are running this island. Maya is independent."

The young man senses the venom and he nods his head.

"That's better," says the senior officer. It's bad manners not to answer a question. Did you know that?" The senior officer looks at the superintendent and chuckles. "Do we town's people have to teach these country people everything?" He looks at the women. "CLEAR THE GATES!"

Another worker raises his arm to draw attention: "Our children can't get work in Bon Aire," he says. "You keep those jobs for yourselves. You ask for this and that qualifications, and when our children get them, you think of something else. You are trying to keep us here tied to this hellhole. But you will not succeed. You cannot stop time. You cannot stop the wind, how then can you stop people? Remember that when you fellas sleep."

The officer is shocked. He cannot believe he is witnessing such an abandonment of self-preservation in the face of authority. But before he can decide how to deal with this 'gross insolence', the young man's courage has strengthened the women and Kamelia decides to speak again.

Something has happened. Her demeanour has changed. With help she stands upright, easing one foot, standing on the other: "We women are not moving from this bridge, and mothers everywhere are with us. I warn you, listen with care. If you cross this bridge, you and your children and your children's children will become as poor as we. This curse is now rising from the earth where our young children are buried. We see it. It twists above you like smoke. It will cling to you as your own skin if anyone crosses this bridge. If you cross, you choose death by your own hands. You will remember me when you are dying, falling like flies all in good time, one by one. You will know your time has come, for you will feel my long shadow on you, even in the midday sun."

The superintendent is stunned. He wonders what could he say back at headquarters, to postpone this confrontation. His heart is no longer in it. He has been hoping that the mere presence of the tractor's razor-sharp blade and the masked driver would be enough. But the instructions to break the strike are unambiguous. "DO WHAT IS NECESSARY". He knows what that means. His thoughts flow past him: Do they understand that the driver is doing his patriotic bidding? Do they understand that he has been given the cover of *no accountability*? How can I get out of this place without losing face? I can see their stand, but they don't see that there can be no turning back for me. If I turn back it means the Prime Minister has turned back. He made that plain. I can only leave here with his authority enforced.

The senior officer's voice cuts through his thoughts. "Shut your mouth, woman, you know who you speaking to? I am Senior Officer Samson. You hear me? You people read the Bible?

A sniggering comes from the lorries.

"They worship stones and paintings," someone cries, and the men on the lorries laugh.

"They're not Christians I can tell you that."

"Heathens."

"You can tell by their names."

"Is many gods they worship."

There is more sniggering and chuckling.

Senior Officer Samson says: "GET OUT OF THE WAY, SCUM. CLEAR THE WAY. GET OFF THE BRIDGE. THIS IS YOUR LAST CHANCE. YOU LEAVE NOW OR NEVER. He is heaving. He wipes his wet face. His role plays its part before this audience and leads him. He is unaware of the force of its momentum. It is the part he decided to play on his way to Hope Bridge, for he comes from a school that says there is only one way to play a crucial role. He strides in the free style of an athlete and blows his war cry to the wind: "GET THE TRACTOR MOVING!"

The masked man hesitates.

"COME ON, COMRADE. DO WHAT IS NECESSARY TO CLEAR THE GATES."

The tractor moves forward onto the bridge. The heavy lumbering wheels roll – one complete turn, then another. The broad steel blade is lowered – waist high. The women are still seated. The blade dazzles in the fierce heat. They sweat. The circumference of the wheel is large. Flickering light bounces off the moving blade which cuts apart the space before it. The chain of human hands jerks intuitively. Then tightens. The chain strains, pulls, jerks. Again it tightens. The blade approaches. Thirty centimetres close. Seven women still span the bridge. They stare. Stunned into a clay mould of terror. Mouths open, lips apart. No sound.

The driver is moving along the track, along this rail track. The earth rotates; it revolves. Thoughts and realisations are cut off, sealed – entombed within vessels from which songs once flowed.

The crowd stands as if of inert clay.

The circling corbeaux are descending. They smell blood spurting. The blade is splashing red. It pitches, trickles, then congeals. Two pieces of a body entangle. The blade takes them. A twisted ankle, a swollen foot constricts movement forward for it hangs before the closed gates like a cross bar.

The soldiers leap forward firing shots in the air and into the ground. One aims at a corbeaux and laughs. The army opens the gates. The tractor moves forward. Two pieces are clinging to it. A hundred yards inside the factory gates, Kamelia's body parts and falls.

The army fires.

A corbeau is stilled.

The backs of the other women are broken. For some life ebbs mercifully. There are two survivors – unlucky ones – they were at each end, pushed like loose earth by the blade into the trench. They are paralysed and will lie on their backs for the rest of their lives. They breathe; they cannot be made ready for burial.

The masked driver is escorted by armed soldiers into the police officer's BMW which leaves at full speed. The strike has been broken.

Cutlasses are wielded in the fields by the scabs to clear a path for the harvester.

Who will inform Kamelia's mother?

The living must be protected, so let the two pieces of Kamelia be put together before they receive her mother's tears. What will her young daughters make of this? "Take her to the hospital," an old lady says. "I go stay with her until her mother comes."

In the capital, there are great expectations for the Prime Minister's regime from his supporters . His voice is in their heads and his face in their mirrors.

3   MARGUERITE'S RESOLVE: FOR WHAT WILT THOU KILL?

I, Marguerite Devonish, sister of Robert Augustus Devonish, President of Maya, have decided today that I will commit fratricide whenever the opportunity arises. I am resolved.

More than two decades have passed, yet it seems like yesterday when Kamelia was sliced in two. I recall this and more with clarity: the remains of the Bon Aire fires – cavernous scars, unhealed beneath the ashes. Deep in the forest around Ica, the blood smells still cling to the earth.

Eyes circle my dreams, round and round. I am a pivot for voiceless faces – Vasu and Gavin cut down in their prime. Two honourable men guarding ballot boxes gunned down – young Shivnarine shot in the back. The murdered Catholic priest, the nun obscenely humiliated; the bullied; the tormented with fearful, anxious faces, terrified of the police; the army – men in uniform terrorising the weak.

Oh how mercilessly my brother mauled Emmanuel Pottaro. He led his pack of leopards for eighty days encircling Mayan democracy – suffocating it, setting Bon Aire alight – and so prepared the path for his enthronement.

Maya was not a place to leave when my brother and I were at school. Under colonial rule, we had a first class education, which greatly enhanced us to ordinary folks. Later my brother went abroad and observed larger lifestyles. He returned with the skills of an advocate and the taste for never-ending privileges. But the desire to have what no one should have surged early within him.

In our youth, this was a place where showers of butterflies and falling leaves pretended they were each other. I recall attempting to remove a leaf resting on my toe, only to find it lifted itself and flew. It was a time when the morning sun turned dew drops into rare crystals, beams of flickering light, and I was fearful of witnessing their disappearance as the sun rose over the mountain tops. That something vulnerable, translucent, trembling with its very being, would be lost forever saddened me.

Throughout these dark years I continued to take my daily walks, avoiding fallen yellow poui blossoms, not wishing to tread upon their silk. But today the burden of my thoughts so engrossed me that I stepped upon the petals over and over again like an ox threshing rice. The silken blooms bled, staining the grass.

My resolve weighs heavily. I must act before my brother's operation brings his voice to life again. *His voice will be our undoing*, mother once said, and it has come to pass.

Country Mayans say Kamelia's curse rests on the land. Thousands have fled, gone to any port that would have them. Grey rotting kokers dot the coastline, looking like mournful places of execution. The drains are lost, and when it rains the udders of milking cows are drowned and sheep and goats have to be tethered on any mound that rises to the occasion. Meanwhile the sea relentlessly pounds the coast, intent on reclaiming it.

When the idea first struck, it was unclear – broken, zig-zagging like lightning and was dismissed. Dispatched with speed, chased by chants about the sanctity of life, the unbreakable loyalty to one's blood line. Later, a more ancient force appeared, bedraggled as if long entombed. I turned to see its face but it was hidden by these words: *The grave whither thou goest there is nothing, therefore for what wilt thou die? Moreover for what wilt thou kill?* This I pondered long and hard. An answer has at last come. So now I must act resolutely, swiftly.

Fate has long played in my brother's favour and seemed to have done so again, for at the very moment I came to my resolve, Robert Augustus stood before me in soft slippers. I could so easily have been alarmed, bowled over to see thought becoming presence, unannounced and smiling in that all-knowing way. I could have endangered myself by alerting his suspicious mind, which he claims is attuned to the inner truth of men. Of late, it has become his way to run the affairs of state.

His smile profuse, he placed his arms around me. "You are the only one I can now trust, Marguerite. See how they don't spy on you, are not on duty when you are with me. I have arranged it so."

"Trust is the most important thing one has, Maximus," I said warmly. "When it leaves, life is a barren plain. I am happy that it binds us."

We embraced.

I received a letter from Aasha in London. Our friendship began on my first day as a pupil teacher and she a pupil in standard one. We formed a silent pact – she partaking joyfully in what I offered. And I grew in courage by her understanding. The warmth of her letter, the grief it reopened and those many circling faces have helped to fortify my resolve. For Maximus is no ordinary fox and I shall need to be no ordinary hound, yet not one of Actaeon's pack, bewitched to fill their mouths with their master's flesh and hair. I would have preferred an end, close to what Aasha once described – a handmaiden of Narsingh or Narsingh himself, the avatar of Vishnu.

"The privileges of a housekeeper in a politically ambitious household are not to be scoffed at, my dear Marguerite." Those were mother's parting words when she left Bon Aire to live in the countryside, across the Azon, with Aunt Maude, her matron sister, not long retired from Bon Aire Public Hospital. It was her wish that I continue to be part of Robert Augustus's household staff. "You are not to compromise yourself, yet do not give up on him, Marguerite, for I believe that your daily presence, quietly depicting another way of thinking, another way of living, will in time have an effect. He needs our prayers. Nothing else can save him."

But that it should come to this?

Mother's rapid decline came, I believe, when she realised that the governments of our Region and our AUL wished Robert Augustus to gain power and hold on to it at any price. The price Mayans paid encompassed the depravities of racism, dictatorship, dire poverty. She saw how his grand style and his confident manner endeared him to his supporters, who attached their self-esteem and their psyches to his voice.

Sitting here on the sea wall, Aasha's letter calls forth too many ghosts from the past. It was her favourite place and Vasu's. How

strange the circumstance that propelled him to the polders where his
forefathers cultivated rice and fed the region in war time. There he
toils today and speaks no more unless addressed by a passer-by. Yet
I hear him clearly, a young man not tied to the rigid dictates of either
Left or Right. His vulnerability lay in his willingness to re-examine
what was held sacrosanct by the politicians' gurus – our all-
knowing AUL who strutted about the Region's campuses with the
same intense righteousness as the early missionaries, declaring
that state ownership and control were the paths to life and growth.
With the flare of bright feathered cocks in a farmyard, they strut,
strut, strut. Peck, peck, peck at what they do not wish to understand. To this day it remains their style, which they call radical.

"We are hemmed in by our own constructions," Vasu would
say, "by a debilitating dependence on walls on which we lean,
which limit our view. Robert Augustus's path leads to serfdom. We
need the rich mix of energies outside our walls to become stronger.
Let us learn these new ways. If we don't, who will buy our goods?
Will we say, "If you don't buy our wares, you don't have a heart.
You want to see us die?"? Will we seek charity and claim our
independence simultaneously? What craft will enable these two
claims to stand tall together?"

But they kept saying, "We permit a Trojan horse at our peril.
Beware capitalist technology, the ideology of those with appetites
to colonise. Maintain our walls, else we perish."

Urban Mayans, the elite, the educated, tutored by our AUL,
scoffed at Vasu, calling him a colonialist, an expatriate, not a true
Mayan. My brother's supporters pushed and shoved him about,
taunting him to respond. They disrupted his meetings while the
police stood and watched, not moved to uphold even a semblance
of the law.

Years have passed and the lumbering state bureaucracy
suffocates the imagination and drains the energies of our people.
Robert Augustus has paralysed his supporters so that they are
stuck in the one groove that sings, "Government must take over
more to give us more. Where are our entitlements? Before
Independence, you spoke of our entitlements over and over
again. You hoisted our expectations, our dreams. *We are the
chosen ones*, you said, *we have the psychic inheritance to rule*, you

proclaimed. We have been patient long. *We are the chosen*, you say. Let it be."

In the breast pocket of some of his supporters rests an old, crumpled list, neatly done, which Robert Augustus recited on Independence night, and many times since. It is a list of things he will do to create the new Jerusalem, and this they carry even now, for there is no release from expectations that were planted with pain, watered with tears, and nurtured with the people's resolve.

Vasu was a lone voice. A prisoner of the Region's aviary of learned, campus birds, their advocacy accountable to no one whatever its outcome. They had supped on State nectar, so energised, they soared high, too high, above the ground where life's struggles beat. With such beaks pecking at him, Vasu stayed as long as he did because he tried to honour his commitment – a son's promise to his father – that he assist the constituents of his village polder. In the absence of the rule of law, no one was safe and he assisted many to leave. Vasu, too, was about to leave with Aasha when they knocked on his door and took him away. He never came back. He may have expected them, for he managed to leave his notes, his photographs, camera and film of that altar in the hinterland, in a safe hiding place, which only Aasha and Aunt Maude knew.

They were to be married in the cool weather, when the poinsettia wears its cadmium-red deep silks, the tall slender Long Johns crown themselves in an overabundance of white blooms, the crocus wood wears yellow and the logwood's clear nectar flows freely and calls to the bees.

That was not to be.

Later Aasha married Arun, Vasu's elder brother. At school we referred to him as Arun the silent. He was dignified, wise, saying only what needed to be said. Nothing more, nothing less. I thought he was from another planet – an alien – so unlike Vasu, with a warm humanity in his every step.

Aasha and Arun emigrated to London with her son Nyasa. It was at the airport that I last saw them, joining the long line of professional men and women, standing side by side with raped families and workers from the rice-growing polder lands, all seeking a new country. I recall our last embrace, her crumpled written farewell and her barely audible voice, soft as evensong: "We Country Mayans have become birds without skies, Marguerite. Pray for us."

That night I reread her farewell.

Dear Marguerite,

Vasu is slowly dying, a part of me with him. He is lost, but his walking frame does not know it. He is beyond my reach, the doctors have explained. What is left is less than a shadow of his former self. Can this be true? Vasu? Who you knew to be filled with the ecstasy of life and of the freedom that comes with understanding what it is to be human. That such a mind be lost, Marguerite? No essence remaining? If gone, where to? One day I may be able to look at him and see he is not there, but today is too early. His scent remains with me and stirs me. The warmth of his embraces still cradles me.

Those in masks say Maximus was merciful. "Opponents of governments in other lands," they cry, "are sent to die in the cold Northern wilderness. Vasu was allowed to live. Give thanks to Maximus. He has no Gulag nor Devil's Island."

Yes, Vasu walks to and from the rice fields in the polder land where the setting sun transforms every flooded field into sparkling silver lakes. He ploughs and plants and harvests the grain for the family who shelters him when the work is done. Each morning when he is led by a child's hand to the fields, he can see what has been done, what next should be done. The land reminds him, nudges him to recall his yesterday, and if he becomes disconnected, it shows him yet again. A patient teacher, the land. It will not tire. It has marked where he ended and so where he should begin.

Aasha writes that she will visit Subah who looks after the Nath's family house. But now Subah too is leaving. Her daughter Veena lives in London. I see abandoned grey houses, gardens and yards gone wild. Weeds seed. I know Aasha will go to meet with Vasu at the polders, though her letter is silent on that. Her loss is still sharply felt, unweathered and will continue to be. She measures herself against the unbending philosophy of an ancient world, with its own large miracles, its concepts of honour, its women who walked upon pyres, its dignified resignation to other worlds to come, believing, *there is no end to life. We are immortal, a thousand forms await us. We are part of everything.*

Time has separated us. I am the sister of Maximus, living under the same roof, and Aasha cannot be sure how much weight our friendship can now carry, preferring to be cautious. Now with my resolve and Robert Augustus' suspicious anxieties increasing, it is as well. I too must walk with extra care, though he accepted the long established friendship of our two families – the Naths and ours. Aunt Maude and Vasu Nath were next door neighbours. Vasu was never really a threat. My brother knew that Vasu was always a one man bandwagon, harmless, at most a nuisance. Besides, it was a feather in my brother's cap, improved his image to be able to say we had an opposition.

I know Aasha comes to meet with Vasu... must wonder how much he recalls... must want to know... must ask herself whether had she stayed with him against all medical advice and that of Arun, there might have been an outside chance that he could have become whole again. She had long argued – "There is much healing, Marguerite, that medical science does not yet understand."

I suspect she believes that they are connected in some cordless way and that her close daily presence might have sparked something that enabled him to regain himself. Perhaps even now she lives in hope...

Not for a moment do I trust what Maximus has just said, coming upon me soft slippered. I see it as a ploy to encourage me to let down my guard. He knows that, like him, I carry my feelings well. This disposition runs in the family. Mother's control was perfect. Aunt Maude's is flawless. Since he left my room I have been asking what request will he now make of me, knowing he expects to be paid in kind for the compliments he offers.

He has been having difficulty with his voice, which from time to time gives up altogether as if tired of being used. This has further intensified his anxiety over the collapse of the economic power upon which his strategies depend. A growing irritability clings to him. Twice this week I heard a continuous low murmuring, an unearthly sound, watchful; then wild and sinister escaping his room.

Sometimes I think Mother is conversing with him, for round and round this orator paces, as if the surrounding walls were a sitting jury and he in some high court. His mind searches for comfort, not understanding this chained position. The recent town walks in disguise were meant to take him out of himself, to the people. Instead it brought this affliction.

4 AASHA AND VASU

The clouds parted, the emptiness of the blue opened above him but Vasu's thoughts were not of its immensity – space without shelter; that would come later.

Now he was lying on bed rock – the sea-wall – a Dutch creation, three hundred years old, built to last by men who knew how to build. This engineering feat withstood the daily breaking of an ocean – two thousand pounds per square foot – which in times of raging storms became a battering ram, quadrupling in intensity, dislodging blocks of concrete more than a thousand tons in weight as if they were pebbles.

And yet, the sea-wall stands. Built to last.

This engineering feat engrossed him. The sea-wall he likened to the custodianship of good laws, protecting the low-lying rich alluvium from being submerged, from being lost to a culture that improves and cherishes; a culture of sowing good seeds, expecting nothing today, but sometime in an uncertain future when the sower may not be there.

He saw the sea-wall restraining destructive forces, repulsing and scattering irrational ones; enabling the creation of another order, one of abundance, allowing large ideas to thrive, where once the high tide marked its place in ooze and barnacles. Sorcery!

Oh to have such a sorcery to build a stand within us and without us against ugliness!

"To build to last," Vasu whispered. That was not what Devonish had been doing. He had sought an all encompassing conquest. How well he succeeded. What Vasu did not wish to contemplate was that Devonish was not only the first but, for an entire generation, the only prime minister Maya had .

Lying on the sea-wall, the past quietly encroached. After the crimes of the State against those women on Hope Bridge, he'd had to restrain the young men and women seeking justice, wanting to capture the tractor driver, to see the face beneath the purple mask. He'd had to point to the armed soldiers and ask, "How many of you will be killed before you are able to disarm two truck loads of militia? Whose sons will be sacrificed to this cause? And when the army and police reinforcements arrive, what then? How many more burning pyres will flare along the coast?" It was better to leave quietly, build a future in another place, he had said, though he knew the insurmountable problems that beset such a path.

Their throats were on fire at their powerlessness. A young woman, someone's granddaughter, with a scholar's face, perhaps visiting, walked up to the front and cried, "Go to another place, you say, Mr Nath? Tell me, are we birds? Our forefathers came here more than one hundred and thirty years ago. Are we to move again to try and build again in another place? Where is this place, Mr Nath? Give us its name. What do you say to our old men and women, to our sick and disabled? Where should we move with them? Who will take us with these cares?"

Voices cried out, "She right, that girl, right."

A young man stepped out. "This is not new," he said calmly, struggling to keep his pain from spilling. "They are bullies. The Prime Minister is the biggest. They bully us at school and everywhere we go – in the hospital, government offices, everywhere. They choke and rob us on the streets. My ajee, they robbed she in Bon Aire."

"They wearing purple masks, kicking down front doors, taking everything."

"Masked men combing the place; the women and children trembling under the kitchen table. One of the masked fellas keeps a gun to your head, while everything you have the other one taking."

"The police don't want to know, they getting a kickback. Who you go turn to? God? He too slow. I say, get yourself ready for them."

Another man said, "They telling us we don't belong here, and if we don't leave, they will do whatever they want with we just like today. Oh God, look at today? I hope there is a God. When I see what they get away with, I have my doubts."

"We belong here, this is the land of our birth, my mother's birth, my nanee's, my ajee's, so we should stop suffering at their hands."

"I say match like with like. Set up 'No Go' areas, defend our places, our wives and daughters. It is the only way now open to us."

"Who could manage to leave, I say, leave before you lose your life. Which police you think will catch that man on the tractor and bring him to justice? Which one? Name one, just one. What does today tell you about us and about them? Who has a future here?"

"Garrison constituencies?" Vasu had queried.

"Yes, Mr Nath. Are we cowards?"

He had told them that garrison constituencies must not be their legacy, despite the crimes against them, despite the daily grossness, this denial of their place. Wherever such self-enclosed garrisons take hold, they become a curse. See the Northern islands where they were common. They had become a cancer. Mr Pottaro had set his face against 'No Go' areas. It was one of the best things he had left them. They should uphold it for it was good.

"You talking rubbish, real rubbish," their voices challenged. "Have we a choice? We being butchered here. You blind or something?"

"Pushed out of politics, pushed out of jobs. Mr Pottaro's legacy is for the weak, for those who fear bullies. Why should these makers of hell go scot free? We shouldn't fear them. We ask no favours. We need no masks. We demand our rights as citizens."

Another asked: "Mr Nath, listen to me, if you was Kamelia's father, husband, son, what then? What would you say, Mr Nath? Tell us what you would say now."

"Speak up, man. Let us hear you."

A rush of voices followed. "Tell us, Mr Nath. Tell us, na. You tongue-tied now?"

Many wept bitterly saying nothing. Their tears silent, their faces still. They were naked men, without the rule of law for clothing, men without representation, powerless victims.

He had no answer. They had moved away. He was shattered, broken, inadequate. How to offer comfort, how to give hope? Nothing came. What he had said was all he could offer in the absence of the rule of law, in the presence of the horror he had just witnessed, and the earlier hells – the Ica pogrom, the long strike, the fires, the daily muggings in the streets of the capital. He was humbled before those young despairing eyes, the many silent voices that turned away from him. What could he say to these youths appealing for just laws? Unarmed, in a hostile Region, how does one think in this situation? Escape?

But he knew that when they asked "Where to go? Which island? Which place? Who will let us in?" There were no answers. Each man was on his own, had to seek his own sanctuary. They had to look outside the Region, the Region that had sung and danced that its *raison d'etre* was – "All ah we is one brother. All ah we is one." They had to look outside this community for an understanding of their plight.

Vasu sat up. Walking towards him was Aasha, the woman he would marry before the year ended, before he left Maya. As his eyes held her smile, the sea-wall receded, its sorcery lifted. They were two vessels of joy converging. The whistling wind was blowing through her hair, caressing his cheeks with Aasha's scent.

They walked together upon the sea-wall, laughing with the ocean wind, holding hands, happy in their first Spring to see the glorious yellow poui in bloom, the poinciana aflame, to see everything anew. She whispered, "I'll race you to the pole," and slipping off their shoes they ran and felt the sun's warmth on their soles.

When he allowed himself to catch up with her, he would not pass her by, preferring to keep their long shadows together, to run with her. Seeing this, she stopped and they embraced, enclosing the beauty, the mystery of a life-giving ocean before them, while the wind danced round and round.

He called wildly to the emptiness beyond as he lifted her, a suppressed intoxication released. He spun her and she became a twirling top. Again they embraced. The earth stood still. But when she said, "catch me", she misjudged his feelings and by the time he was awakened, she was outside his reach.

They met again and again, parting reluctantly, wishing that time would not quicken its pace when they were together. They walked in the city, sometimes gazing through shop windows at goods meant to give pleasure – sparkling vessels for drink and food and light, furnishings to lie and sit and walk upon, or hang on walls, but they were all found wanting, for they had each other.

On one occasion, in an old weathered shop piled with the clutter of time, they came upon a bronze statue of *Shiva Nataraja* dancing in a circle of flames and were drawn to it. Dust rested thickly upon it, yet failed to veil the vibrancy radiating from the god's prelude to movement – his sweeping exploration of the fitness of the firmament – before he tells his tale of the ecstatic births of suns, an extension of himself through dance.

"You know dancers are inspired by *Shiva Nataraja*," she said, "and when a dedicated dancer combines hard work with a rising imagination, Shiva leaves his circle of flames and inspires her to excel."

"How do you think this happens?" Vasu asked, unconvinced, smiling at this explanation, charming and childlike in its simplicity.

"To be possessed by the spirit of dance, Vasu... I have often wondered what it would be like to witness Shiva's dance and be possessed by the spirit of dance itself – dance in its ultimate form – its essence distilled." She hesitated, "I would be exhilarated to witness this even in the privacy of my thoughts."

"Why there?"

"I do not think at present it can be a public display."

He did not understand what she was saying, yet felt restrained from exploring its intimacy further. Instead he said, "Now that you have joined the master dance classes, I would like a demonstration of being possessed by the spirit of dance."

"When I have perfected a piece I shall see if I can lift it further."

"I shall give you time," he said, "for time we have, Aasha; we are young."

"I shall work at it, and it will be. I shall dance for you, Vasu," she said, smiling, caressing his cheek, as a child offering a gift.

But no sooner had she said that, standing before the bronze sculpture of *Shiva Nataraja*, a sudden inexplicable feeling of deep sadness came over her, a feeling of loss and anguish. Propelled by it she held his hands and, without stopping to think, found herself saying to *Shiva Nataraja*, "Vasu and Aasha ask the Creator of Movement, that energy should flow to us when our need is greatest. We ask in the name of the beauty of movement, which is life itself."

5 MASKS
Marguerite Devonish

I could see that Mother's health was deteriorating. She began to have nightmares of the Devil embracing her son's soul.

He remained an enigma to Mother right up to her last days. "Why?" she would ask over and over again, even whispering this monosyllable as she became weaker. It was as if by repetition a door would open to understanding.

I tried. "I am inclined to think, Mother, that certain phenomena of the human mind were present at the beginning of life itself. There is no other explanation, Mother, for Robert Augustus's all compelling ambition."

"Thank you, Marguerite, you are a comfort to me. You should not be troubled when I ask why. It is a question that mothers will continue to ask."

My words were not only meant to comfort Mother, to be some balm. I believed them. For I could remember, even as a child, that few things roused Robert Augustus as much as *the idea of privilege.* To observe a privilege in another that was legitimately denied him, tormented him. My perception of privilege was too ordinary for him. "I am not referring to the mundane privileges, you go on about, Marguerite, like enabling the illiterate to read and write. My kind of privilege is bonded with awe, fear, reverence. One example should suffice: to be a Caesar in the Colosseum, Marguerite, sitting high on cushions of silk, surrounded by succulent fruits, satisfying my tastes while the death struggle of two gladiators entertains me. To have the privilege of taking a man's life or permitting him to keep it, by a mere movement of thumb this way or that. Well, Marguerite, that is privilege. It is not only that the wretched man saved from imminent death will be eternally grateful, but once the signal is given, the action taken, the judgement rests. There is no questioning Caesar's decision once that moment has passed. It becomes out of reach, not to be re-examined and questioned laboriously."

It was privilege without responsibility or accountability, without duties and obligations. It was privilege without boundaries.

He yearned to drink this heady cocktail and came to believe that, to attain supreme authority and total commitment from his supporters, he needed to offer them a benefit, some all encompassing privilege which would satisfy their psychic needs. His desires and their needs would be one.

I recall my first encounter with the masks, which changed the course of Maya's history. It was very late, well past midnight, and I was tired. I had been driving through the darkness of the long country roads for some two and a half hours on my way home from Aunt Maude and Mother. I had to depend entirely on my car lights and tired eyes as I penetrated the long darkness. The lights of the capital were a comforting change, and I became more at ease.

Halted at traffic lights, I looked around and to my surprise saw my brother's car parked outside the house of Selwyn Thomas, a fine Mayan painter. My brother was then leader of the Opposition. What could have brought him to this artist's home at this hour? My curiosity was awakened.

An old friend of Thomas, I felt free to join them. Selwyn had long been working on masks and was evidently pleased to show my brother his display.

"He sees a mask as a piece of sculpture," Robert Augustus said to me. "And these masks... well, masks similar to these were worn before the dawn of Christianity in Europe...." Selwyn Thomas was smiling. It was clear my brother had just learnt this and wanted me to see that he had an understanding of the subject. He gazed at the masks and then said firmly and clearly, as if it had been rehearsed, "Together, Selwyn and I will create a new dawn here in Bon Aire."

"Who wore them?" I asked.

"If you look closely at this one," Selwyn said, putting on a grand mask, "you would conclude it was worn by a man who wielded power. Now, if I turn the lights low ... this mask enhances the power of the wearer. All I need is a slow ominous beat on the drum – a lone drummer's beat, Marguerite." I laughed, but he was right. He touched his drum. Just four beats. But in the darkness, we all heard a march to the steps of the guillotine.

Staring at the mask you became less and less, until finally you were like a dewdrop trembling at the approaching dawn. Somehow, too, you knew that were you to cease concentrating on your own sense of being, you would be no more. The concept of human consciousness would have vanished, leaving no trace.

As I stared at the mask I could not extricate myself. I was held by it, to a deep sinking feeling of being encircled in space, falling, down, down, to an infinite depth of nothingness. Then I sensed movement, something approaching from nowhere, something swerving unsteadily, stumbling its way towards me by some primordial reflex, receiving signals from the surrounding space that here, within close range, was warm living matter – matter to be consumed or crushed.

The mask, a terror camouflaged, a veiled horror, led you beyond the paths of reason, beyond moral laws inherent in reason itself. I was petrified. Selwyn removed it, saying calmly, "This mask was meant to create a fearful awe, and may have been worn by a high priest or ruler of a kingdom – hence the colour purple, signifying royalty – sanctified authority, blood, kinship, sacrifice."

"Did you know," Robert Augustus said, turning to me, his face warm and cheerful, "that amongst certain tribes in Africa, men always carried a small mask?"

"The size of the mask," Selwyn explained, "indicated the share of power, the authority of the holder of the mask. Of course, if they were larger and more widely worn, one would have had a 'Cult of Masks', becoming a law unto itself – operating outside the codes of society. If not tightly controlled, the power felt within the mask, freedom without reins, could become a human horror. It is something we would not want to envisage. But the potential is there."

I had associated masks with merrymaking at carnival and at the circus with smiling clowns. They were open, light, colourful – a cardboard make-up of fun. I expressed this, and Selwyn said I should not confine the mask to evoking one emotion.

Then he led us to a more dimly-lit room with a crowd of masks of varying purple hues – purple moulded faces – hanging from the ceiling, hanging freely as if they were once attached to bodies, and were now relieved of that weight, but on becoming too light in themselves, were jostling each other for space. The atmosphere was hot and still, yet the masks were swaying and they began to play on my susceptibilities. I saw not masks but open cavities, dark cavernous chasms – decapitation. In the silence, the surrounding stillness and darkness, my imagination had become unwholesome.

"Which ones is Robert Augustus having?" I asked, my voice echoing. On hearing this, the hanging masks began to sway, hurling themselves boldly from side to side as if they had a life of their own and were trying to say something.

"Listen to the rush outside," Selwyn said; "how much the wind has picked up. The masks are conversing... I have never seen them like this." The frenzied motion increased and the masks came close to damaging themselves. When I left I must have become disoriented, for how could I ask, "Is it that the masks do not wish to be taken, or is it that they don't wish to be chosen by Robert Augustus?" This voice startled me. I had been in a suggestive atmosphere and become vulnerable to the irrational. I dreaded to think what repeated encounters with the masks would do to my psyche, my willpower, my concept of self. A growing sheet of apprehension covered me.

"The Chief has something quite special in mind. I believe I know what he wants," Selwyn said.

"When our supporters wear this mask, they must feel an inherited superiority throbbing in their veins... A mask that the unmasked would be in awe of, would fear, a mask to shatter the self-worth of those it faces. A mask that would make them long for its privileges," Robert Augustus said.

An inner glow came upon both men who seemed intuitively to understand each other. Art and politics embraced, and in the exchange each received renewed strength.

But something was not understood. For the wearers of masks, there were long-term internal repercussions which were not per-

ceived at the time. It can be likened to carrying the Gorgon's head
to the enemy. The carrier must be calm, controlled, resolute. He
must ensure that at all times its naked face is turned away from
him, his family and friends. If the journey entails passing over
lakes, clear streams and pools, the carrier must be watchful. At no
time, even momentarily, must he catch a reflection of the Gorgon's
head while resting on their banks, for if he does, he loses life,
becomes a barren stone. Carriers of the Gorgon's head could so
easily be left in a landscape of stones – a place without life –
merely rocks and pebbles varying in size, structure and colour.

That is what has come to pass in Bon Aire, throughout the
landscape of Maya. This land has become a place without life and
so without hope.

Within a fortnight Selwyn Thomas arrived with a tall hat box.
He held it carefully, placing it gently on the table as if it were a
Pandora's box.

"Where is the Chief?"

"On the telephone."

"Busy man – a lot on his mind."

"If it's not the trades unions, it's the newspapers, civil servants,
the police. Keeping in touch with many levers. He is meticulous,
keeping the party activists informed to see his plans through, step-
by-step. He does it all. A true Commander-in-Chief."

"That is public life. He has the stamina for it. The Chief is the
man for the job. A long-term planner. A master builder."

Selwyn lifted the cover of the tall box and before me were five
purple masks of different hues. They were works of art. The more
intense the depth of colour, the more awesome and fear-inspiring.
Again that feeling returned, silently exuding from their faces.
They were *terror camouflaged*, a *horror designed*.

Later, I saw that as these masks became worn, losing their
pristine freshness, as their smoothness wore off, as the surface
colour, the art began to fade, the underlying construct, the frame-
work of terror beneath came to life in all its starkness, its gut
energies.

Terror sculptured, made acceptable, to be worn. I touched the
cord that would hold it in place, bind a man's head, his thinking,
his reflective self to it.

"Is the cord viscose, polyester or silk?" I asked.

"Not silk," he said, "close to viscose. Feels good doesn't it? Who can tell the difference?"

I wanted to know what the world would be like for the wearer of the mask, to see it through those specially designed spherical hollows, so I held one in place over my face and stood before the mirror, not knowing what to expect. I saw what the world was seeing. This I had experienced at Selwyn Thomas' home. But now for me, the wearer of a mask, I was the movement within the living, breathing mask. It embraced me. Privileged. Released from a thousand canons, rules and codes. I was swaying with a sweet intoxication of pinnacled supremacy. I was lord of what I surveyed. A conquistador. Then slowly, something from within the mask began to irritate my skin. It became worse and I pulled at it, only to discover that I was allergic to the material and had developed a rash.

Selwyn said, "With prolonged wearing of these masks, the skin receives too little oxygen and could suffocate, even be gradually absorbed by the mask; the skin might then adhere to it, becoming one with it. I would not recommend prolonged use without absorbent cotton placed between mask and skin. But then that would not be necessary for once the power of the mask is established, it will have fulfilled its purpose. To our opponents we would have become the masks and there would be no need for us to continue to mask ourselves."

It was a work of art. The modelling was precise and I could see the brush strokes of purple paint across the mask as waves of rhythm moving to the dark hollow orifices of mouth and eyes.

"Are these to be displayed at independence. Is there going to be a pavilion of arts and crafts?"

"No, Marguerite. You lack imagination," said Robert Augustus from behind me. "I shall wear them. You repeatedly confirm that I was justified in dampening your early political enthusiasms. You would have been outfoxed." He took the grand mask closest to Tyrian purple and went to the adjoining room where there was a large, full-length mirror and closed the door behind him.

"Whose design?" I whispered.

"The Chief's."

Justified? No. Outfoxed? Yes. I gave up too early. When I was young, I was an innocent. Inexperienced. I was outmanoeuvred – like Emmanuel Pottaro was soon to be, though at the time I was unaware that my brother had large plans and that they were already in place.

Mother had made us feel that even one individual could make a difference on the political scene. So enthused, I began one evening to look at a map of the constituencies and expressed a wish to put my name forward for nomination at the next Party meeting. My brother was already a Member of Parliament and I was excited.

Before Mother could respond, Robert Augustus, uncoiling his legs, lifted himself from his chair as if about to strike, and hissed: "Why don't you stop fooling Marguerite, Mother? You must know that no one will vote for her with a face like that and a club foot to boot. Somebody has to be realistic in this house, now that Father is no longer with us. Stop fooling her, Mother. She is ugly and that is a fact. You continue to hide the truth from her. Good looks and a fine voice go a long way in politics. Can you imagine posters with Marguerite's face on it? I will not be made a laughing stock."

Slowly Mother removed her feet from the pedal of the old Singer sewing machine. She stood tall as a chieftain of old, her eyes comprehending the thinking, the soil that would have sprouted Robert Augustus's words, and diminished him there and then. I am of the opinion that her words clawed within him, never left him and eventually brought his demise.

"Your voice will be your destruction, Robert Augustus. It will enable you to live comfortably with illusions of your own making. And as it cradles you, you will forget that the sounds your voice plays for its own pleasure and exaltation are nothing more, nothing higher than the vibrations of the moment. May you be offered the grace, my son, to sit with your soul before it leaves these shores. For this I shall fervently pray. I sincerely hope you shall one day see all Maya with true African eyes, eyes that look with an all-embracing affection at the world though the world recognises them not. We are a gracious and affectionate people, with the warmth and magnanimity of gods, but your lust for power will be a mighty setback for us all. Today you embrace radicalism, first cousin to Marx, while pretending you and Pottaro are miles apart when you could be Siamese twins. You can fool university professors, son, but not your mother. I have watched you grow from the cradle and shall pray for you daily. I dare not think that you are beyond the reach of prayers. Night after night I sit here and ask, 'Why are you as you are? You could have been all that is beautiful and good, you have been greatly privileged with many diverse talents, yet you choose to become a rascal wearing a crown. Why, my son, why?"

Robert Augustus kept his mask of deep purple and took another. I was left with the remaining three. My first reaction was to firmly seal the lid with tape. Then I thought of Mother and Aunt Maude. These purple masks were handmade and had a strange compelling allure and excitement. Their colour entranced, mesmerised, perplexed those who faced them. They were comforting to touch. Clearly it was a privilege to don such a mask. I decided to keep one and offered the other two to Mother and Aunt Maude.

I explained that if things deteriorated rapidly, they might need them in the future for their own personal protection, or they might wish to offer one to a friend. They listened. Reluctantly Aunt Maude agreed to keep them in their place, which she said, "was in its closed box, in a faraway cupboard." Mother examined them closely, and then said, "The day we need to wear these for our protection, Marguerite, will be a dire day for us and for those who have forced us to wear them. It will be a signal that we are already amongst the dead and know it not, my dear. Thank you for thinking of us."

Robert Augustus enjoyed wearing masks of deep purple. He donned distinctive masks for different audiences – the cabinet, our AUL, foreign donors and dignitaries, the media, Party meetings, the British and American Governments, the CIA.

At mass rallies, Third World rostrums, and Regional Government meetings, his specially designed masks became his characteristic style. His supporters found much pleasure in what was referred to as 'the Chief's costumes'. He was as excited as children are with a new-found game.

6   A FOX

My brother, Robert Augustus, still then Leader of the Opposition, asked me to order from Selwyn Thomas a number of masks which he distributed amongst a select few.

The power of the mask, the privileges it opened up to the wearer, were talked about in hushed tones. Then, from the old guard of the Party there came the urgent call for a meeting. They felt they were being bypassed, were not being offered the privileges of the masks they felt were their due.

Then what I had feared took place with frightening speed. The chairperson chosen for this meeting was a leading Party functionary who began by pointing out that the purple masks were not all of the same colour or hue.

"Just like life," someone shouted.

"The masks are of five different shades or intensities of purple," he continued, "and the time has come to utilise these differences, to put them to constructive use. Masks of the deepest purple should be offered to the few who are most loyal to the Party. It has been suggested by our esteemed leader, that all present should today be given grade-one masks, or those of the lightest purple, which signify party membership only. Thereafter each one of you, young and old, will have the opportunity to earn the privilege of wearing a more intense purple."

Someone stood up and said, "Mr Chairman, before you go any further, I would like you to clear up for me, and no doubt for others too, what everyone I believe wants to know, and that is, what an ordinary party member like me would have to do to get a deeper purple mask and all the privileges that go with it. Maybe I shouldn't say this, but from what I have been hearing there is much to be had. It seems to me that the light purple mask which, by the way, is not cheap, is all well and good but really there isn't anything in it." Then voices flew from the floor like paper missiles.

"No meat in it, comrade."

"Too lightweight."

"The colour wash out already."

"Too faded, comrade."

"Not good enough for poor people like me."

"The Party can do better for ordinary folks."

A few laughed and a young man called Gavin turned to the last speaker and said, "Keep it up, comrade, take nothing for granted."

All at once a tumult of voices broke out, each trying to express a point of view amongst friends sitting near and far, ignoring the Chair. The young man, Gavin, kept saying, "The Chairman must know that without us there is no Party, and if we don't know what's going on, the Party will stagnate and we will have no democracy."

It was clear that the Chairman had lost the reins of the meeting and was about to strike the desk, to call the meeting to order. But Robert Augustus was pleased with what was taking place and stayed his hand. As the voices were petering out, the Chairman called the meeting to order. Robert Augustus touched his hand and was offered the floor. He rose to his feet: "Our patient chairman continues with the task before him and I as Party leader have asked his indulgence to make a few observations. We see here today true democracy at work – people expressing them-selves, openly and without fear. This is the main aim of our party. And we welcome it. Of course, we can't get there at once, but a party must have ideals. Neither must we rush into anything blindly or without lengthy consultation. This is what I, our Chairman, and the executive members of the Party have in mind. I am not a mind reader, but I know this is the main aim of all present here."

"Before I hand you back to the Chairman, let me say something more. Since our Chairman is a gentleman and wouldn't say it, I will have to, because I am the kind of man that if something has to be done for the benefit of the party, I will do it, no matter the cost to myself. I am not seeking popularity; instead I am taking the risk of putting this party first before my own well-being. So let me say now that if there is anyone here who does not believe in the little man, let me tell you that you've joined the wrong party. There are other parties that would welcome you, but we are not here to give you our time."

"I will not waste your time in enumerating the aims of other parties – whether they are to make the rich richer or to deny the presence of the Almighty and put a Marxist ideology in His place. You, the citizens of Maya, are here I take it because you have weighed up what the other two parties are about and have chosen to support us. We welcome you wholeheartedly and encourage you to make a valuable contribution. By working together for a common goal, we will make the little man a real man."

The Chairman then explained that with each promotion to a deeper purple hue would come privileges already experienced by the few who had ably assisted the Party to come this far. In addition, there would be certain specific rewards – all of which would in good time be disclosed to Party members. He then suggested that such an important task as to who should decide on whether a member qualified for upgrading should be left to a man of deep insight – Robert Augustus – who was not only the creator of the purple masks but represented most admirably what the Party stood for. There was much clapping from young and old, and looks of admiration, especially from the ladies.

Save for Gavin, who abstained, it was unanimously agreed that the purple mask of the leader of the Party be different from all others and of the deepest purple – grade five plus.

Robert Augustus stood erect as a pillar. "Comrades, I see I have no choice but to accept, albeit reluctantly, this honour you have so graciously and generously bestowed upon me. My reason for accepting stems from the Chairman's insistence that to do other-wise would greatly upset the old stalwarts of the Party who, he says, know the full measure of my contribution. Those are his words and I repeat them here for I want everything that is agreed to be as clear as spring water. But I am a democrat at heart and feel strongly that such an important task as deciding who should be honoured with the higher grades of purple should not be left only to me or to any other individual. In view of this, I am proposing that I would be greatly helped if three colleagues of long standing, well known to you, stalwarts of the Party, were to assist me in this task. I refer to three upright, honourable men – Mr Read, Mr Wright, and Mr Goodfellow."

There was nothing to be done but to accept Robert Augustus's proposals. I could see that a few members were disappointed, hoping that those who would be sitting with Robert Augustus should themselves have been nominated and elected by the floor, but the Chairman pushed on, saying that as time was of the essence and as the leader of the Party had an appointment with the press, he asked the indulgence of all present that promotions to grade two and grade three purple masks should be decided by a second committee comprising of two upright and sound Party members. Only two members were required, he explained, because both committees would be working together to ensure a smooth flow from one grade to another.

There was silence from the meeting. "I can see that it will make sense, comrades," the Chairman added, "if the three, privileged to sit with our leader, did from time to time also sit with the selectors of grades two and three. I know I am speaking for the Committee of Four when I say how useful it will be if these honourable men just chosen by you were there to be consulted by the two members yet to be chosen."

Robert Augustus again asked the indulgence of the Chair. "If I may be so bold, Mr Chairman, as to suggest that as we already have four men, the floor should propose two young ladies to sit on this Committee, for by so doing we would be paying tribute to women, beauty and youth. May I publicly confirm, well before you make your choices, that the views of the two committees will be respected and adhered to by this party as long as I am at its head."

This decision was unanimously approved as the working of democracy at the highest level within the Party. Two very attractive young ladies were nominated, one a fashion model, nominated by her aunt, the other a former beauty queen, nominated by her godmother. No other young ladies presented themselves and they were duly elected.

A few specially handmade 'presidential masks' of the deepest purple were exhibited in a glass case. Party members surrounded these exhibits, very excited at the thought of being in government, in power, with their very own president.

The Chairman was about to bring the meeting to a close when Gavin stood up. "Mr Chairman," he said, "a number of us here are becoming a little uncomfortable at the speed with which important decisions were being taken without approval of the rank and file."

"What are you referring to, young man? You are making a very serious accusation. May I remind you that much time was taken up in the informal discussion and exchange of views, which you may choose to call chatter and to ignore, but this is the way our party members have always expressed themselves and will continue to do so. It is the way of the 'little man' – informality makes it easier for the shy and underprivileged to have their say. I trust you are not from one of the other parties. I was under the impression that everyone here...."

Gavin shook his head slowly. He seemed to be resigned to the voice he was hearing.

"Yes, I noted you abstained," the Chairman added. There was a disquieted hush. "I was under the impression that everyone here wished the leader of our party well and wanted to empower him so that when he stands on any circuit at home or abroad, representing us, the people of Maya, he knows he has the full support of the Party and does not have to keep looking to his back. You can get a stiff neck doing that." A few giggled.

"Mr Chairman, none of the important decisions taken at this meeting were brought to the rank and file of the Party. You cannot seriously say that this meeting was called so that our views might be heard. We came and merely witnessed what was already agreed to by one man, and it became Party policy."

"Are you," the Chairman repeated, "are you from another party trying to undermine us, plant dissension in our midst to weaken and disorient us? It would not be the first time a political party was infiltrated. We cannot be too cautious."

"I have paid my party dues," Gavin said. "Besides, if every time anyone criticises the workings of the Party, his loyalty is questioned, this alone will deter everyone, save the brave or foolhardy, from expressing differences of view."

"Please remember this," the Chairman said, "Even Christ acknowledged that, 'He who is not with me is against me.' We are all Christians here."

The older men and women murmured approval. This was a

Christian party, which would be looking after the small people, too long ignored by the colonial government.

Robert Augustus passed a slip of paper to the Chairman who, on reading it, said: "Listen sonny, the leader of our party is willing to forget all this and would like to nominate you to join the two nice ladies who will be deciding on the grade two and grade three promotions. I'm sure the ladies will welcome you with open arms, for they can see, as we all can, that you're a good looking fella."

Gavin was livid. It was taking a great deal from him to control his anger. "You pretend," he said, "not to understand what I am saying, and I can see no place for truth here. To use the very method I am criticising to nominate me turns me into a fool, at best, or a fox, at worst. Do you think I would rise to so hollow a bait? That you should have even proposed it brings home to me too clearly that I do not belong here."

The meeting was brought to a close.

All this while, Emmanuel Pottaro was crossing the Atlantic pleading with the governments of the United States and of the countries of Europe for investment funds to build roads and bridges and factories, to help maintain and expand the drainage canals of the town and the irrigation systems of the polder lands. This last investment was essential to increasing the production of sugar and rice and the introduction of ground provision farming for the rapidly growing local and regional market. It was widely recognised and further endorsed by a visiting Nobel Laureate Economist from the Region that it was in agriculture for export that the Mayan potential for substantial and rapid growth presently lay.

Not long after the distribution of the purple masks I noticed something contagious had taken hold of Robert Augustus's supporters. It was vigorous, consciously defiant to reason. The editor of the *Daily Carrier*, which was owned by Lionel Gomes, was offered a grade three purple mask and became Robert Augustus's carrier pigeon. A select few from the army, the police force, the trades unions and the upper echelons of the civil service were also honoured with fine purple masks.

The battle had begun.

7 FIRES OF BON AIRE
Marguerite

Much heat was emanating from the centre of Bon Aire. Even two miles away, mothers opened their windows 'to catch the breeze'. After a while they noticed slender stems of ash resting on beds, dressing tables and chairs, cradled too in cobwebbed corners.

Something large was being consumed by fire.

A cloud of black, billowing smoke covered the capital and would have obscured the sun. Raging flames leapt upwards and sideways licking the air, transforming the business sector into a furnace without walls. The curving wind swept it along and the wooden buildings fed its fury. Two masked men retreated. Their bright, halogen-purple faces gave the impression in the dark of night that they had come from the fire.

Men and women stood and looked. It was three-dimensional and on an expanding screen – something they would talk about for some time to come. But here and now there was the excitement of the leaping dance of flames, the hubbub of crowds, the rapid transformation of buildings to cinders – a gigantic incinerator at work. And in the absence of understanding how this might affect the tomorrows of their daily lives, they were spectators enjoying the awe and wonder, the thrill and excitement of an open cauldron. Before the fires raged in all their fury, there was time for rioting and time for looting. For three hours the looters ran, pulled and heaved at merchandise. Two women struggled with a refrigerator. Fit young men saw in kerosene stoves a hot, fast-moving stock, and stocked up. Chandeliers were carefully removed. Wall-to-wall carpets were hauled and pulled along the pavement and later squeezed into tenement rooms. Radiograms were moved out by boys. Bolts of cloth were carried high on heads. Bags meant for baser things were filled with shoes, shirts, socks or as an aged lady said, 'With freeness, my dear'. A tired looter was resting on a Chesterfield settee on the pavement, while stolen merchandise such as mattresses and cushions were sold to onlookers. A young man tried to wheel a piano out but he couldn't manage and his mother said, 'Leave that, come give me a hand with this,' as she struggled with a large refrigerator.

It was a free for all.

At the Bon Aire hospital, a man dripping blood, his hands clasped to his head, his body trembling, had been rescued by a fellow looter. 'All ah we is one,' his helper had said to him. A piece of glass had gashed his head and lodged there when he had tried to enter a jeweller's shop by breaking through the show-case. The opening was not wide enough, but thinking that he might find the contents of an Alladin's cave within, he decided to push through, but could not make it and had to retreat.

It was said that Country Mayan shops were targeted. That might have been the intent, but neither looters on the rampage nor spreading fires made such a distinction. And so it was that a diverse group of investors – from Maya, the Region and further afield – suffered enormous losses since few had taken out an insurance against civil strife.

Despite the heat and ash, Bon Aireans felt removed from the scene, removed from the loss. They will keep this feeling for the rest of their lives. They were spectators at a show, seeing nothing beyond. For to them there *was* nothing more. When asked, they say the owners of such enterprises are 'not we people'. Businesses collapsed into the mouth of the furnace like the rim of an exploding volcano crumbling into the centre. With them went the very foundation of enterprise: trust, the heart of growth and industry. Those who lost everything were at first dazed by what was before them, then crippled by the stress of repaying their enor-mous debts, unable to think. Our AUL were silent. Their unex-pressed premise was that those who had lost businesses were not of the complexion of Robert Augustus. When the story about the man who had tried to break through the jeweller's showcase reached them, they perceived it as an example of desperation, of a spirit enslaved by history seeking salvation through his own efforts. The store owner could afford to lose his stock, they said, and, no doubt, the mark-up on the goods for sale exploited the poor. Such actions, from time to time, had their uses, they explained. They helped to level an uneven playing field. As a most distinguished academic in the Region added, "this can become a freeing of the entrepreneurial spirit of the nation's 'Have Nots', who need to reach out."

These views were widely reported, and the Region's empathy, guided by its thinkers, was with the man who sought to reach out. The wider world of investors and traders noted such pronouncements. Our professional middle classes shrugged their shoulders.

The historical theme of overseas predators is painted on large canvasses again and again throughout our long archipelago of islands. Hardly a single canvas varies from this one concern. No one dares to portray another experience, not uncommon – that of the unashamed exploitation by corrupt governments of their newly independent states. Nor that of the ever-trusting, hopeful poor, becoming poorer still after political independence, while their new leaders enjoy a standard of living better than that of the colonials they so mercilessly criticised.

In time the spectacle palled, and Bon Aireans retreated to have their sleep. In the morning *The Carrier* newspaper would interpret what they had seen.

In the morning smaller country *marchands* come to their caged stalls to find them vandalised. An old woman and her grandson, still in primary school, begin to pick up the odd trampled sock, broken soft drink bottles and soiled paper bags scattered around the empty shelves of her stall.

"What we go do, Aggie?"

"I don't know son. I don't know." They hold on to each other and weep. The stolen clothes, strong baskets and drinks have to be paid for. What will the old lady say to the wholesaler? How will they start afresh?

Next door is the stall of her friend, Nancy Perkins, who lives in Bon Aire but was away in the country that night. She sits down and says: "What dem son of a bitch think they doing, Mai? How they expect we to live now? O God! If I had known that is what those shits were up to, if God had given me just one little sign, Mai, I would've stayed back and looked after mine and yours."

"I know, Nancy. When you're here, I safe. I know that. What to do now? I so tired, must be me age, Nancy. I don't know what to say to dem wholesalers."

"I understand if they want to rob the rich, Mai, but why we who struggling to make something from nothing, catching we ass here. Madness! O God! What happening to this place? Eh! eh! Like everybody going mad? Some mad sickness bout?" Nancy Perkins sits down and bends her head to cover her anguish. Her entire frame shakes. How to start again without money. Who to turn to? "O Saviour, sweet Jesus give me strength. Stand by me, sweet Jesus. Please stand by me, Lord. Stand by me."

Much later, after she wiped her face and pressed out her dress again with her hands, the little boy comes and sits down with her. "When I grow up, Miss Nancy, and I start to work, I will take my Aggie with me to America. I going to work hard, real hard like you and Aggie and I will send for you too when I save up."

"You do that, Rohan. Take your Aggie from here. No future here for you .... for me too. And you send me a nice chocolate with nuts after you save up real good, boy. You go to America, Rohan and get so blasted rich that nobody, but nobody can touch you. And you walk them roads in America with you head high so that your Miss Nancy will feel so proud. And don't you forget them chocolates now."

"I shall send you a whole big box of chocolates, Miss Nancy, with plenty, plenty nuts and pretty pretty ribbons, just as I know you like."

"You do that, son. You do that for Miss Nancy." And she embraced Rohan as he wept, for her tears and pain had evoked from this child a compassion and affection that stayed with him.

But in *The Carrier*, there is neither guilt nor shame nor regret over what had taken place. Indeed, *The Carrier* blames Emmanuel Pottaro for the fires:

> The fires are a sign that the workers
> mean business and will not be put off.
> The Marxist, Emmanuel Pottaro, has

brought this about by refusing to withdraw the budget or increase wages to compensate the workers. The workers have nothing to mourn. They are frustrated. The strike is legitimate. Down with this Government. The Government should do the decent thing and resign. Down with Communism. Much work is left to be done. The strike continues. Any concessions by Pottaro's Government are now too late. He and his Government should resign for the good of the country. Nothing less will appease the strikers.

8   THE CHIEF FIRE OFFICER

The morale of my staff was not high because of our ongoing wage dispute with the government. A few shouted about their right to strike as the way to better wages. But I made it clear that unless we placed our duties as firemen before such rights, we must expect to find our rights themselves undermined. But a muted anger, a smouldering resentment remained against what I had said.

When we arrived at the scene we were surrounded by onlookers who puked hostility and viciousness upon us – an unusual experience for fire fighters on duty, which we are unlikely ever to forget.

I then received a message that someone had set on fire an electric pole near the power station and so I had to divert the energies of a number of my men to attend to that monstrous act, though it was clear from what was before us, what we faced, that we were already greatly understaffed.

In the centre of the commercial sector of Bon Aire, the raging fire was fierce, large and spreading. Flaming, fanning, blown by the wind, fiery tongues were jumping over streets, burning tops of buildings which were breaking and scattering. Burning pieces of wood carried by the wind to nearby houses soon raged within the buildings, instantly enveloping them in smoke and heat. We received our first call at fifty minutes past midnight. It was clear that the fires had started at least half an hour before, judging by what we saw when we arrived. Yet no one had sought to ring us. Feelings carefully cultivated had ripened.

It is my experience, from all my years as a Fire Officer, that the men and women standing around a burning building do their utmost to assist by complying with our requests. There is a great respect for the swift destruction of fire. But in this instance the onlookers tried to hinder us by a considerable disruptive interference. More electric poles were set on fire and on one occasion we firefighters came under gunfire as we faced the impossible task of trying to prevent the raging fires from spreading further into a capital of wooden buildings.

My task and those of my men were impossible. In the midst of this open furnace, we discovered that someone had cut and removed one thousand, two hundred and thirty-one metres of fire-fighting hose. Then those operating the power supply went on strike. This meant that the waterworks could not be operated. This stoppage by the strikers I have never forgotten and even now I am unable to forgive. They were on strike for three crucial hours. It was the time when water was most needed.

The sky was obscured by the rising thick black smoke. The few fire tenders I now had were wholly inadequate to deal with what was before me. In the absence of water from the mains all that I could do was to turn to the trenches and canals, but as you will appreciate they were not always available in the areas of great need.

All this while the crowd bayed at us. I and my few dedicated men could have been in the jungle surrounded by jackals.

Two weeks later I applied for early retirement. The resentment of many of my men was suffocating. They were angry that I answered the call. The few who felt as I did, that the fires should not be allowed to spread, were soft spoken, often inarticulate and silent, but they were also serious men with families, with hungry mouths to feed, and jobs were hard to come by.

9 THE ICA POGROM
Aasha

To this day, in the forest in Ica, the cries of mimic birds echo the anguish of the tormented. Vasu and I, all those years ago, heard them piercing the skies. It was the day before the Purple Masks celebrated the British transfer of power to their leader, Robert Augustus Devonish, in a ceremony called the Independence of Maya. And we, unable to celebrate this gain of ignominy and barbarism, came to Ica, the sacrificial place, with offerings of remembrance, for it was here that hundreds were tormented – raped, torn, battered to death.

Today, I make this second pilgrimage alone.

I come by helicopter to Ica, a service town that provided food and small necessities to the miners up river. What was not grown in Ica, the merchants had to bring in by a hazardous boat journey. Ica was cut off from everything save those it served.

The miners – supporters of Robert Augustus – wore their purple masks on that day.

Some say Ica is only a clearing in the forest, but from above it looks like a fresh wound, a deep gash in the bleeding earth. From the safety of distance I watch, fearing ghosts – lives cut down, innocence stilled in houses, their restless energies seeking sanctuary, moving with the forest wind in and out of rotting frames to the main street, byways, bushes and the river bank from where many were thrown.

I see it from afar, fearing the last soft tremulous cries ossified within the walls, afraid to look at the unhinged broken doors of cobwebbed cupboards that could give no sanctuary to mothers fleeing with their children, stumbling, trapped; trying to escape where there was no escape. Those huddled together, hiding in the forest were hunted down.

I have not the courage nor strength to walk again in Ica and see
standing shadows, gaping hollows where mouths and eyes once spoke.

They faced an orgy of violence from men who hacked and bled
the earth. The end came ruthlessly upon them. Death was not
permitted to move swiftly – its torment long, cupped to overflow-
ing in the forest and in the minds of men – unfortunate survivors
who even now cry out in asylums, or in their sleep beg to be spared.

Facing the chopping and the plunging of curved blades, these
men were forced to witness the multiple rapes of their wives,
sisters, daughters, the destruction of those tender bodies, soft
thighs whose pleasurable warmth once coaxed life to come, life
that with a primeval prescience hesitates and must be willed to
come. Here these bloodied wet thighs trembled then quivered
before becoming stilled for cremation. The broken bottles that
probed, that found the soft kernel of their beings remain. Here
fathers heard some unintelligible murmur guttering from within
their daughters, before the unendurable takes them and all is silent.

All this while the policemen, enforcers of the law, watched from
behind purple masks. From horseback, they watched over Ica and
stood still. They guarded the doors of the doomed to prevent
escape, and witnessed the execution of someone's son, then
another's father, and calmly saw how on each occasion the human
body crumpled, the rich red liquid oozing silently from freshly
blown brains. Eyes open without tears, for that belongs to life.

Their horses, though bridled, clasped by gloved hands, were
not immune to human pain, to human anguish. Their ears quivered, their hooves lifted. Alarmed, their necks thrust forwards,
wishing to flee, but were held back, tightly reigned in.

Try as I do, I cannot contain the wretchedness, the despond-
ency that surges within me. This pogrom was just noted and
dismissed by powerful democracies with their own cold war
concerns, sanctioned by silence, the silence of all. It remains
buried, unrecognised.

On cold winter nights, when heavy snows pull branches down
and the wild northerly wind makes the aged cry for warmth, the
children of Ica gather round fires in strange lands and ask what
were the crimes of their grandparents that they were so viciously
denied breath. Was it that they were brought from the East as

agricultural labourers to save and restore the fast diminishing sugar industry? Was it the fine weave of the family codes with which they wrapped their nakedness and their difference; their relentless hard work on the land, with a disposition to postpone self gratification, to save a farthing from the pittance that the emancipated called slave wages and would not touch?

In the forest in Ica, they were cut off from the source and tributaries of their customs, the ancient customs that shaped a morality, the belief that took the emptiness without and the void within and embraced them with a miraculous meaning, a code that sheltered all – ants, birds and fishes too and trees as well. Here they were cut down.

Now Ica is no more. Travellers in the forest say ghosts weep at nights and walk on rusty roof tops by day. Not too far away there stands a church. Its white cross, freshly painted, glimmers in the morning sun. Beside it, upright, another cross. The message on it reads: No sanctuary here for Non-Christians nor Communists for this is the House of the one true God. Glory be to God.

For the perpetrators of this crime the outcome of Ica was as they had anticipated. Those Country Mayans who were able became a new wandering tribe, leaving behind their lives, their homes, their life's earnings, to seek asylum in their middle years, their winter years, with children and grandchildren, at any port, willing to put their hands to anything and everything, to begin afresh, as their forefathers had once done in Maya.

Retaliation in kind? Looting, burning, raping, murder? An eye for an eye? No. Silently they moved away from Mayan shores.

The horror at Ica closed one chapter and began another more prolonged. It was dismissed as an aberration by the Region and the Colonial powers, neither wishing to see the pogrom for what it was – a prelude of what was to come. Ica sent a green signal to the Purple Masks – of the power of violence to control, to direct and to rule. The complicity of silence hoisted by the British and the Americans signalled clear messages to Mayans of who amongst them should rule and who be the ruled, and how this could be brought about.

I was thankful that, further on, the forest covered the earth, kept it moist with branching shade and falling leaves, and would with time, I trust, take Ica's ghosts to its warm bosom.

10   FROM MY WINDOW
Marguerite

It is time to begin at the beginning.

From the window in my annexe I see the dullness of desolation. At nights I am in a land of ghost travellers. Lights on the streets have gone; footsteps echo in emptiness. When the sun rises in Bon Aire, the aimless, dragging walk takes visible form in the solemn stressed faces of passers-by – loyal supporters of my brother, the 'little men' who suffer in the silence of despair. This has set me wondering again and again of the 'might have beens', the 'if onlies'.

It began with the profits that lay in the cultivation of sugar-cane. Many waves of labour were brought from afar to this end – chained in varying degrees of servitude. Our forefathers were the earlier arrivals, later emancipated from servile work on the land. Then the ancestors of Country Mayans were brought to take our place. Because of this, I believe, our view of them was the view we had of ourselves when we were agricultural labourers in servitude. Then our opinion of ourselves was far from flattering.

Country Mayans came from distant shores, quite different from our own, and spoke in foreign tongues. Their apparel was strange to our eyes. They brought a different way of seeing, thinking and living – new seeds to grow, new foods and spices and scents unknown to us. Their jewellery crafts, patterns, designs and colours, their homes were unlike our own. They brought their philosophy, sacred texts, songs and dance and hymns, ceremonies and rites. They brought their gods, as our colonisers did before them. They had a respect for money and managed it. It was this last attribute which at first disconcerted, then alarmed the politically ambitious amongst us, for Country Mayans were not merely managing to live on a pittance; they were growing. This bred an anxiety within us.

Some who left the sugar estates early were improving themselves by hard work, thrift, and a meticulous care with everything they owned – accumulating capital for investment, almost without end.

They were not like us, their colour, features, hair were not ours and they preferred their own, favoured them to the exclusion of all others, even to the European colonisers. As their numbers grew, our forefathers, the Notables of Bon Aire, displayed their anxieties and fears, and a growing resentment towards them. This was expressed at length in the Memorial they sent to the Secretary of State for the Colonies in 1906. The Notables sought the repatriation of Country Mayans in a way which echoed the manner our own people abroad were at times regarded. How much like others we are when our interests are similar!

The Notables request was not granted and this only further increased their resentments and anxieties. And so it was that they relayed the baton of their disappointments and fears to their offspring. It was almost two generations later that Robert Augustus seized this baton and ran with it, for he could see the time was ripe for another attempt to halt the Country Mayans in their steps and even force a departure.

His main political rival, Emmanuel Pottaro, depended in the main on the support of his fellow Country Mayans. He became the Premier of Maya and sought independence from colonial rule while openly espousing Marxism, as the way to counter a soulless capitalism, the capitalism of servitude. Pottaro wished to capture a higher worth for ordinary men and women, an equality for all, as the early Bolsheviks themselves had once envisaged.

But Robert Augustus knew that the conservative, tradition-loving, churchgoing urban communities of the working and middle-class Bon Aireans, to which we belong, would be appropriately scandalised by the word communism – a system without God. We were Western-educated with a strong Catholic influence in our elite schools, where the leading men in the governments throughout our archipelago of islands had for generations been educated. He sensed that the wish among urban Mayans to contain these aliens, as Country Mayans were perceived, and enhance themselves, would permit the creation of a political climate in which one party and one man would rule.

Robert Augustus saw what he, Lionel Gomes, the leader of the third political party, and the Catholic Church needed to do. Together they pulled democracy apart and with it the rule of law in their desire to topple Pottaro's democratically elected Government.

America, ever wary of the propelling energies of the 'domino effect', became a powerful ally. She had already been outfoxed by one of the Northerly islands where a Marxist government had come to power. The loss of this one island was unfortunate, but to lose two would be seen as the epitome of carelessness.

My brother had learnt something from the failure of the Notables of Bon Aire: *Weave the interest of the super power and your own into one strand*. That strand would hang his opponent. The path he took, the courageous, upright, men and women he felled on his way, is not merely my tale. It is theirs to tell and they must tell it, for to keep silent is to lose our humanity, and make us less than we are – an affectionate, loyal, forgiving, hard-working people with a high sense of beauty and style.

But I have moved on from the beginnings to which I now return.

We, the most privileged descendants of the first immigrants, were now civil servants, many of the highest calibre. We saw ourselves in an unassailable position and wished to keep it so. At the workplace, though not socially, we moved with the colony's expatriates, whose ways and methods we quickly assimilated, including their prejudices against things not European, which meant Country Mayan's ceremonies, beliefs, customs and rites – indeed, their very names which seemed strangely unpronounceable, alien to ears attuned to civilised sounds.

We had long been expecting to replace the British in government, and assumed that it would be fitting for us to have an air of inherent superiority, a disposition which was manifest by the Notables of Bon Aire, and which they expressed with confidence in their *Memoralia*, as you will no doubt hear, as Robert Augustus keeps it on his desk.

The years rolled past, we became the entrenched middle classes. We benefited from the many and varied amenities provided in our gracious capital – our wide leafy avenues, gardens, parks and libraries, concerts and plays. We were comfortable and secure, with Country Mayans providing us with fresh fruit, vegetables and rice, boosting the main exports of sugar and rice which helped to pay our salaries. We had a sense of wellbeing, for the quality of our lives was especially good.

In the meantime, Country Mayans were crossing the mighty Azon to become our *marchands* and dry goods merchants. At first they settled in our secondary streets and then used their profits to move into the main streets of Bon Aire. But this did not alarm us. They were providing a valuable service, and their numbers in Bon Aire were very small compared to our own. A number of them realised that in order to climb our social ladder, they must fashion themselves to our liking. They changed their surnames, their religion, their habits and thinking. They even began to walk and talk and dance as we did. Their very mannerisms were our own. The zeal of some to be associated with a fine correctness – our region's representation of western culture fashioned by our AUL – was so intense that they even laughed and mocked their own, their roots, to show how far removed they were from the traditional culture of Country Mayans. This pleased us greatly.

But those Country Mayans who were refashioning themselves should not be judged too harshly; they were trying to better themselves socially and economically, and were taking the only paths open to them. (Later, a few of such 'evolved' Country Mayans gave their support to Robert Augustus, and rose to high positions both inside and outside Maya. These men were greatly honoured by him for their loyalty and invaluable public relations services in international forums, which provided him with a sophisticated rainbow cover for his tyranny. But I leap forward again.)

Meanwhile, the numbers of Country Mayans had been steadily growing until they had become the majority in our population. Most of these remained in sugar production, the most exploited section of the labour force, and were not truly represented in electoral politics until Emmanuel Pottaro made them aware of its machinery for changing poor conditions. He explained that the role of government was to facilitate their basic requirements for paved roads, piped water and street lights, so that they could in turn help themselves.

Emmanuel Pottaro gave the rice farmers and workers on the estates a political consciousness, another dimension of self – *a political self.* So it was not long before Country Mayans were seeking to play a part in politics that reflected their numbers and their large contribution to the economy. This was deeply disturbing to urban Mayans: to realise what you believed was your own special place was never really yours, but belonged to everyone; to begin to suspect that it is the monopoly you enjoyed that made you appear larger, and that the differences you placed such high value on were not inherent within you, but thrust upon you by privilege, is too much a displacement of your worth. So the Country Mayans had to be stopped.

But they lost because they were ill equipped for the fight, because they were peasants leaving the countryside, entering an urban environment of political intrigue for the first time. We were experienced civil servants in charge of the wheels of government; we were articulate, endowed with political craft and an intense desire to ensure that they did not succeed. We won.

We won with the help of the CIA, by breaking the rule of law, by violence and by British complicity in changing the system of voting used everywhere else in the archipelago to another which would benefit us. We won. And by rigging every election we presided over later, we kept on winning. We were winners. We became perpetual winners, and with the power of patronage for we controlled the economy.

Pottaro's supporters were caught between the millstones of racism and communism. Many of those who had left the estates could see that it was only their own enterprise which would throw open the gates of agricultural serfdom. Yet they supported Pottaro because they had no one else. Being a true Marxist, he neither represented nor reflected their cultural inheritance. He cared nothing for their culture – their ceremonies, their philosophy, yet they voted for him. He was an honest man, a man of principle whose concern with improving the living conditions of the poor formed the pivot of his life, and that was enough for them. This was understandable among the poorest of the Country Mayans, the sugar workers, and the small rice farmers, but the large and medium rice producers and the growing band of businessmen also favoured him. Were they unaware of the encumbrances a heavily bureaucratic state control would have placed on their enterprise and initiative? This strange complicity between a leader and his supporters, whose inclinations should have put them on different sides of the political spectrum, reveal the power of race and kinship in our politics. My brother drew a similar unquestioning support from urban Mayans, though in this instance, their preference for him, for government jobs and his ambitions to nationalise the economy were in perfect harmony.

Pottaro's Country Mayan supporters were trapped as I have said between racism and communism, but that was not all. His dismissive Marxist attitude to their culture and philosophy left them naked in the face of the assault that was to come. It came in the shape of a trumpet call from our Region's AUL that Country Mayans should abandon their culture – whose loyalties, they said were to foreign shores – shown by their way of life. In its place they were to adopt our culture, in other words a style which our AUL approved. This placed Country Mayans at a psychic disadvantage, corroding their sense of self.

This call to sameness, our AUL frequently explained, was essential to nation building, the formation of community. The word community meant sameness. Differences were disruptive and should be abandoned. The idea put forward by Country Mayans that differences could be expansive, enlarging, creative was quickly smothered by our AUL, was seen as near treason, too threatening to be allowed.

Country Mayans were being reduced, while we had a rich source of politically conscious, articulate brothers and sisters from America who infused our campus with righteous energy. Country Mayans were on their own, making do with what was handed down to them by custom. We had Atlantic modernity on our side.

Most Country Mayans kept their heads down and continued as before. Those who saw that their prospects were improved by becoming AUL-approved Mayans became AUL-approved Mayans. And so the seeds of strife and resentment were sown, between those who knew who they were, those never in doubt, needing no help from our AUL and those who, guided by our AUL, climbed to prominence by fashioning and espousing a culture of a single sameness for all. Needless to say, such divisions played their part in disabling any opposition to my brother's project.

11 MAUDE AND JESSICA

From the start, my late mother Jessica and Aunt Maude were anxious about our independence, and spoke of little else. Nothing that happened later would have taken them by surprise. Their clownish truths and laughter protected our sanity.

One Sunday after lunch they were enjoying a tête-à-tête.

"The last thing we need, Maude, is Communism. We're a God-fearing people. I see Roman Catholics in Bon Aire are out to stop him, and they will stop at nothing."

"Emmanuel Pottaro's supporters have faith, are God-fearing too, yet they vote for a Marxist."

"We were taught at Church school, dear, that their religion is not the right one, Maude. Still, the majority of them *are* out there in the polders with mud, tall wet grass, cows and more mud. They need someone to pull them out of that. Besides, who else can Country Mayans vote for? They can't vote for Robert Augustus."

"True, Jessica."

"They have enough sense, Maude, to know that Robert Augustus is not for them. My son is for himself. I see the remains of the Bon Aire fire – people who lost everything. Will Country people now put their savings here, see a future here, you think? Call this home? My son created that situation. It was as if he piled the wood for the fire, poured the petrol and left. In truth, that is what he did. I pray that even now he may find salvation, do the right thing."

"The Masked Ones then did what was expected of them, Jessica. Yes he roused them, true. He allowed them to go amok, and then distanced himself from the violence and the looting. It is his style. Years ago when he was a schoolboy, I could see he was not one of us, not a Cummings. Never was. He is a Devonish through and through. The Devonishes are new arrivals, dear, they are confused in the midst of plenty. We Cummings are not bowled over by anything. We ponder, we understand the purpose of education. We never let it down."

"Imagine *The Carrier* saying it was understandable if people did anything to release themselves from Pottaro's communist grip."

"True, Jessica. In any other place the *Carrier's* call would be condemned as an incitement to violence. But here our middle classes and the Church said nothing. Not a single dissenting voice. Our respectable middle classes were happy to encourage the working man to overthrow Pottaro's government, then hope to enjoy the spoils. They are at church every Sunday. Don't trust them."

"Do they really understand what their silence is doing? What they are saying to their children, to all the children of Maya?"

"A kind of vicious ugliness comes from *The Carrier's* editorials, dear. It has grown into an ugly beast. God help Maya if it comes to sit in our heads."

"An increase in wages would have been nice; that was what this long strike was about, we were told. Everyone wants an increase. It was long overdue, but we couldn't afford it, Maude."

"Emmanuel Pottaro said that, but no one believed him."

"All politics, dear. What you believe depends on who is saying it. They would have believed if my son had said the very same thing. Servitude under Robert Augustus would become whatever he tells them it is and they would bear it patiently. I fear for them... I grieve for them. They were on strike demanding a substantial wage increase to compensate, they say, for the tax-raising budget. But wasn't that needed to improve our roads, electricity and water services?"

"We want everything."

"The Government's wage bill must be something else, I tell you. It employs too many, Maude."

"Part of the problem is we have not yet become a people who ask where the money is to come from? We are still at the 'gimme gimme stage', as Mother would say."

"Yes, well, Mother did speak her mind, Maude. Independent. That was Mother. I think we have taken after her. Marguerite too. It must be a female thing."

"Robert Augustus's strategy is to play to people's fears, then to present himself as the healer."

"When he was at secondary school, Maude, I observed how he ripped two close friends apart, and then presented himself as a go-between."

"A politician through and through, Jessica. Pottaro could have printed more paper money and given them an increase."

"Yes, but Pottaro wouldn't do that, Maude, for then the weak would have suffered most. And whatever we may say about him, Marxist or Leninist, he is truly the poor man's politician... Well, that's his problem really. A poor man's politician needs rich friends, private investment, successful enterprises, but Pottaro does not address this. The problem is complex and his remedy is simple. He sees the world through the eyes of exploitation and colonialism."

"While we need jobs, training for our young people."

"I agree. We need people to invest in us. If you don't know how to bake a cake, to package it and advertise it abroad, you have to attract fine bakers. You have to pay to learn."

"But who will they attract with the kind of rhetoric he and Robert Augustus are continually spouting – bashing foreign investors?"

"Now the big talk is of how we're going to own everything on this island. Nationalisation? Foolish! Forget it! God help us. We're putting the cart before the horse and talking big."

"What we call rhetoric, Jessica dear, is the fashion of the day. Bashing foreigners turns our bashers into saviours."

"An expensive indulgence if you ask me. Tell me, when ordinary trusting folks hear this, what message comes through to them? It is – don't take responsibility for yourself. Blame foreigners for every goddamn thing. You and I know that.... If Pottaro had given them what they wanted, Maude, they would have found something else, some excuse to stay out on strike."

"A political strike, dear."

"As clear as day."

"Robert Augustus brought in his *Culture of Masks*, then he climbed on his rostrum and conducted the strike from there."

"My son's cunning makes Pottaro, Lionel Gomes and all the others look like schoolboys. Have you noticed, Jessica, how senior civil servants, trades union leaders are all rushing, falling over themselves to do his bidding?"

"Still thinking slavishly. It becomes a habit."

"If only he had kept his political craft, but had Pottaro's heart."

Aunt Maude got up and looked through the window. Mother was silent. Then she said, "Pottaro broke under the strain, Maude."

"The strike's success was the beginning of our night."

"What a fool Pottaro was. His ideology made him blind. That could never happen to my son. He would use ideology, not be buried by it. Pottaro was no match for his cunning. Even now my son and his supporters are still battering down the remaining walls of decency. Look at those wretched cartoons in *The Carrier*."

"Look at those gross open letters, published unsigned. No editor should publish unsigned abusive letters to anyone, still less to Pottaro – he *is* the Premier of our country. It is the silence, Jessica, the silence of our citizens throughout all this that worries me to death. I am terrified. We are teaching our children to become big bullies whenever things are not going their way, for they can see that bullying pays. We are saying to them that lies, misrepresentations, strikes, fires, riots and looting are means open to them whenever they find themselves as the opposition. We are saying there is a respectable, valid place for destruction in our politics. And that is not all. We are conditioning them to be insensitive to the hell we create for others, Jessica. We are saying to our children: accept violence. Be silent when we are its perpetrators. Our children should be screaming at us, at the hell we are building. We brought evil and wickedness into politics, and we are teaching them to close their eyes to it. Oh how we prepare ourselves for burial! Dear God, why this long night? Tell me, Jessica, you didn't expect the Christian Churches to protest at the ugly way a communist was being undermined, did you? The Church is tied to its own interests. It is human, Jessica."

"Like the rest of us, Maude... But is the Church not supposed to say: 'Stop this incitement to loot. We are accountable for our actions. We are responsible to a Higher Order'?"

"Christ may have said that, Jessica, but Christ is not the Church. The Church is not Buddha, you know. No cross-legged meditation here. No shanti, shanti, here. Only holy wars. Crusades. Remember how the Spanish Christians slaughtered those trusting Amerindians?"

"You have to admit that the Churches' umbrella is only for their own. No wonder that to Country people Marx's umbrella seems wider."

"The Church cannot be for a Marxist, Jessica, nor for those who will vote for one. It cannot be for those who merrily say that their own religion is their path to God, and that it is but one among many pathways. "We respect your way and our way." That is their dictum, dear."

"Yes, fancy expressing faith so simply."

"The Country Mayans' attitude to religion, their very concept of it, is different from ours."

"The differences are the problem, Maude."

"No dear, it is our attitude that is the problem. We believe there is only one path and we are on it. We go around the world with our missionaries saying, 'Get on our path or hell awaits you.' Country Mayans believe there are many good paths and you are on one and they are on one. But we simply will not have that. We want to be "The Way. The Truth". Not merely another way, another truth. We cannot water down our authority like that, my dear, now can we? We are salesmen. When we move from door to door with our articles of faith, we say, "This is the genuine article, all else is fake." You see the Country Mayans are not salesmen in this way. Have they ever tried to convert you, Jessica?"

"No."

"They respect your religion, but we don't respect theirs. No! No! We believe theirs is an inferior man-made thing, and ours divinely inspired."

"You know, even at the eleventh hour, my son could have prevented it. Why didn't he? Why didn't he, Maude?"

"What, dear?"

"The fire. The Governor asked him to tell his supporters to disperse, to go home."

"Yes. I remember. He was asked but refused. What he said to the Governor is best left unsaid. He would not stop the mob. He needed their energy and recklessness to overthrow the Government."

"My son had long seen himself as the master builder of an Independent Maya. By refusing to intervene, he showed Pottaro and the British Governor that a violent force resided in Bon Aire

and he controlled it. It was his own Pandora's box. I feel it in the
air. It is suffocating me. I can't believe he came from my womb and
my spirit has no effect on him. It does not make sense. I tried,
Maude. I gave him the best. What else can a mother do? If the best
environment cannot do the job, if the best education does not do
the job, what are we left with, Maude? What am I left with, dear?
My spirit has left me. I have to detach myself from his activities to
keep sane. When he and I are together it is all surface talk. If I
attempt to bring up what is covered, he tells me, 'Mother dear,' in
that paternal old-fashioned way, 'you do not understand politics.
It is another world; different rules apply. Leave it to me; I will give
our people a better world. I will give my supporters every opportunity to train and learn new skills when I'm in government. Every
scholarship will be theirs. I will be responsible for training the new
rulers of a developed Maya'."

"Yes, that sounds like him. The purple mask is tied to our
heads, and it covers the face God gave us."

"Houses looted, burnt if they are not in the right political
district."

"We are not at risk here in the countryside, Jessica, though we
are surrounded by Pottaro's supporters."

"You're respected and cherished as their Nurse Maude, their
Aunt Maude, their sister Maude, their good neighbour Maude. I,
as Robert Augustus' mother, cannot expect the protection that
comes from *love*, can I?"

"No but from *fear*, Jessica. They would fear Robert Augustus'
mother. I am wavering as to which is the stronger."

12   THE MIRROR

It was her brother's request that his discourses be recorded that
led Marguerite Devonish to be sitting at her desk. Her posture
erect, firm. Five vibrant green pulses flickered before her. She was
the only one he trusted and the timbre of her voice was close to his
own. The discourses were in his hand, which had grown progres-
sively light and feathery like the flapping of a moth:

Were it not for recent experiences, I, Robert Augustus Devonish,
President of Maya, would not have felt driven to record for posterity
certain crucial facts concerning the first thirty years of my country's
independence from colonial rule, and my governance of it.

My voice has now left me. Broken. The local doctors say the loss
could be permanent unless I have an early operation – a simple
operation; they smile to reassure me. I have also been advised to
go abroad for treatment. It is the state of the public hospitals, Aunt
Maude whispers, but I will remain here. I trust no one.

I have used my voice shrewdly and unsparingly to diminish my
opponents. It has been my chief artillery piece. No one has
survived it. Only my late mother knew the extent of my artifice in
using it. She may indeed have lost the will to live when she heard
the Region's intellectuals crying 'An orator has risen amongst us,'
in response to my sonorous words, words that expressed my own
ambitious agenda and theirs.

Two experiences came upon me on the same day, and their
combined impact wells up within me. They may indeed have led
to my vocal loss. The first was born in another world – my mother's
doing. The intensity of it is her style.

When dawn was still far from coming and darkness stalked my
thoughts, I found myself walking in an abandoned construction
site – a harsh, barren, windswept plain. I wondered: What ideas

had spurred the builders? Why did they fail? Was it a malaise within the environment or within themselves? What brought its collapse? Was the project bankrupt from the start? Were their very methods unfit? A shoal of questions swam around me.

I stood scanning the mix of strangeness and familiarity, when my eyes caught an aperture – the mouth of some conduit. It was a long covered corridor of baked earth almost hidden by a tangle of weeds which were the only signs of life in this desolate landscape.

I left the path and descended a steep incline to get to this opening. Why I entered I cannot say. It seemed safe. I had not travelled far within, when I heard footsteps coming from the tunnelled darkness, shuffling as if overburdened, weighed down. An incoming shaft of light revealed this enclosure. It was clean and dry as weathered bones. The footsteps grew closer, more distinct. I saw the figure of a man coming towards me. There was something strangely familiar about him, exactly what I could not decipher, though I tried hard to ascertain what it might be. Suffice to say I was well disposed to him and found myself asking why he had walked into this deep fissure? What could possibly have sent him there? On his coming into a shaft of light, I saw that from his steps squelched the secretions of a decomposing infection.

I looked about me fearing to move, yet wishing to avoid the putrid vapours. The footsteps of the approaching figure also ceased. Again I turned in his direction and saw why. He had grown gross. Blubs of fat were hanging from a frame which could no longer support this excess. This gross voluptuousness re-sulted in his inability to move forward or backward. The walls that now held him had become alive. Some ancient ossified bird of prey had been stirred to life, roused from a Pre-Cambrian slumber by the dripping mammalian fat which was now firmly bonding to its giant reptilian gullet – the walls of the conduit.

I knew I was lost. Had lost all form, had become a waft of floating consciousness. All this while the human figure con-torted, as a worm clasped in a sharp beak wriggles in an attempt to release itself. A most piteous sight! Each time he moved, the muscular walls compressed further and his body became more deformed, so unimaginable that I could not help crying out to him: "Be still!" I pleaded. "Stay still," hoping that by so doing he would conserve a semblance of his shattered visage – his fast diminishing humanity.

He must have heard my heartfelt cry, for his head, which had been lowered in an attempt to bend and crawl on all fours, made an effort to rise. As he slowly and with great pain lifted his bulbous head – a swelling ugliness, once bone encased – blood oozed from the multiple folds of his neck. I felt at one with him. His pain was mine. For an instant, a deeper, sharper shaft of light spirited itself tumbling headlong onto the stranger's face, and I saw he had been wearing my mask of Tyrian purple which had fallen, and what was before me was a mirror.

I was thankful for the sanity of awakening, for the ordinary and the commonplace. Before a standing mirror, a gift from mother, I examined my limbs. There I saw what I had hoped, save for one thing – my eyes were those of the tunnel's mirror.

That morning, the need to be in the open pressed in on me. I walked to the town centre in disguise, wearing a common mask. A number of vendors were drinking coconuts, enjoying the soft jelly with coconut scoops as they chatted around the laden cart.

"There was a time when coconuts were one dollar," a woman said, her outstretched arm handing thirty-five dollars to the coconut vendor.

"You can't get them at that price today even for love, meh dearie. Now you talking bout ancient history – when this Government was in opposition. But then you see, people right here in Bon Aire went about in bands, marching and shouting, waving placards saying: *If Pottaro wins we go to pots*. Even my neighbour had a placard saying, *If Pottaro wins, slavery begins*."

"Well," said an elderly gentleman, "we know better now, for in the meantime prices have gone up so many times and wages have deteriorated. Is this not servitude? We have a currency that has lost its worth. What good is that? This Government has robbed me of a pension. My pension is a pittance. And that is not all that grieves me. They took the money I had in the bank and bled it to death. I am left with useless printed paper – useless – no one wants it. It is a living shame to hold it. This is not money. It is hell to be brought so low when you're old, knowing that all your savings are being turned to ashes by this Government. Take something as ordinary as condensed milk...."

"Only the President can take condensed milk, Mister. It is not in the supermarket."

"What about civil servant's salaries, Mister? They said they come out on the long strike not to bring down Pottaro Government but, correct me if I'm going wrong, for an increase in salary and a lowering of taxes. It was for a better juicy life. Am I right, Sister? I remember people on the pavements, and the sidelines, and all those looking through them upstairs windows and doors, right here in Bon Aire – smiling, happy to see Pottaro fall. *Ahh pulling down Pottaro so*. That, Mister, that was unconstitutional. The Church think we foolish – we know they don't like we non-Christians. They wouldn't like to see the *Geeta* in the Prime Minister's office. I know that, you know that. Colonialism does make you think like that. Mister, it has to be the old Bible or nothing. So they kill two birds with one stone. Think they smart talking bout Communism, over and over, while joining with the devil they now have. He outwitted them. He used them. They couldn't control him, but the Church help to get him there. God not sleeping I say. The Church is one big joke. The pundits here are a bigger joke still – they explaining nothing to the people, treating we like children. Telling my wife, put this here, put that there. And she and I don't know why. They all looking at their own interest. We poor people better start copying them. I give thanks that Pottaro is not with us."

"Why?"

"No shame."

"Who?"

"Dem unions have no shame, Sister. No shame at all. Thank God, my wife say, that Pottaro is not living to see how the unions crawling about the President's foot. Thank God she say. I say God is merciful even to shameless sinners. But then he is God, na. What you expect?"

"If I were Pottaro," the gentleman said, "and lived to see how the trade unions are today kept in their place by the President, I would leave politics. I despair for our country. If you think on these things you would lose faith in our culture, even with education. I say this with a heavy heart, for educating the young was all I had to give."

"You know, Teacher, education is all we have to separate us from the jungle. So we have to hold on to what we have. What to do? The culture here in Maya is like an old car. Sometimes it takes the family where they want to go; but then again, sometimes it wouldn't start, even in an emergency. My friend has an old car and it stay just so. No use saying, come on, come on man and kicking it. It can't do what it can't do. We have to upgrade the culture. But if we can't afford to upgrade just now, my mother-in-law say, we should at least make sure the car is in a good condition for emergencies... That is woman talking."

The former teacher, standing with a trained uprightness, having refreshed himself with a jellied nut, again joined the banter:

"We can all remember when prices were lower, when we had bread to eat, when living was within the means of most of us, but I tell you, this has become a place to leave. I told my son only this morning that he has delayed too long. He is wasting his precious youth here. This is no place for young people." The man paused. "Come to think of it, no place for old people either."

For a long while there was a stony silence around the coconut cart. Then, staring in front of him as if he had just seen a passing shadow, the upright man said in a faraway voice, a voice that was not his own, "Maya has become a land of horrors. A land of horrors where neither the living nor the dead can rest. Those of us who pretended we didn't know the hidden agenda of the President and connived with him in silence – beware! Vengeance is mine saith the Lord. And there shall be fatal accidents and terminal illnesses. No one knoweth when the Lord striketh. For when he comes he will blow neither trumpets nor beat drums. The Lord works silently as a passing cloud."

"But what can we do, Brother?" said the vendor. "Who will take we?"

"It is a place to leave," the man repeated. "A place to leave."

As I was returning to my residence, the road sweeper stood eyeing a bank note blown by the wind, waiting for it to settle. When it did, he scooped it up with the surrounding trash and emptied all into a foul drum.

13   FOR THE LOVE OF MY NAME

A place to leave.

It has become a place to leave, the man at the coconut cart had said, wiping his lips. And the others readily acquiesced. When this is voiced in the open, I ask myself, what is whispered in closeted rooms when shutters are down? I go a step further: What is thought and not spoken, fearing that walls have ears, fearing the wind that lifts sails and kites and voices?

Should I take comfort in his 'has become'? It is the perfect tense, for Maya was a place to leave many years ago, after Ica, after Hope Bridge. But then you see, that civil servant, headmaster perhaps, would have felt he had a stake in the society I was creating for him and his son. And therein lies the rub. My supporters on every rung of the ladder are happy when I make space for them to climb upwards, by facilitating the departure of others.

When I came to power, I did not use meritocracy as a criterion; that would have been Mother's way and Aunt Maude's, for they learnt well the methods of examinations, a legacy of colonial power, which makes the assumption that the opportunities to do well in examinations are widely distributed. They prized this, their means of climbing out of an underworld into the sunlight – the respected realm of civil servants and the professions.

I will concede that when it came to examinations in Maya, we, the town's people, had an overwhelming advantage over those from the countryside – the sugar estates, rice lands and polder land. I doubt if a single library exists in those places. So we did capture the feast of opportunities each year, but I required certainty. My preferred criterion was nothing new – though often veiled in sophistry in foreign lands. It is an old, much used one: loyalty to myself and the Party, which in truth became the same.

Let me state my case: For an entire generation, I gave my supporters, year in, year out, numerous opportunities – scholarships, exhibitions, grants and loans. See how educated they have become, a lifetime of benefits has accrued to them and their families. No doubt they are reaping a good harvest here or elsewhere. But most of all I am proud of the fact that I offered them more places at our university than they themselves could possibly have imagined. I have earned the title 'The Master Planner'. I brought in the stratagem of national service as an essential requirement for university places, knowing full well that those Country Mayans who clung to their old cultural traditions would not want their children, especially their daughters, to be deep in the hot, humid, forested hinterland, cut off from them, for long periods, in an overwhelmingly male, macho climate, designed by my Party and flavoured by its culture. This idea did two things that were advantageous to my people. Far more gained a university education than would otherwise have been the case, and they also benefited from a military training.

Consider having all these advantages for years and years, as well as government's other favours – good jobs abroad, the topmost positions here in Maya. Consider again the priceless psychic and emotional advantages I bestowed upon them, by merely staying in play, being the government, with the power of patronage. It changed their very stride, their voices too.

I was a recipient of a variety of aid for I was perceived by the Western democracies (no mean feat on my part) as a bulwark against Emmanuel Pottaro and communism. When one is skilled, the misconceptions and exaggerated fears of the powerful can be harnessed to pull one's own cart uphill.

Pottaro's foolhardiness even now overwhelms me. His political naivety made him unfit to rule. I am intrigued, though, that half a century later he should have erred in the same way as my forefathers, the Notables of Bon Aire. He did not learn from the Notables the lessons of history as I have done. He did not ask whether his concerns were compatible with the interests of those far more powerful than himself, and if they were not, how to make them so.

It is a child's question, yet did he ask it? NO. His ideology had become a cult. He was a true disciple of Marx and as proud of it as a bragging teenager. Such indulgences! What folly! To think that rights and wrongs are absolutes, and that he, in a particular place and time, held the essential truths for all time. It became his religion. He was blinkered, uncompromising, like the early mar-. tyrs, to the bitter end.

I used his communism to despatch him. By then politics had become a game of poker for those of us who understood that we must align ourselves to powerful forces we could not control or influence. Those forces imprisoned him. He was imprisoned, made to scrub floors, while I had an understanding and walked out into the sunshine. Enough! Think no ill of the dead the old folks say. Ahhhh, but I know the ways of men.

Now my supporters, having eaten and drunk, and reaped what I made possible, have become a dissatisfied, complaining, ungrateful lot. The Governor of the Central Bank informs me that the cupboard is bare and this is what my middle class supporters call *disillusionment* as their grasping hands reach further out and find emptiness.

"It has become a place to leave". I hear his voice again.

In the solitude of this room, I see clearly that for posterity I cannot allow the men I lifted from history's cul-de-sacs and placed in positions of prominence – about which they had been incapable even of fantasising – to write the history of Maya's independence. I understand full well the meaning of *Lebenslüge*. (I can see members of my cabinet picking up their dictionaries. This is the measure of the men on every side of me.)

Lebenslüge is a lie, the lie that is absolutely essential to the continued existence of a particular life. Without it that life perishes, be it the life of an individual, a people, or a state. It is a lie so necessary to their living that though people know it to be a lie, a falsehood, they need it and so embrace it. It becomes sacrosanct, for without it they are lost. Without *lebenslüge* their consciences would act as Damocles's sword upon themselves and they would be diminished. *Lebenslüge* becomes life-giving to them, and they will defend it with their lives, for what becomes of their lives without *lebenslüge*?

Lebenslüge is already in the market place, and the need to oppose other versions of it will guide my thinking. Let it be known

that it is for this reason, and no other, I will from time to time record
my innermost thoughts – my private discourses with my conscience. They are my 'Revelations' – my voice – which will not be
silenced. I can see its therapeutic value – the release of the
growing disappointment that comes at nights.

I have been let down by the Region's AUL. Their philosophy
manifested self-interest, envy, chains of the past, a raging impo-
tence muffled by dynamic words. Strange how I see so clearly now.
Is it because I have chosen not to walk along the corridors of
government daily, but rather to gather my reflections in solitude,
removed from the tiring day-to-day battles of politics?

When I return from the operation, I shall look at all this again
before I certify it as ready for posterity. I may change my mind
and so my tack. *Some things may be therapeutic and having served
their purpose, they need not be disclosed.* Yet there is Marguerite,
whom I trust; she will record my work. I leave my choices open
until I return with a new voice.

My recent experiences in the market place strongly suggest it
is only a matter of time before I am singled out for blame,
harnessed to the burden of failure, then crucified on its wooden
pole. This must not be. When I no longer stand here, the voices of
the living will protect themselves, by directing the shame of it all
on the dead. *So for the love of my name I shall say it as it is.*

[*The President's pen is poised. Touching nothing, he is thinking, "I shall not be the victim of lebenslüge." And this leads him to
ask, "What of its victims?". Time passes. His pen is lowered, drawn
to the sheet and from it flows:*]

The mouths of the victims of *lebenslüge* are more often than not
rotted, unable to speak. The old meanings for which they fought
and died, those old feelings, once charged with the sun's intensity,
decay with time in a fast changing world and like old words lose
their poignancy, then their usage and so themselves.

The questions that *lebenslüge* will not allow the living to ask are
legion. But since my recent experiences, they have filled every
interstice of my brain. Why did the Church and our celebrated
academics, as well as our professional men and women, the
governments of the Region and their leading institutions support

me so ardently, knowing that their confirmation in public places, and their timely silences, empowered me?

Why did Santa Maria, rich in oil, continue to provide me with the energy I needed to stay in power, aware that I could not repay then or in the foreseeable future? Why was that Government so enamoured of me? Why should the democracies of this Maritime Region, knowing that I was disenfranchising more than half the citizens of Maya through ballot-rigging, choose to look the other way?

Why did my supporters so take to the masks? The demand for masks was far greater than the stock we held. A substantial number was sold on the black market. Alas! no more. 'Disillusionment' has become the 'in word' amongst the erudite. It protects the user from his earlier accord with me, while enabling him now to climb to a higher moral plane. Oh the invertebrates that surround me!

Of all the support I captured, the one which I thought would stretch my political skill to its limit, and so give me most pleasure in the taking, was the biggest disappointment. It came from the AUL. They were so easily won. Their combined consciences should have been screaming at the way I was so effectively neutering the opposition at the ballot boxes, denying them access to all media venues to the public ear. Instead the AUL offered me a silent loyalty, a quiet affirmation.

These are a group of men and women who speak continually of academic independence and integrity, yet found it all too easy to keep silent when I had to do things which, let us say, brought *real politik* into conflict with the niceties of human rights. It grieves me to say that these luminaries, whose salaries and privileges are paid by all taxpayers, who travel in curtained comfort on their chosen flights – which they call 'objective thought' – turn out to have ideas that enabled my own to thrive. I marvelled at these comrades' amoebic flexibility – their capacity for double-think – but then, such men have their uses.

The more disingenuous among them now murmur some disenchantment with my government. But their distress is not so strong or sustained that they are prepared to jeopardise their positions. They have no intention of trying to bring down my Government. Why? They find fault with my management of the economy, with my failure to reach targets, my large expenditure on the militia.

But not once did these honourable men, articulate advocates of human rights, focus on those disenfranchised, those forced to leave. Why? Our AUL were flattered no doubt by the attention I gave to our arts and culture – such an overriding attention is rare amongst governments.

Let me remind them that I accomplished what was not thought possible. I changed the very economic landscape of Maya and did so with remarkable ease. The goddess of fortune has long guided my throw of the dice. Rice production in the polders, the industry of Country Mayans, would have become the main source of their rising prosperity. I brought this to an abrupt end. I offered rice farmers prices they say were too low to make it worth their while to continue to cultivate the crop. I did this with the intention of providing cheaper food for my supporters in town.

With this in mind I also brought in cassava mills, at great cost to my government, with the idea of having my supporters grow cassava which would be processed into cassava flour. In this way, in time, cassava flour would replace rice. Were I to unwrap my intent, it was to coax my supporters to return to the land, to make this move attractive to them, so that they and not Country Mayans would be the main providers of the nation's food basket.

Country Mayans dominated land ownership and had benefited from the support given to agriculture due to its crucial importance in our economy. It always was, as I too found, far more difficult to produce manufactured goods in Maya for export than to expand agricultural production on our fertile riverine alluvium. I have now offered my supporters this opportunity to take over from the rice growers, by seizing their leases and offering them to my people. This is my call to them to return to the land.

I am honest about the purposes of my project, but where were the so-called objective voices of the AUL? Why was I allowed to encourage the emigration of the Country Mayans, while opening doors to my kith and kin far and wide throughout the archipelago? Why did they not question this from the safety of their university campuses? Such cowards! Such hollowness! Conduits for their own gut prejudices which they are at such pains to deny.

I was ensuring that this island would belong to the great grandchildren of the Notables of Maya who at the beginning of this century tried to stop the immigration of labour to the sugar-cane estates, but failed. Country Mayans are largely the great grandchildren of that resented labour. I bestowed to the great grandchildren of the Notables the priceless experience of governance and the favours of patronage. It was no mean feat. I did it single-handedly.

Sadly, nothing came of the cassava venture. The cassava mills are today abandoned in the hinterland, a nesting place for rodents. Production was poor, inefficient and unreliable. It never really got started. Mayans preferred wheaten flour to cassava flour. As the Head of the Government I tried to offer new and challenging opportunities to my supporters. I need to say it lest they forget.

Support of my race was the pivot of my own political and economic strategy. Yet the Region's intellectuals and professional men and women pretended it was not so. It is as if care must be taken that certain 'crimes' should at no time be said publicly to have touched us, lest we lose our innocence – our claim that we are solely victims of this violence, never perpetrators. For this is too sweet a song, so very sweet to hum, so comforting a tune.

But do not for a moment think I was alone in my pursuits. Sportsmen, literary and other professional men and women from within and without Maya came to my assistance. A stream of learned men knocked at my door to support the direction I had taken. Such a wide personal support from the intelligentsia gave me the reassurance and the hand I needed when, at times, in the privacy of my study, I would reflect on the path along which I had taken Maya and wondered and wondered.

The loss of my voice has brought my mother's to the fore. I hear hers clearly when I write. She is within my head in a way she was not when alive. But I am tired and shall write another day.

My present solitude has brought an inner stillness, a detachment. A cleanliness. I am no longer fearful to speak the truth, now that I have lost my voice. My pen and paper are somewhat detached from this time and place. Is it my mother's doing? Or is this some deep inner malaise being comforted, soothed – bringing its own release? How to tell the difference? Or is this some deeper inner anxiety that is being comforted – and brings its own release?

14 WHERE IS THE MAGIC?

After lunch, Aunt Maude and Mother had their Sunday nap. When they awoke, I had tea ready. Mother's coconut cake with sultanas and ginger and cinnamon had been sitting temptingly on the top shelf of the cupboard, carefully wrapped. As I cut the cake, its rich aroma released itself, adding to our engaging circle.

Aunt Maude said, "Since yesterday I was eyeing that cake, but you know how your dear mother is about cutting a cake. She turns it into an occasion."

"At our age, my dear, we create our rituals. Having Marguerite with us is an occasion that beckons." She sampled it, smacking her lips. "Delicious. Who could have performed this miracle, Maude?"

"I wouldn't be able to say until I have tasted it, dear."

Aunt Maude drained her cup. "This new system of voting he is asking for in London is sure to be granted. Mind you, the British have not implemented it themselves. Look around. No other island in the Maritime Region has it either."

"Maude dear, do try and understand it has nothing to do with what is right, or suitable. What the British will implement is what will remove Pottaro. It is what the Americans want. We're in their back yard, they say. They will change the voting system in my son's favour. Isn't it funny?"

"What is, dear?"

"The British giving legitimacy to his unscrupulous ways. When he possesses power, he will do the same – change the rules to suit his own game. He has been shown how by old masters of intrigue."

"How do you imagine the Country people will respond?"

"Who can tell, dear. But I know what they want. It is to own their leased land and work it. Farmers or merchants, that is their way."

"They are being ground between Pottaro and my son. They will be crushed, for both men believe the state should own the land ."

"Country Mayans believe in private enterprise, yet they vote for Pottaro."

"Sister Maude, Emmanuel Pottaro does not go to the heartland of his support and say: "If you continue to vote for me you will never be given the opportunity to own the land you're working, for it belongs to the state and shall remain so.""

"To mislead ordinary folks is unforgivable, Jessica."

"Especially those who have placed trust in you, Maude; you have a moral duty to come clean."

"They will pay dearly for this misplaced trust."

"Maybe they should be voting for Lionel Gomes."

"No way, Jessica. Not after the part he and his *Carrier* played. How can they? Besides, even if he was untainted, Lionel Gomes' head is wrapped in that Portuguese mantilla that prevents him from understanding Country Mayans. Their traditional homespun weave, with its strange designs and beautiful colours make no sense to him. He does not understand them and that is a handicap for a representative, don't you think?"

"But Maude, he understands the essence of free enterprise. It is his way. It runs in his family."

There was a pause as my aunt and mother refilled their cups.

"Private ownership has its other side. A daily grind, Jessica. Its motto is sacrifice – self sacrifice, family sacrifice. It's like a greedy primeval god belching out one syllable – more, more, while being fed with sacrifices."

"Hmmmm. For me it means having to do without things at the start, ploughing back everything into the business while you walk about in old clothes and sandals like the small shopkeepers do."

"Better to work for the Government. Your salary slip is in that satin-smooth brown envelope, waiting to be picked up even when you're sick, my dear Jessica."

"Who will want to leave a good thing like that?"

"But you and I worked hard for what we were paid."

"True dear, and there is all that power and privilege you have sitting behind a government desk – deciding when to be helpful and when to show who is boss."

"When your salary is secure, you can turn your attention to asking what life should be about. Do you think Country Mayans ask this question? No. They know. Life for them is whatever they're doing. Imagine cutting up salt fish, parcelling flour, rice and lentils. Imagine, Jessica, a life of dust and wrappings. Not my style. It is for young Vasu, the Independent candidate, not Lionel Gomes that Country people should be voting."

"But he does not have a party and he is not a politician."

"True. He is dutifully carrying out his late father's wish – representing the old man's constituency in these troubled times. Not a politician by disposition, I agree, but he is far better than his elder brother Arun, who should have been an astronomer in a monastery, high up on a mountain side. Tending bees in his spare time."

"Why bees?"

"It would suit him. He would need to don protective wear and that would keep people at a distance. It would be the bees and he. The one buzzing, the other listening."

"Would the bees be listening?"

"Have you ever heard him speak?"

"No. But he says good morning and good evening, bows and smiles. Courteous, like a gracious mandarin of old, but with a young face. But why an astronomer?"

"Vasu told me that Arun's mind is always on higher things."

"Who else is there?"

"It has to be Vasu Nath, Jessica. He's a Country Mayan who has not grown apart from his roots. He's serious about his politics, too. Look at this pamphlet he's put out. I don't agree with all his ideas. Too idealistic – and too capitalist for an old socialist like me. But he's sincere and honest – his heart's in the right place. He talks constantly about freeing the system, letting the people's energies flow. But he seems to think we are *all* imprisoned by a poverty of ideas. A real young man speaking. But see for yourself, Jessica."

"Good looking photograph. I like the smile."

"I knew his father, Jessica; he was handsome too. Decent family."

" 'State ownership of the whole productive sector,' he writes, 'is like tying the growth of a country to a dead dodo'. A dodo would have sufficed."

"Not for Vasu."

" 'A country', he writes, 'can move from poverty and handouts to managing itself with pride and dignity, exporting quality and excellence'. Look at this, Maude: 'Competition is like having a built-in goad at the heart of business. It encourages discipline that leads to efficiency. The country benefits. This is the magic of the competitive system. The producers have to be ever watchful, alert to new materials and fashions – to change. They must show their best mettle, day and night, thinking creatively, to improve, to do better. It is a way to grow'."

"All very well but it sounds like being tied to a turning wheel, Jessica – constantly bestirring yourself. Life becomes a spinning wheel. Fancy being tied to such a rolling, moving thing, eh. I can see no magic there. What about life? He have forgotten about living!"

"Maude, listen to this. 'We don't have a choice'. He says, 'If we don't, our next door neighbour will, and we and our products will be left on the shelf'."

"It's not a gentle world our Vasu paints is it, Jessica? So what happens if, after bestirring yourself, it doesn't work, or you are second best, or your products are not quite up to mark? Not every producer can come first."

"The loss is yours, dear, you carry it. If your product is second best, well you receive second best prices."

"You mean the loss belongs to the enterprising?"

"It happens."

"But what if it is one's parents' pension money that is completely lost, Jessica, or one's own life's savings or a burden of debt you and I incurred to start the enterprise in the first place? What then? Ah! I see the magic now – swiftly and silently, everything you once held in your hands, all your hopes could go up in smoke and no hokery-pokery will bring it back!"

"But think of the energy and thought you would put into getting it right. That is the essence of private enterprise, that is the goad."

"Energy? I would not need a goad. I would be raging like a storm. Verging on madness. But you, Jessica, you would be pitched high. I can see you with your glasses sliding down your nose, serious; smiles buried for good and your eyes pointed, like a hungry vixen's watching a farmyard. That was the way you looked, dear, if you want to know the truth, when you were inspector of schools, trying to see beyond what the headmasters were saying and displaying. You should be in quality control, then we would receive first class prices for our products. Look at our rice. Where is the control? It's so bad, nobody outside Maya will eat it. Ah, with your inbred discipline, Jessica, you would become a tycoon, a true capitalist."

"But why not you, dear. You managed that hospital so well in the old days when we could still be proud of our public services. Just think, how you would feel if you succeeded in some enterprise. You would be creating another world. It would be as if you were in a land which had only strong winds, no oil and little sun, and you invented the windmill – beautiful, clean and useful. That is the magic of the system – the marriage of man's ingenuity and the wind. That is enterprise!"

"But what of the days when there is not a stir in the air, or when hurricanes devastate the sails on my mill? You can't run a hospital like a business. Not enough sickness around – get rid of some beds and nurses – and then an epidemic comes along... No, no. There's much to be said for public services, sister Jessica – not to say having your salary waiting in a sweet brown envelope. It wouldn't make me rich, but I prefer it that way. Anything wrong with that if I manage my own affairs without asking for help, the way Mother did? Is this not also serving the country? Is this not to be called living a good life? What frightens me, Jessica, is that with Vasu's system you are out alone, in deep space. Alone. By yourself, with your thoughts and yourself. You and your inner self and Nothingness. No shelter. Just you and you and your own consciousness in space. And when that conscious energy leaves you, you ask, "Why am I here? What am I doing?"

"Is there no saving grace in space, Maude?"

"No dear, you can't expect that. The market is not a religion even with all that fervour."

"You know what Vasu is really saying, Maude? We have to work at our own salvation as never before. Soon there will be no more special arrangements in our favour. We need to be responsible for ourselves. If it doesn't work, you alone go under, and you don't take the poor taxpayers with you, though we may learn from your experience."

"It doesn't sound charitable to the enterprising ones – those who were way out there in the frontline, Jessica. Those who dared. Shouldn't we all take some of the risk?"

"It has nothing to do with charity, dear. The taxpayers are spared the burden of your carelessness, incompetence or plain bad luck."

"A system with no heart for failures?"

"You don't have a choice. You have to use your head to have a heart. I think that is what Vasu Nath is saying."

"How times have changed, eh? There was a time when it was all heart, Jessica."

"Since when, Maude? It only looked so. It's the Church's business to stress heart. You and I, my dear, have to get the balance right."

"I agree with you there."

"You know, we women ought to leave the house and child-caring to the men and go back to our traditional place – take our enterprise to the market – the world markets. Come to think of it, Maude, this open market is not new to women. We're not afraid of it."

"Well maybe so. Vasu once said to me, 'Nurse Maude, the business world lost a real entrepreneur when you decided to take those nursing exams'."

"Flatterer."

"Eh! eh! What makes you think that I couldn't have been the most enterprising business woman this side of the Americas? He knows what he is talking bout."

"I see. I beg your pardon, dear."

*　　*　　*　　*　　*

I left Aunt Maude and Mother and went out for a long walk along the cart track – the grassy fields in flower on either side – to breathe the air, to take the breeze from the cool eastern highlands. Sugar-cane stems were swaying; two boys fished in the canal. Here was a sweet gentle solitude – a place to assuage troubled minds. I should have been cradled – the sweet sugar-cane breezes should have lifted my spirits, but my thoughts lay heavy.

On returning to the house I said, "I am worried about having independence when so much acrimony is loosed upon the land by my brother and *The Carrier*. There is no balm, no restraint, no empathy with the victims. Look at what *The Carrier* said after the Bon Aire fires – when the black burnt-out buildings looked like the path to hell. My God! The political victims were blamed, and the perpetrators were told that they must 'keep up the fight, keep to the

path, do not falter'. Good God! And Country people are expected
to build their hope and trust for the future on such a foundation.
They are expected to join in our Independence celebrations– the
prize of a bully. Who is fooling whom?

"Have we ever stopped to ask how they must feel, knowing how
Independence came about? No doubt at midnight, when the new
flag is raised, Robert Augustus will be on the rostrum allowing his
voice full measure and then he'll go with open arms and magnani-
mously embrace Pottaro and Gomes. *The Carrier's* photographers
will snap these embraces and their headlines will shout: A NATION
UNITES. PEACE AT LAST. ROBERT AUGUSTUS DEVONISH HOLDS THE
COUNTRY TOGETHER. What a farce! "

"A new name!"

"A new overlord!"

"A new hymn!"

"Independence frightens me. What will it bring when it's built
on so much hate, pain and deceit? Remember Ica? Do you recall
when friends of the raped and murdered came to see Robert
Augustus privately and asked him to denounce the horrors that
took place there, and how he refused? He refused to denounce the
pogrom. Hundreds of families then left Maya. Do you know why he
did not denounce the horrors? That refusal unmasked him, left
him naked. Remember how before the fires of Bon Aire, when a
reckless crowd was gathering, an ugly momentum growing, and
the Governor asked him to help persuade the crowd to disperse,
to ask his supporters to go home, my brother actually said to the
Governor that the little petrol he had in his car he would use for
Party business, not to appeal for peace. 'To appeal for peace,' he
said with his trained advocate's voice, 'to ask the crowd to
disperse, would imply that I had, in the first place, asked the crowd
to be violent and to plunder. I did not ask this of them, so how can
I ask them to stop?' That is the measure of the man, who will
become the architect of this country's future."

"Leave him to heaven, Marguerite."

"What will our Independence harvest under the rule of such
thinking?" I asked.

"Marguerite, we shall reap what we have sown. So will he." That
was Aunt Maude's response.

15   AN ORATOR!

There are many instances – I am spoilt for choice – but amongst
the more memorable occasions on which my voice lifted and
carried the entire House was when, effortlessly, I removed the
right of appeal from Her Majesty's Privy Council in London to the
Court of Appeal of Maya.

History, my people's history, was my main ally.

"My learned friends," I said, rising to the occasion at the
National Assembly, "you must, by now, have observed that there is
an inherent inconsistency between our having gained independence from colonialism, and I trust also from colonial thinking,
having decided to become a republic, and to find that our final
arbiter of justice still rests elsewhere, outside our land, our culture
and the deeper needs and understanding of our people."

"To allow this to continue, my learned and honourable friends,
would be to adhere to the belief that we are less than other men,
that we are not yet free to think, nor to make judgements on matters
that affect us greatly, nor to run our affairs in their entirety. I trust,
therefore, that there is no one in this House who would wish to
oppose my proposed amendment to the Constitution, to let the
right of appeal, to let the final arbiter of justice inhere in the Court
of Appeal of Maya."

Need I say that this well-aimed shot struck bull's eye. I had my
way and this last bastion of power outside my control was now also
mine, the others being the police force, the army, the civil service
and the trades unions. Oh how it embarrasses me to say that I did
not even have to court the representatives of these institutions!
They willingly gave up their rights inherited from colonial rule; all
and more they handed me on a platter. There is something about
the word platter, that brings to my mind the head of John the

Baptist on sparkling silver. Like Salome's, the platters offered to
me are never bare. Poor Pottaro.

It is said, perhaps among my more fickle supporters, that all
this stems from the seductive quality of my voice, but I know
better. They are hoping that by this common flattery they can
neatly extricate themselves from the consequences of their whole-
hearted support for our common artfulness over the years.

Since in these discourses I wish to state the truth, I need to point
out that a single – and one must give him credit – courageous voice
rose in opposition. Vasu Nath, an Independent member, the only
one in the House. A gifted young man, handsome to women, with
an intelligent demeanour. He had travelled, seen other societies,
I was told later when I began to make enquiries. Though I
understood he was a friend of Aunt Maude and Marguerite, I
cannot say I knew him well.

He looked around after I had spoken, to see whether anyone
would oppose my motion. No one stirred. He became anxious, for
he could see my strategy.

When Emmanuel Pottaro, then leader of the Opposition, but
frequently my 'critical' supporter, a man weighed down by the
ideology of communism and a hatred for the colonialism exempli-
fied by the sugar estates, when this man rose and could only
suggest a regional court of appeal, Nath became physically ill at
ease. He knew that a regional court would be too long in coming,
and that I would question why we should wait to implement a
fundamentally good thing since no one believed that we in Maya
were less responsible than our brothers in the region. When I saw
Nath's anxiety, I was reminded of a young asthmatic in need of an
injection, who knew there was no help at hand. When Nath looked
around , he saw himself surrounded by men who were dependent
on me and he knew he would fail. Yet he decided to stand up and
challenge me. Brave lad, a loser from the start. As I looked at him,
I was amused, as Southern courts in the United States must once
have been, when they looked at my kith and kin pleading for justice.
I will admit it. I had an affinity with him for a fleeting moment.

Nath saw that I had played on the same sentiments on colonialism often expressed by Pottaro and the extreme left within my
own party. While Nath suffered, I was exhilarated that I had deftly

turned Pottaro's own fire-power upon himself, weakening him and strengthening my hold on the country. What an irony that Pottaro and his close colleagues – and some in my cabinet – were so attached to the writings of a European – Marx. How colonial! The most radical among us sup at the tables and libraries of Europe and America, pretending an originality to an electorate that is none the wiser. I shall leave their disingenuousness to heaven, as my mother would say.

Nath rose, looking like a fresh sixth-former in the midst of ugly, battle-scarred men. There was something gracious about his manner. I was reminded of my father's generation – those old family photographs – when men showed the clarity of their thoughts on their faces. Now we all wear masks of our own making. I have before me the record of what he said.

"My learned and honourable Members of Parliament, I beg your indulgence to listen to another point of view before you cast your vote on a matter whose importance forms the central pivot of freedom and justice, without which our democracy would be meaningless, a mere sham.

"History will judge us more harshly than we can possibly imagine if we let loose the forces of a new enslavement, if we allow ourselves to be led by appearance not substance, by ethnic advantage not human integrity. Our abiding loyalty must be to upright laws and the qualities in men that will do their utmost to strengthen and uphold such laws, not only for ourselves but for our children's children. Merely to change the colour of tyranny will make a mockery of our Independence.

"Justice is the main pillar of a thriving society. Without it societies crumble. Our democracy, our political independence is still fragile, newly born. Let us, therefore, give it time to find its feet.

"There is within the walls of this House a contrived rapport between us, but outside, racial and class mistrusts are high. Building trust among ourselves is important for stability, but it is crucial to our courts, to the rule of law and to the growth of democracy and prosperity. Let us, therefore, give our courts in Maya time to build this trust and our confidence in them as independent institutions. When all our diverse peoples can confidently say our courts have earned their trust, Honourable

Members of this House, the time would have come for added
responsibilities to be placed upon them. Allow our judiciary to
earn this higher privilege, do not thrust it upon them, lest they
become vulnerable to the leverage of politicians seeking advantage.

"At the birth of political independence in disadvantaged
countries, loyalty to government, to prime ministers, to party and
kith and kin rides high in the forums of government. In heady
climates of expectation, loyalty will be tempted to knock at the
doors of our guardians of justice, to stay their hands. Because of
the imperfections of the processes of justice, we cannot afford to
take unwholesome risks, for once an infection enters our system,
it is difficult to prevent contagion.

"My reason for what may appear an excessive caution to
learned Members of Parliament does not suppose that we are
inherently less honourable than other men, but recognises that we
are particularly open to other, longer-held loyalties. Our population is small. We know each other. It is highly likely that where our
loved ones are involved with the courts, in our attempt to protect
our family, we may be tempted to do all we can to ensure a less than
just punishment for a crime which may be worthy of the full force
of the law. That temptation lies within all men in all states. It is
stronger in small states when one's uncle may be a judge or one's
brother a police superintendent and where the extended family
is to be found in almost all sectors of the state.

"By acknowledging these dangers, is it not better that our
citizens could seek judgements outside the extended family or
political party, especially when they feel cheated or coerced into
accepting what they see as an unsatisfactory outcome.

"Honourable Members, such an arrangement would not be
unique. We have special agreements with our former colonial
power for our sugar and bananas. It is to our advantage to have
them and keep them. When the day comes that we do not wish to
have these, we will terminate them. We can follow this prescrip-
tion for Her Majesty's Privy Council.

"Some will say that bananas and sugar agreements are far
removed from the issue of justice. I say they aren't. It only appears
so because we have divided human activities into departments in

order to facilitate our understanding of them and then we forget the purpose of these divisions. All these arrangements have one common aim – to give protection to the disadvantaged, to improve our people's quality of life. I know the day will come when we will need special arrangements neither for our farmers nor for our advocates of justice. My learned friends, the future direction of this fledgling democracy rests with you. We stand at the cross-roads. I appeal to the evidence before your eyes. There is a growing injustice that is fast spreading through this island. It is the plunder of the unmasked. We either stop this contagious ugliness now, or it consumes us. Honourable Members, I rest my case."

Need I say that I admired his courage? But when the vote was taken, it was overwhelmingly clear that his effort had fallen on deaf ears. This young man made the very error that the inexperienced in politics inevitably do. He appealed to reason, to what is good for the people or the state, when politicians are concerned with their own survival, especially when they look at the stark alternatives before them and see a bleak landscape. They will vote for their interests, for the policies and the party that will enhance them.

I have found that the strongest loyalty often comes not from those who fervently believe in what is being done, but from those who are indifferent, yet need more than ever to stay in power, because of the privileges they enjoy, and in many instances their personalities require it, for they have become addicted to power. How can Vasu Nath have expected to obtain even a single abstention from any member of my party after I had spoken, though they knew that I was throttling the last gasps of democracy. Their future was tied to mine. Such is the nature of men. I have not made them so. I merely use their proclivities. I hope history will not attribute to me some mind-bending power over men with the ability to think for themselves, for after all the men I favoured had a choice. They did not have to accept the scholarship, honour, post or title. I can honestly say, with my hand on the Bible, that at no time have I forced anyone to accept my gifts.

I will admit to this, that even now the ease with which I was allowed to transform what Vasu Nath calls a fledgling democracy into what my enemies call an authoritarian state still alarms me. Yet I understand why this is so, and will in due course attend to the causes with the fullness they deserve. Good Night.

16   LOYALTY AND KINSHIP

I appealed to that primordial attachment that comes to a clan, a
tribe, a people with a common experience of birth, of life, growth
and death. Let that experience be humiliation and the adhesive
that comes from their anguish will withstand death and not fall
apart. The strength of this attachment comes from antiquity. It is
handed down in song, tears, and whispers in the night.

Its energy – primeval, encompassing not merely the forces of
earthquakes and typhoons, which are the murmurings of an age, but
containing the mystery, the propulsiveness of the birth of suns and
planets. It was present at the churning that brought forth earth's
elements. Some say this force – this solar core of pulsation is blind,
without direction, and if not harnessed is destructive.

I say it has the instincts of all matter; that the instinct of survival
and primordial attachments are one. It is not surprising to learn
that it secretes a sticky substance called loyalty, which adheres to
its own, and individuals quickly become a group, a clan, a tribe,
a nation, which if made to feel threatened can bring hell on earth.
This may one day change. A higher perception, a larger behaviour
across cultures and tribes may be in the making, but its time has
not yet come, and will be long in coming.

Imagine the circumstance in which I was placed. I had only to
be myself, nothing more, nothing less, and I would be handed a
crown, a sceptre for the rest of my life. What would you do? The
excitement was overwhelming. The benefits enormous.

The people of Bon Aire saw themselves in me. I did not ask this;
it is not a request one makes. Yet it is in the nature of kin to make,
though when made in sophisticated circles it does not declare
itself openly. I could do no wrong. Bon Aireans felt not merely good
seeing me in the highest office of the land, but exhilarated – for if

I was there, they were there. The history of our region and the
history of the world helped them to believe that loyalty to me was,
in truth, loyalty to themselves. Men will fight, kill and be killed,
driven by loyalty to king, kith and kin.

I think of the time of the pharaohs – the anointed one, half-god,
half-man – when the people over whom he ruled felt they could not
create wonders by themselves, that they needed his divine power
to change the course of nature's flow, to capture its richness. These
sources fed my imagination to create the purple mask and with it
a loyalty akin to that of ancient Egyptians to their pharaoh. It was
the magnetism of loyalty I offered through the purple masks –
which consolidated my victory.

This power of kith and kin not only worked for me. It worked
with equal vigour for Pottaro. Consider this: here are a people who
see that government-created jobs are not wide open to them, and
know they must take upon themselves the business of making a
living. They become engineers of private enterprise, and yet they
vote for a man who would not have allowed the main engine of
growth to rest with the private sector. Here were men and women
whose personal understanding of growth was more akin to that of
the United States than of Russia, yet found themselves in the
unhappy situation of being deprived of political power by the
former. That is the nature of kinship, though a few may say it is also
the nature of ignorance and backwardness. In fairness to Country
Mayans, there were many among them who worked in sugar estates,
whose servile relationship with their colonial employers created an
environment better suited to the expositions of Marx.

The Region's intellectuals, to my surprise, were the most
susceptible to the magnetism of kith and kin. They made little of
the contribution of Country Mayans. I know of one instance where
in an account of Maya's history, Country Mayans were not mentioned. Indeed, my own education department published a little
book on villages for primary school readers which makes no
mention of the rice-growing villages. When to ignore completely
these Country Mayan villages became a threat to their credibility,
our writers gave them short thrift, a kind of footnote. In the main
histories of the region, they were relegated to a page or two in books
of hundreds of pages, though they formed near half the Mayan and

Santa Marian populations, and this despite a long history of attempts to encourage the immigration of my kith and kin from the Northern islands.

Like the force of gravity, the magnetism of kith and kin should at no time be underestimated. It takes many forms. Few of us are able to resist it. I am often amused by the contortions the Region's intellectuals make when criticising me. Many accuse me of not fulfilling my own predictions of what the economy should be doing. But they cannot bring themselves to face the truth, for under their masks of objectivity, they were supporters of my main policy thrust. This is understandable, for when they look in the mirror, they see my face and theirs meshing, and this brings them just as much unspoken satisfaction as it brings their poorer brethren. These sophisticated men needed to have the dignity of political independence far more than the unlettered, whose main concerns were always security of employment, a stable currency and sound economic management to keep inflation at bay. But here and elsewhere, within and without the Region, the better informed make slaves of the disadvantaged. It is the way of the world.

At no time have the Region's intellectuals accused me of ethnic prejudice, though it formed the very pivot of my economic policies. They were more than able to see race prejudice in Pottaro and his supporters. Even the declared Marxist intellectuals amongst my critics found fault with him. 'He was not to be taken seriously,' they said, without stating why, their camouflage being that he was not a true Marxist. On the other hand they were silent or made excuses for my failings. In my speeches they heard an orator, in my philosophy and policies, they found profundity, their *raison d'être*. I could do no wrong that deserved open, public criticism.

As I noted earlier, Santa Maria permitted me to accumulate an enormous burden of debt. Here was a democracy giving help to an authoritarian state. Such is the power of kith and kin. It is a blind force, without reason or compassion for its victims. A disease of the mind. And we have told ourselves and our children that, unlike all others, we have built up a remarkable resistance against it. This view smacks of *lebenslüge*. To say otherwise would take from us, we would become sullied too, infected with the contagion against which we have claimed an inborn immunity. Those we have denounced, have spat upon in our history courses, on high rostrums, would have been brought a little nearer to us. This was unthinkable.

It was easier, more comforting, to keep our children safe from certain facts that could not be accommodated in our thinking. Common knowledge was that slave traders were Europeans and Arabs. This was easy to handle, but who were the sellers? Who the captors of captives? The Ashanti kingdom grew in wondrous wealth, the kingdoms of the traders grew in grandeur and power. The profit of commerce was understood by all. Such a past could not easily be dealt with. Yet, how favourably my governance compares. For even today the trade continues. There are sellers and buyers – it is the nature of commerce. It is also in the nature of things that where there is a large discrepancy of power among negotiators, their transactions will favour the stronger. History taught, guided my direction. But to give up the moral high ground we've monopolised would have been devastating.

These unhappy truths our young minds would not be suffi-ciently robust to endure. Our AUL have for years consistently denied them a balanced diet. Instead, what was fed were sweet-ened fast-foods, simple, easily prepared, giving a rapid flow of energy. In truth it made for a monotonous, debilitating diet. Such is the power of kinship – to ease pain or remove it, whatever the cost, and to eat and drink without questioning. *Lebenslüge* is alive and well not only in Maya but within and without the Region, for it is an important ingredient when brewing *isms*.

Now you may better comprehend the reason for my discourses – conversations with my inner self, my sanctum, where truths are to be found – my need to understand my governance. He who is without sin.... for there are lessons to be learnt, another under-standing to grasp. Power matters. Nothing else.

The pitch for my play was well prepared by our AUL, the Region's governments, and foreigners. Over and over they rolled their own heavy agendas on the ground. I have batted well and long, making good use of a pitch so well prepared, playing brilliant shots. The applause echoed throughout the Region. It would be absurd and unmerited to hold only myself responsible for the direction of my play, when the wicket was prepared for me by so many.

Though our intellectuals have denied Pottaro his relevance, of his contributions, one stands out. It is his offering to the future economic recovery of Maya. In keeping with the truthful spirit of my discourses, it must be stated, and I will admit that it was Marguerite who pointed it out and stressed its significance: There is in Maya no opposition tribe, armed, permanently at war with my Government, fighting a guerrilla war, as exists in some of the Northern islands. There are no fortress constituencies, no 'No Go Areas'. I disenfranchised the Country Mayans and they left. It is not the way I or my brothers in the Northern islands would have responded to such a blatant denial of our basic rights as citizens.

My intelligence services confirmed what I suspected. Pottaro's heart was never for a military or violent confrontation. He would not permit his supporters to acquire arms. My army, police and militias monopolise the firing power in Maya. The Country Mayans are defenceless. By personality and temperament, Pottaro was a domestic cock while I have always been a prize fighter, with sharpened beak and claws, prepared for the kill.

It will thus be far less difficult to knit this island together than it could have been. Retaliation has been minimal and I hear no call for retribution. The victims have left quietly. When I return there will be the whole of Maya to play for, not merely Bon Aire. Who knows, I may even consider selling agricultural land to the remaining Country Mayans (not merely leasing it to them as Pottaro did), so ensuring their votes, showing how much more I can do for them than Pottaro would have been allowed to do. They would realise that backing me was backing a doer, a winner.

Winning them over should be easy. They are now disorganised, without direction; their leaders, and many of the more able among them have left. We have long placed them and their culture on the defensive. A people so long dismissed by us, can be won over. An European Marxism is no substitute for their ancient culture; they have traded in, as Marguerite tells me, a spiritual complexity for a monotonous, simple answer to everything, and so now without roots their self esteem will be low. I will harness them one by one to pull my chariot, with a little inducement – a lick of molasses, an honour, some special insignia attached to their harness with purple ribbons. The more educated will, no doubt, prefer insignias culled from the 'Historical Houses' of power and splendour of the first world. This can be arranged. I have one serving me who is capable of any acrobatic legal feat I request. I am beginning to feel ready for another term.

17   THE MAKING OF A YOUNG COMMUNIST

Emmanuel Pottaro was born on a sugar estate, far earlier than his mother expected. It was reaping time. She had been bending, stooping, rising, crouching and standing.

At about 5.47 am, the early morning dew cools the baked land and the sweet sticky air spreads above the sugar factories that can never sleep. Day and night, trucks piled high with sugar-cane stand in lines waiting their turn to empty their harvest. Pottaro's mother crouched once more to pick up the cut canes and tote them to the waiting vehicles when her son thought he was in a good position to leave the safety and comfort of the womb and see for himself what the upward and downward stretching was all about. The women in the fields rallied round her and the men kept a respectful distance.

It was during the August school holidays when, at the age of seven, he was sent to spend time with his uncle Mahendra in Bon Aire, that Emmanuel Pottaro's curiosity about the large differences around him was first aroused. He began to ask himself a child's questions, which were political questions though his mind had not framed them so. His uncle was in the wholesale and retail distribution trade and Emmanuel was left in the charge of his two elder cousins, Leela who was nine and Mala who was eleven, for his aunt had died a year earlier.

On the day he arrived in Bon Aire, he was met by Judy, the housemaid. She offered him lunch – lamb cooked slowly with a home-made massala, enriched with onions, garlic and peppers. There was dhal puri and fresh beans, steam-fried with tomatoes – and a bowl of warm dhal with the aroma of jeera which he was convinced had been stolen from a royal kitchen.

He was invited to stand before an open refrigerator, and asked what he would like to drink. He said nothing – confused by the many colours and shapes. The maid, seeing his difficulty, said,

"You from the country na? Then you wouldn't want coconut water or fresh orange juice. Have this cola drink, na?"

He was shown a large, scrupulously clean washbasin and offered soap. He was thrilled that the waste water in the basin swiftly spun round just once, gurgled and speedily ran off, out of sight and not into a stagnant pool outside the house visited by mosquitoes. Judy had forgotten to put out a hand towel so young Emmanuel, with the aroma of his lunch rushing up to him, quickly dried his hands on the sides of his trousers. He did not use the neatly ironed white handkerchief his mother gave him. This he would not spoil, thinking it was necessary to keep it in good condition for the town's people to see and think well of his caring mother.

He saw the cutlery on the table but simply rolled up his sleeves and began eating with his fingers. His mother had taught him this art – only the tips, the soft sensitive part of the fingers to take the food to the lips. His fingers are warm, an extension of himself, and his mouth is caressed each time his fingers bring this delight. Fingers and lips engage in such pleasurable play that neither wishes to part.

The cold cutlery lay unamused to be dismissed in such a way. Such habits, it concluded, can only come from the unlettered. However, when this fine cutlery saw that it was being displaced by so flexible and superior a means – whose hold and grasp never failed – it felt threatened and trembled as it endured this sudden shock. It was then it happened. The young man moved his left hand outward; the cutlery fell off the table.

He had every intention of picking it up, but alone, enjoying his food, in the privacy and comfort of this room, he did not hurry to crawl under the table to retrieve the cutlery. He was contemplating licking his plate, having licked his fingers, when footsteps crowded through the front door. Leela and Mala entered the dining room and stood before him, as two upright pillars amidst ruins.

Mala saw the cutlery lying on the floor, trying its best to attract her attention by gleaming and beaming in the sunlight.

"You've been eating with your fingers!" she said in rising fury.

Judy came out of the kitchen. "Miss Mala, some people in the country eat with their fingers."

"This is not the country. It has nothing to do with town and country; it is just uncivilised. He's barbaric. My God! Imagine if

I had my friends with me. What would they think? My cousin eating with his fingers! And look at his trousers! He's wiped his hands…"

Oh!.. Oh! I forgot to put out a towel for him, Miss Mala, but it would soon dry. Don't fret yourself; boys are like that. Don't trouble yourself, Miss Mala, If he sits in the sun – come here and sit, Emmanuel. You will see in two-twos that trousers would be as good as new."

"Look at his shirt, Judy!"

Emmanuel looked at his new shirt and was puzzled, for he had taken care. There was no food on it, not even a speck of dhal, which showed the care he had taken, as he had promised his Ma he would. He looked at Mala with his curious, clear, childlike eyes, watchful and alert, sensing the closing-in of a hunter. At home, his mother would have wrapped a clean towel round his neck but here... well... besides there was no need. He was rudely awakened by Mala's judgement.

"That is real coolie-coolie colours, that bright yellow and red. Daddy said to take you to the sea wall, but I will not be seen with you in that."

Leela said, "Go wash your hands. You have other shirts?"

"I like this shirt. I like red, yellow, orange and purple. When the sun is setting behind the rice fields, these colours stream out and make the whole sky happy. You should see these colours on the tail of the kite my pa made for me." And his eyes smiled, seeing his kite flying high against an infinity of blue. He paused, gathering his courage, for the disdain in the eyes and mouth of Mala could not be borne. He said, "Besides, Ma says these colours are like jewellery."

Mala displayed two rows of cutting ivory between lips of contempt and said, "Only the poor would think like that, only poor people would say that."

The young boy ran from the room, feeling the need for his handkerchief and his own company.

As he settled into his uncle's house, Emmanuel was amazed that there were so many taps in a single house, that water did not come from a drum or tub in the yard or a well; that at nights there were street lights, and the bathroom facilities were shining clean, beautiful and indoors. Indoors! He was enraptured and inclined to believe that similar arrangements existed only in heaven. He began to ask himself why the people in the country, close to this plenty of Bon Aire, were so poor. His love for his parents and his affection for his neighbours led him to feel that what was in the town, in his uncle's house, should also be in the countryside. It could not be the difference in the length of hours town and country people worked that caused it, he said to himself, for in the countryside, men and women worked before the coming of the dawn and long after dusk had fallen, late into the night, with flambeaux, when insects call and frogs croak their tales.

He imagined all the houses in the countryside transformed by magic into town houses. What was it then that made this difference? Emmanuel Pottaro began his search for an answer.

The roads in Bon Aire, he saw, were wide and smooth – not pitted with hollows for a hen to crouch in during the quiet of the day. They had pavements on either side where he could walk in safety, even read a book while walking without stumbling or breaking an ankle. It was exhilarating! He shared these thoughts with his cousins. Mala was not amused. Leela giggled. "We shouldn't have to explain to our friends," said Mala, "that our cousin is from the country and all this is new to him!"

The public library fascinated him. That there was such a place where anyone, even the son of a rascal or a good-for-nothing, could come and borrow books appealed to him. Who could have thought of such a thing? Did all the people who borrowed books actually return them? That was something he would have liked to find out, but did not know how to ask, without revealing how little he understood the workings of Bon Aire. With the humourless Mala beside him, whose face changed without warning into an alligator's pointed snout, he was going to keep his thoughts to himself.

*　　*　　*　　*

When Emmanuel was nine, his uncle advised his father to send him to Bon Aire to prepare for the competitive eleven plus exams.

"Leela is going to take the exams this year; it will help Emmanuel if he comes now and give himself more time to catch up with the children in the primary schools in town. If he stays in the country he wouldn't stand a chance."

Two years later, with Leela's help and persistent work, Emmanuel gained admittance to the finest church secondary school in Bon Aire, with its staff of scholarly, committed teachers, many of whom were priests from Ireland.

He grew into adolescence an idealist, an avid and questioning reader of everything, including the Bible and foreign newspapers, spending long hours in the library. One day, his form master, Brother Peter, a delicate and dedicated novice from Ireland, overheard Emmanuel joking with his cousin Leela, as his uncle's chauffeur dropped him off at school.

"Beyond the grave whither thou goest, there is nothing, so whatsoever thy hand findeth to do, do it with all thy might, pretty cousin."

She laughed and said, "Shhhhh. Not so loud, Emmanuel. You mustn't say that here."

"It is in the holy book by which you swear, cousin," he said smiling mischievously with boyish glee.

"Shhhh. You'll be burnt on the stake or beheaded, Emmanuel, if you're not careful."

"Will I? Will I?"

"It has happened before, Emmanuel Pottaro. Remember Joan of Arc? Sir Thomas More? John the Baptist? It can happen here too," she said, winking. "The holy book knows this too."

Later that day, he was summoned by Brother Peter. His form master's study was a long narrow room with the crucified Christ at both ends. It contained only a highly polished mahogany table that comfortably seated twelve and a straight-backed, narrow, chair. Emmanuel had to walk the length of the room.

"Do you know why you are here, Emmanuel?"

"You asked me to be here, sir."

"Do you believe there is life after death, Emmanuel?"

"I do not know, sir."

"Do you believe, Emmanuel?"

"I have no way of knowing, sir."

"Do you know the Church's teaching on this, Emmanuel?"

"The Church believes, sir."

"What does the Church believe?"

"In life after death, sir."

"Do you know from whom the Church gets the authority to spread this revelation?"

"I know little about that, sir."

"Do you believe in God, Emmanuel?"

"Sometimes, sir."

"When do you not believe?"

"When the unjust prosper."

"And when do you believe?"

"When a man lays down his life for another."

Brother Peter looked up at the crucifix and was relieved. But Emmanuel was too young to understand that in certain circumstances an ambiguity may save one, while a greater clarity may take one to the rack.

He thought it would be misleading to allow the priest to conclude he was thinking of the crucifixion.

"Let me give one example, sir. I learnt it by heart. During the guerrilla war launched by the Malayan Communist Party against British colonial rule – it was called the "Malayan Emergency" by the British, sir. Well, both sides hunted each other in the jungle. One day as the British lay in ambush, six guerillas, Malayan communists, sir, emerged from the jungle. Well, sir, the British storm of bullets burst upon them. The first three staggered and fell at once. The others bolted for the trees. Two made it; the third folded to his knees a few yards from sanctuary. The British waited, expecting that someone would return for the wounded man. A humane act, sir... to return. They waited. And then it happened. A man ran back from the jungle. They waited for him to take his comrade under the armpits, and as he began to drag him to safety, weighed down, endangered by friendship – willingly offered, sir, they blasted him. And the honourable British congratulated themselves, sir. Who would want to fight on the side of capitalism after that? It is a kind of hell, sir."

"What *is*, Emmanuel?"

"That kind of thinking, sir, that makes you gloat after such savagery. And they did, sir, they did, they did."

"I see," said Brother Peter, intensely annoyed, but trying to keep calm as he heard Emmanuel saying:

"I had great admiration for that guerrilla, sir, especially when he did it not believing any heaven awaited him. I only hope that for a few moments the man who was being dragged to safety was conscious of the deep friendship for him in that act of returning. It has troubled me ever since, sir. I would so much have liked to know whether the wounded soldier knew, sir, whether he was aware of the friendship, the affection, the sacrifice, sir, his comrade was making."

"And if the terrorist didn't know. Would it have been a waste?"

Emmanuel thought for a long while and then said softly, "In this instance, it would have been a waste, for if you don't know, sir, if you died not knowing that someone would gladly give their life to save yours, or had tried to do so, it is as if it never happened to you. Knowing is important to the dying, sir, knowing matters even at the point of death..."

The young Pottaro had not quite finished; he seemed to be searching for something. His form master waited. Then he said. "Even if the dying wounded soldier never knew, onlookers on both sides would know, sir. And when they relate it to others, those who are listening would know of it too. Maybe, even if no one will ever know, it is right to give your all. Yet how I wish he knew, sir, how I wish he knew."

When Brother Peter discussed this conversation with the Principal, it was agreed that since Emmanuel could not be convinced either of life everlasting or of God, he should be asked to leave. The ideas he had expressed might well do harm if they were loosed on other young susceptible minds. "To have a deep admiration for the Malayan communists in the jungle – the enemy, the Godless," said the Principal, "is far beyond the pale. Emmanuel will have to go. Let his parents know that he has brought it upon himself. I know he is from the country. It is clear we need more missionaries out there, Peter. For too long they have worshipped false gods and this has begun to affect their reasoning. It is our duty to help them."

Emmanuel Pottaro was expelled from school.

18   POTTARO'S PERCH

Every man surveys the world from his own perch and Pottaro's perch was a wooden cross.

He pointed it out to me once when he was the Premier of Maya, long before he was ousted by Robert Augustus.

"Vasu," he said, "you are not a communist. I know that. But climb that abandoned pole and you may begin to understand my point of view. I don't guarantee what you will see; you're a bourgeois at heart."

The teak pole had been erected to carry electric wires. A wooden crosspiece was attached to it, a few centimetres from the top. Later the pole was abandoned, never to become a transmitter of light and energy. It remained a tall wooden cross.

I was amused by that weighted word – bourgeois.

"Human beings are like icebergs, Mr Pottaro," I replied, "you only see one tenth of the whole."

"Capitalists are all transparent," he said, smiling.

I laughed heartily, for he had so much righteous energy. We were of different generations and though this had the potential for dividing us profoundly, yet we were similar in two ways. We both strongly believed we were right and we both wanted the country to grow and develop.

He knew my father well and had a deep respect for him. This is how I got to know him, for he would stop by our shop from time to time and have a chat with my father who was a businessman with a dry goods shop and a rice mill. My father wrote letters for the villagers, sorted out disputes between neighbours, gave advice on anything – from investments to marriage. As we had the only telephone for miles, my father took messages for others and sent messages on their behalf. In a few instances he gave credit to farmers for the entire year, waiting for their sugar cane to be sold to the sugar factory, or their paddy to be harvested and sold to the Rice Marketing Board. Looking back, we were comfortably off, with electric lights and a refrigerator, for with our rice mill next door, we had to have a generator.

I did climb Mr Pottaro's perch, which had been erected as I've said to take electricity to the poorer districts deep in the countryside where he grew up. It would have been a new beginning for the agricultural labourers – to be able to see their way in the dark, for they had no metalled roads, only bullock tracks and lanterns. But nothing came of it. No one knew why. It just stayed there – a hope unconnected, a cause shelved. It stands there to this day, nothing but a landmark, a temporary perch for migrating birds.

When he was seven, Pottaro expressed the wish to climb the pole and his father made it easy for him and the village children to do so by attaching crosspieces of bamboo, transforming the post into a ladder. The topmost crosspiece of solid wood (which was part of the electric pole and meant to hold the electric wires) was firmly fixed at an angle. It was an angle to a view which directed his political thinking long after he climbed down the pole.

In the cool of the afternoon when the pole's long shadow fell across the sugar-cane field, young Pottaro would climb it and sit there alone. Before him, the red roofs of the manager's big house and its outhouses seemed foreign to the alluvial plain of sweet grasses upon which they stood. Near them were the deep yellow cricket pitch and the lawn tennis grass courts enclosed by white gates and green mesh. What thoughts came and went, what voices whispered to the young Pottaro, we will never know, but his father told me that his son sat there for long hours, sometimes even until the magical dawn greeted him. "He enjoyed the breezes and the view," his father said.

There, the young Pottaro would have seen the arrivals and departures of vehicles. He knew what they were, for the lifestyle of abundance excites a child, and for this reason he loitered around the wide high gates of the great houses on his way to and from elementary school. The movements were of commercial vans bringing bread and potatoes, flour and meat and freshwater fish, cooking oil and crabs and the sweetest shrimp in the western hemisphere – the Mayan small red shrimp. Wheel barrows piled high with crisp leafy spinach, succulent long beans, and deep purple, satin-smooth, aubergines, ochroes and squash and pumpkins the colour of tropical sunsets and sindhoor and were trundled to the kitchen door from the ground provision plot in the manager's compound.

He saw that the yard was the depository of an abundance. The sweet aromas of baking and cooking lingered and met him as he passed by the wide iron gates. He saw house servants and yard boys, hastening messengers, the hurrying, eager doctor when someone in the great house was unwell, fine horses groomed and fed, all in a constant movement of energy directed and ordained by men with power from another sphere of thinking – the clip clop sound of authority riding high. At the gates, the barking dogs and overseers questioned him: 'What is your business?' This world was far removed from the ugliness and poverty that was the lives of the agricultural labourers in their logies – unsanitary rows of dwellings like hen coops in factory farms. They were without piped water, proper toilet facilities, electricity and roads, their babies at the mercy of gastro-enteritis, and biting anopheles mosquitoes.

Up there, perched on the wooden cross, his view made by its angle, he was seeing the movements of another way of life, on another stage. It was fascinating and exciting, as opulence is when seen with the clarity of a child's eyes, from its own environment of endemic poverty.

It was this experience of living side by side with gross inequalities, woven with his naked experience of the arrogance of the powerful, which not only shaped the way Pottaro saw the world but how he assessed it. Understandably, he was unable to escape the assumptions of his time, the Region's history of colonialism, and the perceptions and writings of the social philosopher – Karl Marx. He wanted Maya to be a place where there would be freedom and plenty for all Mayans. Unfortunately for him and his supporters, his Marxist model was unacceptable to the large powers close to him, and the democratic means he chose to accomplish his vision made him vulnerable to their unscrupulous interference in Mayan affairs.

19   I BELIEVE

I didn't have any difficulty finding Mr Emmanuel Pottaro's house, for this was his constituency. But the road to it was hell. I would not be surprised if it is the worst road on an island of poor roads. I stopped before a modest wooden house with a well-kept flower garden.

"I am pleased that you are on time," he said. "It is my mother's birthday, and I promised her that on this occasion I would not be late." He greeted me with his warm, winning smile, his hair flying in the wind.

"You had no trouble, I hope. The roads are bad and it is the rainy season." Refreshing coconut water was offered me, straight from the large green nut itself. He did not mind my having the interview on tape.

"What would I have done differently? This question is put to me again and again. My answer remains the same – nothing. Now why is that? You see I believe a man's behaviour and his beliefs cannot be divorced. They are the two sides of the same coin. My conscience and my understanding of ethics and morality are tied together.

Look. Examine the forces that overthrew my Government. I was overthrown by a direct order from the President of the most powerful democracy. The CIA connived with Devonish. Gomes and his newspaper *The Carrier*, and the brute force which Devonish unleashed on Bon Aire with the strike and the fires of Bon Aire, were funded by the CIA to destabilise my Government. Have you seen the handbills that were issued by Devonish's party?"

I had seen these handbills. They were callous, remorseless:

LET US NOT BE AFRAID TO SHOOT OR STRIKE .
LET US NOT BE AFRAID OF ANYTHING, VICTORY IS AT HAND.
IF VIOLENCE BECOMES UNAVOIDABLE, WE MUST BE RUTHLESS

AND MORE DESTRUCTIVE OR BE DOOMED FOREVER.
POTTARO MUST RESIGN OR BE DESTROYED
FOR THE BENEFIT OF MAYA.
THE TIME IS RIPE TO FREE MAYA TODAY, OR ELSE WE'LL HAVE
BLOOD TOMORROW, COMRADES.

"Well there were people inside and outside Maya (with far more power and resources than I could muster) prepared to overthrow a legitimate, democratically elected government. It was a coup d'etat, British style. People ask why I trusted the British. The British have managed more than any other people (and I include the developed countries) to convince the rest of the world that they are fair and just at all times. I did not believe this misconception, but at the same time I did not believe that they would change the constitution and introduce a voting system that they themselves did not wish to have, and which they had at no time introduced elsewhere .... Well, the British proved that I was wrong to think so. It is all history now.

"Communism? A word like Capitalism, or Liberalism isn't it? It can get its meaning from its detractors. I am as anti-colonial as the Americans before their war of Independence. I want my country, though small, to be independent, not only politically, but economically. They go hand in hand. You can't be independent if you are poor. I am a democrat. I believe in preserving the liberties and freedom of all Mayans. When I addressed the press in Washington, I reminded them that I did not come to power by a *coup d'etat*. I told them what I have always believed in — parliamentary democracy, the rights of opposition parties, freedom of speech and of worship, regular and honest elections, an impartial judiciary, and an independent civil service. But they wanted to believe something else.

"Now why did they not judge me by my past record? When I spoke to the President of America, I don't believe he was even listening, for if he was listening, he would not have given the direct order to overthrow my Government. These are some of the disadvantages of poverty that the heads of poor countries face. Superpowers believe what they want to believe. I asked for assistance to build up the infrastructure of Maya, but as I said, he had made up his mind. The only thing America gave Maya was a legacy of bitterness and strife. That was a barbaric act. Barbarism and Americanism often go hand in hand. History is full of the legacies of superpowers – the hell they leave behind.

"You ask why he was not disposed to believing me? What can I say? They could see that I was prepared to pursue a policy of neutralism as India had. I was attracted to the policy of being open, not tied to any one sphere of influence. I intended to seek aid from whatever countries were willing to assist our growth and development, though I repeatedly said that I would not accept aid that threatened the sovereignty of Mayans. This third way is not new. But clearly our poverty made us vulnerable, and they wanted to dictate who our friends should be, what direction our decisions should take. Well, I had no intention of turning Maya into an American satellite. We must be allowed to follow our own paths to the salvation of the good life for all.

"Yes I heard you. You say that Czechoslovakia and Hungary are trying to disengage themselves from the USSR while I am embracing it. American propaganda is something one has to be aware of. I have experienced it myself, as you know. I have no way of knowing what is really happening there. The anti-communist illiberalism of postwar United States and its open and covert support for tyrannies in Latin America, Africa and Asia, provided that they espouse anti-communism, I am well acquainted with. Who could trust them?

"As for *embracing*, as you call it, it's a loaded word. I was trying to get assistance to develop my country. The West was uncooperative, they destroyed my Government. They decided what I would do, and then said I had done it. The world is a dangerous place for all undeveloped countries, when superpowers behave like this.

"I have always struggled to create a better tomorrow for all Mayans. I wanted them to live quality lives in freedom and enlightenment. The social and economic development of all Mayans was the sole aim and objective of my life in politics.

"I am a socialist, and by this I mean that the workers should reap the full fruits of their labour through public ownership of the means of production, distribution and exchange. Let us not forget that it was I who first proposed and got entrenched in the constitution, the Bill of Rights, guaranteeing every Mayan his fundamental rights, including his right to hold property.

"Yes I heard you. You say that Country Mayans have suffered because I am a Marxist and they voted for me. That it was a foolish thing for them to do. You say that Maya's path to independence would not have been so violent and disrupted by civil strife if I had not been a Marxist, for then the Americans would not have interested themselves with the internal politics of Maya. I am not evading the question.

"You and I have no idea of what would have happened in Maya. You have seen the editorials in *The Carrier*, read the reports of the speeches of the then opposition. Racism and poverty, greed and ignorance stoking the fires of a jealous ambition to govern can easily erupt into a hell on earth. The history of ethnic and class struggles for power is pitted with pitiless massacres.

"Your question assumes that America has a monopoly of good ideas for the betterment of mankind and that what America wants each country wants, and that America has the right to disrupt and destroy any government outside its shores if it does not like the colour of its politics.

"Your question flows into a wider sphere than you perceive. For it follows from what you are saying, that America must then have the right to build more and more sophisticated armaments of destruction, while destroying the armaments of others so that she may continue to dictate to others on the colour of their politics. Have you asked who decides if America is right? This was a democratically elected government that America undermined and destroyed with the help of the British. This is not the first time America has placed its spiked boot on the soil of others, nor is it likely to be its last.

"Consider what feelings of resentment, frustration and anger grow within people in developing countries who are ill-used by America.

"Perhaps my greatest weakness was that I expected others to live by those standards I believed in…"

He looked at his watch and I knew I should show him the same courtesy he offered me. I wished him good health and left. He sped along the pot-holed road to his mother's birthday party in his old Morris Minor.

As I tried to negotiate around and between the pot-holes, I couldn't help feeling sad. Here was an idealist, a man with a serene face, taking on a mighty superpower, with only a single lever – his theories of how an economy grows and how the quality of life of its participants might be improved. He was unable to seduce America to assist his Government, and his perception of the flow of history could not hint to him what was to come – that Russia would soon be seeking capitalism to improve the quality of its people's lives.

I did not think that he answered one question fully, not because he was being evasive, but because he couldn't. With hindsight, Pottaro need not have expressed himself in the language of an old text – ponderous, heavy and suspect – used on the other side of a high wall. He was politically naive, an innocent, an idealist, out of his depth in the swift currents of savage politics. He was also a young man in a hurry, who firmly believed that he had found the scientific answer to achieving equality and fairness, to abolishing dire poverty, human misery and despair. He was impatient with an indirect, curving path to his destination, the cautious, grey language of British social democratic Fabianism, when a rectangular plan of straight, direct routes was on offer, complete with traffic lights and directions on high, clearly signalling where to turn and where to go, a system neatly composed from a German scholar's vision by a centralising Russian with a modern rule.

He had come to the President of America at a sensitive time, dressed in politically incorrect apparel. His supporters suffered dearly for their leader's political ineptitude, his inability to set sail with the wind. He needed to have a touch of Machiavellianism. Yet how with hindsight we become wise.

PART TWO: THE MASTER BUILDER

20 FROM WHENCE COMETH MY BURDEN?

It was long-harboured fear, and envy too, which was my inheritance and the goad that spurred me to succeed in seizing power for my people where others before had failed.

The first attempt to capture and control a leverage of power, which was then the supply of labour, was made at the turn of the century by my forefathers – offspring of the emancipated – the Notables of Bon Aire. They were men of vision who foresaw the problem that would come with the arrival of the indentured agricultural workers, whose offspring we later called Country Mayans, to demarcate our urbanity from their rusticity.

Proud, serious men, the Notables acted promptly. There are some things that are difficult to accept – sharing power – especially with those one believes to be less than oneself. At the time, the Notables thought that their perception of the indentured agricultural workers was shared by the colonial power. But as the correspondence I have before me shows, this was not so.

It was in the hot month of July 1903, to be exact, that the Notables of Bon Aire sought to terminate indentured immigration. They sought to reduce their numbers, fearing their future influence on the island's political development.

The Notables saw that with one strategic move they could secure for our people – the free offspring of the emancipated – the monopoly of the labour market, with all the advantages that would bring in the eventual gaining and holding of political power.

In this contest, the Notables failed. It was left to me, almost two generations later, to effectively disenfranchise the descendants of these indentured immigrants and so force them to leave. It was neatly done and I was greatly helped by the fact that there was no hue nor cry from the region's free, independent press. They must have understood what I was doing and were not troubled.

Attached to the Notables' 1903 petition to His Majesty's Secretary of State for the Colonies – J. Chamberlain – were thousands of signatures representing the mounting anxieties and growing grievances of my people.

Today, with a clearer understanding of the interplay of interest and power, it was a contest the Notables could not win, but that they should have come together to despatch a Memorial, armed with those many signatures, gives some measure of their determination and foresight, as well as their deep resentment and fear of the agricultural workers.

Throughout the Memorial they placed the agricultural workers in opposition to the rest of the population. It was a masterly move. The detailed tax measures they recommended to reduce the profitability of the sugar industry as well as to impede the infant rice industry reveal the extent to which, by the turn of the century, they knew whom their enemies were.

I have long needed to clarify this, for it is felt quite wrongly that it was I who introduced dissension between country and urban Mayans, while in truth it goes much further back in time. Let it be known once and for all, that I inherited what I have described.

The Notables advanced their case for the cessation of the immigration of agricultural workers on two fronts. They proposed that it was economically unsound to have them. The cost of their transportation and medical facilities, they argued, outweighed the gains of their production and their presence was injurious to the fortunes of free men – here called indigenous Mayans – who were capable and willing to do the work but, as a consequence of the cheap source of labour on hand, were now suffering hardships. It was a disingenuous argument perhaps, one that is as old as the hills and still used effectively in faraway places when boatloads of immigrants arrive from the poor South to the prosperous North.

The Notables made their case to the Secretary of State for the Colonies in the language of the civilised world not yet understood by Country Mayans, who were unaware of this formal request to terminate their contracts and so their presence in Maya. I present selected extracts of the Notables request:

"The emancipated worker and native Amerindian are unwilling, from their more civilised habits and greater needs, to work for less than a fair living wage such as the indentured agricultural workers, with their free housing and medical attention, are prepared to accept. Moreover, even if after the five year period of indentureship, these agricultural workers came to be regarded as Colonists, and were they of a class to yield to the Mayan community as full a benefit as is the case with other classes of Colonists, yet colonisation on conditions such as those on which they are introduced is scarcely calculated to achieve its own objective, and for that reason alone, should little be desired.

Their earnings are small both during indenture (very often less than the statutory amount) by reason of low wage rates, as also after indentureship, due to the lack of regular and continuous employment. Moreover they are of a miserly disposition – saving the greater portion of such earnings, small as they are, which they are able to do by their habit of life and very limited needs, and sending these savings back to their own country, which little benefits Maya. Moreover, the project of the Government to settle them in the colony by means of a commutation, for land, of their right to return passages, has resulted in failure and been abandoned.

Observation also shows that of the articles on which duties and taxes are levied, they consume very few. This must be an embarrassment to the Government while adding to its hardship, for it is natural and reasonable to conclude that because of these habits, their contribution to the revenue of Maya is negligible.

You ought also to note that rice, their principal article of food, is now so extensively grown by them that the revenue formerly raised on its importation cannot now, alas, be reckoned upon. Their presence makes a sad tale."

*   *   *   *

This Memorial, was written by free men, educated men who understood the finer syntax and grammar of the English language, and who moreover were at ease with the subtleties of its intonation. They were the natural inheritors of the culture of Empire, its customs, tastes, religion and ways of thinking; if not identical, they were in full alignment with civil servants of the highest calibre anywhere in the old Empire or Dominions. One also perceives that in asking for better wages for the free workers, the Notables were thinking of further improving the quality of life of this group to facilitate their future entry into the civil service, as they themselves had done.

The Governor of Maya in his dispatch to J Chamberlain responded to every remark, observation and statement made by the Notables, which were not only numerous but often complex. And though the entire correspondence is fascinating from the point of view of the thought and consideration given to it, as well as the evidence it gives of the Governor's wide knowledge of the local scene, I shall confine myself to those aspects of the Governor's reply which played no small part in the development of my own perceptions on the nature of power and self-esteem and my resolve to have both.

The Governor's response helped me to prepare my political agenda – which I fulfilled with such astuteness that even now the children of those I dispossessed are asking how it was possible that I, with the support of little more than one third of the population, should have become Prime Minister and then the Executive President, in full control of government, and have remained so to this day, unchallenged.

From the nature of these correspondences before me I realised we were on our own and that I had to place my people at the commanding heights of departments of Government here in Maya, and to enlarge the power and wealth and ownership of government. I envisaged how our economic and cultural achievements would lead to envy and respect. The alternative was unbearable. It may sound arrogant, but when I perceived what was required and saw the men who were around me, the men upon whom this task would fall, men afraid of their own shadows, I knew that I would have to do it single-handedly. There was no one else. Of course, many jumped on my bandwagon after I got our wagons moving along the trail to permanent governance. Now they are quietly dissociating themselves from the ideas – indeed the gut feelings – that made it possible for me to succeed without hindrance and with celestial speed. But enough of these craven faint-hearts!

*　　*　　*　　*

From the Governor of Maya to the Secretary of State.
Government House, Bon Aire, Maya. July 21, 1903.

Selected Extracts:

"It is to be regretted that among the many statements made by
the Notables which are not germane to the 'prayer of their
Memorial' is the ridiculous one that the emancipated worker,
described by Earl Grey in 1849 as being in a semi-barbarous
state, is more civilised than the indentured agricultural worker
with his three thousand years of civilised ancestry.

The emancipated worker has abdicated his former position
as the agency for the production of sugar, cotton and coffee.
Since emancipation he has renounced continuous agricultural
labour and were it not for the indentured agricultural workers,
Maya would have lost its prosperity, which is solely an agricultural prosperity and is likely to remain so for some time to come.
The Colony's pattern is as follows: the value of the export of sugar,
rum and molasses is at 2.2 million pounds sterling; that of timber
and charcoal 25,000 pounds sterling, and that of all other products
12,600 pounds sterling, while the cost of imports amounts to 2
million pounds sterling.

It is to be regretted that in the case of cotton and coffee
production which is solely in the hands of the emancipated
worker, and not withstanding the wall of protection they receive
by an import duty of 21.00 pounds sterling per ton on foreign
coffee, one finds that the locally produced coffee falls short even
of the local demand, while coffee in full bearing can be found
neglected, growing inland.

One should not have to acknowledge here what is plain for
all to see, that the contribution of sugar production to the
economic and social well being of the entire population is
extraordinarily large and that includes in no small measure the
very salaries of the civil servants of all Government departments,
many of whom may have signed this Memorial.

Moreover, what is often forgotten is that the production of sugar enables the Colony to be physically habitable. It is again regrettable that one should have to remind the Notables of Bon Aire that the settled lands of Maya have been wrested from the ocean and the mighty rivers by a costly system of dams and dykes, laboriously constructed during the long Dutch occupation and kept up only at a vast annual expense. For not only must there be a front dam to bar out the sea or river but there is also a back dam to every estate to keep out the waters which accumulate in the low-lying savannah lands of the interior.

Every estate is obliged to keep up its own dams and drains and in some cases to maintain steam pumping engines. An idea of the expense of this may be gathered from the fact that the Government is now spending 10,000 pounds sterling a year on the dams and sea-walls of two government properties Best Hope and Thomas Good which are on each side of the mouth of the Oro River.

Where abandoned estates have been sold out in lots and settled in villages by free men, the dams have been neglected in almost every case and have only been kept by loans from taxpayers. The prospect of the repayment of these loans is very remote and so they become an additional burden to taxpayers. In the case of sugar cultivation, these expenses are carried not by taxpayers but by the industry itself and so, in reality, by the workers and management of the industry.

With regard to the future progress of the Colony, I confess, speaking individually, my regret that instead of merely 150,000 agricultural workers we have not ten times that number in Maya, for we have lands enough and with a natural supply of water available, they could grow enough rice to supply this hemisphere.

Already, chiefly by their industry, the local price of rice which twenty-five years ago was thirty-two cents per gallon has been reduced to sixteen or eighteen cents. By their industry all have benefited. Here in Maya there are enormous opportunities for the industrious. I refer to coconut planting on a large scale and to the savannah lands for cattle farming, a business which is very popular amongst the agricultural workers.

It is true that the Government no longer offers settlements to these agricultural workers who have opted to stay in the Colony, but it is not for the reason the memorialists have here represented, instead it is because these workers have been so successful in providing for themselves that the Government has decided that they can be successful without land grants. This Government's action could be interpreted, quite legitimately, as penalising the industrious, but the agricultural workers have at no time asked that this be rescinded. They have said nothing on their own behalf.

It is so unfortunate that they are attacked for their thrift, which is most commendable, especially in a country where the need for local capital is large and what is available small. Their substantial savings can be used as a leverage for investment and long term prosperity. It is hoped that the Notables would, in time, come to see that the agricultural workers' contribution to the increased revenue of the country and so to its cultural advancement is very much greater than they are disposed to represent."

*   *   *   *

Well, I staggered under the yoke of that appraisal and was forced to ask, what is it that draws men together if it is not, as I had thought, a common language and religion, habit of dress – the cultural luggage they share? What makes men feel at one with another? By what are men judged?

I can see that the Notables overplayed their hands by referring to themselves as indigenous – since our forefathers too were brought to Maya in ships and their presence and that of the coloniser's administration were not conducive to the growth and expansion of the culture of the truly indigenous peoples. Our presence here, if truth be told, contributed in no small part to their decline and eventual demise.

What acted as a mighty stimulus for the direction I later took was my recognition that the perceptions of J Chamberlain, the Secretary of State, and the Governor of Maya were widely held in the larger world outside. I saw at once the need to remove the problem – Country Mayans – and that by so doing I would be creating space for my people, increasing their resources per head of population, in much the same way the colonisers of the New World perceived the need for a greater space – by pushing

back for three hundred years the space of indigenous peoples far
and wide in every continent.

That you may fully understand my resentment, consider the
arrival of agricultural labourers who speak in another tongue, who
dress differently, wear little on their feet; whose food and its
preparation are unknowns; who, while we are baptised and give
our dead a Christian burial, cremate their dead and pour their
ashes into running streams. Consider those men and women who
rise with the dawn and as heathens honour the sun with prayers
and offerings, who indeed honour many gods, while we worship the
one jealous God of the civilised world. We sing his praises in our
homes and the fields, in our churches and our schools.

We were the inheritors, true replacements for the Empire's
civil servants. Observe the elegance of language in our communi-
cation with the Secretary of State. At the time of the Notables'
Memorial, you would have been hard pressed to find a dozen men
from among all Country Mayans who would have been able to think
and write in that manner. How then could anyone expect us to
share power with the sons of agricultural labourers, or worse, to
find ourselves in a political situation where they would be in power
and we in opposition for the foreseeable future? That could not be
borne, has not been borne. The political system then in place had
to be changed. Power had to be in our hands and remain there.
Only a fool in government loses power. Emmanuel Pottaro was a
fool. I did it all single-handedly. I, Robert Augustus Devonish,
brought about this change and transformed the very stride of my
people.

21   A FOX DANCES WITH A DRAKE
Lionel Gomes

At the London Conference on Mayan Independence, Robert
Augustus and I presented an amicable united front. We received
what we wanted and more, while Pottaro cried out piteously, "It is
unfair, this is unjust," which it was.

The whole exercise was executed by the British Government
in Lancaster House with the appropriate dignity and decorum at
which they are masters. Let us not fool ourselves. Their sole
purpose and that of the CIA was to overthrow Emmanuel Pottaro.
They introduced a new system of voting that would ensure he
would not form the next government that would take Maya into
independence. He was a communist but had won all past, democratic elections fairly.

Under the new flag of Independence and the new voting system,
with the support of my party, Robert Augustus would become the
first Prime Minister and, in the understanding we reached, I would
have the Ministry of Finance. I saw this ministry and its portfolio
as central to Maya's development – my foremost responsibilities
being to enlarge the productive sector. We had to encourage foreign
trust in our government so that it might bring capital and skills to
assist in expanding the creativity and productivity of Mayans. This,
some would say, is the language of a businessman. It is and I make
no apology. Development needs business. It is a large word; every
economic activity is tied to it. I was excited and wanted to make the
first government of an Independent Maya work for Mayans.

What I had not envisaged was that assisting Robert Augustus
to destabilise the island (we could not legitimately overthrow
Pottaro's Government) and enabling him to become the first Prime
Minister was all that he required of me and that thereafter I was

dispensable. With hindsight I had dug my own grave and had been seduced to stand near it. What I had not foreseen was the very short duration that I would be allowed to be Minister of Finance. You see, it was a position negotiated at length and agreed to in good faith. We had fought together to be where we now were. So the kind of vulpine cunning that went for my throat so early, I was not prepared for. Pottaro's supporters would say that Robert Augustus and I had plotted to destroy Pottaro's Government. But the two circumstances cannot be compared. As a Roman Catholic, I had a duty to destroy a Godless system – and my *Carrier* did indeed play no small part in toppling Communism. This is true of the *Catholic News* too. I have no regrets.

As Minister of Finance, I wasted no time in rescinding the gift and property taxes on the rich that Pottaro had introduced in his budget in an attempt, he said, to promote equality and to increase government revenue for Maya's urgently needed infrastructural development. I regarded such measures as not only a waste of time, but also plain foolish. As the rich in Maya were so few, it was like passing a law to save pennies when what was needed was millions of dollars of investment capital as well as new, sophisticated skills in production and marketing. My strategy was to encourage investment, while negotiating the best conditions for the future. I removed foreign exchange controls. 'The free repatriation of profits', the Left howled. But if investors know they can take out what they've brought in, they are more likely to trust the system. In addition, Pottaro's savings levy was declared unconstitutional, since forced savings are counterproductive. The system itself must encourage it, by providing savers with an incentive. It is a far healthier way.

These Pottaran measures I removed were, let it be remembered, those ruthlessly criticised by Devonish and his left-wing comrades when they were in opposition. However I should have seen that Pottaro's thinking was ideologically at one with theirs – the Left in the cabinet – the hierarchy of the Party, and their criticisms of him in opposition were wholly hypocritical and opportunistic. Their bare-facedness surprised even me. I recall now how they accused him of being a communist, while simultaneously saying that he was against poor people. It gives you some idea of the quality of the political debate at the time.

My political thinking was far removed from Pottaro's and I had not opposed him to have the road to serfdom – total state owner-ship, which is what communism is – brought in by another name in the quiet of the night. This is, of course, what happened under Robert Augustus' rule. He outfoxed the CIA by using their substantial assistance to overthrow Pottaro and then established a system of state control far more authoritarian and comprehensive than Pottaro would have dared. Pottaro was always containable, for Robert Augustus would have incited his supporters to disrupt Bon Aire, the seat of government, in the style we know full well.

I should have recognised that at the beginning of his political career, Robert Augustus had undoubtedly joined Pottaro's party in good faith and that the main reason for their later separation was his overpowering ambition to lead the party. When his two attempts at leadership failed, he formed his own party along racial and urban lines with the help of the CIA.

In truth, even with CIA help, Devonish could only have gained a base by playing the racial card, since though there were ideological divisions within Pottaro's party, he knew that when push came to shove, the real fault lines were racial. He could not defeat Pottaro within the party, so he had to break it up, separate one racial group from the other. To ensure that the division remained permanent, *mistrust* and *fear* between the citizens of Maya had to be intensively cultivated. Shrewd politician that he is, Robert Augustus saw the means. The majority of Pottaro's support came from the countryside, particularly the sugar planta-tions. This enabled Robert Augustus to shout to the urban commu-nities in Bon Aire and elsewhere that a vote for him ensured that Country Mayans would not be flocking to the city and its surround-ings to vie with them for white collar jobs and the urban facilities they enjoyed. Country Mayans would be kept in their place – workers of the land. This pleased the professional and urban middle classes, and whatever pleased them was welcomed by the urban poor, for they trusted and respected erudition.

When the Left grumbled that I was facilitating the repatriation of foreigners' profits abroad, Robert Augustus said nothing, en-couraging this dissension with a wry smile, a shoulder shrug, a wave of hand. He allowed their displeasure to simmer. As their resentment intensified against my competitive, market-oriented economics, he would say calmly, "He is our Finance Minister; we must give him the same freedom as other ministers have." Again when the rich welcomed my removal of Pottaro's property taxes, the cabinet again complained: "If Lionel is allowed to carry through more of the same for the full term of his office, it will be 'suicidal' for the Party. Our supporters will rightly shout treachery at the next election, particularly if they remained untrained and unemployed." It was not long after that rumours began to spread throughout the civil service. No one seemed to know how it started, but in no time everyone was saying that the Prime Minister was unhappy with me and would soon be asking for my resignation.

After two years as Minister of Finance and Director of Audit, I discovered that foreign earnings running into millions of dollars were missing from the treasury, unaccounted for. When I began to investigate, I met either the uncooperative silence of the Left, or the individual self-preservation of the ambitious. As my enquiries met a blank wall, my discomfort grew, for it was clear I could not be responsible for a Ministry and not know how it was being plundered or who was responsible. I could see that it would be unwise to continue the charade any further. I stood alone, with no friends in the coalition, so unlike the days when I owned *The Carrier* and it was pummelling Pottaro

Fortunately for Augustus, since Pottaro's fatal car accident, no member of the Opposition seemed to have the ability, energy or political craft to confront an increasingly totalitarian regime effectively. The Opposition was ignored and treated with disdain by the Government; even the most common courtesies tradition allowed them were now openly and blatantly denied, such as the customary allocation of rooms in the parliamentary building. The very name – *Government's Opposition* – was denied them. The word *Minor* was substituted, though in reality they represented a larger proportion of the population than Robert Augustus's party.

The virtual absence of an opposition outside the ruling party did not help me. I became as stranded as a whale in shallow water. Seeing this I said to myself, why should I resign and make it easy for the hyenas circling me? Let them work at sacking me. I looked forward to seeing how Robert Augustus would camouflage his pronged harpoon as he hurled it at me. Yet I knew he long wanted the Central Bank of Maya to be at his private disposal and would do whatever was required. In view of this, was it not preferable, I asked myself, that I left now before the reserves were depleted, which I prophesied would soon come to pass, for by then I knew the full measure of the man.

The day-to-day running of government began to take second place to the question – *When will Lionel Gomes be asked to go?* Matters soon came to a head, when someone chuckled, as he said to Robert Augustus, that no one would think he was the Prime Minister, that he was in charge; to continue in the way he was going gave the impression that the Purple Masked ones were afraid to sack me.

On the following day I was called to the Prime Minister's office and noted with displeasure that the Prime Minister's secretary was going to be at this confrontation, especially when I was told that her presence was for my benefit. Robert Augustus then swivelled his chair around to face me. "Lionel, you can see the predicament I am in. I have been trying to stem the tide of opposition against you in the cabinet, and among the senior ranks of the civil service. I see you're making no headway with your enquiries. This must be frustrating to someone so thorough. The sums involved are too large to cover up. Everyone is calling for your head over this large discrepancy in our public accounts. You have not been vigilant. People are asking, 'Who watches the watchman?' "

"Being Minister of Finance in these circumstances is not an easy task," I replied. "There is obstruction going on. I am having great difficulty in getting at the root of this crime against the people, for that is what it is – stealing taxpayers' money. I will come straight to the point. You have a choice, it is either we try and stop this rot from setting in, from becoming part of our Government, or we allow fiscal profligacy and unaccountability to spread like gangrene which will eventually destroy us. We'll become mendicants, knocking at doors, pleading for other countries' taxpayers' money, when we have the natural resources and the ability to be productive and pay our own way."

"Brave words, Lionel. Your stand is commendable in desiring our economic independence. Yet you have gone overboard, you overstate the position – but you're at present a man under stress. Sometimes I wonder about your political grasp. We're not mendicants, we're merely asking for a small part of what was taken from us. You know this. I shall forget what has been said, for we must be generous to each other... There is this other pressing matter. You have been introducing measures that the Left in the party cannot live with, and on the contrary you show no willingness to accommodate their agenda of state ownership and government jobs for the masses."

"I am addressing those issues by trying to make this place attractive to a culture of producing. Firms must be attracted to come here, to invest here. The number of competitive, enduring jobs that government can create are limited. Besides, our job in government is to govern, not to run a business. We should leave that to people who are better at it. They will make a profit. Government is unlikely to do so."

"And this profit they make, will they repatriate it under your schemes? What next?"

"I am all for transparency. It is better that foreigners work within the laws of Maya, and we are able to monitor them, otherwise they will employ the best accountants and our under-trained, under-qualified staff in the tax department will be no match for them. Or they will offer bribes that our poorly paid civil servants would be unable to refuse. But to answer your assertion: Our job in government is to assist the right kind of businesses to come and build a future here. We will need to be selective. Having an endemic anti-private enterprise culture here is the last thing Maya needs if it is to grow. We can negotiate packages which state that within an agreed time so many quality jobs will be created, so many trained and so on. We need to sit down and plan comprehensive measures. You cannot do that by being anti-business. Nothing I have said here is new. These were my views long before this Government came into being. You know this."

"When we agreed to form a coalition, it was understood that we were ideologically far apart. We have done well so far because, as the cabinet says, and I have to agree with them, I am making all the concessions. We intend to nationalise, Lionel, all private companies. We intend to own the economy and give it direction.

The people of Maya are going to rely on the people of Maya to further the interests of the people of Maya. We will make the little man the real man. You will notice I have not once mentioned the word foreigners, for I have faith in my people. That is our course. Even if I were to go along with your understanding of how we should grow, the cabinet would rebel. The Left is strong and vociferous. I am inclined to move a little with you, but I would not be supported by the cabinet. We would be outvoted. You and I would be sitting around empty tables. The truth is, you have neither the trust nor the confidence of the Party. They accuse you of taking from the have-nots and giving the well-to-do. Their choice of words is far more incisive; I shall not repeat them for they would be offensive to you. This large difference will continue to be a festering sore. Whenever your name is mentioned, the word treachery inevitably comes up. I am left with no choice. It is not easy for me to do this. I wish your views and those of the Party were one. I kept defending you by saying you planned a spring cleaning of your thoughts on development, and that you would soon be making certain adjustments. But I have been proved wrong."

"I knew this day would come, but I did not expect such unseemly haste so early in the alliance. I had hoped that you would have permitted the economy to grow strong and then asked me to leave from a position of strength. But, you say, the cabinet is in a hurry. If so, they are hastening the fall of the Government, like something possessed, unable to stop the rush over the cliff. When the Government comes to this precipitous end – but my metaphor is wrong, when the fall comes there will be no mighty crash. No! You wouldn't hear a sound, because there would be nothing there – puffs of hot air. State ownership as you prescribe it will create an illusion of power. Only when that illusion is broken will development have a chance. Men who are constantly concerned with redistributing other people's earnings to themselves and their favoured ones, and who are not equally obsessed in engaging all to produce more than they can use, such men's days are numbered. Sadly you and your colleagues seem unaware of this, dinosaurs all, grazing in primeval swamps, when what we need is the rocket power for space flight." I walked to the door, preferring to see myself out. "How long will you continue, Prime

Minister," I said, "to sing these outworn tunes? What I am proposing would make colonial exploitation an insignificant thing of our past, while what you are set upon will make it the scapegoat of your failings, and the words of all your songs."

With my departure, Devonish firmly grasped the Ministry of Finance. However, he insisted on saying an official farewell to me. It galled but I felt I had no choice but attend the party he held in style at Government House. It was, of course, not for my benefit but to serve as a warning to other members of the cabinet. Augustus reminded them of how well I had served in overthrowing Pottaro's Government. "Where would we have been without Comrade Lionel or *The Carrier* and his very obliging editor?" A silence fell that pierced, humiliated, embarrassed, as well as delighted – so varied were the receptacles of the chilled white wine. Each one present, however great their past services, now knew that he was dispensable. My departure was confirmation of this.

I walked down the steps of Government House to my own car – my Jaguar – old, cared for. I was pleased that my chauffeur had remembered to remove the ruling Party's flag from its bonnet. As the car sped along the road, I knew I had been forced low, spat upon before Robert Augustus' secretary and again at the function. I had been used, humiliated by an ugly cunning that had showed its true self – its ruthless, overpowering ambition. It was too painful to think that I had brought wind and sails to Robert Augustus' ship, which had taken him to port where he built his own engine and discarded the sails. Could I ever have been blind to his true character? Was there no other way to deal with Pottaro's communist threat than to sup with Augustus? As a good Catholic could I have done otherwise? My Church encouraged a 'righteous fervour' against Godlessness in the quiet, covert ways which it does so well, but did I need its encouragement to fervour?

I will admit to my discomfort with the fact that most of Pottaro's supporters were men of another faith. The Christian church hand-in-hand with government was natural and wholesome. But a communist kept in power by the pantheistic supporters of many Gods! Oh the anomalies Maya accommodates! And there was that other unspoken thing among my business colleagues – our fear that the monopoly we enjoyed in the commercial sector was being challenged by a few of Pottaro's supporters. We felt it too large a humiliation to have coolies challenging us, men who yesterday had pulled and carried, and dug and bore burdens on their backs, now showing such an aptitude for commerce, climbing ever upwards, and with time joining us. Already they were in the side streets, those closest to the main, grand street, the pride of Bon Aire. It bred insecurity to be challenged so effectively by simple men.

Why was Pottaro so reckless in his inflexibility? Why did he have to spout communism so openly? It was a heretical creed I had been taught to fear and despise as a child in an instinctive and unreflective way. Did my fervour make me blind with rage, encourage the half-truths we used to destroy Pottaro – and create the climate in which Augustus' lies could flourish? I slept little that night. In my wakefulness I wanted to cry out: "Pottaro, you could have helped the poor to lift themselves out of poverty by their own self determination. Why did you think you could do it for them and they could not do it for themselves? Fool, fool, you destroyed the country, yourself and me with you. You were misguided; honest and principled, but you forced us to choose Augustus."

That same day, Robert Augustus said to Marguerite, "Lionel Gomes had to go. He was dangerous. Look at the kind of editor he employed at *The Carrier* – a man without a heart. Do you recall, my dear, that even after the city's centre became a grey ruin of ash and firewood, he would not relent. 'Stir yourselves', he told the silent town that could not believe the destruction they had wrought. No feeling of remorse. Such a destructive man no government can have. Besides, does he take me to be a fool? Did he think I could have him controlling the economic direction of this Government? That he should think so is clear evidence of his colonial disposition. It is understandable that men are loath to lose old habits of thought, knowing that the comfort they provide departs with a new coming. Lionel Gomes had to go. He must have known that the alliance had to be on my terms. There could have been no other. "

When Gomes died ten years later, a disillusioned man, it was a quiet affair. He had wished it so.

22 THE PROLETARIAT

Through the grapevine, the revelation of the missing funds reaches the rum shops, cake shops and corner shops. At the barber shop, on door steps and street corners the urban poor of Bon Aire express themselves freely:

"The truth is we don't know what happen to the money. It might be a little slip on the government part. But we don't know and is early days."

"Give the man a chance to sort things out. He coulda be in a jam. Who don't get in a jam now and then?"

"This is our Prime Minister and we party."

"We now in government."

"That's true."

"Everything will come right, you wait and see. He smart too bad. You ever hear that man talk. A true orator, a natural."

"I does have to sit up and ask meh self eh! eh! how come he so good? When you see he walk in a room, all ah we feel proud. He knows good how to carry himself. The man is a natural."

"Whatever it takes, Robert Augustus has it. You take it from me."

"Nobody, but nobody could come near this man when it comes to brains, I telling you."

"He could tie up anybody and put them in he fob pocket."

"How you think he got where he got? Sheer brain power."

"I say leave it to the PM. He go know how best to handle this."

"When you come to think about it, is a damn lot a money, though."

"Yes. Somebody having a good time."

"I wouldn't mind if a little woulda come my way, comrade."

"But no eye witness. Who see? I say let them talk who see."

"No witness, no trial."

"Anybody coulda take it... even Lionel Gomes." They laugh at the boldness of the suggestion, and the relief it carries.

"Who is we anyway to judge the PM – a big man like that."

"Little people wouldn't know what happen to that kind of money. Boy, that is big big money."

"Some people too quick to point a finger. You would think they were right there when it happen from the way they speak."

"We have to back up our Prime Minister, give him ... unconditional support, especially after he try so hard to get where he is, and that ain't easy."

"Besides, with him there, we stand a better chance."

"A much better chance, comrade."

"Gomes think we stupid or something? Casting aspersions on people like we. That is what all this is about, when you come to think about it. He trying to say that we don't know how to manage ourselves, furthermore the country. I say, give the PM a chance. He will surprise everybody. I telling you that from now."

"Gomes could talk from now to kingdom come. He can't fool me. We know he is not for poor people."

"He is for those higher ups in big business."

"I intend to keep meh head down and mind meh own business. I advise everybody to do the same."

"When you come to think bout it, is a good lot of money, though, to go just so eh?"

"To tell you the truth, I don't have trouble with the amount. My only hope is, if it gone for good, that is one of we getting rich, going up the ladder, having it real good. I wouldn't mind a little something meh self, ah mean if it comes my way."

"But I can't get over it. You mean it gone just like that?"

"That, comrade, is called A Master Plan. I can find no other word for the mastery of that stroke. No witness. No trial." He laughs. "Boy, that neat. That is what is known as professionalism."

"When push come to shove, I say, your own is your own, no matter."

"No matter what anybody say, tell me who else we have in that class?"

"A maestro stroke – call it by its name, na."

"All we know for certain is that somebody having a whale of a good time. I wish I knew where the party was."

*   *   *   *

Amongst the civil servants in the Ministry of Finance, the attempt to follow the flight of these funds was met with blank incredulity – how come the Minister of Finance didn't know, yet expected poor vulnerable people to know and to assist him in belling such a large, ferocious tomcat.

No senior civil servant was willing to shed any light on the matter, while junior ministers, in the privacy of their homes, said they needed to keep their jobs and their heads.

Among the more junior ranks who knew what was happening, the prevailing sentiment was, "I not as foolish as I look, comrade. No one paying me to be policeman or watchman on this island. As far as I can see, you have to look out for yourself or else you finish, brother. Besides, the hand in the till has a long smooth reach, stretching from way way up. Everybody knows that. Only a fool or somebody with a strong death wish will open his mouth to any enquiry. If you know what is good for you and your family, you clear out or shut up. And listen, comrade, if you decide to clear out, and you leaving relations behind, think of them before you open your mouth, I beg you. Think hard, comrade, before you say anything."

23   THE PLEASURES OF ROSE WOOD

There was another side to him which we were privileged to witness... Well that was what we were told, he being the President and all. It was after little Jamie and he not wanting to know, didn't show any interest. It was then the scales dropped from my eyes. Funny how, when you're in a corner, you see all before you plainly. I had my A levels at the time... shorthand and typing too... but was out of work for a year when I was asked to join Rose Wood. Looking back, I should have left Maya rather than go there, but you hope when you shouldn't... When there is nothing else, you hope more. Besides, go where? Visas? Money and passport? All that was another world. I didn't have any of those ... Well outside my reach then. In Maya you have to know the right people, have contacts, be prepared to give favours to people to do just what they are supposed to do – I mean their job. I didn't have those kind of contacts. To tell the truth, what favours could I give?

I was too young to understand what was really going on at Rose Wood. At the time I took people at face value, thinking it was a fast track to becoming a first-class secretary in the President's office with all the perks and status that went with it. You see, what you must understand, nothing was straightforward. There was not a set of rules for anything. Everything depended on who you know. I can tell you it was not a place for getting secretarial experience. There was nothing there and in Maya there was nothing else. Before Rose Wood I had all those grand pre-independence speeches of how we will move forward and do great things ringing in my ears – and there was something else. Don't laugh, fresh from the sixth form I thought men and women tried to reflect the ideals of their high offices. And I can honestly say our headmistress did. In a way, I was walking in the world she spoke of every morning at assembly and on speech days. With hindsight, Rose Wood was nothing but promises made to the vulnerable... Yes, those promises were bait... Nothing else.

I was reluctant at first. But I had been frustrated for such a long time – having left school with good grades, yet getting nowhere with them. And I have to admit, the atmosphere inside Rose Wood was cheerful – all that colour, and more than enough of everything while you there... I mean food. I suppose we were like insects attracted to a flower for the nectar, only to find it closing in upon us, and the sweetness becoming less and less as we were compressed within.

Many stayed, but as I said, the scales dropped from my eyes when Jamie came. Somehow, don't ask me how, I managed to climb out. It was a rude, heartbreaking awakening, I tell you. I was so young and foolish, if I tell you how foolish! I was made to feel large when I was with him and believed there was at least some truth in his comforting words. That is all behind me now... Yet in some ways you carry your past with you, don't you?

Looking back though, as you have asked me to do, it is clear that at Rose Wood he received some strange thrill, some sorcerer's joy even, from the spectacles designed for him. There was his cigar throwing from a balcony to members of the armed forces below. He would watch the way these men, his own supporters, in brand-new uniforms, scrambled and pushed and snatched for his 'throwaways;' How their eyes and mouths and teeth would bare themselves! This excited him.

Then there was his Dionysian side – the way he made his grand entrance to Rose Wood plantation on horseback. Trumpets and drums would announce his coming as he approached. The gates, decorated with palms and red roses, would open to a fanfare – it was like an historical movie. At first the villagers jostled each other to have a better view, to see him galloping on his snow-white mare – adorned with garlands and bells, and bracelets of rose wood. She, on entering, having been trained to perform for the sweetness to come, would lift herself high at the gates, standing near upright on her hind legs, defying gravity and her own weight and that of her rider. And he would press his warm neck, dripping face and moist lips on her trembling coat, soothing

her with his purple gloved hands. And then all would applaud and
shout hurrah! hurrah! And the trumpets and drums would sound
their appreciation of her balletic feat, while we young women
would playfully offer her sugared morsels.

As the President rode slowly down the long carriageway of Rose
Wood, a shower of balloons imprinted with his large smiling visage
– smooth, puffed with warm air – would float from the trees
encircling him. It was well rehearsed. Endless practice at this task
enabled the young boys hidden among the branches to throw these
multicoloured balloons which rained down upon him, sailed
before him as he, switch in hand, rode on down the bridle path.
The boys were taken out of school to be trained by the Director of
Mayan Art and Culture. They were made to feel special by being
allowed to wear Rose Wood ties with the President's personal
insignia – his white mare 'Abundance' – her forelegs reined high
above the ground, like a flying horse, the carrier of the gods. We,
too, had his insignia on our more intimate garments. Not all the
girls... the prized ones – the chosen.

The attractive and charming director of Rose Wood was an
intelligent young woman, an artist by training and disposition. It
was our duty, she said, to meet the psychic needs of our President,
whom she called Maximus. He found pleasure, she said, in the
pageant of outdoor theatre.

He would of course say, when asked by the journalists of the
government-owned newspaper – there was no other – that he
visited Rose Wood to see for himself how his brainchild, the
growing and reaping of a variety of marketable hot peppers, was
faring. Well, he had a way with words. He liked "the fiery colours
of the peppers", we were told by the Director, "their distinctive,
arresting allure, their satin, glossy-red and yellow flesh, their
pungent piercing pain that awakened desire and a taste for silks,
brocades lavished on floors – in all, a pleasurable oasis." Her
words... Clearly, she had learnt some things from him. She should
have left, all the supervisors too, but they were blinded by
nationalism and wishful thinking, believing they were dedicating
themselves to the greater future of Maya.

Leaving the intense heat and glare outside, the President
would enter his cottage tucked away deep in the interior of the

plantation, in the shade and the cool, where he was refreshed and remade.

"Peppers fetch a good enough price in the London market," he would say to us, "and the Party coffers are bare. We all have to ensure that we remain in government, that Rose Wood remains ours."

Within the plantation itself the supervisors were hand picked. These young ladies were wrapped in a sheet of raw silk of deep purple. Two scarves, the colours of Maya's flag of Independence – purple and yellow – with the President's personal insignia, hung from their waists in symmetry, one at the front, the other at the back. Their tails were quite fetching. It was those little extras that added to the cost of running Rose Wood. But the Director had her ways... she made things happen. Rose Wood was well kept – a butterfly on a bomb site.

The pepper reapers also wore alluring costumes – close-fitting buttoned blouses – that ended well above the waist, and flaring miniskirts. The workforce was well disciplined. There was no stopping work when the President was inspecting the fields from the bridle paths, switch in hand. Each young lady kept her head down irrespective of the visiting parties. Visiting socialist dignitaries would be told, as they accompanied him either on horseback (which he preferred) or on foot, that the task was being carried out solely by volunteers – young well-wishers of the Republic. One noticed how engrossed the visitors became in the reaping process which entailed the women bending, stooping, lifting and carrying the baskets of picked peppers on their young heads. The reapers were told that Rose Wood was the President's showcase – his scheme – and they played their part for their President and for Maya.

At first there was much enthusiasm for the costumes and the few favours attached to the task, such as paying no duty on groceries sent in barrels and other necessities from abroad. This was particularly valuable when food imports were banned or essentials severely rationed. But as these barrels of 'gifts' could not always be arranged and as the cultivating and reaping of the peppers were unpaid tasks, there was a reluctance to give up one's spare time or one's Saturdays to this favour.

However, whenever the absentee rate increased significantly, a roll-call was taken and being absent on two consecutive Saturdays meant the loss of one's ration card. Flour and cooking oil, salt and onions were among the rationed items. The supervisors and the Director had their way of keeping us all in line.

After Maximus inspected the work, he would be offered lunch, rest and privacy in his beautiful cottage. It was a retreat that offered delight and refreshment, and so it was that we chosen ones became a prelude to the more serious affairs of state. But as I said, it is all far away from me now. I managed to get a visa and a passport and money. You see, I learnt some things at Rose Wood. Since my arrival, I have worked hard at night school for a degree and at present I have a good job here in New York – secretarial work – and now I'm working towards a higher degree.

I want to have a greater independence. I have sent for Mother and Jamie. I hope Jamie does not look like him when he grows up. It is not comfortable to be reminded, visibly all the time, of Rose Wood ... I am hoping that Jamie will not have a way with words as Robert Augustus had, for this art would destroy him and those around him. This is my prayer.

24   THREE MOUNDS OF EARTH
Marguerite

It is an uncanny feeling to think that, from the beginning, every step my brother took in his climb to the pinnacle of privilege was, in truth, a slide downwards, a fall. It was as if in reality there was no pinnacle to climb, save in our minds and his.

Some may explain this as the result of a self-deceiving illusion, others may even ascribe the phenomenon to mass hypnosis. Both responses veil the truth from which we hide. Look at how he gained power, and the manner in which he exercised it. Nothing has come of it. We have become a Haiti – left with the ashes of failed ideas.

Of late even the urban Mayans have been expressing their disenchantment. Severe import restrictions have meant empty supermarket shelves. The printing of money has reduced its worth. Add to this the absence of wage increases, particularly in the state sector. Poverty pervades the land. Yet there have been no strikes, no open opposition. Where there have been grumblings and skirmishes, these were snuffed out. He knows how. The women of Hope Bridge, seeking better, have left the memory of their fate. The Master Planner has seen to that.

What has shocked Urban Mayans and Country Mayans alike is how the virus of depreciation has permeated everything – not only their currency but also their houses, the very land upon which their houses stand and their labour. What they do not quite understand is that worth is tied to future expectations, which in Maya are not contemplated. Robert Augustus and his Party rule over poverty and decay – but it is the ruling that matters most to them.

I see him on the rostrum, after his operation, returning to perform his war dance with words: "What do you think will happen to you if they win the next election and we lose? Don't you know?" He chuckles, then laughs. "Are there any of my comrades here who don't know?" No hand goes up. "Those of you who are cautious, and it is a fine attribute to be cautious, I say look at the evidence. Slavery. Apartheid. Servitude in its multitudinous forms. To be abused, wronged, murdered. To endure a perpetual war on all sides, yet we had the courage and the strength to emancipate ourselves. We were on our own. No one, but no one was with us.

"Trust your own and your own will set you free. Together, we shall build our new citadel. It will not be easy, for there are many bent on destroying us. The virus of inflation from outside has entered our shores. The enemy within will try to divide us. Comrades, be vigilant. I, your President, give you my word that as long as I am here, we will walk together into the light. This temporary darkness now upon us we will overcome as our forefathers did. They fought tirelessly against inhumane tribulations placed in their path. We, too, will overcome. We will overcome by the grace of God. Today I promise you this: Together we shall build our citadel. We shall build our own Jerusalem and trumpets will blare and bugles will sound to welcome us. God bless you and keep you."

Oh how pitiful it is that his supporters should be so susceptible to this cunning. But if my brother's voice created the substance of our illusion, or if we were hypnotised by his words, our perceptions were held in place by state terror. For the graves are there – not least the earth mounds that cover the bodies of two men, representatives of Emmanuel Pottaro's Party, who were shot dead during one of our early post-Independence rigged elections. Two unarmed men dared to say to the soldiers that they should not remove the ballot boxes from the polling station. I witnessed the incident in silence from an open window.

Nothing of their death remains. There is no headstone which says how their ends came. What could their families record on these headstones? *Killed in action against state terror*? No! There are no words on stone to mark their place in Maya's post-independence tale, not even a simple stone inscribed with the date of their end. Their families heard the whispers that it would not be politically correct to erect headstones, so they keep the headstones of their dead in their houses and hope that one day this night will end and they will see to place them, see to let them stand. Meanwhile, footsteps press upon their earthen mounds and flatten them.

Monuments are for those who have the necessary qualifications, the psychic inheritance prescribed by our AUL. These plain
earthen mounds cover simple men – farmers, unsophisticated
country folks, accustomed to speak with the clarity of prayer – who
saw that to steal ballot boxes, to tamper with them, was wrong.

These two men from the Opposition were there because it was
an honoured custom, inherited from colonial times, to have two
representatives of each party present at each polling station to
ensure that the electoral process was free and fair, reflecting
correctly the wishes of those who cast their votes.

As the polling station was about to close, the soldiers entered
the polling booths and picked up the ballot boxes, quite contrary
to the rules. The representatives of the ruling Party sat silent. One
of the representatives of Pottaro's Party said, "We can't let you do
that." The other said, "It is not right. You can't do this." That was
all they were given time to say before they were silenced.

I was a bystander looking through the window. A silent witness.
Unseen. Unheard till now. It occurred years ago, at the very first
post-independence elections, but I have lived with it in recurring
dreams. The soldiers placed the boxes in the army vehicle and drove
off leaving the two bodies behind.

Savagery is, I have concluded, when one pretends such a thing
never happened, or makes an excuse for it. Savagery is when
nothing, not even a whisper in the market place, or a question
amongst the professional classes impedes such an action from
taking place again. I was part of that savagery.

But thereafter, in my dreams, the men would struggle with
the soldiers and I would enter the polling booth wearing my
purple mask. Seeing me the soldiers would retreat, understanding the significance of that awesome mask I took from Selwyn
Thomas' tall hat box, meant for my brother.

The cold reality was that the boxes were taken away and
brought back a day later to the returning officer who opened the
sealed boxes and counted the votes in the presence of others,
adding them to the grand total of Robert Augustus' winnings.

As chance would have it, on that very day, on my way to Bon
Aire, I offered a lift to the two young ruling Party representatives

at the polling booth. They wanted to tell me about it, unaware that I had witnessed it:

"When I told the army fella that he didn't have to do that, you heard what he said? 'They can't tell us what to do. We are the Government. When will these people learn who is in charge here'."

"He had a lot to say."

"What did he say?" I asked.

" 'These people are illiterate,' he said. 'They shouldn't be allowed to vote. When their grandparents or whoever or whatever came here, they didn't speak English, they talking gibberish. Is true. They heard us speaking proper English and learn from us. Yes, from we. Ungrateful! When people don't know their place, they must suffer. They must be shown where that place is. This is Independent Maya'."

"Imagine, Miss Devonish, Country Mayans," and she laughed, "want to sit in offices, behind a desk. They will be very uncomfortable. I know they will. I am telling you. Their place is in the fields."

"That army fella said, 'They are happy when their foot is squelching mud'. This is true. They are happy there."

"He didn't have to kill them to take the boxes. He could have knocked them out cold," one said.

"Country Mayans would do the same to us, if they were in power."

"That we do not know," I said, "and we have no way of knowing." I paused. "Young ladies, we are not ever likely to know, for we are going to be here, in government, for a mighty long time." The incident had left me with a mountain of guilt. I found myself saying: "For the sake of argument, just in case by some miracle Country Mayans were to come to power and did not seek justice for themselves or their families, how would we cope with that?"

"Never, Miss Devonish. Never. If we were them, you think we go take a big political thing like that sitting down? Why would they be any different from us, eh, Miss Devonish? It stands to reason they will want our heads. Only I wouldn't be here. I tell you from now, the first fishing boat come my way, because I can't do better, I will be on it, sister."

"Miss Devonish, no way will people not try to put wrong things right, if they in power. A lot of people will be in prison. I hear the

Treasury has no money left. Well somebody will have to pay for that. We know what to expect, Miss Devonish."

"Country people have no sense, Miss Devonish. They bring these things upon themselves. You think I going to stop anybody holding a gun? You think I crazy or something?"

"I agree. No sense at all. Country Mayans stay so. As far as I'm concerned, sister, the army can take all the ballot boxes, for at the end of the day I have to stay alive, you hear me."

"That is the bottom line for me, too. I ain't ready yet for them worms. I too young for that."

"Now, look where that got them. Where are they? Nowhere. Nowhere at all. And whose fault is that? You have to look after yourself. That is one thing the President always say. And is true."

"You have to give him that. He knows what he is talking 'bout. The President speaks the truth. I have to look after number one. We can't depend on foreigners."

"What about the glass factory? It is there because of the taxpayers of foreign countries," I heard myself say and realised I must now be more discreet.

"That is glass, Miss Devonish. I am talking about what I know. I don't know 'bout glass."

"You are right. More of us should follow you," I said, "and only speak of what we are really competent to talk about." I was pleased that I was able to contain myself in good time, for I could so easily have said, 'Thanks to foreigners we are in power.' After that, I would have needed divine intervention on my own behalf.

"Thank you, Miss Devonish. But believe me when I say I try to tell the man to cool it, to cooperate with the army, for I could sense what was coming. Once you see them soldiers wearing the deep purple mask, I say, give way, for they could do anything, sister. I mean anything at all, Miss Devonish. Once you see they have on that mask, you see me here, I will let them have anything."

"I hear some people with expensive masks are finding it difficult to remove them."

"You have to protect the skin with cotton and oil and lubricants before you wear them. I hear those masks are powerful, they have a life of their own. They pick up the skin, you know, and hold it tight, turning the face into a mask like them."

"It is like pressing a coin real hard on the soft part of your hand," I suggested. "The coin leaves its face – a stamp of itself."

"Even when you use oil and all that, and with luck take it off, it already left a printout of itself on you. Not nice. I know a rich lawyer who had plastic surgery done abroad. I haven't seen him since. I wonder what his face must now look like, because he wore it all the time. He did real good business for the government. He must be so rich, I tell you, he can afford to buy more than one new face abroad."

"I am in a state. You remember that Saturday?"

"Yes."

"Well that is what I mean."

"Don't talk about it."

"Miss Devonish, we were picking peppers at the government farm. You know we have to make a contribution to the Party."

"Miss Devonish, we speaking plainly to you, because we know that whenever you can, you try to help poor people. Like you giving us this lift. You know what a big help that is, especially as the buses not running."

"Pepper prices are paying well, though. In London those bird peppers selling at about two thousand three hundred Mayan dollars per pound."

"You joking."

"Yes, per pound. You hearing right, sister. I'm telling you what I overheard. Some of the higher-ups were talking. I didn't mean to listen. You know how it is, I just heard."

"But at the farm they not telling us that."

"You stupid or something? Why would they do that... I mean if they want free labour. Anyway, as I was saying; we did more than our share really on that Saturday. But you know how it is with them. You trying to keep in they good books – doing whatever extra they ask you to do, hoping they go top up the ration card a bit."

"To get a little something at the side, Miss Devonish."

"We were walking home from Rose Wood because the buses again not running. And we dead tired."

"Stop it, na. Miss Devonish doesn't want to hear those things."

"I want to hear what happened," I said.

"Well there was this little nine year old name Shivnarine. He

normally just selling newspapers and cold drinks by the corner. We
were in the back street. All of a sudden we hear two shots. By the time
we ran up the road and turn the corner into the main street, I can't
tell you what we saw. Nurse Maude was covered in blood. She
holding onto Shivnarine. She saying: 'No! No! No! Everything will
be all right. Everything will be all right, son!'."

"She held him close. I think she knew."

"Of course she knew. She is not just a nurse you know. She was
the Matron of Bon Aire Public Hospital. You have any idea at all
what it is to be the matron of a large public hospital? You have to
know everything!"

"Boy, you shoulda hear she scream. I thought she too was shot."

"Tell Miss Devonish what she did after she closed his eyes."

"She took out a purple mask. I have never seen one so grand.
As grand as the President's."

"Oh God! Miss Devonish."

"Something from another world, Miss Devonish."

"Tell Miss Devonish what she said."

"Nurse Maude put on the mask and she gently turn the little
boy's head to her and she say: 'Look upon your handiwork, Mighty
Spirit of the Dark. Your time has come to turn in upon yourself.
Behold this child. He carried no grudge against you. Release is
here. Self-destruct and find rest with kindred spirits. Feed no more
on the innocent – Rachael is weeping for her children and would
not be comforted because they are not'."

"Yes. And like she seem weighed down by some heavy burden
inside. She bowed her head and the purple mask and the boy's face
touch."

They said nothing more.

What alarmed me was that these two party members saw
nothing especially strange or irrational in Aunt Maude's appeal to
the spirit of the masks. And things began to come together for me.
I understood that nothing now surprises Mayans. They are removed from what they see and hear. They behave as if the world
outside their inner selves is a long-running film – and they are
watching the actors, the changing landscapes, the dialogue. The
actors' words become a musical soundtrack to support the action
– nothing more. They will happily recall any scene or 'action' they

see in the 'show' if you wish. It does not have to make sense. It is out there. It does not touch them in any personal way. Their immediate concern is the struggle to find bread to eat, a job to hold.

I was brought back from my thoughts by their voices.

"I heard you saying to the two men, 'Let them take the boxes. Let them take it'."

"He was so stupid. He kept saying, 'It is not right. Is not right. We have to protect the boxes'."

"They shot both of them – bam, bam. Oh God, the blood!"

"Is funny how when you dead you can't wipe the blood from you mouth."

"You foolish."

"And all for boxes. You see me here. As soon as I can put something together I leaving. No future here."

"No future here long time, sister."

With every election since the burial of these men, ballot boxes have continued to turn up a day late at the Central Bon Aire Counting Station. These latecomers are at all times protected on their final journey by outriders from the army and the police force. There have been no more murders at the polling booths, despite the open rigging of elections. Country Mayans have learnt the lesson the President of Maya intended them to learn and a semblance of the legitimacy of election results can now be maintained, for there is no longer any protest in Maya. Country Mayans are using their ingenuity to leave the island, to build a home in foreign places, not to prevent ballot boxes from being tampered with.

Aunt Maude reminds me that it is also savagery when one accepts and enjoys the special honours, the feastings and other spoils provided by the President, and not see the earthen mounds. Our AUL and professional men and women of the Region and I were present at the last feasting. We sat at his table. My aunt, needless to say, has always declined these invitations.

Of late, the unchallenged confidence of the Government has led to another form of brutality. It flows smoothly from the mouths of our AUL within and without Maya. I once tried to be a devil's advocate in such a circle, saying, "Gentlemen, if a member of the Opposition were to say this and this and this to you, what would your response be?"

Their words streamed past as their mouths opened. They understood my question well. "Why should we concern ourselves with the deaths at the polling station, or in Ica or Hope Bridge. Why repeat those tired old songs. What you have asked us to consider may never have happened, but for the sake of this discussion, we'll take your premise on board and, to satisfy your curiosity, will consider it – though the truth is that those deaths, or what is claimed as election rigging belong to a time that has gone. Why relive the past? We think of the future. We look ahead."

At the time I sincerely hoped that Mayan ghosts were asleep.

"What good is there in remembering victims? What is there to be gained by raking up the ugliness of the past? What need are you satisfying? You cannot bring back the dead. Build anew. Look at the Second World War, you think the countries involved in that spend their time recalling their past discredits? No. Those countries look ahead. They succeed because they are forward looking, leaving the past behind in its legitimate place."

My demeanour must have showed a meshing of pain and disbelief. One said, "Well all right, mistakes were made and you do well to remind us, Comrade Devonish. All governments make mistakes. If you knew the truth about other governments, you would have no qualms about singing the praises of the President – for there is so much to praise that is good about this President."

He did not spell out what these praiseworthy things were, but our society had already reached the sad state in which to state something was proof enough of its existence.

Our AUL would be survivors. I smiled. They shook my hands. "We understand, Marguerite, that being who you are, you will from time to time meet people with unsavoury suggestions, such as those you brought before us. But you will just have to take the line we have taken. I hope we've been helpful."

I couldn't help recalling Vasu Nath saying: "How you present your thinking is itself a moral issue". What I said was: "Gentlemen, you had a difficult proposition to respond to, and I dare say you have done so with the President's sword."

"Any time," they said, "any time at all. Think nothing of it."

"Presidential?" asked one smiling. "Did you say presidential?"

25 MASQUERADES

There were times when I felt, though Aunt Maude did not, that Good Luck had built a nest for Robert Augustus and that power and he were too intertwined to be parted as he marched on and on to the citadel which he had prepared for himself – the Executive Presidency of Maya, accountable to none. An abomination legitimised. It lies in our Constitution.

So when the promises of *Free and Better* crashed before us, they were not recognised for what they were. The full consequences of what was to come were not understood.

For too long, Aunt Maude and I had been like other Mayans – mesmerised by his gains – his long-running good fortune. There was the public and covert support of the governments of the Region; the silent consent of our intellectuals to the death of democracy; and the ineffectual response of the opposition to their disenfranchisement. These circumstances energised him. A natural end of his rule could not be envisaged.

But now Lionel Gomes' spectre stood before the bare, plundered treasury. Wheaten flour, oil, salt, lentils and split peas – in truth almost all imported foods – were banned. The Lord's prayer in public places – *"Give us this day our daily bread"* – was perceived by my brother's Party as an outright provocation – a plea for a banned product – an act of deliberate transgression of government policy, and so a slight alteration was made: *Give us this day our cassava bread, Oh Lord.*

It was when bread was added to the long and growing list of banned products, and remained there, that even in Bon Aire – the heart of the President's support – anxiety increased and overflowed onto other shores.

Bon Aireans scurried in all directions like ants from a disturbed nest. Some tried to come to terms with the empty supermarket shelves, and their implications for the future. There were those who had forgotten how to think for themselves, how to unmask the masquerades, demystify the illusion. I overheard an old man say to his companion at a bus stop, "The President is right when he tells us, 'If there is no bus, use your feet. God gave us feet so that we may put them to use'. Now you see," he emphasised, "I wouldn't have thought of that," he paused, his shoulders hunched, to catch his short asthmatic breath. "You see, my friend, I would have waited and waited, hoping the bus would come. He is a clever man, the President. Soon he will provide us with cassava flour and rice flour. Large mills are being installed in the hinterland, I hear. 'Make use of what you have.' There again you see what I mean. He thinks in new ways."

"My wife," said his companion, "managed to get a little cassava flour and rice flour. All too heavy for me. Not like bread. Nothing like bread. I would like to go back to the bread we know, the bread my mother and my grandmother, and her mother before, baked and ate. I don't understand it. Something is going on that I don't understand. Something basic is not right."

"Government business is like that, comrade. It beats understanding."

Now that the cupboard is bare, the Party sings a new tune. The billboards scream: THE PRESIDENT OFFERS POWER TO MAYANS. TAKE IT!

Beneath this there are short slogans:

OUR PROBLEM IS IN YOUR HANDS, TURN IT INTO A SOLUTION.

BE PATRIOTIC. *GROW YOUR OWN FOOD*

SAVE FOREIGN EXCHANGE TO PURCHASE ELECTRICITY

WE NEED MORE ELECTRICITY FOR OUR HOSPITALS AND SCHOOLS

THE PLIGHT OF THE SICK AND THE YOUNG RESTS WITH YOU

STIR YOURSELVES. SAVE SCARCE FOREIGN EXCHANGE. WE DON'T NEED FOREIGN FLOUR, WE HAVE OUR OWN

YOU HAVE THE FUTURE IN YOUR HANDS

Not everyone knew how to stir themselves or what exactly was meant by it. There were many who had neither the land nor the skill to grow food. After all, his supporters lived in the capital and suburbs. He had already told the cultivators of land what he thought of them. Growers of food in the countryside knew that if they were to plant, the Purple Masked Ones could so easily reap the toils of their labour and they would be powerless to stop them.

A thriving trade in contraband began, opening the door to another wave of official corruption. The risks involved in the business of buying or selling on the black market were high. Heavy fines were imposed by the police and magistrates who cooperated with each other, working as a team. Prices reflected this. The poor could not afford it, and even for the well-to-do, eating bread made of wheat flour became an adventure of risks and escapades.

There followed a growth in beggared rummaging and scavenging. In these times, even the purple masks became an absurdity. Whereas in earlier years, when there was something to be had, the wearing of the masks, *the camouflage of privileges conferred*, had been an asset – now for them too the shelves were empty.

Even Aunt Maude (after years of adamantly refusing to use one of the finest purple masks I had given her) wore it to get to the head of the queue when she heard that oil and wheat flour were available to the Party elite. She succumbed to stop the dreams of her once-upon-a-time, golden-crisp morning bakes, with specially dried local fish, topped with onions and black pepper, from recurring. She smelt them, held them and tasted them. "Dear Marguerite," she wrote, "I did what I had promised myself I would never do save in a dire emergency. I wore that mask. When others saw it, they stepped aside like tall grass in the wind to make room for me at the head of the queue. You would have thought I was Robert Augustus himself. I have at last eaten. My craving is satisfied. I have tasted the privilege of absolute power and felt the force of its seduction. The enticing aroma of my breakfast of warm bakes still fills the house with goodness, dear. I thought I should bury the mask deep lest I become weakened by it. But I am glad that I kept it for I shall be lending it to Vasu Nath when he goes to the hinterland, where he'll need whatever help we can give him. Though we support his going, I know he will be walking into a mine field. It was my suggestion, but now I'm not sure whether this is the way to learn the truth of what is really going on there. Time, Vasu argues, is running out for the victims and he will go. But I am deeply troubled, more now than ever before, and do worry so for him. I cannot bring myself to think of failure."

*   *   *   *

Now all Mayans, the Purple Masked Ones as well, want to leave. Country Mayans have long been searching every port for employment, facing humiliation at the hands of custom officers. Not only young Mayans, but the aged too, with trembling hands and stammering speech, have sought sanctuary in cold inhospitable climes. Unwelcome guests.

Our neighbouring islands, on the other hand, should have brought some comfort to Country Mayans; for is not 'Regional Community' – to which the archipelago of islands all belong – an embracing phrase? But there is another meaning not understood by Country Mayans fleeing political persecution. Robert Augustus, his supporters and the governments of the Region have no difficulty with any meaning of the word 'Community'. There is an understanding, a conspiracy of silence binds them.

*   *   *   *

The Santa Marian immigration officers stand at the arrival gates awaiting an aircraft from Maya.

"So you here on holiday?"

"Yes."

"You know when you come on a holiday, you don't go and get a job, eh?"

"I know."

"I take it you also know that imprisonment and heavy fines are imposed if you're caught working?"

"I am on holiday."

"You will be staying at the Hummingbird Hotel, I see."

The woman is silent. Stress envelops her and all that she was told to do or not to do when she faces an immigration officer has abandoned her. Her memory is too confused. It is leaving her to cope alone. Her hands have become too moist.

"How nice. You know it?"

"A friend recommended it."

"Everyone from Maya stays at the Hummingbird."

"I don't know many people."

"So you don't know it closed down three months ago?"

"I will find another place."

"Listen. You people come here thinking all yuh smart. Well you not fooling us here in Santa Maria. No! Let me come to the point. You not fooling me. You understand that? Why all you Mayans lie so much, man? You should all study law. What you think of that for an idea?"

"It isn't bad."

Uniformed. Confident. A man in authority doing a job. He returns the passport and waves his hand as if wafting a fly and shakes his head from side to side. He turns to exchange a few words with a smiling colleague whom he knew was admiring his performance.

Another Mayan awaits her turn. She would now like to cross out her destination – The Hummingbird Hotel – but what could she put in its place? As he turns his back, she sees a gap in another immigration line and moves there, trying not to let it appear as a move, merely a need to exchange a word with a friend.

In another part of this airport, suspended above their heads, slowly swaying, is a sharp-edged rectangular block. DEPAR-TURES. A long line of Mayans are shuffling their feet. These weary feet are not chained. It is not 1682. It is 1982. Yet they are shuffling in stops and starts, moving in line, pushing and pulling overbearing burdens.

Overburdened. A thin trail of wheat flour marks the Mayan line. Anxieties frame their faces; worry and stress crease their fore-heads like Chinese fans. Their eyes, like low-powered torchlights, are trying to discern what is ahead.

Before them the scales stand firm. "It is solid. It will not collapse," they are thinking, neither will the needle move in their favour. They fear the scales. They see it as their cross.

How can they see that for the safe and efficient operation of an air carrier, their too weighty baggages need to be regulated, their excesses costed? Their very sanity depends on another percep-tion. This truth and others must remain covered, for these are humiliated psyches. Survival is stronger than truth and Robert Augustus knows his supporters well.

The day is done for the sweeper at Santa Maria airport. As he gathers himself to leave, he is attracted to the long trail of flour on the terrazzo floor, which he has just swept. He stands before them awaiting an explanation. He points to the floor. "So what is this? A bag with a hole?" He scans the queue but the women are looking ahead at the check-in counter. There is no place for civil niceties, for apologies, in the stressed lives of women without rights at home. They are too close the edge. The airport sweeper sees the spills of flour on the floor, not the spills of self-worth exacted by Robert Augustus' long misgovernance.

Many Santa Marian employers understand too well that illegal immigrants have no right to work. One or two Mayans are lucky, their employer treats them generously and this experience they are taking back with them. They are enlarged. Back home they will be the envy of those who wish to follow them, hoping that they too would be smiled upon by some caring Santa Marian employer.

These women in the queue are many in one – daughters, mothers, sisters. They are hunters and gatherers. Now they are returning with wholesome things from an enterprising place for their mothers and children, with whom they are losing touch, for whom they weep and worry. In exile, they are greying rapidly in solitary rooms, bare, save for framed, fading photographs. Who dares to whisper their deeper thoughts? Who dares to ask? And if their silences can be read, what fears do they reveal? "I am far from my children and they are drifting away. They are drifting away with no guide, without the maps we would have made as we talked together, ate together, played together, fought together. What makes it so? Why am I here? Must it be so? Why could Maya not be as Santa Maria? O God, tell me!"

When they arrive at Maya's airport these women will need to warm the palms of the custom officers so that they can bring in the flour sealed in polythene bags. Their bodies are no longer the temples they once were. Their age of innocence has passed. But they will survive its desecration for their children's sake.

And it is for their children's future that they struggle on alone, aware that their own futures have passed by in the immeasurable toil of their sad lives – that, somehow, does not accumulate bankable worth though they give their all.

The day they return to Maya is like any other. All around the drains are silted. Overflows and pollutants stagnate. The grey kokers stand rotting, sad spectres of the times. When it rains the udders of milking cows are drowned and sheep and goats are tethered on any mound that rises to the occasion. Meanwhile the sea pounds the land relentlessly, intent on reclamation. Those who can do no better must stand and wait like drowned houses for floods to subside, while others secretly seek a future in foreign states – the very states much abused on Mayan political platforms.

*   *   *   *

On this particular day in London, England – in South Kensington, others are travelling too, leaving the outskirts of the metropolis for the centre. Purple-Masked Mayans are gathering in a cold, poorly-lit room. Each one in attendance knows the way. They have managed the stairs over the years, though the bulb has long blown. The old escalator, nervous and trembling, takes its time coming and going. "It is just as quick to climb the steps," the regulars say, puffing like steam engines.

In time, all thirty stand gathered around an oval table, looking as solemn as if it were a coffin. Then comes a whispering from one end of the room; each in attendance takes a glass of white wine. They hold it, not taking it to their lips. It must be held with care for that is all there is. Everyone waits. Then from somewhere, a voice. It is difficult to ascertain the source. The room makes their number almost a pressing crowd. All eyes are turned to a photograph of the President of Maya sitting on his white mare 'Abundance'. His purple gloves and purple switch are meant to catch the eye. And as the restless eyes turn, the same voice comes through again. It says "MAYA". Nothing more. No adornment. A simple, single statement – *Maya*.

Those in attendance raise their glasses a few inches higher as if the better to examine the liquid, and they repeat the sound, *Maya*, before swallowing and shaking hands and smiling. *How do you do? So good to see you. Where are you now? Any news? Have you been back since? What beastly cold weather. But I had to come.*

After other pleasantries, they walk out to the equally cold but better lit London streets. They nod as they pass, acknowledging once more each other's presence at this – their celebration of the Independence of Maya, at the Mayan High Commissioner's London residence.

A group of tired men, their old masks removed, are wrapped warmly as babies, uncomfortable in the bitter cold. They have come from far and know that something is amiss that they should have to return so soon to their homes. They recall when Maya's Independence celebration was an all-day affair of dancing, feasting and fetes. One or two, if pressed, would say with some unease that for them Independence had meant freedom to think, to build a country, to thrive, to honour the land where their parents and grandparents toiled and laughed, wept and danced. They tremble in the cold and quietly move away.

The journey they have all made has taken longer than its stay. It was a journey prepared for – garments brushed and pressed, hung out in the morning sun, aired for their annual celebration. And so they linger awhile, unsure, uncomfortable in the glistening hard frost, for *camaraderie's* sake. It is an old, warm, comforting word from childhood, another time and place long gone save in their memories. They are old men becoming older, taking with them the dignity that comes with age, the disappointments of life, its lingering hopes of a larger recognition. They supported Robert Augustus, have always done so. Stalwarts. He has disappointed them. But this too they will carry, for they are men.

"Couldn't let the day go by without coming."

"No, Sir."

"We holding on."

"Still holding on."

"Yes, we are."

"Yes, brother."

"Still there with a fighting chance."

"We will abide."

"A rough patch."

"Cannot stay rough forever."

"No, Sir."

"It stands to reason. Whatever goes down must come up."

"Everything in motion."

"Hang in there."

"Yes man. Hanging in. You can't give up on your own."

"No, brother, you can't. It's all we have."

"Today, you have to be for yourself, for the world looks after its own."

"Mind you, we deserved better."

"Better. .. Better."

"Yet it is all we have."

"Will come right. Must come right. Can't stay like this forever."

"By the grace of God, must come."

"In God's good time. He will see us through."

"Deserved better."

"Change will come. Must come."

"Good night, Comrade."

"Good night."

The echoing sounds of fading steps sadden the night air, and are swallowed up in London's rushing flow.

26   TWO WOMEN MEET
Subah

Dorothy Gittens would have come today and I would have looked forward to her coming. I miss her. Everyone who once lived here has left and I, housekeeper to Vasu and Arun Nath, have become keeper of an empty house. My feet echo everywhere.

These are my last days in Maya, and as I walk about the vegetable garden, I relive happy moments such as finding a full ripe pumpkin hidden by its broad, palm-shaped, prickly leaves, laughing a deep laugh on my finding it. Memories of this kind I will take with me to London. I shall miss the smell of green, the coastal Mayan breezes sweetened with sugar-cane juice. When London's spring and autumn come, will I recall the warmth and burnt sweetness of sugar harvesting?

It is here that I see the spirits of my parents, my husband, my mother-in-law, my father-in-law. I hear voices of the living too – my daughter Veena, Arun, Vasu and Aasha. I say farewell to all this as I prepare to leave for London, to live with Veena. Yet I feel an undertow within me, pulling. It is asking why should I have to leave? I know why, yet I still ask.

Again my spirit reaches out to Dorothy. She wears a fine hat of red, pink and yellow roses.

"Subah, I have to keep up appearances. You can't let go. Just hang in there."

That is Dorothy.

But at first I didn't want to know. I met her when she came round the back, by the kitchen door. Everybody was suspicious of everybody. It was that kind of time... It is that kind of time.

"Good afternoon, sister."

I said nothing. I watched.

"You want anything today?"

I shook my head. When I saw her laying her bags at my door I felt I must make myself clear.

"I don't want anything today, sister."

"I know that. I heard you. But what I trying to figure out in this killing heat is how you don't want what I have in this strong bag. How you don't want what breaking my hands and wearying me down, when you don't know what I have, especially these days when the shops have nothing. I can see from here that you grow a lot of things – spinach, ochroes, beans, squash. But you can't grow everything."

[*Subah has that kind of face that draws you to it, especially if you are lost, have taken the wrong turning, and are now well and truly confused. She combs her hair in that simple classical style of eastern women – a middle parting, hair combed neatly back and held in a smooth bun. Hers is an intelligent face, but it is her eyes that seem to be listening intently when you speak, listening for what is not said, jumped over or held back. She had wanted to teach, but under different circumstances she could have become a fine judge. She is slim, has always been slim, because she cannot stay still. Even at nights her pillow falls to the floor. But when she smiles or laughs, which is becoming rarer, you know you have been given a treat.*]

"Listen, I don't know you and I don't want trouble. No sooner you leave, you'll send your policemen to search this house for contraband. Whatever you have, sister, I don't want. You hear me. I know this setup too well. It wouldn't work with me. The police will come pretending they looking for contraband, meantime they looking to see if this house worth raiding. They busy-busy looking at the windows and doors to see how they can break in later. And when they leave, I find I am missing a gold chain or a gold ring or money, because they searching the bedroom, everywhere. And you don't have time to put things away. They don't have a warrant. They tell you straight: "You hear the President say he is judge and jury? Well policemen are warrant, prosecutor and magistrate.""

Dorothy said nothing. She could have been a passer-by listening to a complaint. I had to be on my guard. Everything she had in her bag, and more, were banned. Ordinary everyday goods that

were not available in the shops: salt, flour, butter, cheese, oil,
onion, garlic – just to give you an idea. I knew if I bought anything
and a police search were to find even one pound of flour I would
be charged in the magistrate courts. Every day people are fined in
these courts. I call them hijackers courts – with the seal of the
government. I have a good idea who eats the flour the police seize
and the magistrates condemn. You can't afford to trust anyone.
Trust is too expensive a commodity here. It is that kind of time.

A fortnight ago, it happened before my eyes. I was coming from
the market and a nine year old, as fine as a needle, was caught
carrying a twenty-five pound bag of flour on his head. Later, I
found out that when the driver carrying this contraband realised
that the police were tipped off, he threw it out of his jitney. This boy
saw the flour on the verge, picked it up, intending to hide it, but
there was no shelter either for him or the flour. Seeing a purple-
masked policeman he began to run. The police told him to halt. He
didn't have the sense to drop the flour and run. He ran with it.
Maybe what kept him going was the thought of being able to take
it home. Maybe he saw the joy in his mother's face and those of his
neighbours, if he managed it. For though weighed down by the
flour, he was doing pretty well. Then he saw Nurse Maude and
began to run in her direction. She saw what was happening and ran
towards him, but before they could reach each other, the police
shot him in the back. He didn't fall at once. His blood flowed from
him. He didn't let go the flour. Seeing Nurse Maude, the police
drove away.

I came round to see better. Nurse Maude held on to the boy.
The blood kept flowing. She tried to stop it, but she knew. His
hands looked for hers and he spoke so softly. She bent low to
hear. "Aunty Maude, dem ah kill me. Me go dead. Take me home...
Help me, Ma, Aunty Maude... dem ah kill me... Me... gg..."

She knew. And Nurse Maude brought him closer, embracing
him tightly as if she was trying to press her very life into him. After
a while she released him and closed his eyes and opened her
mouth. A sound came from within her – a cry from hell. Her crisp
white coat changed colour. I left her side to pick up the flour before
it disappeared. A crowd had gathered.

"Subah, this is Shivnarine," she said. "I delivered him nine years ago. Help me take him home." She placed the flour in the trunk of her old Morris Oxford. "Indu is his mother, she would want to cremate the flour too. I know she wouldn't be able to eat it. I don't think his five year old sister Leela would understand what happened. What do I tell her? How to put to a child where this island going?" I sat in the back of the car with Shivnarine's head on my lap and Nurse Maude drove in silence. Later her voice entered my head. It was strange: "A voice was heard in Ramah, Weeping and great mourning, Rachel weeping for her children, and would not be comforted, because they were not... When Leela grows up, how does one explain why this can happen and the policeman can rest in his bed fearing nothing. What hell ties us to this? What binds us to this, so we can't speak out? Lord have mercy on us." We were both silent for a long long while and then she spoke again in that strange way. "We have given my nephew Robert Augustus Devonish all our rights and we are reaping the consequences... *And there was a great earthquake, such as was not since... so great an earthquake, so mighty... And every island fled away, and the Mountains were not found.* You cannot build a country by denying to yourself that it is a hell you have created for others. You cannot build on lies, on other people's torment. What sort of structure would that be? The ghosts of your victims, the spirits of the tortured would undermine you. Your innards consumed, Subah, and you become a hollow vessel echoing the passing wind."

Two days later the cremation took place. He had such a slight frame. The ghee and the rich yellow crystals of fine Demerara sugar his mother placed on his small chest would help him burn well. His sister Leela lit the pyre on all four sides, while the pundit performed the sacred Sanskrit rites. The flames were framed, for the pyre was skilfully constructed. Shivnarine did burn well. His sister and mother watched as the fire consumed him and he and the burning wood were one. We watched. In silence, men wept. Later, much later, the tall pyre was brought low and Shivnarine's warm ashes entered the mighty Azon.

*   *   *   *   *

I was brought back to the present by Dorothy's voice.

"I understand everything," she said. "Except that if a police-man come here, is not me who sent him, or is not me who asked somebody to send him either. I don't expect you to believe that, because the policemen and I have the same birthmark and people choose who they trust and what not by birthmarks."

"I go by who I know."

"Good for you. You wouldn't mind if a tired lady catch her breath. I going just now. You not to worry bout my staying. I could see you busy."

There was something about her eyes and the way she leaned against the kitchen wall that made me bring a chair for her. And her fine hat with roses, red, pink and yellow, seemed to be smiling at me for bringing the chair. I know it sounds foolish, but that is how it was.

"Thank you. I didn't want to ask but my feet and I are thankful."

She was perspiring so much and the sun was really hot. I brought her some water from the goglet. She drank and I poured her some more and she drank. She adjusted her hat and smoothed her dress with her hands. She wiped her brow. "I needed that too bad. Thanks."

She had beautiful eyes. You wanted to keep looking at them, but they were shy eyes. She smiled and turned away. She didn't even look at me when she said, "You know what I like bout you. You plain speaking. You telling me what you think, and giving me a chair and water to drink and telling me you don't trust me one damn minute. I like that. I like that too bad. That is good. That is really good. We stop doing that in this country. That is half the problem."

"You from Bon Aire, na?"

"I come all the way from Bon Aire." She shifted herself in the chair and I thought she was preparing to leave. But she sat quietly for quite some time. So quietly I thought she fell asleep. "Thank you. I going. I know you don't want anything today. Just let me show you what I have. I don't want you to buy anything. Next week, if you want anything, you will let me know. Check me out with Ramlakhan, the one with the cows. I understand you have to be careful. I have to be careful too. But you wouldn't believe that. Here in the country, I know all you country folks believe that we in town have it good." She laughed a cynic's laugh. "Only we know, sister, only we know."

She opened the bag. "I have flour and onions and garlic and salt. I could get milk powder if you want. I don't have butter, cheese, coffee nor split peas. But I can get split peas for you, if you really want it. But it would be expensive."

"Dhal was always cheap."

"What is your name?"

"Subah."

"Subah, you tell me anything you know today that has not gone up six times since Emmanuel Pottaro's time. The money today is no money. One of the worst thing the President did, that killing we poor people who put him in power, jump up for him, wear his face on our backs, is to rob us. He took his hand, put it in everybody's pocket, took out the money that was there and put in its place a counterfeit, lightweight thing. You need six times of his new money to make one of the old, and add to that, wages have not moved up in years. So what all that add up to for poor people? Mind you, the police, the magistrates, everybody in the same boat. Everybody scrambling, you hear me."

"Why you telling me that? Because I know, if there was election tomorrow you would still jump up and vote for him. So put that aside. I remember well how you Bon Aireans went on a long strike against Pottaro, how you people brought a good man low. God help you all. Now, all you not on strike, all you quiet as a mouse. People get what they vote for, I say. And God not sleeping, sister."

Dorothy looked at me. "Subah, I don't have time now, but one day when we know one another better I will tell you why we don't go on strike now."

I did check her out with Ramlakhan: "She has good reasons for keeping far from the police." That is all he said, except to add that in these times the less you know the better. "She calls herself Dorothy Gittens, but I wouldn't be surprise if that name is not on she birth certificate. You right to be cautious. You don't know who is who these days, but she alright."

The next time I bought a pound of flour. It was expensive and I held it as if it was something too precious to eat. I really had no choice after she said:

"I don't know when last you had a good hot paratha rotie, flaky and breaking up in your hands. I can see that nice honey-looking

ghee you have up there on the top shelf, home-made; good quality
that ghee is. Now that would make them roties soft and nice, and
with pumpkin or your own fresh chowrai bhagee or bygan chokha
and bird-pepper, you will be having a feast, Subah."

"How come you know bout chowrai bhajee and bygan chokha?"

"But eh! eh! You living here and I living here. I copying from
you, you copying from me. We pretending that not happening.
We playing hide-and-seek. You know where I hiding. I know
where you hiding." She laughed. "But we pretending – grownups
playing children's game. I trust we will soon get tired and come
out of hiding, and walk this road together, Subah, because if we
do, we will create the next best thing to heaven right here. And,
by the way, I know bout tomato chokha too."

I grew to like her. I couldn't believe anyone who voted for the
President could think like that, talk like that. I am not easily
convinced. Ask my daughter Veena about me. I began to think that
something else might be going on under the surface. Trust takes a
long time to catch, even on good soil, and the soil around me had too
many earthen mounds covering our sons and daughters.

I brought some cow manure from Ramlakhan and began to grow
more of everything – ochroes, bygan, squash, pumpkin, patchoi
and beans. I felt I could barter with her for the flour on some days.
If not, I could sell the vegetables. I went to Bon Aire market myself
one day. It was a whole day business. I saw the prices the market
traders were selling their vegetables for, and so was better
prepared to bargain with her. I told her what I had done. Business
is business. I didn't want her to think that I didn't know what the
market was doing. I didn't want the arrangement I was thinking
about not to take off, just in case she was tempted to overdo things
because of the pressure she had. I could see she was a woman
striving to do what could make anyone go mad – support a family
on little.

Between us we worked out something that gave us a fair stake
in the production and selling of fresh vegetables, and we were in
business. I wanted her to succeed, not just because it meant that
I too would be making something, but, my God, she deserved to
have success! She had a van and that helped her and helped me.
I learnt more about the van by chance.

On that day I could see she was disturbed. Even her fine hat didn't smile. And her business of 'keeping up appearances' seemed to have left her.

"I think they've been trailing me."

"Who?"

"The WSM."

"What is that?"

"Subah, you don't know the WSM?"

"I don't read papers any more. The Government banned the import of newsprint long time now, so no opposition newspapers. The only paper you can get is pure government propaganda –*The Carrier*. I will not buy that. If I get one for free I will have a look just to see what new song they singing. The last time the song went like this: 'We're a poor man, poor man government. We will give him shelter, give him food and give him clothes too. For we're a poor man, poor man government'."

"You have a good voice, Subah."

"I've been singing bhajans all my life, but this tune as 'rendered by me', as my daughter Veena would put it, is a real come down...."

"You don't say, Subah. You are something else, I tell you."

"So what is the WSM?"

"The Women's Socialist Movement."

"Is it for real?"

"What you mean? We have a uniform, a flag..."

"A motto and an anthem?"

"No, Subah."

"Tell me."

"We're the women's arm of the Government and I'm a member."

"Oh. Here we call you WAG – so why they after one of their own?"

"How come you think I can be here every Tuesday."

"You come in the van."

"So you think I own the van?" She smiled. "That is nice. I wish it was true. No, my dear, I use the WSM van. I have the use of it on Tuesdays to come down to persuade you to buy and eat cassava flour and rice flour. We mixing it now, you know."

"You never brought me any."

"You want some? I have it in the van."

"I prefer to boil cassava and boil rice."

"This is what people telling me here. You see the President has a cassava/rice flour project. It is a United Nations project. The President has contacts with inside people, so they trying to help him out. We in the WSM have to go round and talk about how superior cassava/rice flour is to wheat flour."

"But you never told me anything about this."

"You think the cassava/rice flour is superior to the flour I selling you?"

"No."

"Well then."

"People try it. It heavy too bad. It riding on the stomach for days. I can't afford a doctor and my daughter away in London. Any time now she will send for me. So the last thing I want is to have something riding on my stomach when I riding the air waves. The truth is I don't travel well, Dorothy. I have to be careful."

"Me too, Subah."

"Things not easy in London, mind you, but plenty better than here. Anything you want, provided you have the money, no problem. The supermarket shelves, Veena tells me, are bulging with anything and everything. Cheese from all over the world, nicely wrapped so when you open it you want to hold on to it and smell it deep. Cheese from Holland, Denmark, Switzerland, Norway, France – from all over the world, Dorothy. Coffee, too, from Colombia, Costa Rica, Kenya, Jamaica and so many other places I can't remember now. It's as if the whole world rests on one shelf, and you can cross thousands of miles of sea and jungle, mountains and deserts, worry and trouble, mosquitoes and alligators with a step, a trolley and a hand-stretch. Because somebody has already done all that searching for you. And Veena says supermarkets vie with one another for your custom, so you get all this service at a good price. Value for money, Dorothy."

"That sounds like a special place. That is quality living, Subah."

"No, Dorothy, Veena say that is ordinary living for them. Take bread. You know here you will be charged for eating it. Over there bread is not something to hide, cover over with a brown paper bag when you see somebody coming. All kinds of breads are sold at bakeries in London. If only I could put my hand on that letter now, you would get hungry. Farm loaf, French loaf, Cholah, bloomer, bagel, whole wheat, rye bread, granary, multi-grain. Dorothy, that is not all. On top of the bread now you have different seeds – sesame, poppy seeds, aniseed, rye seed, and, oh yes, crack wheat, oat flakes and a variety of nuts."

"And you telling me ordinary working people can eat those breads?"

"Yes."

"Is it a socialist country?"

"No, Dorothy. Russia is a socialist country."

"Funny how I used to think that socialism would be just like that. Everybody, the higher-ups and the small people, all eating the same good quality bread, according to their needs."

"And according to their appetites too, na? Seems to me socialist bosses tend to go that way, Dorothy – the appetite way."

"No! no! Subah. According to their needs is socialism. But according to their appetites is capitalism."

"Is that so? Well, Dorothy, you will at least have a greater choice with capitalism, because some people have an appetite for egg loaf and some for granary and so on. So the capitalist baker is baking a variety, catering for all appetites. While with needs, Veena says, that has just to do with energy – any old plain bread will satisfy energy needs. A greater need means more of the same."

"Subah, I used to think that under socialism, when you go to the socialist bakery, the place would be clean, smelling good good. The workers busy busy serving you. Bread would be hot and the paper bag would get wet with the heat and it would be so nice inside the shop. The baker would be smiling, asking you bout yourself. But... now I wonder, Subah. Now I wonder."

"Me too, Dorothy. I wonder how all this childish foolishness get into our heads? Who put it there I wonder?"

"Coming back to this cassava/rice flour. I'm supposed to say that we must become independent of foreign things. Eat local."

"Look at my vegetable garden. Country people eating local. We have been doing that from birth. You mean to say that we carrying out government policy? We too law-abiding down here. That is our trouble. We should have set up our own underground resistance. Veena says so."

"As a member of the WSM, I'm supposed to say to you ... look Subah, it's written on this card: *Eat local so as not to have to import foreign foods. Save our scarce foreign earnings to purchase petroleum for our power stations.*"

"Well what about the President's cars and his helicopter, his brandy and his cigars and those grand government banquets with imported wines and fancy nuts and olives? Nurse Maude keeps me up to date."

"Subah, stop. One day you going to find yourself in jail, eh."

"Dorothy, you think I will speak like that to a WSM lady?"

Together they laugh a bellyfull.

But trust is a shy, fragile bird. It takes a lot of hard work and a long dedication to it, before it will leave its sanctuary in the forest to come and sit with you.

*   *   *   *

The last time Dorothy came I could sense that things were tightening round her. "Subah, would you be interested," she said, "in having a purple mask?"

I was stunned. The purple mask for us country people was not merely something that should be destroyed, it was something we despised. We associated it with Ica, Hope Bridge, the burning of Bon Aire, and the anguish of cremating the innocent. We saw it as the face of hell. Women like Shivnarine's mother had left. Kamelia's daughters were adopted and their grandmother later joined them in New Jersey.

If the purple masks were creating problems for their wearers, I saw God's hand in it and thought it high time too. But as everybody knows, that was not the designer's intention. We were his targets, and he struck us – bull's eye – again and again. His victims are everywhere. New York, Toronto. Go there and listen to their whispers. Hear their tales. Country Mayan families in every port.

And now this? Why does Dorothy not understand that I feel nothing but contempt for the very idea which brought these masks into our lives? What could have made her bring this so close to me?

"Let me show you what I have," Dorothy said. She sat down and carefully removed three cakes of sweet soap, five packets of milk powder, small sachets of salt and then a plastic bag. From this, she brought two folded masks, placed them on her lap, removed a handkerchief from her bosom, wiped her hands, then opened the masks and pressed her hands over them as if to iron them out.

"See if you would like these. They are grade one purple masks. These are the rank and file WSM purple masks. They are not the masks of the higher-ups in the movement; you have to have Presidential contacts for those, or know someone on the PMC, the Purple Mask Committee. But these have their uses. They are plenty better than nothing."

I did not want to touch them. But I had to do something. I held a mask and was surprised that it was made of such cheap quality cotton, so lightweight. The colour must have left it some time ago. In fact, it was not purple at all. It looked a washed-out, faded blue. Lighter than the blue soap poor people use for washing clothes. It was dull and poorly stitched. Was it for this that the poor in Bon Aire voted? Overthrew a legitimate government? Sold their rights in the new Presidential Constitution? Was it for this?

As I held the mask, Dorothy must have thought I was wavering and said, "The purple mask has become an entrance ticket to everything in Bon Aire. It would come in handy, Subah. Besides, you will have some protection from being robbed or molested in Bon Aire if you wearing one of these."

"I am grateful, Dorothy, that you take the vegetables from me so I don't have to take the risk of choke and rob in Bon Aire. But I will tell you this, if I ever want one, I shall buy it from you. I promise I will give you the sale."

"Thank you, Subah."

"Now you must eat with me, Dorothy. I may never see you again, so let us eat together to mark our meeting and parting, na? Come, let us fire one between us." Subah brought out a nip of rum in a bottle without a label. "This is strong rum, Dorothy. Straight or with water?"

"Straight. So when you really leaving, Subah?"

"Next week."

"Next week? You good-for-nothing, lucky woman. You realise that?"

"My spirit has not left here yet. I am still between staying and going."

"You have to let go, Subah. If all that you tell me is true about the bread – and all the other things about buses and trains running to a timetable and such. Dependable and reliable. I never had anything like that. This Government never provided for us in this way. It does not help us ordinary people. I always had to look out for myself... begging for a lift, a job, standing where I think there might be something I could pick up. I had to. This Government behaved like the father of my children. He just picked up himself one day and left. The Government favoured others – high coloured, not us. Now is I alone with the children. Battling everyday, Subah. But I'm glad for you. Make the most of it, sister. I'm too happy for you. So this is our last meeting then. Eh! eh! What you doing with that camera?"

"Come, Dorothy, stand in front of Vasu Nath's house. He would have liked you to do that."

"Me? Look at me. Why didn't you tell me before; I would have come prepared for a photograph."

"Stop complaining, Miss Fussy. Think your nicest thoughts and smile, Dorothy Gittens. Tell the world who you really are – a fine gracious Dame, as Veena would say, with the dignity of a two hundred year old mahogany tree. You just tell them, Dorothy Gittens, tell the WSM, the PMC – and all that lot – tell them, Sister."

As they eat squash with lots of home-grown tomatoes, and beans picked an hour earlier, lightly curried, and rice and silver snapper seasoned with garden thyme and pepper, fried in home-made coconut oil, both women are silent. The goodness of the meal embraces them, holds them together.

Subah cannot forget the wretchedness of the poverty displayed in Dorothy's handbag, the desperation which drove her to try to sell her two of her masks. She is more than ever convinced that the ideas that brought down such a woman, the ideas that helped the poverty of Maya to grow and forced thousands to leave, the ideas that turned Shivnarine to ash for carrying a small bag of flour, those ideas should be buried deep in the bowels of the earth.

And yet Subah knows this will not be, for Veena has told her that such ideas were still around in influential schools in the archi-

pelago, and their prophets were still enjoying a secure lifestyle on
state salaries.

Subah muses, smiling to herself, remembering what Veena
had said. "If a businessman comes up with an idea that proves
bankrupt, he pays for it from his pocket or loses his job. Why is it
not the same with a man employed by the state if he preaches a
bankrupt idea that facilitates mediocrity, stagnation, or brings
about a creeping hell that suffocates the poor? His salary, his
pension, still rise and his security of tenure remains intact, even
if he continues to disseminate ideas that perpetuate hell."

Yes, Subah thinks, in the long and short run, it's always the poor
who pay for all the bright people's mistakes. Those people learn
ways to cushion their fall. They know how to help themselves, how
to cover their nakedness.

Subah is trying to understand the nature of the force that could
bring about widespread ruin and devastation, without those af-
flicted protesting, when they had in their hands the power to do so,
even to overthrow a government, as they had done in the past.

Maybe, at the beginning, the quality and colour and stitching
of the political masks were beautiful, something of which to be
proud. It was their Prime Minister's design, meant exclusively for
them to feel special and different, with high expectations of further
designs to come.

But a mask is a mask and can only mask what it covers. Yet it was
sold as privilege, power, and became those things too. Was this
faded, poorly-stitched, cheap cotton mask actually purchased by
the poor? Was it not freely given? Was this all that remained of one
man's idea of self determination, of national sovereignty? Were the
masks in Dorothy's bag like her Party? She must stop asking
questions – a headmaster's questions from an ancient classroom.
She will enjoy Dorothy's company for the last time, if she doesn't,
she knows she will look back with regret for wasting this time.

They eat mangoes and drink cool water from the goglet. Dorothy
says, "I know you're not asking me, but you must want to know.
Besides I did promise to explain why we in Bon Aire not coming out
on strike. Look at me, Subah. Look at me real good."

"I have, several times. You have pretty eyes and your smile
looks the way small children see the sun smile."

"Subah, stop interrupting me."

"Not a word from me, sister."

"Now you see this face, these features, this hair; the President has them. This is why people in Bon Aire vote for him. The world stay so, Subah. All about, people do that. They look at their face in the mirror and they look to see who has that face and they vote accordingly. Two weeks ago I was standing for a bus in Bon Aire which never came. I was so frustrated I said, 'This President can't even run a bus service, furthermore a country.' A neatly dressed man, who had clearly known better times, old enough to be my father, was also waiting. He came up to me and said, 'Listen, my child, you shouldn't say that.' 'Why? But is true,' I said. He says to me, 'When you say that, do you not know you're criticising yourself? Do you not know you're also saying that we, the Purple-Masked people, whom this Government has brought to power, cannot run things? Do you want our children to hear that from their parents? Have you thought of the long term consequences of what you're saying? I'm old enough to be your father, and I never dreamt that someone looking like me would ever walk up those steps of the President's residence and run this country. You know what that means to me? We know; the state the island is in matters. Of course it does, no getting away from that, but still, what is even more important to my mind is that we are in power. We are in charge. We are the rulers of this land. We and we alone, and we're going, so help me God, to keep it that way. Holding onto power is our insurance'."

Between these two women there is a silence. Then Subah speaks. "That is bleak and dull, Dorothy. It's coming from an old man who is tired. He's weighed down, carrying the long, long-ago past on his back. He is bent double by it. He can't lift up his eyes unto the hills, as my headmaster used to say. He belongs to my mother-in-law's age. He doesn't have a clue what we want our todays to be, furthermore our tomorrows."

"Subah, don't tell me the President created a hell here. I know that. I am living in it. You don't understand a damn thing. You so blasted optimistic. Take this meal with you – the rum and all – is the best thing I have had in a long time. Sweet Jesus, I don't want to remember how long. And I'm feeling so bad now. I feel I should have made some excuse like, 'I just eaten but I will take it home if you don't mind so you wouldn't feel bad.' Just so I could take it home for the children. You know how I feel inside that I have to tell you this? Look at me, Subah, I'm standing naked before you. Don't you think I know the hell this place is? Don't you think we have to have some pride too? But the old man has a point. Of course I'm saying we not running the damn place, it falling apart. I know. I know. And when it comes to suffering, we have suffered before. Suffering is nothing new to us. So what difference does it make if when you're a colony you suffer, and when you're independent you're suffering more?"

"Dorothy, I hope you don't believe that. All I can say: it is not you speaking, Dorothy, it is still the old man speaking."

There comes a gentle peace between them. Then Subah says. "The difference is too big. I thought of letting it pass but I can't. Besides, I believe our friendship is strong enough to walk with truth. Many times, most times, Dorothy, our suffering comes when we're exploited by others. But when you bring it upon yourself – it can be any mix of – irresponsibility, stupidity, incompetence, ignorance, carelessness. Veena says so and I have to agree. But when a government brings destruction upon its people, it should feel bad. Very bad, Dorothy. It should hang its head in shame and its supporters should tell it to leave. If it doesn't leave, it means the Government is not only messing up the present but messing up the future too for everybody. When you think we have only the one try at living life, anyone who cuts down our chance to make a good try, while he, his wife, family and close friends cream off year after year what is there, some would say he should be shot. I say he should be 'put away', imprisoned, but never be allowed to get off scotch free, irrespective of his looks. You can make a case for the defence, Dorothy Gittens, but Subah is prosecuting on behalf of young children, the old and the poor who have become poorer, to ensure it doesn't happen again. Our lives are as precious as those who govern us. It is time we say so."

But there comes a point when much is left unsaid, though each suspects what the other is thinking. Dorothy, Subah thinks, is displaying a deep courtesy and tact that she would never have expected in someone from the Bon Aire of the raging fires and the

long strike. At no time has Dorothy said to her that in the country
people voted for Pottaro for the same reason as the Bon Aireans voted
for Augustus. Pottaro was a communist. No respectable farmer
would, under normal circumstances, vote for a man who believes the
farmer ought not to own his farm, his land. Yet Country Mayans had
voted for such a man.

Subah knew that Pottaro had leased the polder lands to all
Mayans, but that only Country Mayans had been prepared to put
their all in it and make something of it. She says nothing of this.
Neither does she express her view that urban Mayans saw their way
out of poverty through a nice white-collar job with shelter, security
and pension, not through working on a polder, in water, waist high,
singing, "One, one, dutty build dam". Exposure to mud, rain and
heat was for Country Mayans.

This soft silence, born of the courtesy that holds them, means
that Subah will never know whether Dorothy, if pressed, would
agree that country people had no one else but Pottaro; that Robert
Augustus had never been for them, had seen them as a people in
his path, in the way of his ambition when he was in opposition, and
so dispensable when in power.

Subah does not know whether Dorothy would agree that Pottaro
would have given them a better time, because he was a poor man's
politician – the genuine article; that he would have felt the need to
keep courting those in Bon Aire who threatened him most; that he
would have thrown parts of his ideology to the winds and offered Bon
Aireans the ownership of land, at the expense of his country
supporters – whom he had long taken for granted – just look at their
roads that gave tadpoles and mosquitoes such a good start.

And so though Subah thinks that Dorothy Gittens had admitted
much, she still feels she has not acknowledged the whole picture
of Maya under Robert Augustus: No jobs. Old jobs going and no
new jobs coming. Illiterate school children, rats and cockroaches
becoming bolder – knowing numbers are on their side and showing
that they are no longer afraid of patients in the hospital. A public
hospital without even ample detergents and clean bandages.
Patients are asked to bring their own. And yet Bon Aireans dance
for him. And yet they praise him. To accept this because of the
politics of the mirror was not good enough.

Subah feels there has to be a way out of this thinking that imprisons the victim with his own lock and key. Seeing Dorothy wasting before her, while she was going to leave this man-made mess behind, and with time might even forget what Mayan mess was like, had set her thinking. What does one say to a friend? She had to come up with something worthwhile. Maya needed good ideas, good direction.

"Dorothy, you have to become modern."

"Subah, you're a joke. I'm from the town, the capital of Maya; you from the countryside with no street lights, no paved roads, no telephone, telling me to become modern. I cannot believe it."

"Let me tell you what I mean."

"I see."

"Here I am with many fine old trees around me, flowering shrubs and rice and sugar-cane. A few butterflies. Only insects move between the rushing winds and waving branches. I don't have children nor husband, so I spend my time thinking about everything. Look at that poinciana or that mahogany, or over there the saaman tree."

"Yes, Subah." Dorothy begins to smile.

"They look top heavy."

"Yes, Subah."

"One single trunk holding up such a wide, heavy spread. Yet it is not top heavy. It stays upright, Dorothy, because of all the strong underpinnings, that travel far and wide, picking up strength and energy from a wide area. Doing it all quietly. Not showing off, not shouting about its work. Instead, it goes about undercover, underpinning its sturdy foundations that enable a single trunk to hold up a hundred branches high above the heads of the tallest men. Now, Dorothy, those trees are being modest and modern. Efficient and beautiful is what Veena would say. That is how to go about making good sense. The leaves catch the sunlight, sustaining the tree and cooling us and allowing birds to shelter and nest. That is modern. And giving shade to a weary traveller – that is thoughtful."

"Subah, what has that got to do with you and me?"

"Well, I say if a tree can design itself so well, you and I are supposed to have more sense. So what are we doing? Dorothy, I am designing myself and you must do the same. Don't let anything or anyone or any idea imprison you, even if that idea has your beautiful eyes."

Dorothy thinks long before she says, "Maybe, Subah, where you're going, you can run by yourself, but here in Maya I have to run with my group. If I don't, which group will find a place for me in one of their crowded inns? And if I don't show a preference for my kind of face and eyes, what will I have left, Subah? What will I call my own?"

"You will have freedom, Dorothy."

"What kind of freedom will make up for my own face?"

Subah looks at Dorothy. They are about to part for their own journeys, and Subah says, with tears in her eyes, "The freedom to think, man; to walk and listen too; to learn, to create, to explore; to run and fly; to speak, to imagine the best, Dorothy, to make things in a different way; the freedom to grow stronger and not lose yourself. A freedom that can travel." She walked towards Dorothy and said: "Now you must hug me. I shouldn't have to ask. But this is the world I live in, Dorothy Gittens."

These two women embrace and receive from each other an affection they know will withstand time and the pull and tug of kith and kin, and country. They do not give it thought, but we must hope that, between them, they are placing two stout granite pillars to help with the foundations of rebuilding the Maya of tomorrow.

After using their handkerchiefs, they go their separate ways.

27   GAMES PLAYED

It amuses me to hear men in robes, on high benches, trained in foreign lands, say, "It is how you play the game that matters – not winning. The means are more important than the ends."

But if you have won nothing or the world perceives you as having nothing, well then *winning is all there is.* And the word *game* becomes a misnomer. Players know this. It is a struggle for relevance. Winner takes all: pride, prestige, self-worth, influence, value – all are showered upon a man who has shown himself to be of consequence – until the next game. There is a list too for losers. But for long-term losers two words suffice: irrelevance and contempt.

So if the world perceives you as a long-term loser, would you not use every ounce of cunning, every Anancyish trick, all the help, witting or unwitting, of friend or foe to win, to gain the trophy – the power of consequence? Of life? Once grasped, would you not use every device to hold it? Only a fool gives up power. Even mother superiors in nunneries know this. It is the pivot of freedom, of that greater choice called privilege. This elixir I bestowed upon my people. From this perspective I would describe rigging an election as preparing my vessel for sea, for the next journey, another term in office. "It is how you play the game that matters", is for the comfortable, the habitual winners. I do not expect those who live in places with an excess of winnings, an excess of heroes to understand what I am saying.

For three decades my supporters dined in this hall of winners. At first a sumptuous feast was there. They know this. The whole Region knows, hence the strategic silences which stem from a widely shared understanding and support for what I was doing.

I succeeded. Today my people are in charge of the commanding heights of the economy. They are the bosses. The show is theirs.

Go to the Ministries, to any Government Department, the Mayan Co-operative Bank, the board rooms, the marketing boards, the mines of Ica, the army, the militias and paramilitary movements, the police force, Mayan Broadcasting Corporation, the judiciary, and I say with pride that you will be met with a sea of purple faces – faces of the same hue as my own. I ask a mere ten per cent levy on salaries to accommodate this royal tone. Not quite Tyrian purple but, at the price offered, good value.

My rise to power was meticulously planned. In order to psycho-logically weaken the opposition's claim to the fruits of democracy, I turned for help to the AUL who composed a symphony of sounds that was music to my ear. "Urban Mayans, citizens of cities," they sang, "and no other, have a strong psychic right to inherit economic and political power. In the ancient world of Greece it was so, and this is our inheritance. For it is in cities that men have freed themselves from the larger discomforts of nature to create their dreams – the essence of civilisation. For this reason, a firm belief resides throughout the Region that we, and no other, are the rightful heirs to the British. No other but we." This was the measure of the composition and it became part of our national music and dance, rendered at all cultural events here and abroad.

My style of operation was carried out on Hope Bridge. A wave of this thinking surged upon the mining town of Ica. The Opposi-tion responded as I had hoped. Emigration. These swift methods are, in the long run, kinder than prolonged pain. I do not have the stomach to see a worm still twitching, wriggling after its body has been pierced through with a steel fork. One draws one's line well above that. They were leaving in droves. Leaving gardens and houses behind. Nobody was buying. Everyone was selling. Prices were now well within the reach of those staying behind. This unforeseen benefit of a greater equality in the housing market, I will not take credit for, though it does not escape me. We now have more empty houses falling to rack and ruin than there are occupiers to fill them. And more overgrown gardens, with Guinea grass and tough weeds than there are market gardeners. If people are still complaining it is because they will not adjust their place of abode, and complaining and blaming others have become a favourite national pastime around coconut carts, street corners and cake shops.

I created space for my supporters. A high proportion of the Opposition's middle-class had already emigrated to North America by the early 1970s, a higher proportion than anywhere else in the Western hemisphere. It cannot be disputed that I created this measure of space for my people in a far more humane way than was used by European administrators in the New World in the sixteenth, seventeenth and eighteenth centuries. And dare I speak of the space created during the Second World War? Enough! All I ask is that my regime be seen in a wider world setting.

With the routing of the Opposition's middle class went the cohesion of their supportive culture: their strong family ties, stable marriages, codes of conduct, the deeper understanding of the significance of their religious rites and ceremonies, the reading and exposition of their sacred texts in public gatherings. My loyal Mayan sociologists were happy. I was informed by one eager for the cultural uniformity of our people that the meaningful differences between the two ethnic groups were now too faint to be measured. Those who remained behind were left naked, and in search of an identity. They found us. Understandably they embraced our modes and attitudes with the intensity of new converts. See how they dress, dance, walk and speak! We are all one now, I am proud to say. One culture abides. This would have greatly pleased Emmanuel Pottaro, who also tried in his indirect, faint ways, so characteristic of the man. But he failed to accomplish this cultural uniformity. His supporters did not comprehend the full vision of their leader. He was never enamoured of the culture he inherited at birth – the culture of Country Mayans. It was Marxism-Leninism that directed his every cultural step. All others, to his eye, were irrelevant, either capitalists or a part of the petit bourgeoisie.

How colonial he was in this thinking! How he danced to the political tunes of a European, unaware, Marguerite informs me, that his forefathers offered ragas that revealed other perspectives – one which might have enabled him to bring a kind of socialism to Maya *and* remain in power. But alas, he had already acquired, as the rest of us, a European prejudice against our own. The weaknesses of the Country Mayan's culture appeared large to him and its strength he was never disposed to discover. I said this once to him. The poor chap was confounded, for he never understood the themes or the philosophy of his ancient culture that had withstood repeated conquests without losing its Gods and so itself. He never asked why. I learnt what I wanted from Marguerite in my efforts to understand the thinking of his supporters. When she was unable to satisfy my curiosity, she went out and became better informed. Traditions and beliefs that have withstood the passage, the travail of time, excite her.

Uniformity was not easy to accomplish. A large part of the ancestral culture of Country Mayans was an integral part of their sense of self. But time and time again I have managed the insurmountable. The malleability of people in changed economic circumstances never ceases to astound me. This formed part of my hidden agenda – to change the very psyche of the Opposition. Economic and political power formed the pivot of my potter's wheel.

Our AUL was most pleased with this accomplishment, this suffocation of another's identity to create the desired homogeneity of culture. For some time now, in books and papers and cultural events, they have been calling upon Country Mayans to abandon their culture, while they themselves retained every aspect of colonial culture they found pleasing and advantageous to have. It is in our interest to refer to our retentions as 'urban culture'. If one is honest, these preferences of our Nationalists and our AUL are not consistent with any particular principle. Where men can create a history, or an interpretation of whatever event – past or present – that their fertile minds are called upon to register, such men need only their own private yardsticks – their own undisclosed measures.

I leave tomorrow for the hospital and on my return shall look again at these discourses. I would by then have had time enough to consider what I have already written. I may be able to make valuable additions – and perhaps some deletions. For I have observed that both my tone and what I am prepared to say vary from day to day and even with the time of day. And there are moments when I feel that Mother is here directing the flow of my pen. But I intend that these discourses will be mine, ever wary of *Lebensluge*. There are, however, two humbugs which I shall mention later, for they are likely to turn up again and be used against me.

Today I am weary, for I have said things I have long carried, but never declared.

28   THE FEAST AND THE MASTER BUILDER

As I wrote earlier, I did send Aunt Maude invitations to the annual celebrations and feastings but she always declined graciously, addressing me as her "Dear Niece Marguerite – Housekeeper to the President". Such needle jabs are her style. And yet one year she did come, in a manner of speaking, as you will see.

Few would associate the President's residence with the magic of fairyland, but on that night of the feasting, fallen stars were pulsating on the lawn, circling pathways, betwixt branches, and on rooftops, dancing.

Tender chicken and succulent lamb arrived the day before by air. From the wild outback, bush labba, a delicacy of the President. French loaves and fine cheeses; fresh riverine trout, sweet snappers; bunches of dates, figs, sapodillas and purple-black fulsome grapes; rich, buttery avocado pears as large as Bombay mangoes, leafy-green and sunset-yellow vegetables; and for the ears, calypso players from Santa Maria. I recall an aged fifteen year old rum, a nectar from an ancient world. And I recall too an inviting port – sweet ruby in the light, Blue Mountain coffee, the summit of stimulation, and Cuban cigars adding to the mist of unreality.

Chatter and laughter from extravagant voices. A night to remember, heady with intoxicating aromas and seductive ideas, mingled with the warmth and scents of ladies in their best, hoping to catch even a passing look, a momentary glance from the most powerful man in their orbit – Robert Augustus, in royal purple.

All this while, silently pervading this night, there was a strong sense of make-believe. A strange apprehension came over me that, by some accident, we were outside time, that we had been dropped off at a deserted station, that we were standing still, in the same place, in the same room, expressing these very hopes and plans with such intensity, as if we were voicing them for the very first time and had not done so before – many times over. It was as if we were participating in an eternal Masque, actors in purple masks.

Was this mass amnesia – a community's collusion, silently honouring itself, outside the path of time? How confusing that this identical air of expectancy should have risen again! It had hovered over the celebration of our Independence Night when flags were lowered and raised and the urbane women of Bon Aire were doing their dutiful feminine best to catch the Prime Minister's eye on behalf of their husbands, who were positioning themselves, moving within the new space provided, eager to hear the playing of a string of words: *Would you be interested in ...? You are amongst those I have been thinking of... have in mind for...* All those years ago, a generation ago, they were the new arrivals, jostling to be in what they saw as *their* Government.

Of course, today there is this large difference. Robert Augustus is no longer Prime Minister; he is, instead, the all-powerful Executive President of Maya, a post he created for himself, by designing a new Constitution, so as to further enhance himself, and his supporters without end. Perhaps new positions will be on offer, as tired searching eyes are still trying to catch his.

Are we are on a child's merry-go-round?

Time has passed and we are in the same place. It was easier to believe that this was one long prolonged party, with expectations high – voices and laughter sustaining the long night.

We are a people who know how to laugh and sing. We love life – all of it – and are prepared to work for its fine things. Capitalists at heart you see. We want an overabundance to share with family and strangers and will happily sow to reap a bountiful harvest – to drink long and hard of life's joys. And when we do, it is with such free style, flair, charm and panache that the world is stirred. Our spirits are more at ease with free style than with governed steps, for we embrace life's entirety. Every atom of its pulsating self is too precious a gift to enclose within any kind of restricting dome. How wrongly our AUL read us.

It was so with Mother and it is so with Aunt Maude. Independent minds that will not be contained by loyalties to false gods, believing passionately, from their strong sense of individual responsibility and their deeply religious family background, that things were alterable, that wrongs should be acknowledged and amended swiftly. Their concept of society was a conscious daily effort to make each life worthy of birth, and this is why Aunt Maude was devastated by the death of nine year old Shivnarine, whom she had coaxed into life, into her world.

On that grand night of the feasting, Robert Augustus had climbed to the 'Pinnacle of Privileges'. Towering above all. Out of reach of foreigners, of capitalists, of political opposition. Accountable to no one. Answerable to no court now or ever more. It was as he had wished. Free at last. Privileged. A Caesar in the Colosseum.

The night was a celebration of the ruling Party's governance, its nationalisation of the economy, its long term in office and the replacement of what Robert Augustus called a foreign-formulated, London constitution, with one composed on home ground by Mayans. Laws made by the people for the people's President. He had been well served.

Robert Augustus' academic well-wishers were present, basking in the fruition of their cherished goal of nationalisation – of government ownership and control. "Ownership of all by the people for the people," they explained, "was a long answered prayer. A dream realised."

Delicious Belgian chocolates passed my way and I did partake of one – well two – may have been three, I cannot recall in full, except to say they were so delicious. Who can resist such mouthfuls of delight in such gala company when everyone is moving to the beat? I did sip a little fine champagne cognac – and was warmly disposed to the world.

It was at such an inopportune time that I heard Aunt Maude's voice reverberating in my head. She had a distinctly untimely habit of observing when I am about to lose myself a little. Then, thinking that I have some Dionysian abandonment in mind, she would come into my consciousness and insist that I should not forget something she had once said. More often than not it is something quite dull and inconsequential to my moment.

Because of the frequency of this occurrence, I have concluded that she looks at most forms of enjoyment with deep suspicion. The joys of the natural world are not welcomed at her door. I am sure of it. As the evening wore on and the guests became more accommodating, her eyes developed a piercing clarity more suited to a learned, lean, austere judge than an aunt. These eyes were seldom comfortable to look at and always difficult to ignore when I was younger. Yet she is my aunt and, all in all, a good woman.

Marguerite dear, her voice does come over so clearly though, *these Assorted University Luminaries who are so charming (and you, my dear, are so vulnerable and do not know it) and whom you may recall I christened AUL in Robert Augustus' presence, have conditioned our people to believe that they need a single track through life: government's shelter, government's jobs at home and abroad, government's scholarships, government's assistance in every way. A monoculture of dependence. Have you noticed how nationalisation is an AUL-government's affair?* She chuckled and I knew I needed to be both patient and tolerant.

The direction these AUL have offered to our islands has proved to be the Region's bitter gall, Marguerite. In truth these Luminaries should have been called GAUL, my dear, for they too are government dependent. Their preferences explain much don't they, dear? And she winked so mischievously that I began to smile.

I had thought she had finished, when... *What is it you are drinking, dear? You are smiling too much – without cause, dear. Are you receiving me loud and clear?*

Yes, Aunt Maude. How are you?

We shall all reap that bittersweet harvest of government's dependency, Marguerite. It is another form of bondage if prolonged... a slow, gratifying trance, dear. Like the one you are on the verge of falling into. One becomes addicted to spirits from a bottle as well as those from government planners. A kind of hypnosis. It is far better, dear niece, to enable your own spirit, helping it to cope with life. What did you say you were having? Ah! Yes! Yes! I remember. There is one exception, Marguerite, just the one thing our AUL talk about at length which is not government. It is how to distribute the wealth earned by others. That topic excites them. Have you observed how they warm to it? How they do a slow dance on the floor whenever they are discussing how a redistribution of other people's thrift and savings, other people's hard-won successes should be carried out? On second thoughts, that is government too, isn't it? The long arm of government in your pocket. You have to say this, Marguerite. They are consistent.

Be quiet Aunt, I remarked, as if under hypnosis. It was a cognac courage. *The late Emmanuel Pottaro said that Capitalism was organised selfishness. Therefore redistribution by the state was necessary. Imagine organised selfishness compounded through the centuries, Aunt Maude.*

She chuckled. *I will excuse your insolence, for you are not yourself. That is plain to see. What did you say you were drinking? I am not asking you, Marguerite, for the views of the well-meaning but misguided Emmanuel Pottaro. I happen to know them well. May he rest in peace. He suffered much for holding them, so I hope he is not listening. Were he here, I would have been discreet. He is no longer with us and so I speak freely to you, Marguerite. Any man who has spent his entire life advocating an ideology for which he and his supporters have suffered dearly cannot see light anywhere but in his own camp. The pain is too much. It must be covered with the balm of justification, Marguerite. Men must be allowed to keep their pride and dignity even when time reveals that their ideas are unworkable, flawed. Jessica and I could always see that Pottaro's communism was incompatible with what we were taught and what was around us – democracy and individual freedom. We have always wanted, as you well know, a continuous improvement in our standard of living, but we wanted it to come from the endeavour of each and everyone – people making their own decisions every day on how to improve their lives. Free style has always been our way. We did not want a few comrades planning the direction of our lives. We wanted the excitement of endeavouring to improve our lives to be our very own. Self-worth and dignity come this way. Mother always said that. It is something you work at. No one can give it to you, she used to say, over and over again.*

Do you recall that old Chinese saying? 'Build a golden bridge for your enemy to retreat upon'. For Emmanuel Pottaro, we should have built such a bridge for his Marxist pride to retreat upon. His 'enemy' was an unquestioning belief in Marxism-Leninism. That was fraternity by compulsion, dear. Total commitment is the nature of faith, isn't it, my dear? Come to think of it, it was his religion. If Pottaro was ever to have given it up, he would have had to 'leave

behind' his Marxist friends. This would have been seen as 'deser-
tion'. Pottaro would have found it difficult to leave his comrades
behind, for after all he had become their guru. A guru leaving his
disciples? No! Not Pottaro. May he rest in peace.

But before you retire tonight, my dear, ask one of the Luminar-
ies, there are sure to be a few there – which countries have, over the
years, taken in hundreds of thousands of our sons and daughters,
their mothers and fathers, brothers and sisters and offered them an
opportunity for a livelihood far better than they could have had on
their island of birth? And if they don't know, dear, despite the fact
that ignorance is bliss, tell them. And then ask, "Why do they
continue to batter that system and praise the other one?" Suggest
that it is not in good taste, my dear. Or on second thoughts, what
your grandmother called good taste has become a bourgeoise
thing! That sweet upright woman would have laughed in style.
Marguerite dear, tell them to either say it as it is or to shut up.

One of the Luminaries – Carl Goodbody, a slightly-built man
with fashionable glasses and a taste for the beautiful (no doubt
according to some Marxist-Leninist dictat), caught my smile and
my disengagement and moved in my direction. Strange, I thought,
as he walked towards me, how success makes us handsome to the
world and our confidence grows with it. I now understood what
Robert Augustus meant when he said, "I have changed the very
stride of my people."

"A night to remember," Carl said, caressing my cheek, his
breath conveying a warm bonhomie. "This is what is called
community, Marguerite. This is the beginning of greater things.
And as the President shows, we can do it without capitalists, free
markets, globalisation and all the exploitative stratagems devised
by the developed world to recolonise us, to make us in their own
image. Thankfully, the President is alert and aware of these ploys.
He has refused to have the screwdriver industries and should be
applauded for taking this stance. Here we are, doing our own thing,
Marguerite. Staying the course, holding strain for the good of all."
He was enthused and his entire body moved about as if responding
to an involuntary rhythm. "We have been assigned the political
responsibility to give direction to Maya, " he continued. "And you
see it here tonight," he said as he perused all corners of the room.

"A new thinking is being born – it is ours – created and cultivated by us. I feel uplifted tonight, elated. We have risen to this responsibility which is our preserve. Now we own and control our destiny. People of our ancestry are the rightful heirs to this new order. And it has come to pass."

I thought there was nothing more, but there was.

"Tonight is path-breaking in that our psychic inheritance, our political, economic and cultural control have come together – meshed for us and is being acknowledged here tonight. Look at the walls: our national flag adorns them. There you see our colours, our designs, our souls, no one else's. Here we discover ourselves. This is what this feasting is about. It is a thanksgiving."

A thanksgiving? Aunt Maude butted in. *Looks like the lustful feasting of the elite on the backs of the poor to me. Not a feeding of the poor, the weary and the burdened? Ask him why? Why are you so timid tonight, Marguerite? What are you drinking? You are not your mother's daughter. Tell him, we have never had to discover ourselves, we are quite clear in our minds who we are. Your diffidence, Marguerite, has it to do with the cognac you are holding? Alright... It is a party, after all. I understand. Well, ask him about means and ends, obligations and duties. He is so well versed on his inheritance, his preserve, and his rights. Where are the Country Mayans? Didn't your invitation call this a national celebration? Ask him something, Marguerite. I want to hear his reply... Hyenas all... They wait in the comfort of their academic shelter for the lion's kill. Robert Augustus is the hunter and he drags the kill before them. And there is feasting. Have you no passion left, Marguerite? Being the President's housekeeper, has it proved so costly?*

Leave me now, I said, *it is late and there comes a time to rest.* I then indicated with a nod of my head that I would like to be helped to yet another drop of the extraordinarily fine cognac.

I was in the mood to listen and I'm partial to the Region's university voices, so confident, such flow! They have not puked at everything colonial. They have not discontinued the enjoyment and privileges of their colonial inheritance – the freedom to sing whatever intellectual indulgences take their fancy or whatever ditties are in academic fashion without facing the consequences.

Then I heard Carl Goodbody say, "The President has brought

this about and we have tried in our own way to give him the necessary support. If you look around, you will see that support comes from every quarter of the Region." The cognac made me warm to him. I heard myself say, "My brother knows this. He cannot acknowledge it too openly. The university and its contributing governments have given their support verbally, tactically and in kind, Carl. Much has to be covert, of course, but you and I know there is an understanding. What more can one ask? You must be aware that without this he couldn't possibly have continued. Dependable is the word I wanted. Robert Augustus can depend on the Region. He knows this."

"He must continue. The Region would not allow him to fall. It is no secret that there is a very strong belief throughout this archipelago that, no matter what, he must be supported. Nothing is as important to us as running the show. We have been mere stage-players for far too long. Today we are owners, directors, managers and consultants. We are in control. Our old colonial mentality gave us a propensity to seek solutions from abroad. Now commonsense alone says that a local problem requires a local solution, that reflects the history and culture of our people. And that is what we are doing. Tonight we are riding our chosen path, and we are doing it my way and your way. With our heads held high. This is our show."

"Yes, how you would have enjoyed meeting Aunt Maude, the President's one and only aunt."

"Has she been here?"

"She would have loved to be here, even if it were only to taste these choice Belgian chocolates."

Liar.

"A sweet tooth – you know and yet she speaks of restraints *ever* so often." I came closer to him and whispered (gently circling him, for all things on our planet will rotate), "I'm inclined to think this habit of restraint has reduced her appetite for even simple joys."

Heaven forgive you.

"She knows that Jesus attended weddings and wanted the wine to flow plentifully; how she would have enjoyed herself here tonight. Sadly, my Aunt has become hard of hearing and wouldn't have been able to catch all that you have said and this would have upset her so."

Enjoying yourself I see.

"Carl," I said, warmly cradled by the feasting, "my aunt has one question which I am sure you can answer, and for which I know she would be grateful that I remembered to ask. The late Emmanuel Pottaro was a Marxist-Leninist like yourself. Yet as we know he was hounded by all, while you are warmly embraced by my brother, by Bon Aireans, *The Carrier* and everyone really. What would you say made your reception so distinctly different."

"Well that is quite simple really," Goodbody said. "You couldn't take him seriously."

"Yes?" I was waiting. Surely that was not all? I waited to see whether I would find the meaning behind his response. But there was nothing. "Help me a little," I said, "I don't quite understand."

"Well," he said, in a casual manner, "it is as I have just said; you couldn't take him seriously."

"The Americans did, you know, and the British. And *The Carrier* and Lionel Gomes and Robert Augustus took him seriously. So much so that they did what they did – the long strike, the fires, the changing of the voting system. I need not go on."

"We at the University didn't. He was not an intellectual, you know. The President had to take the reins of an Independent Maya. It was the right thing to do."

Mr Goodbody observed a circle of ladies looking in his direction. He was distracted, and though he played his voice before me, his eyes and interests were elsewhere. One of the wives of our AUL was saying, too loudly I thought, for we heard her above the rising din in the room. "I would weep if the President were ever to lose an election." I did not wish to detain his moving in her direction, but I so wanted to understand the thinking of our Region's AUL.

"Carl, have you ever thought," I said, "how on emigrating to foreign lands, and faced with all those foreigners, and their economic systems, which you call unpalatable, our people do sufficiently well to send us remittances amounting to six hundred million American dollars annually. I refer merely to remittances which come through the banks and to one island only. It would be a most gratifying exercise to tot up what the total contribution to the entire region is from our hard-working, gifted people overseas."

"I would think that in a few of the smaller islands their contribution to the government's budget is significant. There is no doubt about it, their remittances are substantial, but I do not believe our people are happy in cold climates. And discrimination wears them out – a daily uphill climb. Undignified. Our people should not have to face that open, blatant racism. It gnaws at their self-worth. Many become suicidal." He lowered his voice. "Here we intend to make the little man a real man. This is where.they belong. This land is ours. We make the rules. We decide. We are in control." He was departing, hesitated for a moment and then said, "Not thinking of becoming a capitalist, I hope, betraying the cause."

"No," I replied, "just playing the devil's advocate to better understand the nature of your thinking. Aunt Maude asks questions, she observes what is around her and reads widely. Often I cannot satisfy her curious questions. You have been helpful."

I began to search for a single 'little man' in the happily bubbling crowd and couldn't. Then I saw one approaching, all smiles, nicely dressed in uniform. I reached out to what he was offering. "Your cognac, Miss Devonish," he said.

The ladies were opening their circle to receive Mr Goodbody when I said, "After all these years of being in control, Carl, our people continue to leave in droves. Would you dare ask anyone in Maya if he would prefer American citizenship to Mayan? An unfair question, you may say, as this is true for large parts of the poor world. But look at the beauty of our land, our resources, our literacy – a colonial inheritance – and there the wealthiest market, our neighbour. Have you asked yourself what we're doing wrong? What should we be reconsidering? Why has your advice led to a long-term decline? We've got poorer, Carl. Many others have come from behind and passed us."

He placed his finger to his lips, "Shhhhhhh," he said softly and pointed to the rostrum. Robert Augustus was standing there. I knew then we were a community of the deaf speaking to the deaf, and was afraid to ask myself how long had this been so. Had we so devalued words that when we speak they are as light as a feather, so no sounds reverberate? They take no hold, make no mark, float away. Nothing remaining. Maybe that is where we should begin. To weigh our words well, give them their due worth, and then our currency too would gain in value, for I do believe they are inextricably linked.

Robert Augustus had begun to speak. I lifted my head and turned in his direction. His voice held us:

"Comrades, ladies and gentlemen, today we celebrate the dreams of slaves. Having achieved political independence, my Government did not sit idly by. We did not think that was enough. Instead we used it to gain economic independence. Today we own our country. Mayans will be relying on Mayans for a much higher standard of living than that of colonial times when we were subjects, dependent on others. No longer will we be going cap in hand to say, please sir, some more.

"May I remind you that it was not easy. People who have enjoyed the privileges of power to the detriment of the many do not yield their position of privilege. But we have managed to overcome that hurdle and will continue to overcome others.

"The main reason for the backwardness of Maya, I have said on many platforms, both before and after independence, was that its productive sectors were foreign owned – a millstone round the necks of Mayans who wished to fly. The time has come, comrades; we are on the path of progress never envisaged for colonised peoples. It is a path along which the very quality of life of the 'little man' in particular will be greatly improved. Comrades, distinguished guests, ladies and gentlemen, I promise there will be food, shelter and clothing for all Mayans, not only for those who have doggedly supported me but for those minors on the periphery who oppose me. No doubt they will one day see the light, for I am patient. Members of my cabinet tell me that I am too patient, that I cannot wait forever.

"This is a free country and I will not tell those in the countryside, those who continue to vote with the Opposition, how to think. I don't believe they are in anyway less able than we. I say 'I do not believe' because I am by nature a cautious man and I like to give my opponents the benefit of the doubt. It is one of my weaknesses.

"There is another matter which from time to time creates a problem for some people. They are usually men and women of a colonial mentality – a rigid mind-set – who believe that if a certain thing – be it a political system or school syllabus – is done one way in the developed world, it should also be done in the same way in developing countries, despite, comrades, despite the totally different environment of history, culture, climate, resources, expectations and standard of living.

"I make no concessions to those people when I say that my Party, the ruling Party, comrades, ladies and gentlemen, your Party is paramount. It has for sometime now assumed its rightful inheritance of paramountcy over the government, which is now properly the Party's administrative arm. There can be no doubt in the minds of thinking men and women that the ruling Party has been Maya's major national institution and has served us well.

"I wish to call upon all of you here tonight, it is my special and only request, that you enjoy yourselves. Eat and drink your fill for tomorrow work begins. I know that no one here tonight will fail me, and that whatever task he or she is called upon to perform in the higher interest of the Party, you will feel more privileged then, than now, for it is by their works that I shall know them. Comrades, distinguished ladies and gentlemen, I regret to have to say that I have received a message that I am urgently needed elsewhere. Nothing to be alarmed about, nothing that cannot be attended to." He smiles his winning smile.

"However, I do regret having to leave this gala company, but duty calls, and as a few of you know only too well, duties are not always comfortable and cosy affairs. Besides, I cannot ask you for sacrifices and not be prepared to make them myself. I like to be consistent. I see the night is still young and I hope you will not leave before the beautiful platters before you are bare and the last bottle is drained. Good night and God bless you all."

29 THE FALL AND THE ENIGMA

The death knell of Robert Augustus and his Government had been ringing all around us, yet when the end came, Aunt Maude and I failed to recognise it.

It did not come from outside, on horses, pounding the earth as it passed, rattling window panes. Nor did it come from within – a mirror image of Robert Augustus' own rise – in burnings, strikes, a pogrom's cry, or by the covert funding of the Opposition by the CIA.

We should have understood that it could not have come in those ways. My brother was well prepared for such challenges. In opposition, he had seen the chinks in Pottaro's democratic rule, and on gaining power had sealed them.

The destruction of his tyranny could not have come from the governments of our archipelago, since he had their psychological support, their private blessings.

It is ironic that at the time the end came, his political position had become near invincible. With the banning of newsprint, he had effectively muzzled all opposition voices. The death blow came as a thief in the night, soft-slippered. The fall of world sugar prices brought him down, some say. But few understood how a regime could collapse without an invading army. There were no killings, no betrayals.

When the fall came, it was complete. I can understand Aunt Maude's interpretation: 'Justice is mine, saith the Lord. His sword cometh from on high.' It did seem utterly strange that nothing Robert Augustus had so painstakingly put in place to protect himself, even at the cost of bankrupting Maya, was able to save him. Later Aunt Maude said, "Every step Robert Augustus climbed to attain a greater grasp, was a step nearer his executioner."

I could not see this at first but I have come to understand what Aunt Maude meant.

Our export prices for sugar, bauxite and bananas fell and continued to tumble – and with it, the funding of the ruling Party's costly masquerade. The House of Robert Augustus Devonish lay strewn on the sands – the foundation upon which it had been built.

Later, I could not help thinking that he had carried within himself the seeds of his own destruction. The skills and philosophy that had enabled him to capture and control power – his cunning, his ability to scheme, to distort, to mask events, to bribe, to fool, to destroy the Opposition – were not the requisite skills for the substantial, sustainable growth of Maya. His very success at plunder and control, his ability to maintain this without an Opposition, meant he was comfortable and did not have to reconsider, with any urgency, the direction his designed path was taking Maya.

He was not equipped with managerial skills, and during his regime not a single, new, viable export industry was developed. He was wholly dependent on the industries established under colonial rule – and under his governance these became rundown, inefficient and loss-making. The bauxite mines and many sugar mills gasped their last breath.

Instead, Robert Augustus introduced schemes that brought him and his supporters emotional satisfaction. Heavy debts were incurred to nationalise industries that dominated the economy. The cost of servicing these substantial borrowings for nationalisation were enormous. Yet for a time it seemed as if the wheel of fortune was stuck inextricably in his favour. Soon after nationalisation the prices of our exports quadrupled. A little later they fell back to double what they had been before, but all in all they rose substantially and made the servicing of the large debts well within reach.

For three years the unusually high prices of our exports kept aloft. It was to be his 'Indian summer'.

Then the prices of our exports fell and kept on falling like a plummeting aircraft. In the good years, no effort had been made to raise new private capital or bring in foreign industrial skills. Instead, undisciplined, feckless management of the economy meant that nothing was in place to compensate for falling prices. There was no industry whose productivity could be increased. The foreign reserves of the Central Bank had already been consumed. There was not even a week's supply of reserves. Lïonel Gomes' spectre, the humiliation he predicted of our becoming mendicants, overshadowed the land.

The extent of our fall came home to us when the Deputy Prime Minister had to send a letter to the winner of the coveted Mayan island scholarship – a young man who had come first in the Advanced Level examinations set by the Cambridge Examination Board. The letter from the Government was not a message of joy, conveying satisfaction over his hard work and achievement. Instead it explained to the scholar that the Government did not have the funds and so could not finance his island scholarship. It suggested that he sought foreign assistance. His mother showed us the letter. Aunt Maude said she gave thanks to the Almighty that her parents and grandparents were spared this humiliation – to see one of their offspring reduce Maya so.

But within the Party, there was still optimism. Having played on a winning ticket for so long, cabinet members had come to believe in their own invincibility, their power to rule without end, so the falling world commodity prices were first explained away as a mere temporary hiccup. It was suggested with *gravitas*, by middle-aged, experienced politicians, that though oil prices had risen substantially and then fallen, they were still being maintained on an attractive price-plateau. This pattern, the Party's economists concluded, other commodities would soon be enjoying.

It was wishful, childish make-believe that dragged on most painfully over the following years. World commodity prices continued to fall and the Party was forced to come to terms with its changed circumstance, though it should have been clear that few commodities have the characteristic buoyancy of oil. Such is the uncanny ability and strength of wishful thinking.

There was another burden – self inflicted. In the government-owned and controlled economy, the main qualification for rewards was loyalty to the Party. And so we had loyal men and women ill equipped to manage large state enterprises, helping in their own rapid demise and that of their employer.

Soon the economy was at a standstill and it brought rising urban unemployment onto the streets of Bon Aire. Robert Augustus was

aware of the potential dangers of youth unemployment: an out-
break of 'choke and rob'; or worse, political disaffection.

In an attempt to reduce the numbers of the urban unemployed,
a strong source of his support, the Party hierarchy demanded that
more and still more of these unskilled men and women be offered
employment in the civil service, state shops, factories and mines.
It did not take long for Maya to become a land of Lilliputian
strangeness, a place where men were employed at the factory gates
but then found they could not fulfil their obligations to work, since
there were frequently no materials to work on or, as things got
worse, no power available at the work place. The limited amount
of work available had already been stretched out as thinly as
chewing gum. In fact workers got in each other's way. But even
these wasteful schemes were inadequate to curtail the rising
numbers of the unemployed congregating on the streets.

Unemployment continued to increase and government again
printed paper money to carry through its plans for full urban
employment. These schemes were Robert Augustan in character
and style. Expensive government machinery was set up to squeeze
the urban unskilled, like sausages, into the newly formed Mayan
Militia (comprised wholly of urban Mayans) as well as into the old
Mayan Defence Force, which soon became the largest ground
force in the Region. This stratagem was not hard to justify, for there
had been murmurings and political manoeuvrings from a nearby
continental state which produced documents to show that geologi-
cally as well as historically, Maya belonged to it.

Government expenses increased six fold. An expanding army
requires uniforms, artillery, security and telecommunication equipment, vehicles, housing and food. All Mayans, as taxpayers, found
that they had no choice (including supporters of the Opposition)
but to finance the ruling Party's requirements for increasing its
political hold.

There was another Robert Augustan device, constructed with
his supporters in mind – the Mayan National Service. It became
compulsory for secondary school leavers to do a stint of National
Service in the hinterland for a year, in order to qualify for state-
funded tertiary education. These cleverly thought out devices, at
a stroke, precluded a significant number of young Country Mayans,

both male and female, but especially the latter, from qualifying for university places, as parents were reluctant to expose their children to an aggressive political culture, hostile to themselves, without any protection, in an unfamiliar forested hinterland. Within a very short time, Bon Airean school leavers found that there was more than ample space for them at the University of Maya.

And so it was that the urban unemployed, once so visible, were removed from the streets of Bon Aire, removed from the window views of the Party elite. Both the army recruits and those doing their stint of National Service were participating in the government's Hinterland Development Scheme in the deep forest. These young men and women were offered a minimum of welfare – food and sleeping accommodation. These masquerades of employment were not solutions. Our unemployed youths remained untrained and their numbers continued to rise, but there were no jobs.

The young unskilled, either in the Militia or the National Service, were virtually the Party's captives in the hinterland. Their loyalty could be called upon during the elections or whenever the Party bosses felt it was necessary to deter or impede any opposition. 'Only a fool loses power', became the Party's unspoken motto.

The feeling that time was being lost crept upon me, for while the young in the developed world were acquiring skills to live in the twenty-first century, our young people were being put away in the forest, and from time to time would be marched along forest tracks without purpose, exposed to malaria – swatting mosquitoes, not knowing which ones were the blood-sucking female anopheles. 'Hinterland Development' involved the cultivation of land cleared of its rainforest, then furrowed, its loose top soil open to the coming of the first heavy tropical rains. Our inexperienced, urban youths were being asked to repeat the destructive plunder of eighteenth and nineteenth century colonial 'developers' on tropical lands. And so it was that Maya was being governed by a system that was blind to the fact that it was digging the country's grave. The only opposition came from a brave group of men and women, who were too few and without resources. Gavin, who had once been the lone voice protesting at party meetings, was amongst this courageous group.

What is unforgivable is that my brother had available to him the means for developing Maya, but he chose not to use it because of his deep, gut resentment of Country Mayans. The way had been suggested to him by a Nobel Prize winner in Economics, familiar with Maya, its resources and those of the Maritime Region.

It was the way of agricultural production – a wide range of vegetables and rice grown for export on the rich coastal alluvium of the polder lands. Robert Augustus could have begun with increasing the productivity and export of rice, for which Maya began with large possibilities. During the Second World War, when German submarines were stalking the Atlantic, the trade from the North bringing wheat flour, salted cod and canned foods to the Maritime Region became hazardous. In a bid to keep food prices low, to prevent mass unrest, and to keep the spectre of malnutrition at bay, Country Mayans were requested by the British Government to produce rice for the entire region at a low price. In this period of food scarcity, when these rice farmers could have legitimately demanded an increase in their prices, they did not; instead they produced ungrudgingly.

Robert Augustus placed impediments in the way of rice production. It was the largest locally-owned, export industry in the Region. So it came about that rice farmers, even those past middle-age, with leased acreages of rice land, were emigrating to New York and Toronto to start afresh once more at the bottom rung of the ladder – working in cold grey factories and drab warehouses.

In this economic crisis, the large-scale drainage and irrigation network of canals in the polder lands was neglected by the government, and they ensured that farmers' complaints became indistinct murmurings by filling the Rice Producers' Board with their own political appointees.

There is no doubt that these choices must have satisfied the gut feelings of my brother and his Party, but eventually these very decisions undermined his Government, since no country can afford to remove half its population from the development process or destroy productive assets while failing to create new ones.

Robert Augustus did attempt to draw his supporters into the production of rice. He confiscated lands leased to rice farmers, claiming this was in response to their nonpayment of rent. These leases were offered to his supporters who negotiated with the remaining rice farmers for a healthy profit.

Today faded purple masks strewn on the floor are all that remains in Maya of the ruling Party's masquerade in government.

I recall the first victims of the purple masks — soft targets — small families — men with their wives and children working in their small shops, and lone travellers in quiet places. Today we are all victims. "The masks," Aunt Maude observed, "are doing for their wearers what the new constitution has done for the President — made them morally unaccountable for their actions."

Another time of ripe rottenness is upon us. We all reflect the ugliness around. My brother's philosophy, portrayed in his masks, envelops us all. See how even Aunt Maude wore one to climb to the head of the queue, to be able to satisfy a craving for hot, crispy golden-brown bakes.

A pervasive debilitating contagion has spread, changing its structure, colour, intensity and form over time. It has risen to the roof tops, even to that of the highest Court in the land — our own 'Independent' Court of Appeal, where the flag of the ruling Party dances in the wind, proclaiming its paramountcy.

Whenever I pass the Appeal Court and see this flag, and hear it flap-flapping in the wind, I hear again a lone voice — young Vasu's maiden speech in the House. And I think to myself as I watch the flag that Emmanuel Pottaro could never have done this, even if he were inclined to do so, which he wasn't. Such an idea would not have come to him, but had some ugliness stirred him and he had the madness to place his party's flag above the Court of Appeal, there would have been street confrontations in Maya, protestations throughout the Region and before our diplomatic missions abroad.

"Did someone say aggression does not pay?" I overheard a student from across the mighty Azon ask. "Look, does it not fly high over our Court of Appeal, and on hill tops and cities abroad?" She smiled a cynic's smile that appeared grotesque on so young a face.

That smile haunts me. From time to time, it appears in my thoughts in the day and in my dreams at nights, as a hanging mask, dangling from the ceiling, swaying amongst Selwyn Thomas' masks. It seems to pick me out, and when I point to it, Selwyn Thomas does not see it, though all the while the grotesqueness enlarges itself before me.

30 THE PEQUOT INDIANS

There are those who would harp on the few casualties of my regime. In wars there are casualties and when one enters the field of politics one is on a battlefield. There will be plunder and pillage and booty as well as losses and suffering.

I take the world as it is. Compare like with like, I say to my critics, compare my casualties to those in similar circumstances of war. But they do not respond. I am ever mindful of *Lebensluge* so I will. State terrorism against those feared, hated or regarded as 'lesser breeds' is *not* on the lips of citizens who benefited from such actions, those for whom that space was created.

Understandably, a strategic amnesia prevails. The early Americans, on crossing the Atlantic to what they called the New World, made space for themselves and their kith and kin. The extermination of the Pequot Indians in 1637 or of the massacre of 500 Cheyenne women and children in 1864 – and this alas! alas! after the tribe had surrendered. Yes! Yes! Surrendered. You heard correctly. And *surrendered* did have the same meaning then as now. You see, knowing the world helps me to place my space-making effort in perspective.

I have made another observation: Moral disdain is not for the poor. They will flock wherever the water is clean, the grass succulent and the air invigorating, irrespective of the political crimes committed to create this opportunity. More often than not, they are running away from something far worse than that which they may encounter in their chosen place of abode. Moral disdain is not for the wealthy either, if the returns on their investments are attractive. How could I, therefore, so steeped in the awareness of men's pretences and games, not play by the rules formulated by the offspring of terrorists, buccaneers, slave traders, owners of slaves – rascals all.

I have been more honest than most. I acknowledge that were I today presiding over an economically successful Maya, that conversation around the coconut cart would not have taken place. Opposing voices would have been muted. My AUL in Maya could have sung in good faith a song I hear clearly elsewhere, but alas will not now be hummed here: "Comrades, development is an idea that needs time. Development is a journey, a process. And so there will be light and shade. And just as shade is relevant to a painting, adding depth and meaning, the same is true of mishaps and mistakes; they make stronger men of us and wiser, for greater challenges ahead. What others have taken hundreds of years to achieve, Maya will accomplish unaided in a far shorter time. No one should expect the redistribution of wealth, the creation of a level playing field for all citizens to come to pass within a day or a week or to be without pain. Sacrifices are a part of the development process and we, the privileged, should be prepared to make them or else we walk along the road to serfdom or onto the path that leads to the guillotine of revolutions, taking our children with us. Forget past errors, mishaps and blunders, they were disappointments – true – but part of the on-going process. Forget this past, build anew. The future is – a world for you. Your President, Robert Augustus Devonish, has single-handedly laid the foundation for this renaissance. God bless the President."

Words were always *our* commodity in the archipelago. A pity we have not a market for them.

The absence of this song has come to pass because my managers failed me. They failed the country. I provided them with the top jobs but there was no one to take it from there. I have done my best. I did irreparable damage to the Opposition by keeping them out of power for a whole generation while my people were exposed to a vast range of administrative experiences. The value of that experience cannot be measured, purchased or found in books. It is unique. I offered prestige where there was none. Let me be judged by my motives and accomplishments, not by the failures of my managers.

Of course I used the CIA in my rise to power, and why not? Should I not be commended for turning the tables? This is no mean boast, since more often than not this agency uses others mercilessly.

But to bring home the moral bankruptcy of those who pontificate loudest from on high, let me say this. I overheard some of those from the Colonial Office who were engaged in negotiating Maya's Constitution. My name was mentioned, there was a meaningful pause and then one said, "He is a rascal." Another said, "He is a racist, opportunist and demagogue, intent only on personal power." On the following day these very voices offered me everything I asked for and still more.

Poor, naïve, Emmanuel Pottaro, may he rest in peace. He had more guts than you would think. He kept crying out to these two superpowers that what they were doing was unjust, that they were changing the rules of the game because they wanted another result, that the system they were offering him they did not wish upon themselves. His appeal was heart-rending. I was moved and ... aghast. For he spoke as if they did not comprehend the truth of what he was saying, of what they were doing. How strange, I thought at the time, that he should be pleading with capitalists who look after their own interests with the savagery of the hounds of Baskerville. I was puzzled that he should be expecting the very system that he had denounced on every platform, to come to his aid and to practise a morality, a code of behaviour that was of a higher order than that practised in his beloved USSR.

Pottaro walked the political minefield with an unbelievable naïvety. He seemed unable to grasp the full consequences of the political realities around him, and so he was clearly unfit to govern. He lived in an ideological Marxist-Leninist frame of his own making and believed in it with religious fervour. But religion can become a terminal illness. The first symptom is a propensity to believe that one is the long-promised prophet of the proletariat, or that God has chosen you to be his intermediary. Ahhh, the things men believe – that an Intelligence that created the universe would need an intermediary!! Oh how much does wishful thinking make knaves and fools of us all.

What happened all those years ago at our Constitutional Conference in London was that powerful men from powerful states were looking after their own interests, which cut across the humbug of moral codes. Emmanuel Pottaro would have been in power on independence night had he not so foolishly worn his political cards on his sleeve. They would have allowed the democratic process to run its course. The main concern of America was that there should not be a head of state sympathetic to the Russian regime in 'its back-yard'. America, I knew, was particularly allergic to the domino theory. I used their susceptibilities to my advantage.

I said I was not a communist but, on gaining independence, nationalised the entire economy. There is not a single thing I did that a communist would not have done. My Party controls the army, the police force, the media, the judiciary and the economy. It is paramount. I said the Opposition was irrelevant, for to have a communist opposition in this situation is to have no opposition. Poor chap, I stole his thunder *and* used the superpowers to get my way. No mean achievement for a socialist in a Third-World developing country. Now one must pause to ask that all important question on the professed moral codes of superpowers. Maya is a multiracial, multicultural society. What regard did those British negotiators and American advisers have for the Mayan people, especially the Country Mayans, if they believed what I overheard and yet gladly offered me a system of voting that would place me in power for all time!

Had they taken just a little time to get to know Emmanuel Pottaro better, they would have found that he was a threat to no one – a squeaking mouse. Perhaps my propaganda machine against him was too effective and they lapped it up. But then again, they did this because I painted Pottaro in the image I knew they wished to see and hear. How very transparent they are!

Some of what I said in the past embarrasses my intellect. When I was in Opposition, I accused Pottaro over and over again of being a racist *and* a Marxist, of being anti the workers *and* a communist. "His budget is against the poor" was one of my main cries. Yet no one pointed out these blatant inconsistencies. By 'no one' I include our well-read middle classes, my own shadow cabinet, the superpowers and the AUL. The country was ripe for picking. I was in the right place at the right time. The temptation was overpowering.

I was cushioned between the *real politik* of powerful democracies and the ineptitude of a Marxist-Leninist ideologue. I cannot even recall what response Pottaro or his cabinet made to my sophistries. Are they to be exempt from the part they played in the turn that history took? Where does responsibility lie? They all helped to create the present.

I have become weary. Marguerite has packed for me and Aunt Maude is travelling down from the country to see me. Both ladies have always done their duties with meticulous care. On reflection, I find satisfaction in having granted Marguerite that one large favour she asked of me a long time ago – to stop that mission in mid air. To this day I cannot understand how that which held him did not give way; sawn through, yet having to hold while it was being pulled back into the aircraft. It was a close thing.

It was a close thing. She must have had a deep affection for the fella, Vasu Nath, for she pleaded with the dignity of virtue and then handed me the emergency phone. I had little choice, for her manner enforced on me that I would be doing what should be done, despite the fact that he had seen too much, knew too much. She vouched for him that he would leave the island and she would be responsible for whatever he disclosed. In the end I affirmed what she had said, I placed my seal on it. Strange, I did not resent her. I wish with hindsight that my cabinet and our AUL were like her.

I was wrong all those years ago. Marguerite would have made a fine statesman. Then the world was younger; men thought differently. I was impatient and inexperienced. Marguerite may like these plain-speaking discourses. She may even perceive her influence. But would her feelings end there? No! She thinks too much. I can hear her ask on reading each discourse, "Why have his revelations come now?" I shall answer that on my return from the hospital.

Goodnight. Tiredness overwhelms me. Goodnight.

PART THREE: THE PITY OF IT

31 BEYOND REASON AND THE SAPPHIRE

I long sensed that with the wearing of masks something consciously beyond reason – defiant to reason – was loosed upon the
land. On that night in the room of masks in Selwyn Thomas' home,
I had felt a virulent life within them – something independent,
threatening, contagious.

Now late in Maya's long night, there is nothing left to prey upon
and irrationality has turned in upon itself, has begun to consume
itself – its own spores – its source of life – its host. In our midst,
irrationality was self-destructing; the forms it took were gross and
ugly. Virulent among crowds or where two or three come together
with ill purpose.

Selwyn Thomas, the artist, may have realised early the force
for ill his masks possessed, and at some stage implanted within
them a self-destructive mechanism, for I noted that after Ica
and Hope Bridge, the quality and texture of the material and
the design of the masks had changed. It must have been his
doing.

One day I was drawn to inspect the masks more closely and
found that the very touch, feel, weight and scent of those first
masks had gone. Those for sale at later party meetings were from
another mould than the earlier designs, including the five grand
masks Selwyn brought us, all those years ago.

I have tried to protect myself by never wearing a mask, even the
very fine mask I have is in safe keeping. I hope that the need to
wear it will not arise. So far I have managed this even on grand
celebratory occasions of the ruling Party, by claiming a severe
allergic reaction to the masking of my skin, which, to my conster-
nation, I have now indeed developed whenever I am close to a
masked person. Being in a room of walking, talking masks, in my

waking life, has added another uncomfortable dimension of unreality to my night-time wakefulness.

Before his death, I visited Selwyn Thomas. He was confused and embarrassed at the turn of things. He seemed to have lost his confidence and grip on his work. "I never envisaged this," he said, "the deep purple masks were not meant to be used in this way. They were there to be worn with the utmost judicious care and consideration – to avert an injustice – to scare those who were harassing or creating hell for others."

Seeing that the masks had moved beyond his control, it is no wonder he began to design them as hollow vessels – without character, intuitive energy, and thought. "My art, my skill, has been debauched," he said, "and so I had no choice but to provide simple covers, washed out, faded, limp in texture. Too many of the earlier ones that were made in good faith," he said softly, "were already in circulation and in the wrong hands."

*   *   *   *

I know Maximus has not escaped this rampant ailment, this virulent contagion. Of late he has become withdrawn and suspicious, feeling threatened from all sides. A growing anxiety for his personal safety has returned; again his place in history has become his overwhelming concern – the reason for his discourses. I have continued to record them in my own voice, as he requested. On his return from the hospital, he will edit them and, in his own voice, leave his discourses to posterity. No doubt he wants my response though he has not asked for it, and uses my recording as the next best thing in case his operation does not go well.

I see that these discourses have weakened him considerably. He searches for the meaning of his regime, his rule. He seeks some justification for the path along which he took Maya. But the poor showing of the economy and his reduced position have led him to play more heavily than before on secret fears, and on prejudices which he long nurtured and fed.

Only one fast fading element of satisfaction remains. What gives him a sense of wellbeing, what he cherishes dearly, is that old pleasure: the dependency of others upon him – Bon Aireans feeding from his hands as if they were in a zoo. If ever he suspects that party members have forgotten their dependency on him and

are beginning to show an independence of spirit, he sets upon them
mercilessly and reminds them of their place.

I recall one evening after dinner, he asked me to phone Mr
Ishmael, permanent secretary to the Ministry of Health. I was to
make the call at two in the morning and say that the President
wished to see him immediately.

Mr Ishmael had been trying to get outside funding for the public
hospital, which was on the verge of collapsing, but was as yet
unsure of the outcome and had not yet reported to my brother. Only
if he were successful would he have informed the President. But
Robert Augustus saw this as the beginnings of a senior Party
member taking decisions and moving in an independent direction. This enraged him.

As the cover of secrecy rested on almost everything, Mr Ishmael
knew better than to ask what it was about, so he got out of bed and
drove for two hours around narrow, unlit, hairpin bends, climbing
Maya's unprotected, precipitous, unmetalled mountain tracts, his
blood pressure rising. All the while he would have been wondering
what the pressing urgent matter could be – something that could
not even be alluded to on the telephone.

Arriving at about four thirty in the morning, he would have
encountered other hurdles. The guard would not have been
expecting him. Had he insisted on speaking to me, as a last resort,
his requests would not have been met, there being strict instructions from the Head of Security that no one, absolutely no one, was
to be allowed to enter the President's residence at that hour.

In the morning after Maximus had had his full breakfast of
freshly squeezed orange juice, piping hot home-made rolls, ham,
omelette folded with sliced home-grown tomatoes, coconut muf-
fins and coffee, he would have asked for Mr Ishmael who would
have been waiting for two hours in his car, restless, no doubt afraid
to fall asleep, watching the pliant bamboo bordering the neighbouring park as it bends and lifts, buffeted in the cold, damp wind.

Maximus, who had been in bed before midnight, would say to
him, "You took your time to get here. I know you wouldn't have
expected me to wait, so I have had to take the decision on my own.
I would have preferred it otherwise. Now it is too late. However, I
don't hold this against you and will let you know the outcome of my

decision at the appropriate time. Marguerite can offer you breakfast but you may prefer to return home. At this hour, it shouldn't
take you as long as getting here did. There are times when
decisions must be taken on the spot – but you are aware of this. I
am told that if you are *au fait* with the roads, it should be a mere
thirty-five minutes drive."

If Ishmael had risen to the bait and said, "I was in the
countryside, Mr President. I informed your office; your secretary
promised to inform you. I wrote her also to remind you", he would
be further humiliated. Maximus would sneer, "You don't want to
take out your tiredness on my secretary. Grow up, man, shoulder
your responsibilities as a Permanent Secretary should. My secretary carries a heavy post, as you must know. Should I say to her that
you think she is incompetent? In your position you are expected
to be able to manage stress. You appear to be doing badly at
present. I wouldn't be surprised if your blood pressure has risen
appreciably. Cool it, man, you forget you are with the President.
I shall let these foibles pass and again offer you breakfast. I'm
advising you to have it, but I can't force you. That is one thing I
don't do. Nobody is forced, for example, to accept a job that I offer
them. I like to help those loyal to me – men who understand their
position and mine. It is clear that I am loyal to all my permanent
secretaries. Where would they be if I didn't employ them? There
are no large minds amongst them. Jobs are not easy to come by,
especially for middle-aged family men. But enough said. I have
already given you more time than I intended, which makes me late
for another meeting. My civil servants expect me to be punctual
and I must carry the can for others. But that is what is expected of
the father of the nation, isn't it?" And he chuckles. "This is not an
easy country to administer. Too many chiefs, too few Indians."

*   *   *   *

And there was that other case – Rohan Mistry's. It was pitiable.
Mistry was a successful businessman, well established long
before Robert Augustus even thought of entering politics. He
moved his business from the countryside to Bon Aire, when my
brother was still in primary school, and it expanded, for he had a
natural flare for buying and selling.

Then Robert Augustus got into power and began nationalising the economy. A number of small family businesses remained outside state ownership, simply because the government couldn't purchase everything. The national debt, as a result of nationalisation, was already far too large for an island with a growing balance of payment problem.

However, in order to control these small family businesses, without having to purchase them, Robert Augustus implemented several schemes with rigour. One commonly used was known as ATA – Arbitrary Tax Assessment. This was an extortion imposed on businessmen and others to bring them in line or to punish them for not conforming to the Party's expectation of support.

Another punitive measure, which was introduced to oppress men like Rohan Mistry and the small business community, was the need to apply to the Department of Trade for import licences. These were given only for short periods and for a specific item. In reality, businesses had to fill the Party's coffers before they could import goods for their shops. This enabled corruption to attain new heights. A businessman now had two choices: he either paid up or closed down. Many chose the latter, so the Party had to raise its demands on the remaining businesses. Understandably, no new private investment came to Maya.

Rohan Mistry's four children, professional men and women living abroad, pleaded with him to sell the business when the government began nationalising the economy. They wanted him to live with them in a part of New York where there were already a large number of Mayans, and were convinced that with his knowledge, skill and temperament, he would succeed. "Pa," they said, "you're the kind of man the world wants." But as his wife later told me, he said he was too old to make a fresh start in a new country – and one with freezing winters. Rohan Mistry must have felt that, as long as he was prepared to be satisfied with a low level of profit, prepared to keep things simply turning over, he would survive.

But as the economy began to collapse, the Party became more and more shamelessly parasitic. Women with grade-four masks, armed with black ledgers, would be seen on the highways and byways, receiving cash and cheques on behalf of the Party. The business community had no choice if they wished to survive.

This troubling situation began to wear upon Mistry. He had the additional humiliation of having to make frequent visits to the Department of Trade, and the Customs and Excise to plead for import licences, after filling out long laborious forms, designed to baffle and intimidate. One day he asked himself why, at this time of his life, should he bear such constant humiliation. And so, after much thought, he suggested to his wife that they should present to the President a precious gift – a grand Kashmiri sapphire that had been in his family for generations. It was so sacred and precious to the family that Meera was convinced that Rohan, to have made such a suggestion, must be losing himself under the strain,

He argued that if this precious gift enabled him to conduct his now contracting business without having to make constant visits to the Department of Trade and the Customs and Excise, it would be well worth it. "After all, dear wife," he said, "why do we work, but to ensure that in our old age we have friends and a little comfort. My monthly humiliation before those young chaps, I can take no more. They think that power must be seen to abuse and threaten before it can be respected. Going there depresses me. They are trying to make me feel small. I am too old to withstand this. I feel reduced. I have reached the end of the road. I cannot face them next month when our import licence runs out. The President will have the sapphire valued; he would see that it is worth a lifetime of freedom, but I would be asking for a mere fifteen years of freedom from harassment. I may not live that long. And if I do, it will be time to retire."

Meera tried to dissuade him. "Keep it for our old age, Rohan, and continue to give the Party the monthly cheques. Let me go to the Department. Sometimes a man may treat a woman less harshly."

But he remembered the women at Ica and Hope Bridge and could not bear to see her standing there before them, while they made their social calls and pretended she was not there. He could see them sniggering, and she pulling her ornhi closer around her. He had not mentioned it, but he had observed of late that this traditional protective gesture had become so much part of her. It was pronounced whenever that well-dressed, confident woman, the Party's assistant treasurer, entered the shop to pick up their monthly 'contribution'. Meera's ornhi would be quickly gathered around her, long before the woman stood there and said, "How is comrade Rohan today? Everything ready for the President?"

Meera was strongly opposed to her husband's plan, but he returned to it so constantly that finally she relented, for as she said, "It was taking a toll on his health. He could not face that government department to renew his import licence."

As his housekeeper, I was there when Rohan Mistry made a quiet sojourn to the President's official residence and offered my brother the exquisite sapphire. I sat with him in the visitors' waiting room, offering tea and biscuits, which I often did in the rainy season when it would suddenly become cold and hazy as the coastland mist drifted inland.

Rohan Mistry explained to me that he wanted no publicity. It was a personal gift to the President and he would appreciate my explaining this to him. I did.

*   *   *   *

Robert Augustus received the sapphire. It was elegantly shaped. Its beauty entranced him. He was overwhelmed by its strange reflectiveness, more of light than of colour. Its spatial transparency, the subtle changes in its waves of colour, its dazzling sparks and tiny bursting flares that revolved at cosmic speed absorbed him. He seemed to receive an ecstatic thrill as he moved the sapphire slowly, then swiftly, from light to darkness, observing in it a meteoric life that seemed to be still travelling through space. He became totally drawn to its magical play of light that came and went by laws or codes that must have come from another place outside our understanding.

One night, Maximus suddenly became morose. He removed the sapphire from its bed of velvet, and placed it in his dark vault. I sensed that something within him was broken, something dark had occurred, and wished I could instantly warn Rohan of impending danger. But I too had become imprisoned. I had to choose between encouraging Robert Augustus to confide in me, while preventing the very worst outcomes of his thinking. It was a fine balance which presented me with daily dilemmas. The compromises I made ate into me and I knew that I was less than I once had been. This knowledge increased my resolve. The time had come to play my part to bring this suffering to an end.

At breakfast the following day, Robert Augustus said, "Marguerite, Rohan Mistry thinks he can buy me, enslave me, with his sapphire. He and his kind think – the whole business community think – that they can run this country, do whatever they want, have their own way, change the rules, by simply offering gifts. Well, I need to show him and teach others, too, that I am a man of integrity. I cannot be bought. The CIA can be bought, but not me. Don't get me wrong, Marguerite, when people make donations to a political party, there is nothing wrong with that. The whole world is so engaged. The electorate contributes to the party they wish to see in power. Citizens contribute to their chosen charities. It is all above board, but this, Marguerite, this is trying to tie my hands, to turn my good attentions solely to the business community, to make me well disposed to them and to Country Mayans. I will neither be bought nor fooled by any of them."

The following day I changed the course of my daily walk with the intention of warning Rohan. But I was too late. From where I stood, I saw a security guard standing before his house, and a police officer taking Rohan handcuffed into the police car. When the car left, I asked the security guard what had taken place and where Comrade Rohan was being taken. "To Police Headquarters, Miss Devonish. He was found carrying flour, salt, garlic and onions, all banned items, in the shop. People have to be encouraged to be law abiding. The well-to-do must set an example. It boils down to who is running the country, doesn't it? We have to be vigilant, otherwise we lose control."

I knew the set up. Rohan Mistry had been framed. The police and the courts would have their way – and the Mayan Court of Appeal as well; though there, suffocating the truth would be done with sophistry and style, by educated men.

The party hierarchy kept its distance from Rohan Mistry. Those who had annually received his Christmas and Easter hampers wished it were otherwise, but they kept to the Party line for survival. Bail was granted and Rohan's case was to be heard in six months. But he was a broken man. His wife ran the shop until there was nothing left to sell. Rohan's General Store was closed never to reopen.

I met Meera Mistry in the market place, a month before the case was to be heard. "You know, Miss Devonish, Rohan used to speak so warmly about the President to everyone in the shop. He felt that once he could see that some things were not working, the President would bring about change. It was only a matter of time before things were put right. He believed the President was his friend." She had aged, become worn, had lost too much weight too quickly. "I warned him, but he would say, 'Meera, what choice do I have? We have to work with what we have.' I pleaded with him to leave, but he said he could never cope with the harsh winters abroad. Business was his life and he was confident that the country would one day come round. Tell me, because we are so puzzled, and the children are asking, "Why is the President treating him like this? Let us know please." What could I say that would make sense? She asked me whether I would try for her, try to help her husband. I was so overcome by her pleading I agreed.

I knew that Robert Augustus would be attending a thanksgiving service in a fortnight's time, so I arranged with Meera that Rohan would stand at the foot of the cathedral steps and that I would do my best to get the President's attention for five minutes. I could only hope that seeing this fine, old, upright man before him, the source of so much kindness in the past, deteriorating rapidly before him, would move my brother. I had to do something.

During the service it began to drizzle, then the rain came with a mighty roar, thundering upon the roofs. It poured ceaselessly. I had hoped that Rohan would try and seek shelter, yet I couldn't see where he could go, except in the packed church with its two rows of armed security guards at the entrance. Would they let him in, a Country Mayan on bail?

I knew I must not fail him. The rain continued for half an hour, then petered out, the sun coming out and making everything glisten with the laughter of light on drops of water everywhere. The many pools and canals mirrored the land. When we came out of the cathedral a faint rainbow was in the sky.

I had told my brother of this meeting, and presented the case as best I could. I touched his arm gently and said, "Mr President, your one and only sister needs your help now more than ever. You must give me five minutes of your time ; I ask for no more, or else the name of Devonish will bring pain to me. Please hear what Comrade Rohan Mistry has to say. He has been a close friend of the Party and the Devonish family for as long as our dear departed mother needed him, and for as long as I can remember. It would enhance your image; the cameras are behind us and they would portray you as the father of the nation administering to a citizen in distress. The cathedral makes such an appropriate background." He allowed himself to be led by me and motioned to the security guards to remain where they were.

Rohan stood at attention, upright and gracious. His hair and his clothes clasped his skin. Water squelched from his shoes and socks whenever his numbed feet moved awkwardly. He reminded me of a scarecrow in the rain.

"Comrade Rohan has paid you the compliment of waiting here to meet you, though we have had such a downpour," I said. The President turned his attention to Rohan who had developed an ague.

"Comrade Rohan," the President said, "how are you?"

"I am very well, Mr President, just a little cold and wet." His teeth began to chatter.

"It is about his pending case, Mr President."

"What about it?"

"Only you can save him now."

Rohan began to nod, for he could not control his chattering teeth and trembling body.

"But what can I do? Is it not in the hands of the court? I am not a lawyer, am I? Is this the court?"

"No, Mr President," he managed to say.

"You can assist him, Mr President, in a way no one else can."

"My sister is your spokesman, I see, Comrade Rohan. She wants me to disrupt the course of justice. Do you think that is right?"

"I am innocent, Mr President."

"Well, surely that is what courts are there to decide. It is not proper that I should interfere in any way with the course of justice. Don't you agree, comrade?"

"Just a word from you, sir."

"Oh a single word from me? What word is that? Let me hear it."

"Two words he has in mind, Mr President: dismiss and innocent. He is asking you to enable the dismissal of the case against the innocent and, as you can see, he is not well, brother."

"My sister has become a mind reader, I see. I cannot promise anything, but I will see. I will see. I promise nothing. I believe five minutes are up. We must all keep to our word. Get some warm milk; you need that."

Rohan Mistry stood at attention until the President entered his waiting car.

He died a week later.

Soon after, my brother's anxieties over his personal safety reached new levels of neurosis and he further tightened security all around him. He saw my concern and said, "My security guards search all ministers and members of my cabinet who come to my office and my residence. Keeping the cabinet under a twenty-four hour surveillance was not my idea. It came from the head of security himself."

"Would you prefer him not to do this?"

"I pay him well to do a job; I cannot tell him how to do it. Besides, I have noticed in my occasional walks in disguise among the people that they are whispering more and more among themselves. Why are they whispering and not talking as you and I do? We do not whisper, do we?"

"No, Maximus."

"Well then, why should they? It must be something they do not want the government to hear. There are a few ambitious men in my cabinet. I need to be on guard. There is a pertinent question that often comes to me. Who watches the watchmen, Marguerite? We both need to be on the alert. We may find that we need to protect ourselves from our most trusted friends. Think about it, if they know you trust them, they have an advantage. You can trust no one today, absolutely no one, Marguerite. If truth be told, you are the only one I trust. Follow my advice, be on guard – especially among friends. Remember Brutus?"

His paranoia reached even more disturbing levels when he learnt that Meera Mistry's mother had taken to performing Kali puja every morning. My brother, like most Mayans, had a healthy respect for what he perceived as the dark arts of other ethnic groups. On the day before Meera Mistry and her mother left the island for Santa Maria, the President of Maya lost his voice. It was reduced to a guttural whisper, barely discernible. Hence his private discourses and the pending operation.

This may have been nothing more than sheer coincidence. But there is something else. I know it is a foolish thing to say, but Rohan Mistry's Kashmiri sapphire, vaulted in pitch darkness, in solitary confinement, was in some sense alive. It had a strength, some 'larger intelligence' – some phenomenon complex and intricate that we do not yet comprehend.

I became convinced that the sapphire had communicated with one of its own, travelling at the speed of light out there in the vast beyond. This traveller had answered our imprisoned sapphire's call and would do whatever was necessary to ensure that our sapphire's extended self was returned to the freedom of light. I made a promise to myself that I would return it to Meera Mistry.

Why did I feel compelled to say that it was alive, that it was a consciousness from another place that spoke the language of light? It was not merely its alphabet of flares, sparks, beams, flickers and glows which so fascinated Robert Augustus, but something both in-between and beyond, which I know my eyes could not see, nor find the words to express. I believed the sapphire needed light to exist, that something beautiful was dying imprisoned in the vault. I promised I would release it.

How can I begin to explain what I had seen within the sapphire's dazzling spectrum of flares, its motions of light? Imagine we lived on a planet without water, had never seen a liquid, and suddenly we saw a spring shooting from a hillside, which flowed into a mountain stream, that became the Amazon. And as the Atlantic ocean opens before us, what then? What would we say we had seen? What sensations would stir within us? Awe? Fear? Incredulity? What in our telling would we liken this to, in our solid world of boulders, stones, pebbles, rocks and sand? Where is the vocabulary that we could use to communicate a moving, amorphous energy, with waves that could rise as a cordillera, fall as an avalanche, yet leave delicate ripples of lace on its shore? What would we say we had seen?

32   FERRY CROSSING

The water waves as it flows – alive – vibrating with a multitude of fish. Standing on the stelling, Vasu and Aasha await the ferry. It is late. The vast chocolate river moves effortlessly towards the open ocean. The midstream currents and the undertow create capillary ripples. Shoal after shoal swims with the flow; riverine life meets the ocean.

A dark and light green border of vegetation – grass, shrubs, trees and hanging lianas – hem the river's earth-brown bank. "Is it tomorrow, Vasu, you leave for the hinterland?"

"No. The following day I leave."

"Do you have to go?"

"I have no choice, Aasha."

"Shouldn't someone else go."

"Who?"

"I am thinking."

"Look at the situation. The Government has allowed over one thousand non-Mayans to establish a commune deep in our hinterland, and we are told little about it. Some say it is an agricultural commune, others that it is a religious cult. It could be both and I think we should know for sure."

"They are certainly coming to the capital in larger numbers than a few months ago."

"We need to know why they are among the favoured. They wear masks of such good quality purple. Why? They're not Mayan citizens, yet they make party political broadcasts on Mayan radio and television."

"True. They're on any platform they can climb – voicing the government line on everything. *The Carrier* reported one of them as saying it has been proved scientifically that wheaten flour is bad for you. They want us to eat the government's cassava flour."

"Maybe wheaten flour *is* bad for you, Aasha. If you're caught with it by the police, you will find that it is not good for you."

"On May Day, leaders from the commune raised the ruling Party's flag high as they marched with the trades unions. One carried a banner: *Bon Aireans, beware the enemy within*!"

"They are not referring to themselves, Aasha."

"No Vasu. You make light of everything."

"It is more serious. They're preparing to undermine Gavin. He holds his second political meeting on the day I leave."

"Devonish certainly sees in Gavin the first real opposition since Pottaro's death."

There is a long pause. The ferry still does not show itself.

"Why you? Why do you have to go, Vasu? Unarmed? Without a bodyguard? Isn't there such a thing as obligation to oneself?"

"The Government is enabling these commune functionaries to set themselves up as yet another coercive force. We need to know why. Why does the Government need them? It controls the media. It doesn't need additional propaganda."

"Perhaps it's really feeling vulnerable. Perhaps even Devonish sees that they can't forever deny responsibility for the economy. They must be wondering how deep Gavin's support really is."

"His holding a public meeting must have really unnerved them. It may just be the beginning of a change."

"I hope so, yet I know that to write well, to speak well, to have good intentions are not enough either to gain power or govern well."

"True. The agenda of Gavin's supporters in Bon Aire does not attract or embrace all Mayans, though those close to Gavin say he is moving in that direction."

"But would he be given the chance? If there's an election, Devonish's party will fabricate enough fear to counter him. Besides, their rigging machinery remains in place. It is all they have left. The President knows it too and for that reason is probably even more dangerous. Don't go to the commune, Vasu. Whatever the reason, it is only there because the President permits it. It must be in his interest to have the commune there."

"Yes. But what are they offering him that he cannot obtain elsewhere?"

"You will be crossing the path of a frustrated, ruthless dictator with the means to do as he pleases. If you're caught there, expect no mercy."

"We have to take risks, Aasha. Many will be risking the wrath of the Government when they go to Gavin's meeting."

"Gavin is encouraging everyone to wear masks. He's using the Government's own instruments to undermine it."

"Clever Gavin."

"Not so clever. The police may try to remove these masks if they arrest people and take them down to the police station. That may result in untold pain for some whose masks have begun adhering to their skin. Many can't now remove them, even surgically. So they remain masked. In the absence of their faces they will be recognised by their masks..."

" To lose one's face to Devonish's design! The police have first hand knowledge of this, for they have long been masking themselves. The masks were never meant for permanent wear, Marguerite says."

Aasha is silent.

"The police may be more at ease at the meeting than you think, Aasha, for they want to hear what Gavin has to say. They themselves are not having it easy. No salary increase in years, with rising inflation eating into their wages' real value."

"Poetic justice? But I believe his supporters will not be able to judge him. Devonish is all they believe they have. He has encouraged them to see him as half-man, half-god."

"But when the lights go out and remain so longer and longer, and you have to have nerves to put something in the oven to cook a meal, how long will that belief remain?"

There is an anxious restless silence between them as they stand together and look out over the silt-laden flow. Then Aasha says, "Don't go, Vasu. Some risks should not be taken. Live to fight in another way. Going alone is far too great a risk."

"Is the dance ready?"

"Yes, come tomorrow."

"I have been looking forward to this. I shall be there. When I return from the hinterland, we shall get married. I need marriage with you to live, Aasha."

"Why can't we find someone in the army who's trustworthy, dependable. They're in the hinterland, they could visit the commune from time to time, observe, ask discreet questions."

"Nurse Maude would do that if she felt there was someone she could trust in the army. Getting the information back to her would not be easy. Today our poverty means you can trust no one. It has made us realise that everyone and everything has a price. And then, it's more than a day's walk from the military base to the commune. There are no connecting roads."

"Who will you say you are when you get there? What if they phone to check up on your identity? Your security file must be bulging."

"In this region, socialist republics are seldom so efficient, Aasha."

"That is what you say, making light of everything. In the hinterland you'll walk alone. There is no opposition party to look out for you. You'll be alone and vulnerable. Why risk so much?"

"One of the prerequisites of a dictatorship is the absence of an Opposition."

"So what can Gavin and his handful of men and women do? Who has the stomach for fighting Devonish when everyone just wants to leave? Who is so foolish as to face unarmed an army, a police force and the militia? Wasn't that what you were saying on Hope Bridge? And if by some heaven-sent intervention they were to lose the election, would a new government be allowed to govern? Wouldn't Bon Aire go up in flames again at the word of one man? Wouldn't there be strikes, violence, muggings, robbings, assaults? Would being here be worth it? And if you have young children and you know what state the schools are in, why would you condemn their young lives to such a place? It's time we leave. Why aren't we leaving? Let them be, let them rule over the ruins of their making."

"Something ugly is going on in the commune. I don't have a name for it. I shall need to take photographs, get them out to London, New York. Ask the journalists there and the governments that helped to crown Devonish to help unseat him."

"Good. You will have to take your story outside. The Region's newspaper men refuse to see Devonish for what he is. They wear his purple ties and speak of their objectivity simultaneously."

"The families and friends of those in the commune need to know the truth. Democracies need to know."

"Don't speak to me of democracies. It was two, well-established democracies that handed Devonish his crown and sceptre and their blessings... I wish you were not so upright, Vasu."

"You don't mean that... You can't mean that. Say you don't meant that. Do you? God, you're angry."

"We all have a choice, Vasu."

"All right tell me. What choice do you have if a child is drowning and you believe you can save her. Do you have a choice? I can feel your anger raging. Yet if you knew the situation, you would be doing the same."

"I doubt it."

"Nurse Maude says that for some time now in the hospital she has suspected that the so-called accidents – some quite severe – bruises, burns, cuts, broken limbs, falls – were not accidents, for the pattern of the injuries was too similar."

"What are you saying... that they are self-inflicted?"

"Inflicted. Victims all."

"Why? By whom?"

"I want to know why. Nurse Maude stresses that the injuries were too similar, occurring in the same place on the body. It is as if there is some religious rite. Not quite Abraham about to sacrifice his son Jacob on the altar, but certainly an offering... such men have a zeal for the Old Testament."

"So what do you think is happening?"

"The questions are endless. Men from the developed world are deep in our hinterland, cut off from civilisation, with a large vulnerable group of people who are seeking a new communal way of living. Why are we told so little about them by this Government? An island with a failing authoritarian regime is chosen by a religious cult leader. Why? Who needs whom and why?"

"I hear you. But tell me, what happens if you're stalked on arrival. As you take your photographs, someone comes from behind, presses a pistol in the small of your back and says: 'Satan shall be loosed out of his prison and shall come forth to deceive the nations.' He pulls the trigger. You are unarmed and dispensable."

"Where does that come from? Where have you heard that?"

"St John the Divine – *The Revelation*. One of their leaders quoted it. Remember their banner? *Beware the enemy within*? Don't you see you are trying to enter an irrational place without any safeguard? Are you trying to be Abhimanu? He had to face the cruel brutality of madness. That madness is here in Bon Aire and in the hinterland. It wears a mask. It sat on the driver's seat at Hope Bridge and turned Ica into a pogrom. It waits like a spider. Its web is of a fine weave, invisible in places, and you will become entangled, not understanding how it happened. Please try and see what you are up against, Vasu. For God's sake try. I beg you."

"Please believe me when I say I wish I didn't have to go. But how do I live with myself later, suspecting what I suspect? What happens if, six months from now, some brave traveller brings news from the hinterland and publishes it. And we see that had it been revealed to the outside world earlier, many lives might have been saved, torments reduced. How then do I live with myself? What then do I say? ...If only I had known? I had no way of knowing? I didn't know for sure? There was no way of really knowing? Do you think I will seek sanctuary there?"

"No, Vasu. You wouldn't."

"We have to live in the world and we have to live with ourselves, Aasha. We can fool ourselves with sophistry and wishful thinking only for so long."

She embraces him and they are comforted in each other.

"I have been fighting for myself," she says, "for my life with you. Forgive me. How to live apart, separated? How to live with such a loss? My spirit is anxious, goes ahead of me and tells me, 'Ask him to turn around – to walk another way.' Help me, Vasu." They embrace and she closes her eyes, saying, "I understand. My spirit will be with you always. Be at peace. If love has worth, I offer you armours of mine. May they protect you, Vasu. May you have no part uncovered, no Achilles' heel."

"When I return we shall be together. Nothing will separate us."

"How will you go?"

"By one of the small single-engine Islanders."

"Whose?" He can see she is trying her best to be brave. She keeps smiling through her tears, pretending all is now well, and he embraces her again.

"Marguerite and Nurse Maude have arranged it. They're in contact with a few stalwart Bon Aireans who cannot be bought by power or wealth. I shall be thinking of you. I can hardly wait to get married, Aasha. When in the hinterland I walk alone, as you say, I shall be thinking of our future life together. That will sustain me. Tomorrow I come to see you dance. That treat awaits me. A man so blessed should give something comparable when the need arises."

She embraces him and whispers something in his ear and he throws back his head and laughs, holding her in his embrace, spinning her around as he had done on the sea wall. And when the earth stands still again they turn to see the ferry has at last appeared. Even now, it seems to be standing still, reflecting as to whether it should stay where it is. The monotonous sound of the engine drowns the chatter of a crowd of ferry travellers patiently waiting. They have not been aware that the stelling has been receiving passengers all the while, and are taken aback to find that they are in the midst of an overcrowded, hustling, tumbling sea of humanity.

At last it arrives, an old dinosaur of the swamp, churning up the bottom, swirling and rippling the red mud, as if it is breathing into it. It is here, subdued in its old age. Seeing those who will journey with it to the other side, standing, awaiting its arrival; it slowly swings round, silently slides, and reveals its name: TORANI. This heavy metallic dinosaur is not built for comfort, but to carry poor people, traders and their cargo, trucks, vans and cars.

She embraces him again. And he takes his large handkerchief and wipes her cheeks. "Keep it in remembrance of this," he says. "There will be happier times, I promise." She hurries away, clutching his handkerchief, and is lost in the crowd. He cannot see her and he leaves. He knows she would wish it so. Even now she is moving to the other side of this rusty ancient tub, holding onto the railings of the steep stairway to the deck.

He leaves the stelling. An old beggar throws a mango skin at a straying goat; the animal wrestles with it. It is late and there is much to do.

33   THE PITY OF IT

While Aasha was on her way to the other bank of the river, Vasu
returned home and wrote this piece. He named it 'The pity of it'.
Unknown to him it was to be his 'Last Testament' to Maya, and I,
author of *The Purple Masked Mayans*, was tempted to call it
'Vasu's Testament.' But I was asked to keep it as he wrote it and
this I have done:

Tomorrow I shall see Aasha's dance, and it will travel with me
to the hinterland. Now that she has joined the master class, her
dance will be even more stirring – vibrant, exquisite. This theme
runs through her work. To her dance is not only life – the opposite
of death – it is light, a revelation. The dancer in full flight is a
firefly– glowing in the night, dancing across the vast darkness, a
traveller's guide. It is akin to what my brother once wrote:
"Daylight is not the opposite of darkness. It is larger, more
profound, for within a cavernous darkness, things cannot be seen
and so do not exist. With light comes their being, daylight brings
a riot of colour, adds to the form and substance of things; facilitates
our perception. Our very personality and spirit are transformed,
our brains stimulated, and the imagination endowed with wings."
Arun's words stir a deep resonance within me, for they apply to our
condition here in Maya. Our sense of possibilities enlarge with
sustained improvement in the quality of life, while with the night of
prolonged poverty, men forget themselves and know not who or what
they are. Our development should have meant growth, as from seed
to tree, or from a two dimensional plan to a majestic cathedral with
room for all.

It should be clear even to our President that his ideas for
development have not worked. At Independence, his supporters

danced and sang, believing their futures would be secure under his rule. But the outside world opened to them what they were not ready to see for themselves: that under Devonish they were not merely being left behind, they were moving back in time. Now, even his supporters are leaving Maya, a decision which cannot have been easy, since they were made to feel that Robert Augustus' success was theirs. When he had said that yet more was required of them to bring down Pottaro's Government, they obliged. So his failure has been a personal loss. He touched their depressed, sore spirits with the balm of his voice. When he told them they would be underdogs no more, no longer satisfied with morsels from the tables of the rich and the privileged, their resources no longer exploited by foreigners, that they would build their own Jerusalem, fashioned in their own likeness, he spoke deeply to their innermost longings.

I can hear him, speaking to his rapt supporters, "But now we shall own, you shall own all Maya. The little man will become a real man. No more will we go a begging for jobs. No more will we go knocking at other doors asking to be let in. No more to say, 'Please Sir, let me in.' No! That, brothers and sisters, that, no more. We will build our own citadel high on our chosen hill and there we will labour and there we will rest. We will make mistakes for we are not omniscient. We may not become rich, but whatever we have will be ours. We shall own all Maya. We may learn from others, but we will not copy."

He understood the needs of the poor in spirit, but obliterated the realities of Mayan industry and commerce. His sophisms unmask him. For what is the difference between learning and copying to a people desirous to learn? We first learn by copying and then with a better understanding create new ways and do new things. Yet he made the poor think he copied nothing and would copy nothing. It was all part of the rhetoric of the grand but crippling belief that we could rely solely on ourselves. Why say that the need for foreign investment and know-how were the ideas of the ignorant and the unintelligent? We became trapped in a narrow stultifying nationalism. Why did he continue to pretend that what was needed for the development of Maya was so very different from the needs of the rest of the developing world? Why the pretence that Maya was making large strides by his schoolboy stratagems – the first Republic in the Region, the first to place Co-ops at the centre of its development, the first to have its own Court of Appeal? He failed to see that what was important was not whether we were the first to implement anything, but its relevance to our growth, to our development. The acquisition of new skills, of new understandings of the wider world outside, is what we should have been working at, so that we too make niches in the world market, for exporting our creativity. Oh the pity of it all! Wholesome lives lost, a large political opportunity squandered.

He drove us all into a cul-de-sac, and still tried to move, not understanding why there could be no movement forward. His sense of self-importance would not allow him to consider revers-ing. He was following the fashionable ideas of his place and time, fiercely advocated by the Region's AUL – state ownership and state intervention – as if there were no alternatives. This led to his overdependence on exploiting our natural resources. These, no doubt, could have given our country a good start, but by far the more important in the long run is the skills of all our people, their creativity and resourcefulness. It was in the training of our people, in offering an education relevant to the twenty-first century that our endeavours should have been directed. Instead, he chan-nelled the savings of all Mayans into a new phenomenon – the establishment of the largest army in the Region. Oh, the pity of it all!

He was conventional and did not know it, believing he was in the forefront of developing new concepts. Yet behind these self-deceptions lay the temporary advantages of *real politik*. If he saw ownership and control *per se* as synonymous with freedom from economic and political servitude, it was also the means to reward the party faithful and secure their loyalty. He forgot that for an enterprise to be sustainable, it must provide something at a competitive price which many wish to have , provide an attractive livelihood for those engaged in producing it and at the same time be sufficiently profitable, so that the entire process can be renewed with reinvestment. He failed to grasp that if the majority of our enterprises were not doing this, we would become bankrupt. It was the absence of this simple understanding, this simple arithmetic that every roadside trader knows, that brought his demise. Simple concepts of good management, efficiency and competitiveness, he never attempted to fathom, and through this fiscal waywardness and waste, he and his party rapidly eroded the viability of the economy.

The truth is that a covert racism has been one of the main pivots of his development policy. It has been a costly indulgence for Maya and instrumental in the enormity of his failure. Racism is anti-developmental wherever and whenever it is practised. It was in our uniquely rich variety of cultural resources that our dynamic creativity lay. This he could not acknowledge, and has effectively destroyed.

I do not judge his lack of economic understanding too harshly. Historically, colonialism and capitalism were close companions on the road of empire building, and in failing to understand their different natures he could not see that one can unbridle capital from colonialism, from conquest and wars, and harness it to the chariot of growth and development. But this needed a skilled charioteer who understood his horses, the limits and capacities of his chariots and the dangerous curves of the trade circuit. Such an experienced charioteer we never had.

Instead, in this Maritime Region, we had arrogant men who read about chariots and then assumed that this reading alone made them expert charioteers. But then again it was a time when bright schoolboys were encouraged to think that through their reading and writing of books, their flare for speaking on platforms, would come the new dawn. Oh the pity of it!

And what a vehicle our thinkers persuaded our government to build! As we walked around it in its air-conditioned show room, its large, polished, rear-view mirror, its gleaming hub caps, its splendid, technologically advanced tyres were brought to our attention with pride. We admired its fine metallic crimson sheen, but when the day of its test run arrived, it could take us nowhere. Our assorted advisers and university luminaries had forgotten to build into it that finest of Rolls Royce engines – self discipline.

There was a time when Mayan butterflies were so plentiful that visitors would cry, "Look how beautiful! The wind carries showers of petals." It was a time when the crotons tossed their heads in sunshine; when the poinciana displayed its silken crimson skirt, and our forests decked themselves in delicate, sweet scented blooms. Alas no more! Now the pink mealybug and the fruit fly are here. Leaves curl and bunch. Flowers remain unopened. Fruit falls unripened. The sea wall crumbles. The ocean waits to reclaim its rich alluvium. Maya is sinking. Yet it need not have come to this. The pity of it all!

I am looking forward to returning to Aasha after this is over. My journey weighs on me. Marriage to Aasha is what I need more than anything else. To be together for a lifetime seems too good to be true. Will I be so blessed? Is it possible to have such a joy ... such a life's companion? Is this my dream? Then let me forever dream.

When all is said and done, I am only too aware that it is the world we have created that leads men and women and their children to become slaves to such a man as Devonish. It is the world we have shaped that leads men and women and children to isolated communes in the forest, the middle of nowhere, seeking the brotherhood of man. And though I know it is a world that from time to time has the capacity to recognise its own failings, still a dread clings to me and compels me to ask: Is this a world where men will say, "To live is to love"? Or will they leave it willingly to terminate their living hell?

Of late, a deep sadness comes over me. And though I tried to appear at ease before Aasha, making light of her concerns, I am as fearful for myself as she. Yet I cannot leave Maya without going to the hinterland commune. Duty is the foundation of rights. Goodnight, dearest Aasha.

Vasu

In case I do not return... I have discussed all with Arun. He is against my going, though he understands my reasons. I hope the Gods are with me. Suddenly I am tired and weary, overwhelmed by doubts, looking for a way out. May I be strengthened by that enormous faith all our Mayan forefathers had when for months they fought and survived the iniquities of power and greed on a ship at sea and when they learnt to survive in mud huts amidst the intense disdain and the accompanying ugliness of an imperial capitalism.

From where do the powerless gain the strength and courage to live to see the next day? From where, when the world despises and mocks them?

This much I know, Aasha, a man must live with himself or else he cannot live. You, the light of my being, must understand this or else I am no more.

Vasu

34   THE DANCE OF AASHA – AN OFFERING

She has composed the room with an adventurer's flight of fancy.
A thin line of saffron surrounds the sacred circle of movement
where the dancing *Shiva Nataraja*, his motion stilled in bronze,
tests the firmament with a sweep of limbs. Soft twilight enters,
bringing new tones and shades, enriching the hanging raw silk.
The cool velvet satin upon which his hands rest develops a
blushing crimson; beside him a jug of wine. Tempted he suc-
cumbs, pouring a fullness, only to refill the glass. The scent of
incense pervades all.

Sounds, held together as in a bouquet, flow to the saffron sphere
with clear identities: solemnity, gentleness; youthful impetuosity,
vigour, fevered intensity; promise of renewed growth and summer's fullness; menacing disturbances; despair, delusions, de-
mons, death. Vasu catches these.

A melody of hope and serenity enters. He misses it, for his eyes
have been seduced by murmuring motions of the hanging, swaying
weaves. When his focus returns to the stage, there she is, her
thighs draped in soft silken folds, as in the frescoes of the Ajanta
caves, her form partially hidden by *Shiva Nataraja*.

She enters the glowing bronze and retreats. It is an intrinsically
varying repetition – the very spirit of dance. Then music and dance
extend themselves in an ice skating partnership. In this prelude
they acknowledge each other's presence, before parting, as buds
must, to open to fuller forms of petalled perfection.

Both movements return and from them comes a harmonious
arrangement, solemn and aloof as a marble pillar. Gradually
Solemnity opens like a fan. Currents of motion reveal that it
understands the truth of reality and will no longer compromise. It

declares that in the past it has attempted to veil the future by religious myth, childlike in offering an unknown, and in promising an unknowable with vehemence. Crashing cymbals tear these veils aside. Silence.

Solemnity moves to another pulpit, "There is another way," it states. The dancer makes angular lines to reach it, but before she can, the music has changed; Solemnity is departing. Gentleness comes and Solemnity whispers, "Now I have accepted the nature of things. It is enough."

Gentleness curtseys. Solemnity bows low, taking its leave.

It is the movement, the melody of soft breezes in an intolerable heat; of shade from trees, of dew rolling on leaves, of caring hands; of friendship in a strange land; the silent flow of sunlight upon the earth at dawn; clean air, the gentleness of cool water brought by a child's cupped palms to parched lips. It is soft. Cool hands soothing, binding wounds; it is the release of chained, dragging feet from a cruel convicting world.

Suddenly, a few strides – fleeting footwork – and there is an entire new arrangement, another path to the whole. A call and a response to two transitional bars, and the weight and pace of the narrative change. Youthful impulses whirl everywhere at once. Space becomes flexible as wings, yielding as running water. The dancer is sensuous, robust, propulsively energetic. Space is fluted by her movements, expands, deepens.

Along her limbs is a continuous flow of change, its form and character constantly arranged anew in intricate, exquisite ways, like drifting snow flakes. As the impulse reaches the outermost extremities of her limbs, another fresh impulse is born, followed by another and another. This impermanence of beauty in motion haunts him. And yet in the midst of this transience, there are shapes held in tableau, facilitating and holding the darting of his flowing imagination.

A dance of joy – the dance of a flock of birds, of a tropical forest tossing its head in the wind, wildly coquettish, trunks swaying, moving almost in full circle, forgetting themselves in Bacchanalian abandon. Poinciana petals the paths vermilion and the yellow poui of dawn scatters fragments of the morning star to rest upon the earth.

The dancer draws him further.

Petals and butterflies drift together dancing in the wind, in texture, colour and motion alike. We are falling petals, yet it is bouncing butterflies, the dancer offers: let us be butterflies today, for tomorrow we will be drifting petals, eddying down, unable to soar again, to rise and sit on treetops, expand our wings.

The dancer retreats.

The music asks: Are we gods that we walk upright, run and fly and sail; see vast distances and hear the echoes of distant planets? We are part of earth's bountifulness, its beauty, its motion. We have been granted the fullness of Bramha's imagination to create and to destroy.

Vasu's concentration lapses. On regaining it, he sees Aasha moving against the music, her form in counterpoint to it. Her rhythm moves away from the music to the wings of the stage. In her absence, silences form a sphere of emptiness, a rotating vacuous planet. It is not the silence of stones, but of an absolute void.

Suddenly a forceful chord changes the tone, rhythm and colour of the music so that it becomes ruthlessly daring and irrational. Aasha re-enters in haste, chased, disturbed. Menacing resonances assault her mind and a feverish delusion captures her. These chords give way to the voices of masked carollers – promises in soft sibilants and sweet labials. Their masks fall and he sees that behind them morality has long evaporated. Her nightmares explode and shatter her. Despair enters with its companion, death.

Death sings of a sweet comforting peace, a siren's song. It offers rest from work, shelter from distress. She begins to move in unison with death's leaden steps. They embrace in cold silence. She shivers. Her weary limbs and troubled mind welcome a dignified forgetfulness.

From afar, a lone horn is calling. It awaits another's coming. A companion horn replies. The earth rotates. A new dawn will rise. The earth rotates.

Hearing this, death releases its sweetest siren's song, the allurement of a peace that defies all things, the seductive promise that there will be no more torment or pain, no more weariness. Death stirs her, embraces her, tracing his steps to the coming of an end. She falls.

A distant trumpet calls and calls again. The horns leave. As she rises, the trumpets sing. A flood of sunlight pierces the last night-clouds. Energy flows. Life is energised. It warms her limbs chilled by death's courtesy. Death sees that this is not his day. He bows low and is lost to her. The trumpets rejoice.

She regains herself, circling the saffron sphere, absorbing Shiva Nataraja's imagination. The pulsating dance of Spring begins. The rhythm heightens – celebratory, inspired, joyful. The music rises upwards and up, and she is lifted. A new birth is coming. The music of Eros arrives, a seething, turbulent ferment. Hope dances with life and all the seasons bloom.

The cool freshness of Spring and Summer's ripening heat are played out in vibrant rhythms to exhaustion, and as they go, Autumn, graciously balanced, is busy capturing colour with its long slanting brush of glorious light. Autumn is enthralled to see the smiles of Spring and Summer lingering as it completes its painter's task. Meanwhile, the mulch of Autumn – the falling leaves – drift in heaps for Spring. Winter's outriders are eager to visit and Autumn accepts that Winter must have its time. A gentle melancholy accompanies the twins – maturity and wisdom. They recall earlier conversations, earlier arrangements, and separate the memorable from mere stirrings of the past, reminding us of the exuberance of life and the rest that awaits. Vasu is moved by this fine discernment.

The fierce intensities of feeling that carried the dancer and her audience now release their hold. All that is left within the saffron sphere is a soft shadow of a past melancholy. Today it will not sit and await Winter. It will enjoy the last glimmering fragments of the Summer's sun on the grass, sip nectar and bathe in cool mountain streams. There is a sweetness and a mystery still to explore – the miracle of music in motion.

Finally, with flow in stillness, comes contentment, an assurance of an abiding restoration, a cradling of the human spirit. The dancer and *Shiva Nataraja* are one.

Aasha circles the stage, graceful, sublime.

Within the thin circle of saffron her dance has become a dew drop before the dazzling sun, sparkling, illuminating, gone.

Vasu enters the saffron sphere and calls. And there two movements embrace.

35 THE LONG NIGHT
Marguerite

The President's men were on full alert for Gavin's meeting. An unspoken anxiety hung over Bon Aire, akin to the day preceding the fires. I was tense for I could no longer predict how my brother would cope with this serious public attack on his regime, especially when for the first time he was being opposed by a man about whom he couldn't say, "He is not one of us. He does not qualify. He does not have that psychic inheritance to govern."

I recall thinking that Robert Augustus would need to compose new songs of fear and disinheritance, but he had aged and old men are loath to change their tune. "So Gavin, beware," I said. "You face a man depressed, deeply frustrated, who sees his end is close and will not be pushed. I fear if you unwrap the truth too rawly, you will pay dearly. Take care, Gavin. Show restraint, underplay your hand."

I had been there at that party meeting on the grading of masks when Gavin showed his true colours . Then he was reported in *The Carrier* as a troublemaker, a man to be watched. After the meeting he showed little regard for the pompous sensibilities of the party Chairman. So on the day of his public meeting I kept thinking aloud, hoping that by some telepathy my thoughts would reach him: "Be more prudent, Gavin. Guard yourself, become an older man. Lay down youthful impatience. Cup your anger tightly; duplicity and deception are all around you. Take care, Gavin. Take care."

My brother, the master builder, had foreseen this coming and sought to stay it, by a change to the constitution. It was his last act of self-preservation – President for Life. Ever conscious of the means he had used to eject Emmanuel Pottaro from power, he sought another kind of legitimacy for his regime. Conscious that what he sought (to be democratically elected by free and fair elections) could not be had, he then offered himself full protection from prosecution for crimes he perpetrated in the past. In true Augustan style, he legislated, too, for future acts, hoping to enjoy that ultimate privilege of primeval gods.

Once more the Region's governments, university, non-governmental organisations and press were silent as my brother's absolute empowerment of himself denied Mayans any redress from state tyranny. It was as if we were alone, deep in the hinterland of the Amazonian jungle, cut off from civilised thought, hearing the echoing of our cries from the mountains, the mirroring of our suffering by the streams.

Robert Augustus's new Constitution stated:

"The President of Maya is not answerable to any court for any civil or criminal proceedings instituted against him, in his private capacity or as President of Maya for acts done in the performance of the functions of his high office during his term of office or thereafter."

What a piece of work! Those lines were prepared by a bespectacled, serious man, a Country Mayan who, impatient to display his feathers, crossed the floor from the ruins of Pottaro's party to join the paramountcy of Robert Augustus. "Learned and public-spirited", *The Carrier* called him. Others followed his crossing. I suspect these turncoats were men tired of waiting for what could not come to pass – free and fair elections while Robert Augustus and his Party were in control of the ballot boxes.

I had half expected the last word of that paragraph in the Constitution to be *hereafter* – and found some comfort in its exclusion. Covered by the hallucinatory tent under which we were all living I would not have been shaken if Robert Augustus thought his Constitution could travel the distance from his *therafter* to the *hereafter*, that his sophistry could silence history and beyond.

I would have liked to attend Gavin's meeting, to have got the feel of the public for this young man, knowing it would not be fairly reported in the press, but as the sister of the President that would have been imprudent! I needed more than anything to retain my brother's confidence and trust. The time was ripe for an overthrow.

Robert Augustus was in much reduced circumstance. He had, I thought, nothing left to confer upon his faithful servants. I was wrong. Once more, with his back to the wall, he made an offering to them, this time – a word. As with his masks, he chose with care. He offered the ultimate word *Supreme*. So welcome *Supreme* judge, *Supreme* Superintendent of the Police Force, *Supreme* Army General, *Supreme* Congress of the People, *Supreme* Permanent Secretaries, *Supreme* Ministers – and even the *Supreme* Editor of *The Carrier*.

Alas! These words had been nurtured and maintained by other men, but here in Maya they were mined of their meaning and became but empty shells. I should have known what such a man was capable of doing when he found he had used up his last words to purchase a future.

But neither words nor what he did to Gavin could help him, for the shadow of death had already begun to lead him from one place to another. Robert Augustus, who had wanted all time, desired a monumental time, had become a leaf in a stream gushing down a steep mountainside, moving rapidly to the edge of a waterfall, crashing with the flow of time. It was his last flutter – that of a moth before a lizard draws it quivering into its serrated jaws.

36   GAVIN'S MEETING

"Everything Robert Augustus touches turns to shit!" The crowd roars. Gavin is batting and that is a six, clean over the boundary. Effortlessly and with style, swift, full bodied. They are enjoying themselves. Hands go up in the air. Here and there heads bend, feet and bodies move as in dance. Sweet, pleasurable words that give release, free emotions. Sweet Jesus, uptight for too long – all this bearing up, bearing all in silence, conscious of needs within, and loss of face without.

In the open savannah, the citizens of Bon Aire are listening to a young man who looks not a little like a young Robert Augustus. On this occasion, though, the speaker is using language not to preen himself but to communicate in short sharp stabs, a cockerel pursuing a squirming centipede. "We are now the Barrel People. We say, 'I have a barrel coming, my daughter promised me a barrel. My barrel come'. A nation concentrating not on developing itself but on barrels." A quiet affirmation comes from the crowd.

"Why should a simple wooden vessel, strengthened with staves become so important to all Mayans? What could be in it? Salt? Yes. Powdered milk? Tinned butter and tinned cheese? Coffee? Yes! Cassava flour?"

"No!" the crowd shouts.

"Wheat flour and split peas? Yes. Why are these things not on the supermarket shelves? Why? You know why? Because Robert Augustus is running this country. And we better run too. You read the other day he got some doctor to say wheat flour bad for you. Well, comrades, all I can say, all you can say is *he* must have swallowed plenty. We can't say, for we haven't seen any, still less eat enough to feel bad."

A youngster cries out, "True-true talk, comrade."

"In the barrel you will also find a tin of cooking oil, a box of tissue, toilet paper, sandals, shoes and dresses; soaps and creams. Now we are asking those who were pushed out to put a supermarket in a barrel. That is not all, comrades. We must now all knock at the closed gates of every country and tell a lie to get in. Is this self-esteem, comrades? Is this the dignity of independence? Who is fooling whom? Humiliation, comrades, that's what it is. Where is the dignity in these long years of poverty which turns young men into old? Today, we are jostling to enlist to pick fruit, to cut other people's cane, because *they* have better things to do with their time. Who is fooling whom, comrades? And if you succeed in getting through the gates, you sigh with relief, but after your time to cut and pick and pack is up, and you don't turn up at the exit gates, comrades, because you know and I know the President has left nothing here to come back to, well then, brother, you know you must now hide. Now you on the run, but you mustn't run, though every police uniform in those 'free states' will send a shock through you, until habit soothes away those raw edges of fear. You mustn't keep looking over your shoulder, comrade. Walk natural. Now don't ask me what that is, because I don't know. If I knew I would be a rich man."

"You learn to take whatever those sharks over there give you as payment for a full sixty-hour week and you keep quiet, comrade. Yes, you keep your mouth shut and your head down too, comrade. I know. If they knock you down on the road, don't open your mouth. Protesting is not for you and me. It is not safe, you are an illegal immigrant. Shut you mouth, for the sound you will make and, if you were not primed, the very clothes and shoes you wear are givea-ways. Say nothing to your neighbour. You share that room with twelve others? All travellers in the night. All from newly independ-ent countries with prime ministers whose ideas have got you all over there, jostling in one room, prime ministers who will resign on an index-linked pension, while your pension, your wages sinking so fast you getting dizzy and people thinking you going mad. The other day I saw a lady running to the market. She say, 'Mr Gavin, with the little money I got, I have to try and run faster than it, before it disappear before my very eyes'. Comrades, who fooling whom?"

"If you want to know what slavery was about, don't worry to read about it, you living it. This is twentieth century slavery – shackled by your own. Each age has its own style of servitude, but the same abuse of power. Knowledge and power exploiting ignorance and poverty. Here in Maya, the strong exploiting the weak. And why? Why comrades? You know and I know, it is because whatever the President touches turns to shit, turns to sh..."

The microphone is on the floor. Policemen in protective gear are charging the rostrum. Two women come from nowhere and step in front of Gavin as shields. They are talking to purple-masked policemen. Gavin is being hustled into a car by his colleagues. He is unwilling to go, he is resisting, but the women are being firm with him and they eventually leave with him.

The crowd comes round and watches. They see the army is here too. Rifles are held high. A voice comes through the loud speaker. "Comrades, the President advises everyone to go home. Anyone found loitering in the savannah, singly or in groups will be taken to the police station for questioning. A crime has been committed and the criminal is on the run. It has just been confirmed by the police that the criminal is among you, seeking refuge in the crowd. Everyone in the vicinity is under suspicion. Go home. Return to your families if you are innocent."

*   *   *   *

I had gone to Gavin's meeting both to occupy myself in Vasu's absence, lest anxiety drain me, and as an act of witness on Vasu's behalf. I returned home in an even greater state of nervous dread. I could not help feeling that here was David and Goliath. Except that Devonish was not going to face David. He would send one of his men, armed with the shield of anonymity, *to do what is necessary*, so that as David climbs the hill, expecting to see Goliath standing there, he sees a large upright figure with a visage not unlike Goliath's. As he approaches, he senses he is walking into a trap, but before he can turn around, he is gunned down from behind. The papier-mâché figure of Goliath stands upright; beneath it Gavin bleeds. Goliath blinks, his head drops as if on a string, watching what lies so low. No breath remains. All is still. Was I dreaming? Gavin, beware! Beware!

37   AASHA'S DREAM

*Marriage is what I need to live. Not oxygen, water, bread and work,
as you whispered at the stelling.* The note pinned to her pillow
brings pleasure. *You are misinformed, young lady. This malady
comes from the habit of gleaning information from books, though
a foolproof source – the school of life – daily unfolds before you. This
is an infliction uncommon amongst peasant farmers, yet amongst
the learned, alarmingly high. By the time you have read this, I will
be nearer the clouds than you are and on my way to the commune
in the deep hinterland.*

*I shall see you as soon as I return, else I perish, despite oxygen,
water, bread and work. I hope you are coming round to accepting
this truth.* It was signed: *Your eternal spirit of good will. P.S. Thank
you for being real, Aasha... But are you? Could it be that my
imagination has created a perfection? How will I know? Vasu – the
peasant at heart.*

Two days later she rereads the note. What could be keeping him
in the hinterland for three days? An anxiety which she tried to
dispel a day ago clings to her and she finds herself clutching his
note with excessive zeal, recalling their night – the night of the
dance.

Another day passes and her nights have become disturbed.

She is walking on gradually sloping land, as on a continental
shelf. The nearer foliage is dark green, and darker still beyond.
She sees the vegetation as a boatman at the bow – moving out to
sea. And then she is in the ocean and can feel the sheer weight of
the water pressing in upon her, circling her as if she is an islet. Her
steps are drawn further down the slope. The ooze under her feet is
too silky soft. There is no grip. Sensing the gravitational pull to a
greater depth – a force too vast to counter. Terror holds her, she

sinks further; the water is rising with the sound of rushing streams. She is on the edge of oblivion that has come too soon. This shelf will end abruptly. Feet without eyes stumbling where there is no shelf and falling down, down, down, into the ocean's deepest ooze – lost to consciousness into a habitat of gills.

Turn back! Turn back now! What an effort to wade through the jade-green current, to turn against the encircling ocean. And then she hears his voice, brought by the wind, and the water gradually recedes and there is the yellow poui, its petals on the grass. Sunlight and almond leaves painted in aurora yellow, crimson lake, carmine and magenta. Vasu stands on the sea-wall. He is looking at her, not seeing that the foundation of the sea wall is being washed away, is moving away. She cannot reach him... Her mouth opens... but nothing comes. She cannot warn him. She signals with her hands for him to jump off while there is still time to swim the five metres to reach the mainland. But her voice has no sound. "Vasuuuuu", she is screaming. Nothing. She sees the sea wall drifting steadily from the land. A solitary figure on a drifting rock, with room for one pair of feet. He drifts and drifts away. Yet all this while he is calm, and all at once too far out. She stands and stares alone. Watches and watches until he becomes a speck, drifting into the horizon.

She wakes in tears, feels an emptiness in her stomach, then a pain. She begins to cry, unable to pull herself together, unable to say this is a dream. Then the sound of his name returns to her and she screams, "Vasuuuuu", for the urge to call his name overwhelms her.

38   THE ALTAR

The single-engine Islander is cruising high, and Vasu Nath looks
down. He feels removed from reality. Trees have become giant
broccoli on sticks. Here and there a yellow brush stroke warms the
leafy green. Cirrus clouds chase corridors in the sky or descend to
sit on slopes marking a lost snow-line. Below, a river, uncovered,
opens to the sky, its sinuous line lapping the forest.

Just the two – soaring, vulnerable. The pilot says nothing, but
it is a warm silence accommodating Vasu's restlessness. They are
on their way to the Hinterland Commune, an agricultural settle-
ment where hundreds of people, young and old, men and women
from diverse places outside Maya have come seeking a new life,
close to nature, far removed from what their organiser called the
"Iniquities of Capitalism" (or IC, pronounced *ice*, as it is famil-
iarly known). They are a mixed bunch: a few political idealists,
some 'back-to-nature' ruralists and seekers after some new,
meaningful religious experience. But the poor and disadvantaged,
the naked and the weak, those seeking shelter and the brotherhood
of man are the majority. Here, they are alone in the forest,
surrounded by the unknown. Vasu is sure they are unable to leave
even if they wish to, for his intelligence is that they handed over
their passports and money to their leader. He fears they have no
understanding of where they are. They have trusted one man, and
he holds their means of leaving.

In a word, they are prisoners. Vasu is sure the Government
knows this and yet it supports the leader of the commune with zeal.
Any visitor who wishes to travel to the interior can have his stay
shortened if the leader makes the request. Why? How large is the
contribution the commune makes to Party coffers? What other

comforts does the Government enjoy? Why are the senior members of the commune and the Government so closely knit? What favours does the Government need from the commune leader that it should act so favourably on his behalf? Vasu feels he is going round in circles. Something ugly remains hidden. One man rules there and has absolute power over the poor, the vulnerable and the trusting. This much has filtered out, despite the commune's cover of secrecy.

Nurse Maude has told him she is convinced it is a kind of hell, with an eleven-hour working day and an inadequate diet – monotonous and unbalanced. "We're all travellers, Vasu," she said, "and these travellers have drifted onto our shores. They are totally dependent on the personality of their captain – he seems possessed with an obsessive desire for a following, slavishly loyal to himself. Reminds me of someone," and she winks. "Perhaps he sought a kingdom to rule and, not having found one, makes his own here in the middle of nowhere! He sees our forested heartland as his promised land. So easy to imagine this if you were brought up in the slums of a crowded ugly city." But by gently probing, coaxing members of the commune who come as patients to her hospital with severe burns and bruises, broken and fractured limbs, Aunt Maude suspects a *fearsome thing* dwells there. "I know he has black moods. He is a walking bomb, a danger to us all. And yet why does the government not see this? What is it that covers their eyes? We need photographs, Vasu."

He looks down. There is no place to run to in the dense forest, no escape for those who wish to leave. They may never leave unless someone informs the outside world of what is really going on. He plans to take as many photographs as he can.

He has not disclosed his deepest fears to Aasha, his awareness that he may be approaching a man who has no limits. Why has Maya, he asks himself, become the visionary world of two men whose illusions enabled them to remove their followers and themselves from the sphere of rational thought? One leader rules the forested hinterland, the other the flickering lights of Bon Aire.

The aircraft enters a shower. Sea-green. Sea ferns. Island-green. Sea-blue mountains rising from the ocean. Every shade of grass-green, silver-green. He searches here and there for an immortelle tree – a reddish tangerine and orange to comfort his eyes from this overwhelming green. The engine drones. It continues to rain. Runnels on the cockpit window stream speedily down like chased tadpoles before disappearing.

Out of the shower, they fly into clear skies. Below – tangerine crowns, heads sprinkled with saffron; a singular burnished brown. Are these the colours of marine flora? Are we on an ocean floor of oxygen? He pictures how a falling bamboo leaf dives like a fish, darting to the bottom and rests. Our homes, our lives, our thoughts sit beneath flows and currents of air. Does this pressure, this movement, affect our thinking? How deep is our ocean of oxygen? Is this real? Why am I here? What awaits me? Where am I? Why is the commune here?

Streaks of sunlight come through; the water glistens, filled with piranhas' silver-scissored mouths. Clouds cast shades of elongated loaves. Drumlin-shaped shadows become blue glacial lakes and the sunlight illuminates a laterite road, bleeding through greenheart and balata hills which leads to Ica, now deserted.

Vasu moves between dream and wake. He sits with the pilot. Two men alone. This is only his second trip to the hinterland.

Today, he thinks, Gavin will be holding his public meeting, to test the waters, to ascertain the strength of the support he can muster. He would have liked to be there, to speak on his platform, but Nurse Maude and Marguerite had insisted he must go on the day of Gavin's meeting. All eyes would be on Gavin, his meeting a convenient decoy. They had convinced him it would be easier to borrow the single-engine Islander when the militias' attention was turned to Bon Aire. They had been mistakenly told that the commune bosses would not be in the hinterland, so here was an opportunity to walk about, to speak to people, open doors.

The pilot is calm.

The discontent in Bon Aire is growing. This will disturb the ruling party, put their backs up. They have no solution. Trapped. Cornered. Dangerous. Gavin knows this. He will punch hard this evening. Is the time ripe for a change? Vasu wishes Gavin well, but fears for his chances, without access to armed force. How will he face the largest army in the Region? Take care, my brother, take care.

Suddenly Vasu feels more naked and vulnerable than he has ever felt before. He tries to comfort himself with Nurse Maude's parting words. "I am leaving this purple mask with you. It is special. It has been cleansed by my thoughts and prayers. Do not leave it behind, I beg you. Take it. You need all the help you can gather. I shall be praying. The pilot can be trusted, he will follow your instructions, and ours when it is over. God be with you."

The Islander continues to drone.

The last time he was in the hinterland, the indigenous forest people had gathered to hear what Mayan Government officials, surrounded by armed army officers, had to say about Government incursions onto their land. He had come with Aasha to see what the Government hinterland project was really about. They had heard officials explaining to the indigenous forest people: "This is a Government project and all will benefit. It is in the very nature of development that things will be better. Lives will be improved. That is the purpose, the meaning of development. You must trust us. We will not do anything without consulting you. At all times the Government will work with you."

An old Amerindian, who had been silent, listening, thoughtful, waited to ensure that the Government officials and their armed men had nothing more to say. Then he rose, standing tall and erect as the forest around him and spoke clearly in the language of the tribe, formally greeting his people, thanking them for being there to listen to what these men from Bon Aire had come to say. He also thanked the officials for coming to speak with them. And then he spoke in English: *I cannot speak the language to ask why you are here. Yes, I hear what you say, but I ask why are you here? We know what you must say, we hear what you say but how do we ask? We do not have the language. How do we know why you are here?*

Aasha had been deeply moved by the clarity of his question, the simple truth of his quest. When they returned to the car, she was drying her eyes. "He knows the tribe is dying, Vasu. He knows the Government brings a further destruction of his culture, his way of life, yet he watches us, speaks to us with a quiet dignity, as I imagine he would to Death when it knocks. I hope I will have that grace when I need it. I wanted to tell him that we know that when he and his tribe leave their ancestral land, we too would have lost, but how do I say this to him, knowing the history of his people? And of what use, what comfort would that be – the sentiment of a traveller, a passer-by? How can I convey my thoughts which must pass through complex language codes and barriers of culture before they reach him? And when they do, how changed will they be? Will they arrive as pity before him? And what of my uninvited presence? Was that not an incursion too?"

Vasu remembers these words as, suddenly, high up at eight thousand feet, the aircraft begins to descend. He feels he has become the old man and ponders: Do I have the language to ask the members of this commune – its children, men and women, the old and sick, the tortured and the scared, mothers and fathers, and those without their families – do I have the language to ask why they are here? Why they have come? And those functionaries in charge, what language will they use to tell me why they are here?

He remembers to take Nurse Maude's mask as he alights from the aircraft. He and the pilot have agreed on a code to be used if he falls into danger, and that at no time must the pilot leave the aircraft to follow him. Vasu has studied the area well and knows which direction to take, where to head for if he has to run for it. They have rehearsed it all. The pilot is a young man who works for Marguerite. Vasu wants him to live.

As he walks on the hard dry mud of the commune, he feels he has entered some time-warp – into the seventeenth or eighteenth century, walking along a path to the slave-quarters of a plantation in the deep South of the United States. There is, though, a strange stillness. The commune seems empty. Perhaps its members are out somewhere in the vast expanse of forest.

He hears a voice. A woman is humming a tune he knows. And then she begins to sing, moving in and out of the building. He hears snippets. At times the wind lifts her voice and her song reaches him. "Where are the clowns? Send in the clowns.... Sure of my life. No one is there... Well .... maybe next year."

He sees groups of women washing and baking, ironing, cooking and sewing. The scent of boiled rice is carried by the wind. He meets tired women in the fields, planting corn and cassava and asks to be taken to the Director of the commune, only to be told that he is not there, but that the next in command is there, the Reverend

Ernest Cannon. Two women accompany him and he can't help thinking they feel safer in twos by the way they hold each other's hands. Their eyes are troubled, pleading. He recalls himself as a child eating a sandwich and seeing a stray bitch standing before him, waiting. She was full with pups and looked at him in this selfsame way. He had shared the sandwich.

The Reverend Ernest Cannon is not in his office. This fact disturbs the women greatly. They will go no further, but point, saying, "The church, the church. He is there." They hurry back to the burning fields as if sanctuary lies there. Vasu senses the time has come to wear the mask of deepest purple.

It is not far to go and he does not know why, but he finds himself walking on the grass to soften his steps in this harsh, harrowing place of live spirits, whose presence he feels close by. He looks for cover but there is none save the shadow of the building, a church, simply designed. The entrance is locked.

He thinks he hears something. He listens, he waits, but nothing more comes. He is lost in thought when a whimpering comes upon him, holds him, increasing at a fevered sweating intensity. Then a piercing sound bursts from the church, locks him into it. He waits desperately for the silences, which mercifully are at times prolonged. Suddenly a scream pitches out. Someone is in excruciating pain. And then comes another cry. Is it from a child's throat? Vasu cannot be sure but there are two sounds. He knows then that someone is devouring life, innocence, a child. Two children are facing an incomprehensible terror. They are without escape. He hides behind the building and waits and hopes and wills that it will end. Then the softest whimper, a faint gurgle. Nothing.

Twenty minutes later, a dishevelled middle-aged man with a dog-collar passes by. Vasu smells evil and wants to hurry back to the aircraft, yet knows he must enter the building with its high ceilings, and roof vents or else he will have nightmares that will derange him. He has to know. He speaks on his walkie-talkie to the pilot, explaining what he is about to do. The door is closed. A door handle hurriedly wiped. Chained and padlocked. He listens. No movement. Nothing. No sound. He is desperate to see what is inside, but knows that to stay there any longer would be to endanger himself.

Yet he pulls at the long chain and sees to his surprise and then horror that the padlock is not pressed in, as if whoever left in a hurry intended to return soon. Panic, a stultifying fear takes hold of him. Were he to enter and be observed, someone, seeing the door ajar, could easily padlock him inside, and his end would be swift. He opens the door and is met by a hot and putrid smell – that of burning, the burning of what? It is covered over somewhat with the smoke of incense. He leaves the door slightly ajar, and begins to take photographs in the dark with his flash. He walks in a little further. Two children are on the altar, uncovered, stilled. The door creaks open. He stands stupefied. A wave of wind, a shaft of sunlight pierces in and then a tall shadow.

It is the wind and the shadow of branches, but he knows that he must leave instantly. Yet he takes two more photographs – close ups. He rechains the padlock and moves a few metres away when the feeling that he is being watched becomes overpowering. He decides that it is better to be on the road, but has gone only a short distance before he feels a pistol being pressed into the small of his back.

"So you want to see what is in there? I can show you now, come with me. No one who enters leaves except the chosen few."

Vasu turns. Reverend Cannon staggers, startled by the sudden appearance of the face of the Grand Purple Mask. He is held, captured by its awesomeness and majesty. Vasu asks what is being planned for the coming rainy season, what will be planted. He says that is not his field and asks Vasu what he has seen. Everything was quiet, Vasu tells him, and thinks, God forgive me. He makes sure that Cannon sees that his walkie-talkie is on and tells him that his pilot is in a hurry, that he has another appointment, though he would so much have liked to speak with the Director. Vasu explains he is a travel writer, that this venture of a First World commune in a developing country, in the heart of an inaccessible tropical forest, attracted him as unique.

They walk to the aircraft and Vasu sees Cannon is confused, ill at ease. He knows he could have been shot there and then at close range. He sees Cannon looking at the tires of the small aircraft with his pistol in his hand. Vasu bids him good bye, but when Cannon stretches forth his hands, Vasu fears that his heavy hesitation, his instinctive reluctance to hold his hands, has given him away.

When they are about three thousand feet above the sprawling compound and rapidly leaving it, Vasu knows that he has escaped with his life but that he will have to leave Maya at once. He thinks of the photographs he has taken. Two girls, no more than ten, lying on their backs. Their hands clasped on barely formed breasts, held in place in death. Yet there was something about the heads, the palms, the small fingers – they were lifting, rising above the bodies. He wonders – were they praying or pleading? One thing is clear. They died looking up. What was above them?

"Thank goodness their eyes were closed," Vasu says to the pilot, telling him what he has seen.

"Why?" the pilot asks.

Vasu finds himself speaking in whispers. "What would those eyes mirror?"

"I'm not taking you back to the airport," the pilot says, "that will be too dangerous. Relax. It's over. Your part is done. Leave it to me now."

He brings the Islander down in the countryside among sugar-cane fields on a rough landing strip, which has the appearance of a long abandoned cricket pitch. A car is waiting, arranged by Maude Devonish. The plane takes off and disappears in the direction of Bon Aire. Vasu can't help thinking that, like Gavin, the pilot resembles the portrait of the youthful, even boyish, Robert Augustus that Aunt Maude has hanging on her wall.

*   *   *   *   *

Nurse Maude's window opens. Her torchlight flashes. It is clear that she has been worried sick. Standing before her, Vasu understands the joy of Lazarus' mother. She offers him food but he cannot eat. Then comes a barrage of questions: "What did you see? Whom did you meet? What did they ask you? Were they suspicious? What did you say? Did you find out what caused the broken limbs, the severe burns?"

Vasu describes his experiences. She, becoming more anxious, insists that in addition to the mask he should hand her the film, his jottings, diary and any written material on the politics of Maya for safe keeping.

"The Reverend Ernest Cannon," she says, "is Satan in human form. What does he look like? Has he appeared on our television?" But she sees that Vasu is tired, and says, "We shall decide what to do in the morning. You will have to leave Maya at once if he discovers that you took those photographs. If he suspects, he will take no chances, the security forces will be asked to make sure you are silenced."

Vasu begins to wonder whether tomorrow will be too late. He realises that he has no way of knowing whether there were hidden cameras on the walls or ceiling, whether he has been caught on film. He tells Nurse Maude that he will leave for London the following morning. This thought lulls him but his sleep is troubled. He sees himself in a wide open plain, chased by dogs, Land-Rovers and men wearing clerical collars and dark glasses. He wakes. When he reaches London he will alert journalists to the ignominy within Maya. But he is also thinking: " Aasha and I will marry and our lives together will strengthen us." He reminds himself that his photographs, notes and other writings are in safe keeping.

The President's men are waiting outside. They are expecting him to run for it, to leave the house, but when he doesn't, they wait for Nurse Maude to go out on one of her emergency calls. They close in. They are banking on finding the film; it would mean so many extra perks. They are sure it is still in the house. Though Vasu is saying nothing, they know that when they get him back to headquarters and do what is necessary, he will speak. A pity he is holding out. What a pity!

When she returns, Nurse Maude can see there has been a struggle, that he must have been dragged away, that they were searching for the camera and the film and then must have lost control when they found they were getting nowhere.

She phones Marguerite. A coded message. The security guards are listening.

39 A SCARECROW ON A STRING?

A small two-seater aircraft hums, circling the mighty Azon, whose chocolate coloured water stains the ocean far and wide, making it alive with feastings that lure the hunters of the deep. Men and women working in nearby fields look up. Something is dangling from the aircraft. Is this a stunt? Some advertisement? It is high in the sky – too high to catch the message. Will purple balloons stamped with the President's visage now float down to earth and sea?

The labouring men and women grow ill at ease. An inexplicable fear casts a shadow. They focus harder on what is hanging. It slowly takes form – not a diving hawk, though the head is down and two wing-like extensions reach out. Is it going to glide? A circus act? A trapeze in the sky?

"It is waving – signalling to us," someone offers.

"No. Something struggling in the air," another whispers.

It is brightly painted – red and gold – a Government aircraft. Ah! It is an announcement... No, some warning...

Whatever is dangling must have slipped, for it now hangs further below the aircraft. It looks like a scarecrow. Ahhh, what a relief! A scarecrow on a string! Yet though they cannot hear the droning of the mechanical fly, men and women working in the fields continue to focus on the sagging scarecrow. An emptiness penetrates them as if their stomachs too have left them. No stomach for heights. Peasants all. The strain on their stretched necks and eyes is telling.

The aircraft moves on. It circles the coastline, heading for the open ocean, yet still they stare after the slipping swaying form, as if they know that just as a scarecrow takes the place of man, a man can take the place of a scarecrow. No! No! It is, it is a puppet hanging, a scarecrow swaying, not live bait dangling above the ocean, between an eternity of blue above and below. A scarecrow cannot feel the terror of space without shelter. Can it? Will it disintegrate, its woven fibres weep? Or is something living to be dropped into the sharks' ocean or the piranhas' river and there be stripped of flesh, decay with fallen leaves, momentarily to change the colour of the flow?

At much the same time, not far from the prison wall in Bon Aire – the President's territory, where men and women marched and burned and carried placards and lost themselves for him – there is a mighty explosion. The peasants in the fields are too far away to hear this horrendous thing. A car is ripped apart and its mangled metal body is splattered with a softer matter once called man. A man named Gavin. The street will be cleaned, washed over. It has become a habit now in Maya to look and not perceive, to hear and fail to understand.

High above, a serrated blade is brought to the taut rope. The blade is pressed, it saws across the fibres of a plant, which offers its own resistance, struggling to keep its integrity intact. Yet, under this serrated steel it cannot hold forever. But wait, a telephone calls to the aircraft – an exchange of words – the sawing hand halts, the rope is hauled back slowly, carefully, its weight dangling precariously, for much of its weave has been severed.

The aircraft returns to base with three on board – the pilot, his assistant who sawed, and their scarecrow passenger – Vasu Nath.

Something has happened to stay his fall. What could it be? Look! Something strange has come upon him. It has no voice, it offers no name. It is invisible, yet is felt by the President's men. It shows itself through Vasu Nath's eyes. What does he see?

A quiet soft whimpering heaves his frame and leaves. It is a sound akin to what he heard on the altar, deep in the hinterland. His eyes close. Something as delicate, as compressed as thought has left him as he sleeps. In its place, lie paths broken, disconnected, that lead nowhere. From his fractured self, much has gone. When he awakes, what will have remained? Who will he be?

40   SUBAH'S TALE: THE FIRST WORLD
AND THE CONTRACT

People returning from America to look after their abandoned
houses and yards would say, "Place bleak, Subah. The whole
place sleeping. Nothing to do here. Place dull, dull. Roads bad, no
proper conveniences at the old stelling, same old dirty ferry. Low
water pressure and water na change, still brown, brown, Subah.
Street lights? Even on the one main road, tell me na, you have any?
Countryside na change one bit. My grand aggie woulda recognise
the place good, Subah, if only she coulda bring sheself to raise
sheself from the dead."

I understand. I know what they're saying. But what they should
understand is that nobody is here who could do better. But I'm
wondering if my way of seeing the place has changed when I find
that in my letters to my daughter I am writing, "Veena, you don't
know how dull this place now is." She writes back, "Ma, it was
always dull." That is the voice of young modern people living in
those First World countries. That is the reason I am thankful that
a man like this President is in power in Maya now and not when
I'm old. My only regret is that he didn't come when I had just left
school. Then I would have emigrated earlier. It was easier then too.
Just in case people think I'm going round the bend, I'll explain later.

What my daughter is saying is not true. Dullness has to do with
what you want to do – and there are a lot of things worse than
dullness. My mother-in-law is a good example. She was everything
I disliked about my culture. Veena tells me that her aggie was a
victim of her culture. Well, Veena can think like that because she
was not on the receiving end of her aggie's tongue.

The truth is, this culture I was brought up in survives only
because of the daily sacrifices we women make to sustain it. Yet

I have to agree with Veena that this is a culture that consumes its women. Wears them out. Grinds them to the ground. Daughters-in-law are household slaves. Wives and daughters too. If the home is poor, they must help to provide the daily bread, go out of the home to earn it, and then come home and prepare it. We women must spin straw into gold every day of our lives.

Prepare is a nice word. It is what a modern well-to-do woman in the First World does when she comes home from work. She opens the freezer, she opens and closes the microwave oven. She has a shower, pours a drink for herself and her husband, and then the lady of the house says, "Sugar Plum, dinner is ready". That is called preparing the dinner. (Veena says that Sugar Plum is old fashioned, and is the name of a fairy.) That may be so, but I saw this on American television where I got the gist of modern cooking. I like it.

I am not going to stay in the life of grinding massala, toting water, chulha smoke in meh eyes, having a row of homemade pepper sauce and achar and kutchla curing nicely in the sun for a week, because I agree with Veena, all this has to do with the low cost and low regard for female labour in Maya. Today, anyone in London can buy a nice tandoori chicken and naan and curried vegetables and pepper sauce, just like a modern woman should.

But you see it does not end there. Whoever made these culture rules were big-time planners. They included the future – I mean life after death – the spiritual world. Trust men to make arrangements like these for themselves. I will tell you how it works. Before the deities are called, it is the women who prepare the altars, with flowers and sindhoor, camphor and pitch pine for the sacred fire, and garlands of marigold, creating a place of prayer fit for the Gods. But on the arrival of the Divine Ones, the ladies retreat, and their fathers and brothers and husbands come to the fore with the pandit to welcome the Gods, to honour them, to form a contract with them. One of the women in the village, who is a trader, tells me that in Santa Maria the customs are moving with the times – *panditas* and women themselves inviting the Gods to solemnise their requests and wishes. They are having a direct one-to-one meeting with the Gods. I am glad women are waking up.

Now, I said before I am thankful that the President put enough pressure on Country Mayans so that we all had to try and make arrangements to leave this place and modernise ourselves. Some people will think I'm not making sense. Let me explain. All over the world, town and city people have been emigrating as far back as you can remember. In this Maritime Region, history books tell you people have been emigrating to America as far back as the seventeenth century. My headmaster said that for the Region's poor people, it started in a big way with the building of the Panama canal.

But we Country Mayans went nowhere near the Panama canal. We remained here. We bent our heads, true peasants, letting the land hold us. We engaged in a relentless struggle with this polder land. It was like those long-time marriages. Through thick and thin we worked on the land.

All over the world, you will find, it is people from towns and cities and not those from rural areas who are the first to leave their homes in bad times, for where there is land, the country folks would grow food, they would not starve. But here in Maya, after Devonish came into power, Country Mayans were the first to leave. They left after the massacre in Ica. They left in droves after Hope Bridge and with choke and rob, murders, the Purple Masks on the streets and in your house after kicking down your front door. Then Government came in again to attack from another angle when they killed the rice industry. Well, the entire community in the countryside became families on the move.

Later when unemployment did begin to zoom, those Country Mayans – who would have liked to leave with the others but couldn't – were not spilling onto the streets of Bon Aire. Our able-bodied men knew that getting a living in the army or the police force was not meant for them. Unemployment in the countryside? You couldn't see it, because it did not, could not, confront the Government. It was hidden by the leaves and stems of sugar-cane, breadfruit trees and vegetable plots. So the men settled in the bottom-houses gaffing over what opportunities were open to them. Many had a go with the contraband trade, knowing full well all the problems of bribing the coastguards, the customs officer, the police and then facing up to them same fellas blackmailing them so they could squeeze the traders more. Life was a living hell for them. I wouldn't be surprised if some of them got heart failure or high blood pressure and went early.

The better-off people in the countryside didn't have it easy
either. Nowhere else in the Region did such a large proportion of
the middle-age rural people abandon fertile land, their houses
and goods in so short a time. Their older folks were left behind,
until they were able to reach out for them. Once families understood the immigration 'ropes', there was no holding back. Entire
families left with their grandparents.

Veena writes, "In times like these, Ma, you must look for the
silver lining, or else you will go mad. What is important, Ma, is that
in this upheaval of the countryside, an introspective, conservative
people were able to re-orient themselves, cut themselves free from
the land, which had held them for generations. They soon realised,
Ma, that they didn't have to own a piece of land to feel secure, and
that the key to their security they had with them, since they were
willing to put their hands to anything, and save and strive and
think and plan, and learn new skills. So in a way, Ma, they
rediscovered themselves. They found that they had what it takes
to be enterprising anywhere, despite bitterly cold winters and
the depressing anonymity of large cities of strangers. Ma, give
them time. They will make a few friends among the strangers,
who will find their culture not threatening, as Robert Augustus
did, but a new experience."

Well, that is youth speaking. I am not so sure. Even I like to
walk on a piece of land that I can call my own. It's hard to have to
leave these open spaces, this green landscape, for some harsh,
aggressive, run-down place to begin with, to make a fresh start,
when you don't even know where the bus stop is, which side the bus
running, what the fare is. When I leave here, who knows what
feelings I will leave behind and what new ones I will hold when I've
lived over there a while.

You see what I like about what Veena calls modern culture,
(and I can hardly wait to sample it) is that there is no place for my
kind of mother-in-law. Everybody there has to pull their weight.
You better be useful, find a job, learn something, get trained. "You
have to be informed," Veena says. My mother-in-law wouldn't
have liked it at all. She was quite happy having me working from
six in the morning to nine at night, and at the end of the day I'm
still feeling as if I am nothing because of her attitude towards me.

When I get up there, in the First World, I intend to waste no time, since I am already starting late. I'm going to take a course in interior designing, get a fashionable cut. I am not only speaking of my hair, I mean my clothes too. In time, I will buy myself a car and then I'm in business. First World culture tells the man and the woman the same thing. Get trained, find a good job, be a somebody. Don't give your life away for nothing. I like that kind of culture, so when I get up there and anybody ask me what my culture is, I shall tell them, "Whatever you see me doing is my culture. I am living my culture, my dear."

Now don't get me wrong. I don't intend to throw away the nice things about my culture like the food and Divali, the bhajans and the classical dances and the close family life. Saving and building. And all the warmth of family gatherings at weddings, with the laughter at cooking and eating and dressing-up times and the talk of funny incidents in the past and sad ones too. And when you see all the clever designs in silk, and the fine filigree work in the jewellery, it makes you think of the craftsmen of old whose names we shall never know, but who give us so much pleasure.

I like meeting together in clean orderly family homes, to listen to good music with tabla and sitar or to hear again tales from the *Mahabharata* and the *Ramayana*. And when my day comes to leave this earth, I want to be cremated with ghee and garlands and incense while Sanskrit chants are sung, knowing that these chants are older than Christ and Columbus. I still remember my grandfather singing these chants while he rocked me in a jute-bag hammock. And as I have no son, I know Veena and my grandchildren will light the pyre, their heads held high, for the time has come for women to light the fires.

Come to think of it, I also like the way this old culture tries to protect us from our worst natures. I value our customs, like wearing your ornhi, covering your head properly in the presence of older people and strangers; like knowing how to behave with members of your extended family. Having fathers-in-law and daughters-in-law keep a respectable distance, and brothers-in-law and sisters-in-law honouring the same courtesies. I like the way the very words we use to address each other have been carefully laid down. All this makes good sense. They help prevent improper attachments and remind us of the dishonour of trespassing. For me, this is a culture offering fire-fighting equipment to help us to cope with the flare-up of rapidly spreading fires of passion. This ancient culture has arisen from generations of observation and experience. So I am going to keep my head and pick and choose my cultural attachments, as well as my accessories.

I shall never again take on a whole package, be it a package of songs, dance, music or religion. I want to be able to say, I don't like that dance in this package, but I like that dance from this other package. In Veena's last letter she has a p.s. "Ma," she writes, "when things are in a package they are tied together. It is like being on a package tour, you can't tell the tour director that you don't want to go to a particular place because it's boring, that you really had something else in mind, and that you had only taken the tour because you thought he would see reason and take the more interesting way. Ma, you are still not thinking First World. You have to be streamlined. Ma, you must really try. We worry about you."

My mother-in-law put me off packages for life. She was part of the package when I got married. Let me explain. To begin, I have never heard her say thank you, nor laugh heartily. Glum and dull she was to the very end. From morning till night she sang the same acid tune. It would go like this: "Look how you clean that garlic, look na, come see for yourself, small-small skin left. You go give people that to eat? Where you come from, gal?" I can tell you what really killed my father-in-law. The doctor said it was diabetes, but I know better. If she saw me reading the newspaper, I would hear, "Me na know how to sit down. Me na know how to waste time. Some people know good-good how to waste the whole day." Well I refuse to stop reading the newspaper. After all, my ma and pa did not ask me to mind cows or plant rice. I would only have to sell in the shop after I had done my homework. And I went right up to seventh standard, the only girl in my village to do that. When I look at the education I had up to seventh standard in colonial days and compare it with what students leave with today at the end of their secondary schooling, all I can say is, that the comparison is an embarrassment to the meaning of independence.

I had intended to teach, take examinations every year and work myself up, but then my father-in-law came and asked for me. My

mother said it was a respectable family and that Ajit was a good
boy. The mother is not nice. But the father is a good man. A quiet
man with good ways, a real brahmin. "Subah," she said to me, "you
must not expect to get everything in life just as you like." That is
certainly not First World thinking, but my mother, poor woman,
God bless her, only knew this old world. She told me if I married
Ajit we didn't have to live with the mother for long. "Don't you feel
good," she said, "they come and ask for you, and you a girl? Subah,
you have to look at all these things. It is better for you to be in a
house where the father-in-law come and ask for you, than your Pa
having to go and ask. And you know well, that after you pass a
certain age, your Pa and I will have enough trouble, so please,
Subah, try and see this thing with the eyes of a mother."

I said nothing and then she started again:

"I hope you not going to be like some of these puffed up young
people, Subah, who don't know when they have something they
should hold on to. Teaching is good. But in the long run, Subah, is
better for you to have your own family. Then everybody respects you.
When you single, every man – young, old and in between – think
they don't have anything to lose if they behave like a ram goat,
thinking there is no husband to answer to, na?" That was my mother,
she had a way of coming to the raw edge of things if she thought it
would help her case. I secretly admired her and felt that if she had
the opportunity, she would have made a champion lawyer – the way
she would have removed fluff from her opponents' arguments.

Well, I got married and Ajit and I lived with his parents. My
father-in-law was the kindest, gentlest man you could meet, but
with my mother-in-law I had two years of "The rice not picked
good. Wash the bhajee one more time." And that was after three
thorough washes, not counting the first wash when I had cut off the
roots and allowed the sand and grit to leave. The only thing that
saved me was my ma kept saying, "Always remember, Subah, she
is Ajit's mother; and is not for a lifetime."

You see, nothing in life is straightforward. Since I met Tara (she
tells me she is now a Mayan American), I know I must carefully
examine First World culture when it comes in a nice package. I
will open that package too and pick and choose. I don't agree with

Veena. She thinks that way because she is already part of the modern culture. She tells me everything over there keeps to a certain size, colour, weight, shape – tomatoes, potatoes, cabbages, cauliflowers, and all the rest. So I figure out that if they take all that trouble to keep common foods in line, people must be keeping more important things like their thoughts and feelings in line too – acceptable to the consumer, as Veena would say. I will say this for my daughter, she is trying her best with me and I am learning fast. Her letters inform me. They are lessons on the modern way.

So I'm intending to equip myself, though I don't want to become quite like Tara, Veena's class mate. That young woman is something else. You can say she came here to sell America. She knows people here desperate; sheer desperation is forcing them to break up their homes for an American Green Card. Cut off from everything that holds you back from qualifying for a Green Card was Tara message. God help us! When I think about this I change my mind about saying Devonish should have come on stage earlier. I am ashamed of thinking it. This struggle to get a Green Card is making us lose ourselves here in Maya. Tara had become an aggressive Mayan American. I observed her when she came to our village and tried to put Anil's mind at ease about going to America. She was doing the exact opposite and did not know it. How come she can forget how she once thought and felt? There must have been a time when she was in our world and thought as we. But listening to her and the 'hifalutin way' she expresses herself, you would never think so.

Over here, as I said, Mayan people so desperate they willing to consider any step to get out of this hole. Husband and wife divorce each other so that one of them can marry an American citizen to get a Green Card. Later, the one who gets a Green Card, he or she divorces the American and sends for the former partner. That is how it is meant to work; but can you imagine the heartaches, the loss of trust, the exposure of yourself to whatever ugly comes from this arrangement? This is the hell that many live in, but they keep it closed to the light of day. What was sad is that Tara was now so sure that her way was the only way to go. She lost the feelings she once had for other people's way to move. I was there when she met Anil and his family, to formalise things. His wife Carmen wanted me to be there – a neighbourly request. They were thinking of doing something that went against everything sacred to their understanding of marriage and family. "What would Agni think?" Carmen ask. She was troubled by what the Gods would think, especially Agni as the first of the Gods to be invited to witness the wedding ceremony. "To invite Agni, Aunty, and ask him to be present at our wedding and then make a fool of him, by pulling apart what he had joined, for a Green Card? Only a mad person would do that, Aunty. I can't even think of how Brahma, Vishnu and Shiva would look at a thing like this. You know, Aunty, I'm sick with worry. I can't sit through it. So you must be with Anil when Tara comes. She doesn't understand us, and I might say something to upset her. Then we will have to start all over again with somebody else. At least you and Veena know her, and I am saying to myself if I have a problem I will ask you and Veena to speak to her. "If it was not for the child, I could manage to stay here," she tells me, "but look at the schools... And you see we have to think like them, be like them to get a job. You have to forget your culture. Anil wants to be in a different place to bring up his son, a free place, in a country that is not telling you how to dance, or that you have to dance when they clap. This place is not for us. They want it for themselves. Let them keep it. We only want to leave quietly, but we don't know what will happen at the airport. There is all that body searching, and they asking for some official paper or other they don't ask their own people for. We will leave the house and the land. It is hard to leave all your savings behind. But what to do, Aunty? We have to give our son a better chance."

So, I was there when Tara spoke with Anil.

"A contract– that's all it is," Tara said to Anil. "I will sign. You will sign. A business proposition – pure and simple. No need for me to meet your wife and child. I prefer it that way. Remember it is just another contract." Anil said nothing. He asked to be excused and went to the kitchen. He needed an aspirin.

Tara turned to me. "Veena's Ma, I will speak to you candidly because you will understand. Complications, complications! You offer something straightforward to a Third World person, and they lose it, weighing it down with a cart-load of irrelevancies. Their inexperience and their own excess cultural baggage weigh them

down. See how they totter across the airport floors, how they heave
and lift their burdens, wiping their brows. I often wonder how they
don't collapse altogether. Now look at a First World person.
Streamlined, nothing surplus, keeping it simple, smooth, clean cut,
no friction. They are like the nose of an aircraft; they have
designed themselves for currents and turbulences. But Veena's
Ma, these people here are not attuned to modern living. As for
modern thinking, God help them. Some of them still blowing their
sank, ringing their bells and striking their gongs during their pujas
as if they are living here in Maya, in the open, and not in a block of
flats. Now I ask you, what are they thinking when they do this?
Bhagwan? They're not thinking of their next door neighbour, nor of
the implications for the rest of us. I'm telling you this, Veena's Ma,
I would not be at all surprised if very soon landlords will insist that
we sign an agreement that says, *And there shall be no blowing of
conch shells, ringing of bells nor striking of gongs to call the gods,
even when the tenant feels threatened, persecuted or lost. The
landlord advises a silent prayer in such emergencies.*"

Well! well! Wasn't I relieved when Anil returned. He looked
solemn. He must have been having second thoughts. But all this
escaped bold-face Miss America. She turned to him in that selfsame brass-neck way. I was beginning to feel sorry for him and if
Carmen had not explained their need, I would have tried to bring
it all to a quiet close. I could see that Anil was no match for her and
I'm ashamed to say that I wanted to put a spoke in her wheel. She
began again. "I'm helping you to move with the times. You're so
old-fashioned," and laughed. I felt she was on the verge of saying,
"And for a young man too." But his serious expression curbed her.

"In America, people choose a target and go for it, Anil. So you'll
have to change your thinking when you get there, otherwise...." she
lifted her shoulder to complete her statement. "Anyway, over
there, you'll have to make decisions on the spot, on your own." She
smiled again, encouragingly. "You wouldn't have your family
there to hold you back with this and that. All I'm saying is, why not
get in line now? I'm giving you the opportunity to unclasp that
baggage from your back, straighten yourself, and walk light, man,
walk light. Think about it and let me know. I'm giving you first
preference. I'll be honest. I like you, I want to help you. I don't like

saying this but you yourself must know there are a lot of people here who want to leave and would offer me anything, I mean anything. They're desperate. I told you what my expenses are and what the contract will cost you. It will remain so, no matter what I'm offered elsewhere. I give you my word. I have my reputation to think of."

Anil took up Tara's offer. Afterwards I felt confused, wondering what my mother would have made of this, or even of my sitting there witnessing this unholy transaction. Survival, that's what it was all about. But what won't we do for it, I began to wonder.

41   THE GLASS FACTORY

The purple-masked ladies of the Women's Socialist Movement
had come to the end of their monthly meeting. "Glass, comrades,"
Madam Chairperson said, "as we well know, permits light to enter.
The construction of this factory is symbolic; it marks a turning
point for us." As an arm of the Government these women saw it as
their role to encourage the people to hold strain while the Government turned things around. They did this by adding polish to good
news whenever they faced the public media and by reducing the
pain of the bad. "A glass factory also means sparkle and refine-
ment. Let us not forget that," another said.

This was the kind of technological advance that Mayans,
accustomed to putting their main export in jute bags, had been
seeking from the development process. With independence they
thought local manufacturers would be converting the country's
raw materials into locally made goods. Much time had passed and
this hope had not yet been realised.

The committee members of the WSM would not have dreamt of
being critical of the Government, but their suppressed disappointments found expression in their excitement over having a glass
factory in the midst of so much unemployment and the ever
deepening depression.

It was suggested at the WSM meeting that a glass factory had
other advantageous features not initially envisaged. It could,
unlike, say, a cassava flour mill, become a tourist attraction.

"A glass factory," Madam Chairperson explained, "is our way
of saying to tourists that we are becoming industrialised." Smiles
came to their faces. These well meaning ladies felt there was
something about the word industrialised that had intimate connec-

tions with the industrious, the diligent – dynamic modern economies. "Think, comrades, what a glass factory will do to enhance
our image." It was a voice rolling out a carpet of warm hope.

"Yes," said a young woman, "I'm all for it. There's something
clean about glass; you can see any speck on it. We all like to know
what we're drinking.' She laughed. "It will be good for us to have it."

"I don't mean to interrupt," said a matronly lady, "but this
draws me to compare it with what today is called the tourist
industry, so common in other islands of the archipelago. There are
industries and industries. Glass is certainly preferable."

"I will admit I have been partial to glass for as long as I can
remember. I preferred it to enamel even as a child."

"I give it my blessing. Anything that brings work to the young
people," an old, tired-looking woman said. "If this factory can
teach them some worthwhile skill, God be praised, for He knows
how badly we are in need of jobs."

The matronly lady stood up again. She smoothed her sleeves:
"I'm for this glass factory for all the reasons comrades expressed,
but I go further and say, comrades, it must succeed because what
is the alternative staring us in the face? We have to tread
cautiously when it comes to the hotel industry. From what I have
heard, that industry is running full speed ahead, to Sodom and
Gomorrah. Believe me, comrades, we don't want that kind of thing
here. Poor but decent, we prefer to remain to our dying day. That
is the way we were brought up. I know I'm speaking for all my
sisters here. I know for a fact," she continued, "that in those so-
called prosperous small islands, where there is nothing to speak
of but tourism, white women lie naked... and ... they have a
masseur, a local mind you." She lowered her voice and bent her
head, reluctant to say any more. "That is not all they offer,
comrades. No courtesy is paid to decency, and in all the hotel
bedrooms, I am sorry to have to mention this, but you will find
written large: 'Room service provided'. Now I tell you, comrades,
I didn't know where to look when I read this. All I can say is that this
government should be highly commended for moving a long way
from what is ugly and common, to crafting crystals. I myself can't
wait to visit the place. Maybe Madam Chairperson might use her
good offices to glean a few passes for us – committee members."

Everyone turned to the Chair with an air of expectancy.

Madam Chairperson spoke: "Rachael, you do not understand what is on offer on the room tariffs. What is meant..."

"I thank God for that."

"Let me explain."

"Sorry to interrupt the Chair, but I would rather not know. I am a God-fearing Christian woman and have been so for as long as I can remember, and with the grace of Our Lord I wish to keep it so."

After the meeting much was explained to Rachael. She, though, remained convinced that whereas others might be hoodwinked into accepting the official and conventional explanations for things, she knew better, for she understood human nature only too well... It could not be trusted.

*   *   *   *   *

The site for the glass factory was well chosen. Twenty-five acres were set aside to take into account future expansion and parking – to accommodate tourist buses. It was close to the highway, close to the airport and close to the main ingredient – white sand, rising in vast hills. It was on the basis of identifying this rich resource that sheets of translucent purple prose were printed to seduce overseas grants for the glass factory project. All seemed well.

*   *   *   *   *

On the day the factory's foundation stone was due to be laid, the police band practised two national anthems. A young recruit, unschooled in national sophistication asked his older companion, "Which anthem first, sir, theirs or ours?"

"Listen, son. Until you become rich and developed, and we don't know when that will be, you're not going to have many occasions to put yourself first. The few you have, use them with dignity."

The television crew did a superb job. Viewers were treated to pleasing images of seated dignitaries, gleaming white table cloths, neatly arranged posies, representatives of the Women's Socialist Movement with grand hats and flamboyant headdresses, the local school choir and the police band. They heard their President say, "The future is here and we are all part of it. On behalf of the Government and people of Maya, I wish to thank the donors who know a good investment when they see one, and chose this Mayan investment instead of hundreds of others that come before them daily. Comrades, I ask you to join me in applauding our friends on their choice. We thank you and hope that you will convey our appreciation when you return overseas. There are people, many of them Mayans, who are good at talking about development, but when it comes to investing their own money, in their own future, they send it abroad and place it in foreign banks. It is a sad day when men and women from overseas show more faith and confidence in ourselves than we do. This is one of the consequences of slavery and our historical loss of self-esteem. I have never been one for forcing people to do what they don't want to do, but I can tell you now that what is produced here will be as good as anything from abroad, and cheaper. So it will be in everybody's interest to buy local. We must make the effort to help ourselves and not be dependent on foreign governments. I know that our donors would join me in advocating self-help. Comrades, distinguished guests, nothing less than a standing ovation for our donors."

The camera focused on a mahogany sapling. We saw the President being helped to plant it. He no longer made the effort to smile. My brother was tired, had grown old and worn, his voice weak. This was his shortest speech ever. It was some time after this that Mayans learnt of the planned operation on their President's vocal chords. He would be having it done at Bon Aire Public Hospital.

The following day the newspaper was filled with photographs of the sapling and the President under the headline: "The future is here". Readers learnt that the plant was designed to turn out bottles of various sizes and designs and wares such as glasses, dishes, ashtrays and sheet glass of various thicknesses and size. Crystals were not mentioned. But many hung onto the words 'various sizes and designs' and found comfort.

Nothing was ever heard again of the glass factory. Nothing appeared in *The Carrier*.

A few years later, on my way from Aunt Maude's, I happened to be in the area. A fungus was vigorously attacking the factory walls. The grounds had been taken over by guinea grass and farmers tethered cows there. I made discreet enquiries and learnt that from the beginning it had been a nonstarter. Had the Government done its homework, they would have discovered that the making of glass requires a continuous supply of electricity. Once the process had begun, any power failure would ruin the glass. With the frequency of blackouts, this became a major problem. Two stand-by generators were added. At this stage, not including the substantial funds from the donors, the glass factory had already cost *Mayan tax payers* six million United States dollars. Were you to consider that the exchange rate at the time was one hundred and twenty Mayan dollars, and rising, to one United States dollar, then the magnitude of the waste for so poor a country becomes a national tragedy.

It was also discovered that there was no market for the sheet glass the factory was designed to produce, because of the high cost of its production. Then Mayans were told that there was going to be a section of the plant to produce bottles. I learnt that this section was too small to meet local demand, and it could not be enlarged because of the design of the plant.

Ministers left Maya in search of more foreign capital. Ministers returned empty handed from overseas. The ruling Party began to put it about that foreigners were preventing Maya from becoming industrialised, that they had all along wanted to keep industrialisation for themselves. It was the tune Robert Augustus and his Party had sung for decades, and though they themselves were now weary of it, their supporters were left to sing the chorus. Our AUL were silent, though from time to time they hummed the tune in the comfort of their enclaves.

42   A CHANGED CIRCUMSTANCE

Aasha is aware that another life has begun within her. What would have brought her and Vasu immense joy within marriage, what she would have gladly announced to the staff of the school where she taught, and would have brought congratulations and well wishes, now threatens discredit and shame. In this regard, the culture of the Hinduism of her upbringing and the Roman Catholicism of her work place are one.

Mother Superior has reminded the staff that in matters of religion – which of course covered moral codes – the Church alone has the authority to prescribe what *was morally right*. Christians, naturally, had no choice but to follow the guidance and teachings of the Church. But she has also made it clear that she expects non-Christians on the staff to conduct themselves in an exemplary manner.

Aasha needs to talk to someone, but the thought of making this intimate confession to Vasu's brother, Arun, pains her. Arun is quiet and gentle, he listens to your whispers, attentive to your asides and gestures. He would say nothing unless asked. With him you talk as if with your inner self. Yet it is Arun she fears to approach, for to lose his regard would devastate her. From his manner towards her, she knows he holds her in high esteem. This she dares not lose.

She walks alone. Where is a listening ear in this country of clones, amongst a staff of clones who are certain about *what is morally right*? In her dreams, she bars the voices hammering at her front door, and when she will not let them in, their mouths enter through her letter box:

"Unfit to teach."

"Resign."

"In the name of virtue and duty, do the decent thing."

"Underminer of the teachings of parents, the school, the Church and God."

"You have obligations when you live amongst people of God."

"What manner of woman brings shame to her name, her house, and her family?"

Her dreams are nightmares, her days a torment.

*   *   *   *   *

But there is one, whom she had not at first considered, who brings her comfort.

"Let us think," Marguerite says. "You're neatly sandwiched between the codes of your upbringing and those of your work place. Let us extricate ourselves from these two millstones. Listen, Aasha, at this very early stage, call it an impregnation. This name will move you to a place where you can think clearly and not go under. The word 'child' is too heavy to carry."

This was Marguerite, ever practical, moving through the moral standpoints like a trained veteran in a mine field, with the sensitivity of a leaf and the eyes of an eagle. She would not be weighed down by the perceptions of others. Aasha embraced her and gathered herself.

Then Marguerite said: "Let Vasu's example save you. He always argued that reason has obligations to clarity. An impregnation and not a child. What should you do? Give yourself time to be at ease, to think at ease... Talk to Subah. Choose a time when Arun is not at home. Whatever you decide, I stand by you."

The following day Aasha does as Marguerite suggested. As she approaches the family house, the excitement it once had for her has gone. Vasu will not be there. He now stays with Subah's cousin in the heart of the polders. The kindness and simplicity of these country people make his life working the land as peaceful and contented as it can be.

*   *   *   *

The consultant had said, "There is a saving grace, Arun, though you may not consider it so. Your brother Vasu is not in pain. He sleeps, the sleep of a babe. He remembers nothing; his mind, if you can still call it by that name, is totally blank. His sense of his past disintegrated under the torment. So his stored knowledge, his former understanding of the world, is lost to him and to you. As a consequence each act he performs is just that – an act completed. No storage. No recall. Of course, he need not remain like this. A reconnecting could take place. I would not rule it out completely. On the other hand, it may never happen. We have no way of knowing, but to be honest, his chances do not look bright." To Aasha he had said, "One thing, however, you must not do. I understand you were engaged to be married. I am sorry. This must be devastating for you. What is required of you is not going to be easy. You need to be strong for what I'm about to say. You should not present yourself to him as his fiancée, thinking that your presence will trigger something. It will not happen like that. It will happen gradually, if it does at all – an imperceptible transforma-tion of a complex structure, programmed for survival, searching, adjusting, putting itself together again, responsive only to its own inner rhythms. You will only confuse him and torment yourself if you try to get him to recall who you are. You are likely to make him feel uncomfortable, inadequate. Would you shake a cracked crystal to make it whole? He would be puzzled, vulnerable. He would not understand what you were saying. He would not be able to cope with that. You would do the best for him, Aasha, by leaving him in the countryside to embrace a natural, simple routine on the land. We are unable to help him. I am truly sorry. "

*   *   *   *

Subah radiates a wholesome warmth of welcome. She is warm-ing gulab jamun and the mingling aroma of ghee and cardamom syrup is pleasurable and comforting. Aasha feels she has found an oasis in the desert as Subah listens attentively, slowly stirring the syrup.

She hands Aasha a cold glass of water and says, "You were both already married in thought, Aasha. Your spirits had long em-braced. There was no spiritual obstruction to your union. It brings pain to no one. I am convinced that the Gods would have favoured such a meeting, given it their blessing. As you told me, Shiva was there on the night of your dance offering. It is so easy to be judgmental. And some of us old folks have forgotten what it is to be young.

"Aasha, we think of a marriage ceremony as a public affair, an announcement we make before friends and family. The ceremony is in part a courtesy you pay your guests – informing them. It offers you an opportunity to make the day a delight for them – by sharing in your happiness. And, of course, you invite the Gods, too, and ask their blessings. But Aasha, that is only tradition. There is another way: You and Vasu could wear garlands of sweet marigold, hold hands in the privacy of a room and turn to the East and say, 'We, Vasu and Aasha, have decided to come together as husband and wife and we ask the blessings of Bramha, Vishnu and Mahadeo.' In essence that is what marriage is. I am referring to spiritual marriage. After that you legalise the declaration... That is all a marriage certificate is – a legal document of an agreement. The ceremony is only to inform family and friends. Maybe you could simply pay a drummer to go around the village and make the announcement.

"I will be honest with you, I am happy that a child of Vasu will live. Let Arun give this union legitimacy. He will. I know he will, if you ask. I could prepare him if you like. But if you don't want me to do anything, I shall fill him with gulab jamun and his favourite dhal puri, bhunjal mutton and steam-fried beans with tomatoes. That should put him in a down-to-earth, agreeing mood." She winks. "Good garam masala.... You know he is as handsome as Vasu when he smiles. He has the eyes of a traveller. He is so aware of what is around him, he may suspect something in the air before he eats. When he sees what I'm offering him, he will say, 'Subah, you are celebrating today, have I forgotten something?'

"You must be wondering where I got the cardamom pods, na? We get everything from across the river. I barter my fresh vegetables with the traders and I store these things next door at Nurse Maude, just in case the police come to search.

"You should speak to Arun early. He is leaving Maya. He has been offered a good job in London. Time you don't have, Aasha. You have to be practical. You have to be more like Marguerite.

Here take some gulab jamun for her. I can hear her blessing me for sending them."

Before she leaves, Aasha asks Subah to let Arun know she would like to see him, to mention that she has a problem she wishes to talk over, the nature of which she can hint at, but not disclose. But how is she to put all this to Arun, a man who stands like a judge and walks and looks the part, save for his warm traveller's eyes, distinct; removed from the immediate – yet there.

PART FOUR: A NEW PATH

43   A REQUEST

There is something about her womanliness that Arun has long found alluring. This is now heightened by her request to see him, and on their meeting, by her suggestion of a walk in the open, beneath the sky. A mix of feelings flows through her — pride, dignity woven with threads of mourning — grief glistening through her eyes. Her lips and neck and eyes, meant to be cupped by another's warmth, speak of loss. Vasu was blessed, he thought, and if just a chink of his memory had remained, it would have exploded to expand itself to receive her. He is sure of this as he stands beside her.

They walk to a nearby rice field — tender shoots beginning the growth of an abundance which will one day offer nourishing warmth. His eyes rest on her full breasts, keeping time with her heart's beat like the rise and fall of leaves in a cradling wind.

"I am here to ask something," she says. "It is a large request. The path to this is painful. I wish there was another way, but Vasu is now beyond my reach. I ask for myself and for the life within me. Legitimacy requires me to have a husband, and the child to come a father. I ask this."

They are in a highway of cicadas and have to wait for their passing. Though he faces her, he does not look at her, but speaks as in a dream: "I am pleased, as a brother, that you carry within you a part of Vasu. I am sorry, for your sakes, that the hopes and joys you both embraced cannot come to pass. I am honoured that you should think of me when your spirit grieves. I am willing. And to put your mind at peace, the earlier this marriage takes place, the better for you and the child."

He pauses, considering how best to put so delicate a matter before a woman mired in sorrow. He does not know how to speak to women, yet knows that her thoughts will touch on this and that, and will have misgivings, perhaps even regret, and so wishing her to have a permanent peace, he says, "It goes without saying that there will be no marriage bed." He pauses, but she thinks he has nothing more to say and feels a relief like the splash of cold water on burning skin.

"Thank you." It is all she feels is appropriate.

"That is," he continues, "unless another time comes and brings with it other feelings and desires. Such a time may not flow our way, nor will I at any time force it upon you. I understand that feelings of duty or obligation towards me, because of our circumstance, may never be replaced by a yearning for a oneness of being. If our marriage bed comes, it must come from what is beyond duty. I wish it so." He looks away.

He must have read her inner thoughts, that flicker of eyelash, that change of focus, for he continues, "If desire does not stir, you will be free to separate yourself after the child grows to a height that pleases you."

Her eyes express gratitude and warmth for a man who says little and understands much.

When she arrives home, all manner of feelings surge through her. A deep sorrow for Vasu and herself, and gratitude for Arun's magnanimity; his understanding that her emotions will be in mourning for sometime to come. Even so, a passing thought knocks at her door and asks what may be the effects of day-to-day close contact on her presently cordoned affection for Arun. Could duty ever animate itself into desire? How can she know? Then sensing in the question an intimation that her affection for Vasu might with time wane, she replies with womanly pride at this insolence, *Surely, wouldn't that depend on the quality of the affection and the vessel that contains it? Ah, there is an invisible sorcerer*, replies the questioner, *that enables desire to grow from the closeness of certain attributes inherent to being. And what are these?* she asks. *The passing of time together, sunshine and laughter, good food and healthy bodies, music, scents, and a Brahma-like imagination. Too many requirements... What is the matter with you? Have you never loved in a way that so stirred the earth that it stumbled in its path?*

Later she had said to Arun: "On our wedding day, I would like Vasu to perform *Taag*-Paath or *Raksha Sutra*." (This ritual involved the garlanding of the bride by the bridegroom's brother, signifying that he would protect his sister-in-law wherever and whenever circumstance demanded.)

"You do understand, Aasha, that Vasu will not recognise me as his brother nor..."

"Nor me. I know this. I understand this, Arun. But his physical presence is all he has – all he can offer on that day. Let him stand beside us. His frame is still his, though it does not uphold him. Let us honour his presence, his form, honour it with the dignity we owe its former self. Where will you have him sitting on this day? He must not be in the polder lands nor with the other guests. I would not be able to bear that. I could not have the ceremony without his presence. If he sits with us I will be at peace and the life within me may recognise him. Forgive me. Please bear with me this once."

Arun understands. He can see that desire will be long in coming his way, if at all. He tries to imagine the nature of an ecstasy, whose very shadow suggests an energy of sensuality, intelligence and compassion. He wonders and wonders. Without warning, a great gush of compassion for his brother overwhelms him and he wishes with all his might that Vasu be healed so that Aasha would have joy again.

On their wedding day it is done as she wished, as they both wished.

45   AASHA MAKES A DECISION
Toronto

A year has passed. A long time for Arun and my son Nyasa. Now their restlessness joins my own. I have been living a hermit's life for too long. My family needs a home with Summer's ripeness. I have stayed Autumn and Winter. But no longer. Another time is knocking. It was not so at the beginning.

At first, after our evening meal, I would make some excuse and leave the table, busying myself with anything and everything, my part-time teaching post in particular. He never tried to detain me or keep me at any place longer than I wished. Now I am relaxed with him. After dinner we sit and chat and laugh together, relating the eccentricities of our colleagues.

The power of his kindness moves me. Now, when he hands me Nyasa, who falls asleep as easily with him as with me, his closeness, his scent, gets in my way of thinking. It is night that changes my feelings, releases a part of me once held firmly. It transforms the realities of the day, gives another meaning that daylight would pierce.

When we walk in the park, do our shopping, go to the theatre or cinema, something now stirs in me. It is gaining strength, becoming bolder. I noticed that yesterday I took my time taking Nyasa from his arms. My perfume and my falling hair caressed him. He moved away from me speedily, as if his sanity depended on it.

The strain is telling on me. I have Vasu's photograph at my bedside. He is so alive and well there, smiling warmly, as if waiting to greet anyone who comes to him. There is another with Vasu and Arun and I holding hands. I am in the centre. This I have put away, and though I am now more relaxed about the image, it remains closed in the album. There are quite a few of Vasu standing on the sea-wall, looking like a slender sailing ship, his hair billowing in the wind. And there are some of Marguerite and Vasu and Arun.

In the past I saw everything from my window. Now, the power of his kindness makes me ask, how does Arun feel? What sort of life is this for him? Is it still right that he should carry me and Nyasa as I had asked when we were in a hostile environment? Should I not now do the right thing and release him?

I continue to lock my door at nights, no longer fearing emotions outside my room, but to bar me from those within, so that I would have to make a deliberate, conscious act of taking my feet to the door, then using my hands and eyes to unlock it, to seek some warmth and comfort in the night. In this way I have protected myself from drowning by the sudden bursting of a dam. Nyasa's cot is there, and I have to look at his sleeping face and think of his father and of another time, before I turn the handle of the door.

So far I have nothing to reproach myself for, if Vasu were to come through the door and say, *I am here. I have regained myself, recovered fully*. Yet I have been asking myself, what must Arun be thinking? What is he expecting? He thinks a great deal, so he must see that I am still mentally engaged to Vasu. Or does he think I have become irretrievably cold, immune to life's gifts?

By what code does he judge me? Is it that of both our upbringing, or of these 'modern' times. And what is modern? Is it simply the mores of these technologically and scientifically advanced places? Their manufacturers tell us to use this washing machine or that dishwasher; their philosophers, scientists and physicians tell us at what stage the development of our multiplying cells can be said to have attained humanity. Must we accept their perceptions, their dispositions in all other things? Must we follow in their footsteps, so that our lives are lived as theirs, as they have mapped them?

They tell us that the moon is not made of wholesome cheese that is eaten down to the last quarter and then remade – renewed by the great Cheese Maker. As a child I pondered on the nature of a cheese that would not melt in the day, but would glow in the night, bringing light to dark streets. I searched for such a cheese and wondered and wondered as a child, and so I grew.

I know the world is led by places of industry, by 'scientific' cultures probing the outer limits. Is it my weakness that I find this way of thinking incompatible with what I still hold – a gut feeling that settles like lees and colours whatever enters? I keep asking myself this. I have been trained to think rationally, yet find it inadequate, not satisfying. Is it because of my childhood experiences and schooled expectations? Am I looking for a Cheese Maker to make Vasu whole again?

By which codes will I live? It was to help me find my way that I decided to visit Maya, perhaps for the last time.

Subah has written regularly, keeping us in touch with Vasu, yet I need to see him, to speak with him, to touch, to embrace him and recapture once again what time and distance are taking from the quiet of my days. I believe I will be more at ease for doing so. Arun understands this, but I sense he cannot wait much longer, which is why I am here in Toronto, in this fine hotel, on my way from London to Bon Aire. Tomorrow I shall be in Maya.

By chance, this evening when I went for an early dinner, there was a Country Mayan wedding reception taking place in the adjoining room. The party included people I had once known and I was invited to join them, which I did, grateful to renew my childhood's fascination with the splendour of celebration – of the joining of lives to create another miraculous thing called family.

I watched and listened, hoping to see and hear I knew not what until it came.

45   SUBAH, VEENA AND AASHA

When the car stopped before the house, I knew it was Aasha. I wrapped my ornhi hurriedly and went out to meet her, I couldn't wait. We embraced. She paid the driver in American dollars and he bowed. "When you want me to come?"

"Come five o'clock. Tomorrow," she said, "five o'clock. Don't let me down. I would like to go to the polders."

I turned to the driver. "Where Mr Nath is working, na."

"You can depend on me," he was smiling. "I know where Mr Nath is. Leave it to me. I will be here. Five o'clock you say? I will be here before that, you wouldn't have to worry."

I had spent yesterday cooking and cleaning so that we could talk till late in the night. It was good to see her.

"Aasha, let me take a good look at you. You looking well. You looking good... a bit sad, na? Tomorrow, you will meet Vasu. How are Arun and Nyasa? We must eat now. It is well past lunch time."

"I have photographs to show you. They are both well, Subah. But look at you. You still blossoming in this place. Imagine what you will do in London... Did you notice how the young man bowed? He was paying homage to a foreign currency that keeps its worth."

After that Aasha went quiet. I wanted to comfort her, but she had closed herself. Before Vasu's accident, she was a laughing, talking stream. I knew her problem. Still in love with Vasu, feeling lost – drifting, losing the meaning of living, carrying a burden of guilt. She thinks that despite what the consultants say, despite the risk to herself and the health of the child, and all the hardships in this rundown countryside – that her place is with him. I wouldn't be surprised if she is thinking that if she had stayed with Vasu, that he might have recovered. But the Vasu she knows is no longer here. She needs to get that in her head. Sacrificing, sacrificing – that thinking comes straight from my mother's generation and she would say it comes from her own mother, who in turn would remind her of what the *Ramayana* had to say. This is a sore point with Veena. She says, "It is ancient, Ma. It has nothing to do with modern times." Maybe. My thinking is that for too long these great epics have been interpreted by pundits. We need panditas. We need a new understanding. A life of perpetual sacrifice! Is that life? I don't believe it. Aasha did the right thing. I encouraged her to marry and leave. Vasu was a modern young man and he would have wanted her to do just that. He would have wanted her to have a full life. I will have to be direct with her. I told her this already, but you just have to keep on saying the right thing over and over again. What else can you do?

The other bundle of guilt feelings, I am sure, comes from her relationship with Arun. She herself must have a heap of different emotions rising. No healthy young woman could live with Arun and not want a proper married relationship. The fact that he behaves so well is a great pressure. Her feelings for him must be so full of confusions... grateful to him on her son's behalf and her own, and thankful for the way he respects her. But even if she feels something for Arun, she wants to say by her behaviour – "My love for Vasu was special, this is how I love when I love." I know that. She wouldn't say that. And she must feel so lonely. She needs to be comforted, but stifles this with work, staying busy. I guess Veena is right. It is the *Ramayana* all over again. Veena tells me that our culture is to blame for the way Aasha conducts herself, that it has 'paralysed' her. "My own generation, Ma," she informs me, "will not postpone living. We will live for the moment." Live for the moment? What does that mean? Is the moment lived not attached to the moment before? Does the moment lived have no consequences for the moment after? No? I hope she is not forgetting her upbringing, she will soon forget herself if she does.

Just look at what my daughter Veena writes me:

"I know of no culture, Ma, that demands so much from its women, even when you compare it with other ancient cultures. Look at the ten year Trojan war. The people of King Menelaus' country rejoiced on his returning home victorious with his abducted wife, Helen, and Homer did not ask his listeners to consider anything else.

"But Ma, the culture from which the *Ramayana* comes is not so easily won over. It is not satisfied with the same outcome – that Rama had a victorious war, destroyed Lanka and regains Sita. No. This culture wants to be satisfied that after her years of abduction, living in the home of her abductor as Helen did in Troy, Sita is still fit to be queen. Her character, her conduct are brought centre stage. The criterion for being 'fit to be queen' is pitiless, as you well know, Ma. Valmiki, like Homer, expects the menfolk to fight the good fight and to die on the battlefield, but Valmiki also knows that he needs to show that during the years of abduction, Sita has also been fighting the honourable fight, single-handedly, in that paradise created by her abductor, full of gifted musicians, painters, cooks – designers of seductive delights. Her society expects her to cope with loneliness, and at no time falter, despite temptations that would erode the willpower of saints. And here lies the rub, Ma. When the King and Queen and army return victorious, the society of the *Ramayana* wants to ask whether this fine woman also fought the good fight honourably, in the privacy of her quarters.

Now this is too delicate a question to unwrap even in private discussions. Valmiki knows this. He reflects the sensibilities of ordinary men and women of the kingdom of Ayodhya. They have no way of knowing the answer to their unspoken question, but it is not a society that will give the woman the benefit of the doubt. And since it needs to know for certain, it is uncomfortable with itself. Valmiki knows that these doubts must be removed, before the respect and affection of the kingdom can be bestowed again on their Queen. The decision is taken – she will be tried by the grimmest of laws. The Queen will stand on the pyre. The God of fire, Agni, will judge her. His judgement is indisputable. This will attest that at no time did she for a moment fall from grace.

The people of Ayodhya came. Rama watched. Husbands watched, and sons too. Wives and daughters watched, mothers stayed at home. Sita will be above all suspicion if she survives the test. She does not protest, she submits willingly. She will take the burden of others' doubts upon herself. She walks to the pyre with dignity and grace and, in so doing, becomes the symbol of womanhood for us all. The way she walks to the pyre becomes the way to endure life's hells, hurled by husbands, in-laws, and society's laws and customs.

As you well know, Ma, the fire rages. Those close by retreat; the
heat is unbearable. They can see nothing; the flames are too high
and the smoke envelops all. Women weep, men bend their heads.
The smoke clears, the flames subside and Sita is there unsinged,
her head bent in prayer, her hands clasped.

She walks from the pyre to her husband Rama, who embraces
her. He knew there was no test her honour would fail. Her subjects
rejoice. They are satisfied. She has shown that she is not only fit
to sit on the throne as their Queen, but that Agni honours her. And
so do we, as the epic moves from generation to generation, from
mothers to daughters. And so a standard of womanhood is set in
time and lives in the retelling.

You wouldn't have seen Helen of Troy leaving the pyre, Ma.
Come to think of it, I don't know who would today. Sorry, Ma, I am
referring, of course, to my generation; I cast no doubt on yours. But
Ma, consider this: the loyal subjects of King Menelaus did not
expect nor demand this kind of 'honour' from Helen. In societies
past and present, husbands and wives were and are living more
comfortably than you would imagine, Ma, not wishing to know, not
asking for proof. I believe this thinking is spreading fast. I have
been asking myself why can't our society be more like those?

And what of Arun? How must he feel? He would not want either
to be repelled, or to become a beast. He remembers his own
promise and tells himself, 'If I lose control, I lose everything.' He
wants her respect and her love; for him they are bound together.
He will be patient for the boundless pleasures of a willing,
passionate partner. He knows that even Ravana conducted himself honourably during the years of abduction, hoping that with
time Sita would succumb to the art around her, and he would enjoy
an indescribable ecstasy.

Now don't get a heart attack, Ma. You brought me up to ask
questions. Well, from time to time I do. People are no longer like
the heroes and heroines of the *Ramayana* are they? I believe the
word 'honour' is itself going out of common usage. Yet Aasha
carries this epic within her. She lives by its code. How will she live
in her own time, Ma? She thinks she ought to be stepping onto the
pyre. Ma, you who are adept at designing and redesigning pathways need to consider this. Help her, Ma, as you did before."

46   SUBAH ADVISES AASHA

After Aasha ate – I coaxed her to have another rasmaila, which she had just to please me – I decided to speak. Time was running out so I said, "Vasu is best where he is, Aasha. The consultant was right. The polder land is good for healing... You are still grieving for Vasu, I can see that. A year is too short for some things. You're between the past and the present. Aasha, I must come clean and say what is hard to say. You know I cared for Vasu and Arun when their mother died. They were good boys and grew up to be fine men. I wouldn't like to have to choose between them. Thank God I don't have to do this. But you don't either, Aasha.

"Vasu was a scholar, but he had a warmth for life and was excited by it. His laughter brought light to a room. This Vasu I am talking about, this Vasu you loved and who was deeply in love with you, died in the air. I hear from Nurse Maude that the men who do these things take their victims way out into the ocean, in the shark-infested areas. They throw in a piece of fresh meat, and allow the victim to observe the sharks feeding, then they gradually lower you down. I don't think they drop you there, but that would not be necessary, for after that kind of excursion out to sea, you do just what they ask or you leave Maya quietly.

"All Maya knows what happened to Gavin, enough of him was left from the explosion to identify him, but we don't know exactly what they did to Vasu. What we can say is that the torture was so severe, it cut him off from himself. The consultant was right – his memory lost its roots. We don't know from day to day how much of that day he remembers. I would say he catches some things, he loses others. And then again, he has better or worse days. Nurse Maude, God bless her, visits him during the week. And Marguerite goes whenever she comes down from Bon Aire. I see him on weekends. I don't ask him questions. I just sit with him or work with him. Maybe to him I am like the polder, a part of his world, a familiar thing ... not a painful thing.

"Let me tell you, Aasha, he will not recognise you. Make it easy for him and for yourself. Observe him well, then decide. I can't tell you, of all people, how to behave when you see him. That wouldn't be right. I can only tell you what we know."

"Subah, he was alone in the Hinterland Commune, and a puppet in the air, hanging in space without protection – just a cotton shirt and his old pair of trousers. It was one horror after another. I read his account of the hinterland again and again. I know it by heart. How could anyone absorb that, followed by what they must have done to him when they dragged him from his home and carried him to that plane to dump him. He just snapped. It was too much. Why didn't we see the imminent danger and arrange for him to be flown straight out of Maya to Santa Maria? Why did we all behave like amateurs? They were bound to know, to follow up who the visitor was. He must have been under surveillance as soon as his aircraft landed. They knew he had entered the forbidden place, that he saw more than he should. They must have had a camera somewhere, that would have captured his coming in to the altar, taking photographs of the young girls. They acted with such speed, they were so fast on his heels. They needed to take the photographs from him, before he passed them on. The photographs made public would have destroyed them. It was they or he. The Government co-operated with them. They have an understanding. With hindsight, it was such a waste of a large spirit. Such a naïve thing to do, Subah, to return here after that mission. We should have made sound arrangements to leave Maya immediately. O God, why couldn't I have foreseen this? I was so self-occupied."

"If they were bent on getting him, Aasha, they would have stalked him wherever he went. You have to stop blaming yourself. It does no good to Vasu and it harms you, Arun, and your son Nyasa. Nurse Maude said he would not have suffered long."

"Subah, he would have imagined what they planned, and being up there alone, dangling in space on a rope, he snapped. But how can the doctors say that losing himself was itself a protective mechanism? Shouldn't the body save the mind?"

"For his sake, and for his memory, Aasha, you must try and heal yourself to live. If Vasu's spirit could speak, it would want you to live again. I know that, you must know that too. Now I will come straight. If you lose this opportunity, this chance to live again with Arun, believe me if you were to lose him to another woman, you would realise too late you were a fool. Think of Nyasa. What is best for him? Show me a better father than Arun? Come in the garden and help me pick a few Julie and East Indian mangoes to take back with you... "

*   *   *   *

Tomorrow I meet with Vasu. How much will he have changed? Changed? Can there be anything of Vasu that remains, which the torment could not take? I have come to say farewell, to say it properly. Will there be something that I will recognise when he speaks to me? What will he see when I am with him? I cannot envisage how a changed Vasu will look, speak, feel, smile, think. Subah means well. If all is as she says, then I will need to leave where I now stand. But how? How to leave someone with whom I wished to spend my life, who enriched my life, someone who had become part of me? This Vasu stands before me whole, whenever my memory dwells on him. And there is the entrancing magic of that night, the night of the dance – of giving and receiving. That remains. How does one remove one's skin where kisses live, where caresses abide?

Subah tells me gently to move on. But memory makes us too. It gives direction, leaves a path which draws us back, makes us overstay our time, seeking comfort. Subah is the voice of practical good sense, but my memories yet hold me, embrace me. How to release myself?

47 THE DYING OF A LIGHT

The chauffeur drives slowly along the raised earth road. On either side the rice-growing polder land contains its waters. It is lower to protect the road from its overflow. There is nothing to be seen or heard, save at a distance – white specks beneath the powder-blue immensity – white egrets coming home.

Silence pervades all.

Work on the field is done. The day departs and labour too. Sunbeams sparkle on neat rectangular lakes – embankments built by hand to contain the water for growth. "One, one, dutty build dam," the old women used to say as they worked with the wet clay.

This is the polder land she recalled on many a northern winter evening, seeing these sweet green leaves rapidly sprouting, like common water weeds to the untrained eye. She knows that later they will show their flowering heads above the water, stretching to protect the pearly nut of energy encased in tightly sealed husks. As a child, she would eat the young grain, which is milky sweet, its coat a succulent green that turns yellowish green, then light yellow to light brown, and creamy brown to brown, until the paddy hangs heavy.

All this time she scans the emptiness for a figure whose form is framed within her. The sun is close to the horizon and a flood of dazzle shimmers, rising above the sparkling, jewelled lakes.

She cannot contain her anxiety. Her body lifts – her dancer's heels are up, toes pressed, neck and bosom rise, searching. The chauffeur is helpful. Two pairs of eyes pierce the land.

"Over there."

"Where?"

"By the bamboo clump."

"Please stop. Wait here. I'll walk the remainder."

"Is a long walk."

"I know. Thank you. I will walk."

She runs and walks, runs again and walks.

Vasu Nath is staring intently at the water as if it holds some puzzle he should unravel. When Aasha approaches and stands by him, he should be surprised, but his eyes have grown accustomed to the daily appearance and disappearance of things.

"Vasu," she calls. He turns and Aasha sees the face she knew, the face of countless caresses.

"That is my name," he says smiling, embarrassed, though he cannot explain why it should be so.

"I will not forget it... A beautiful sounding name."

"I am sorry, but I do not know yours. Forgive me. I feel I ought to know it. I have been unwell and a little confused."

"Aasha."

"Aasha... Aasha..." He is unpuzzling the sound.... "Aasha is not here. Aasha is not found here ... though ... I think I know it. I cannot recall it. Am ... yes, I know it." He hesitates, trying to make sense of what his voice is saying. He smiles to cover his confusion. "Come sit. Don't go away."

"Are you alone here, Vasu?"

"I am with Aasha."

"You work the land?"

"The land works. I work. Aasha, I have nothing to give you. Have you had lunch?"

"Yes... I've come to see you."

"Nothing to see here. People come and go. They are here, they are not here. This is the polder. Are you going?"

"Vasu, you remind me of a tale I heard long ago. Come sit with me over here in the shade. Once upon a time there was a young man, his name was Abhimanu."

"I like the name," He feels good and wishes to please the traveller, knowing she will soon disappear.

"He was a courageous young man... may have been sixteen or seventeen. He fought valiantly against the rotten and destructive forces in his father's kingdom. One day in battle, after he had broken through the enemy's formation and wrought havoc, destroying columns of men, fighting his way on and on through their

ranks, crushing the supporters of vileness and wickedness, he
entered the enemy's innermost formation, and there Abhimanu
found himself surrounded by six warriors – men of valour and
experience. They were awaiting him.

These men had fought wars of honour and renown but now they
were bound to their covetous Prince, their own cowardly kith and
kin, and to promises they had made in peaceful times and in good
faith. Now they were men who had lost their way and themselves,
forgetting what above all else they should be loyal to. They were
offering their service to what was demonic.

They slew Abhimanu's horses, then his charioteer. And so,
ignobly dismounted, Abhimanu stood on the battlefield, a mere
boy, covered in dust, with only his sword and shield, surrounded.
His eyes are watchful, bright and clear; his heart and temples
throb like a hounded deer's, seeing no gap in the enclosing circle,
hearing the hounds' cries, feeling their panting breaths, aware of
the closing in of his time.

Abhimanu stood before these warriors and began to whirl his
sword, moving as if he wore winged sandals, not resting on the
earth, his arm sprouting a thousand flails. He held his own against
this cavalry of six – like wild beasts in their desire to diminish him.
Round and round they galloped, again and again encroaching ever
closer upon him, until they tore his shield to tatters and broke his
sword. Disarmed, he picked up his chariot wheel, whirling it like
a discus, keeping them at bay until the sun dipped beneath the
horizon (not wishing to see the dastardly act to come) and they
shattered his chariot wheel. He stumbled, fell and as he struggled
to his feet, one of the warriors, all now dismounted, struck him with
his mace. He lay dying. And with the warm blood gushing out of
him, he called out to his father who was fighting on another front
in this vast battlefield. "Father forgive me, for when you come after
sunset, I shall not be here to embrace you. But ask this red earth
that now cradles me, how I fought against these cowards. Father,
I take my leave of you and salute you. May the Gods remain with
you. Farewell. Farewell, Peeta Ji."

"He was surrounded," Vasu says.

"When they saw him bleeding on the earth, the warriors left,
but the Prince's people danced round his dead body, like savage

hunters exulting over their prey, blowing conch shells and crying, 'Victory is ours'."

"It is a sad tale. He was alone. Where was his army?"

"The birds of prey circled overhead crying, 'Not thus! Not thus!' They protected Abhimanu's body. Another young man from the enemy's camp, seeing what had been done to this brave young soldier, stood before the still warm body and said, 'Today our camp should bury its head in shame and not revel in cries of victory. To slay this fine brave soldier, a mere boy, we had to relinquish our ancient codes of honour upon which our civilisation rests. We slaughtered his horse and his charioteer, which is against our rules of battle, and then we slew him disarmed. We are amongst the damned and know it not. Our danger − imminent; it is here knocking at our door while we feast like cannibals on carcasses. I can no longer fight for men who have done this or for rulers who allow this in the name of winning the war. Today I leave the battlefield for a life of contemplation. I ask Abhimanu's spirit, as it hovers over his now stilled body, for forgiveness. Today is my shame, Abhimanu. Today is our shame. Forgive us'."

She embraces him. "Forgive me, Vasu. Forgive me." He holds her and she recalls the night of the dance. And though his scent is true, and his face and skin and colour, she now knows that what Subah has said is true. This is not Vasu − that exhilarating spark that overwhelmed a passing comet by its beauty, its flames of Sirius.

Vasu said, "Aasha, beautiful Aasha," and wiped her tears as he had done at the ferry. "You carry a sad tale... are you visiting?"

"Yes. Do you know the sea-wall in Bon Aire?"

"I have had an accident, you know. Nurse Maude and Subah tell me so. I am with a family here in the polder. It is good near the fields. Subah and Nurse Maude come... Another lady comes... she comes from far."

"Have you been to the sea-wall?"

"I will go."

"Before this accident I would meet you there. Together we walked between the land and the sea as if we were parting the waves. Tomorrow I will be going to the sea-wall. I would have liked you to be there."

He was happy to learn that she would like to walk with him, that
such a beautiful sad story teller would walk with him. He would
cheer her up. Then suddenly this pleasure left him and he said, "I
couldn't get there."

"I can take you now and bring you back."

"It is too late. Dusk has come. I feel better here. Since my
accident, you see, I do not leave here. Nurse Maude comes. It is
best to stay here. I like the land, the trees. Do you like the land?
People are helping me, and I am healing. Nurse Maude and Subah
say everyday that I am healing. I am not ill. I am not in pain. I will
walk with you on the sea-wall. I would like that. Why you walked
there? ...Did I walk there? ... Why you walked there?... Why?... I
am sorry. I am asking questions. I am confusing myself. I am so
sorry. Will you go?"

"You should ask Nurse Maude to take you for a walk on the sea-
wall."

"No! No! She's a busy nurse. It isn't right to ask her. Please
don't. She has to be in the hospital. She cares for the sick."

Aasha takes him home. He stands at the door and waves to her,
as in her dream, then goes inside.

"I have a feeling he will come out again," she says to the
chauffeur, "that this is not the last time I will be seeing him. Can
we wait a while?"

"If we don't leave straight away, Mrs Nath, we will miss the last
ferry to Bon Aire."

*   *   *   *

Aasha cannot remember exactly where they once walked, for
the deep yellow poui has been cut down. She sees a stump and,
with nothing else to go by, climbs the severely fractured foundation of the sea-wall. It has become unsafe, dangerous in places,
filled with fissures and blow holes.

As she walks upon the broken wall, the short tropical twilight
stays a while, playing with shadows. Swiftly darkness descends.
From the ocean, open and wide, now unseen, she feels a threatening
encroachment that would engulf her.

It is a vast, deep, foaming force, rising and falling with the wind,
roaring and lashing the land, swallowing the shore's life, dragging
it down to its digestive depths. The overwhelming darkness

becomes a fearsome, sinister thing. Vulnerable and lost as in a nightmare, a cry comes from deep within her, a prolonged extended sound – "Vaaaaaaaaaa Suuuuuuuuuu..." It seems to have no end. Her breath, everlasting in its intensity and duration, creates a mighty wave that crosses roof tops, crowns of trees and shrubs, the wide river, the crowded stelling, the sugar-cane and rice fields and reaches the sleeping Vasu.

He awakes suddenly. Dazed. Unlocks the door and runs out into the wind, into the cold open space, out into the centre of the road, stands and looks to the right and to the left, overcome by a frenzied anxiety, expecting some loss to be found... someone's call. Then he knows it is the sad storyteller, beautiful Aasha, waiting on the sea-wall for him. "Aaaaaaaaaaa Shaaaaaaaaaa," he cries and his tears bathe him and a balm, strangely intense, caresses him. He stands alone on the deserted polder land. Fine cirrus clouds drift to veil the moon. The scent of cows and grass moves with the wind. Stillness and dim lights from faraway houses encircle him. A stranger to himself, Vasu walks back to the house, surprised that the front door is wide open, not understanding how it came about.

49   EARLY SPRING
Aasha

I'm back again in Toronto on my way to London. When I passed through here a week ago on my way to Maya, I was anxious, troubled, weighed down with sadness. Now I am at peace with myself. I have travelled far. Subah, Nurse Maude and Marguerite have enabled me to cover this distance. Each told me the same in her own way. I am blessed. What would have become of me without them? Now I must look ahead.

Seeing Vasu has been good. His courtesy remains and his concern for Nurse Maude so moves me. I know they will do their best for him, will take him to Santa Maria when they leave.

I am at peace. It is as if I were in solitary confinement in an underground place, and now I see clouds dance before the rains and stars from afar.

This afternoon I sat with one of the managers of the hotel where I am staying, a Mayan. It was in her futuristic office that I had a chance to look at a book published here – *The Unofficial Tales of the Disenfranchised Mayans*.

Below her tall umbrella-shaped office – a giant mushroom, in the grand dining room, a group of Mayans were having a thanksgiving celebration. They were commemorating their flight from the island and their good fortune in Canada. The atmosphere was vibrant with laughter and chatter, their optimism for the future carried by their voices.

Just before I went down to absorb the warm camaraderie of this gathering, I reread the entry of my last visit.

This music, this dance – so close, yet so distant, brings me deep sadness. Foreign. I fear our beliefs and customs will be lost like a leaf sucked into the mouth of a giant wave. No trace of it remaining.

*Like frail memory-fragments of foam when the backwash recedes
from the shore.*

*Here, private thoughts and feelings are exposed, open, indeli-
cate. 'It is just another way,' a part of me says. Yet I feel we are being
forced to wear a dress unsuited to our form. Feelings once unspoken,
are now openly scattered and lose themselves. Their perfume, as
from an overblown flower, falls away. All privacy is lost and with
it tenderness. No one escapes. We face the sweet seduction of this
youthful culture chanting: 'Empower. Empower yourself.' Confident and smiling, it is self-assured in silks. At gatherings, its
falsities, pretences, its make-believes are masked by easy words —
puffs of nothingness.*

*What is there we have created after our own image? Castles in
the air, self delusions, sticky webs of wishful thinking? They hang
and flap in the wind, in the absence of rational thoughts. But where
is truth, the sacred truth? It outweathers time and place, the sages
say. Thank God it does, for nothing else remains... Yet I have
wondered, wondered as to the truth of this remaining balm.*

*   *   *   *

"They're all Mayans here. Come with me," she says, and we
stand by her open window to have an eagle's view of the merry
gathering.

"These are the lucky ones," she smiles. "The strong, the
survivors are here. Those who made it through the barbed wires of
bureaucracy."

She tells me that some who came here died prematurely, of
heart failure, ever-rising blood pressure; that cultural deprivation
and loss of significance took their toll on these brutally uprooted
spirits. Not all came through. The stress was too much for some.
Alcoholism and personality disorders were not uncommon.

"You will not find many older people among us. Too many
broke under the strain of seeing their lifetime's work and sacrifice
having no value when converted into the currency of commerce.
Here, as I've said, are the lucky ones — those that somehow made it.
Their tales are here." Her fingers tap the neatly bound collection.

"Come, see that lady over there, the one with the fine deport-
ment in the light-orange sari, with the splendid border. She is still
picking herself up. They murdered her son just as he was about to
leave his home for Maya's airport, to come here. She didn't know
what had happened. She waited and waited at Toronto airport,
scanning the passing faces, full of expectations. She told me she
had cooked melongene chokah, young squash with that nice thick
cod fish you get over here, and plump, juicy red tomatoes; that she
could already see the delight in his eyes! She told me they had so
much to say to each other; she waited until the last person on that
flight left the airport. When she discovered he was not on the flight,
she began to feel a heavy emptiness. 'To think your young son, who
only just completed A levels, is murdered for no reason, is a
thinking you will not entertain,' she said. On returning home, she
telephoned, but there was no answer. 'Then I knew,' she said. She
phoned the neighbour, who told her. They must have got wind that
he was travelling, that there would be American dollars, travellers'
cheques and other valuables. They shot him in the head. He must
have died there and then. Masks protect. The police and the
Mayan Government protect. There is no need for restraint. No way
of identifying them, as you well know, Aasha. If by some miracle, you
have enough information to bring charges, what do you say when the
defence makes it clear that you were attacked by masked men and
at no time did the masks fall?"

I must have looked despondent, for she said, "No! No! These
people are healing themselves. That mother has stood up well. She
keeps going... took a course in interior design... is in much
demand... She carries his image in her head and his photograph
in her handbag. That consoles her. She swears he is there, helping
her: 'He was a very bright boy,' she says, 'and I find I am getting
such good ideas from I don't know where. It must be from him'."

The gathering is full of good cheer. There are generous portions
of fresh salmon on five hundred plates and quality wines in plenty.

"Here the wine will not run out," she says, pointing to a framed
Wedding at Cana. "The system here in North America has a huge
capacity; it absorbs thousands of new arrivals every week. It offers
them hope, a new beginning. Not everyone is like her, but many
are progressing, making something better of their lives than they

would have if they had remained second-class citizens in a dictatorship.

"But look around you. You see no purple here, not even on the borders of the saris. That colour they have come to associate with pain... Look over there ... in that corner, neat and remarkably whole, are two sisters whose father was strangled at prayer and his iron safe looted. He was doing his evening puja. The coroner said the old man gave much resistance. His daughters found him on the floor and the safe empty. They had to sell their father's business for a pittance. But today, one is an accountant working with a bank and doing work privately at home, supporting the other at Yale University. They will take turns.

"Over there, on the table to the right, sits an elderly lady who lost her only son, a jeweller. She wouldn't talk about it, but her neighbour, an eye-witness, told me. The old lady lives with her daughter, Indra, there to the left of the pillar. Today, that lady makes the finest gulab jamun and ras malai. The hotel orders from her. She told me she would have opened a chain if she were younger. She is fantastic with pakoras and samosas. I buy from her on my way home. But it was not easy for her. Two Purple Masks came into her shop and held her up. As they emptied her jewels into large leather bags, she pressed the alarm and her son came running downstairs and began to chase after them. He was an athlete and beginning to catch up on them, when they turned and shot him. The neighbour told me, 'We used our ornhis to try to stop the flowing, but it did not help. There was no one to turn to, is you and you alone.' She related how the mother cried, 'Forgive me, son. O God forgive me. Ah shouldn't ah call you, son. Forgive me. I had the best jewel upstairs and didn't understand this.' At the cremation she had to be pulled away. The heat began to spread but she would not move. She wanted to be on the pyre."

Later as I sat in my room I found I had written:

Who will be the guardian of these sacred truths? It is not the Assorted University Luminaries nor politicians, nor Party members. It is these ordinary men and women, formerly Mayans, now Canadians sitting here, enjoying this feast they have created, carrying on age-old celebrations to enrich their lives. They have been taught by the harsh criminal school of their experiences. These people, who were called 'Irrelevant or minors' are saying, 'The past is that other country that has grown dull, so very dull, dark and grey. Poverty and wretchedness belong to our past. We are busy weaving our children's future with fine threads of value, to leave behind a tapestry of worth for them'.

As I laid my head on my pillow I heard again the voices of two generations and two paths. They came from a table to which my hostess introduced me. The head of the table, a healthy, smiling old man who, seeing me holding a copy of *The Unofficial Tales of the Disenfranchised Mayans*, said, "Baetee, we sometimes give too much of ourselves to the past. You would notice there is no purple here. It is a rich colour. We should have purple here. When I say this to old people like myself, they say nothing. They don't say yes. They don't say no. That is good when you consider their own experiences and the bitter winter cold they must now endure in their old age."

"Purple is a colour that was badly used," Utra, the old man's granddaughter, said. "If we had been made to think and believe what was fed to those who wore the masks, I would be surprised if we would have behaved any differently. We are like them and they are like us in the things that matter."

His other granddaughter was livid. "Don't worry with Utra. She has never lived in Maya. Cultures are different, people are different and their experiences are different. You can't say we would have behaved in the same way as the Masked Ones. That's so much rubbish. We did not stand up and fight. We just left and those of us who remained were sheep, and we made lions of cowards and bullies. They roared beneath their masks and walked all over us. We had no guts for a fight. We did nothing. A few of us even crossed the floor to join them, believe it or not. Incredible! Let me say this: If we had done to them even a tiny fraction of what they did to us – burn down our shops, loot our homes, murder our families, rape our women – how do you think they would have reacted? Like us, you think? Now what did we do, Utra? We packed our bags quietly and left, begging and pleading so we could leave. And here we bend our backs and heads with work. We don't go around talking about human rights, no matter what we experience. We don't complain. So much for how alike we are. Utra, I have never heard you with such nonsense!" She drank some water and then said, "A number of our middle-aged men and women even purchased masks to get food and jobs. It was pitiable. Our young women were exploited in this way. It makes me ill. Devonish was a brute and a bully. And as he became desperate, he used everyone, even his loyal supporters.

"But we had no fight in us. No guts at all for a fight. How he must have despised us, quivering under his heel. O God, what manner of people are we? Don't we know that if you do not stand up and fight, the very ground you stand on is taken from you? Bullies have to be shown that it is not only they who can disrupt and immobilise. We can paralyse governments too. They brought down a legitimate government by brute force. We ran away from the hell they created and would not speak about it. That is the difference."

"Rena has a point," Utra said. So this was Rena, the young poet, some of whose work I had read in a Toronto magazine put out by Mayans. So much pain held within. Here and now, the energy of her grief and anger overflowed in torrents. But I thought how calm, how controlled was her fury in her poems. Utra, continued to speak.

"If the army is against you, Rena, the police force is against you, and the Region is silent, and America and Britain fooled themselves that they were fighting communism, it would have been foolhardy to fight. How many government militias were there? And official paramilitary groups were springing up like mushrooms. In such circumstances, one does what our parents and grandparents did. They ought to be praised and not ill judged."

The old man had the last word. "These are my granddaughters. I taught both the alphabet. Yet their poems are different. But let me say this. What Rena said was entirely true and what Utra has told you is not wrong in its entirety, yet, believe me, you have to conduct yourself as if the world is a better place than you know it to be. That is not to say, live in cloud cuckoo land, not wishing to face the truth. To dishonour the truth of our experience is to dishonour the dead and we do this at our peril. You and I need to see in the eyes and smiles of people a new dawn of promise, of hope for a better day. In that, there is energy and life. Rena knows that, too. But it is too early for her. Her torment in Ica brought her to the edge. She has had to try to remake herself. That is painful... Birth is painful. She will succeed, for the earth will lose if she loses, and her affection for the world is great. I am a little older than these two. I am eighty-five. If you follow my advice, young lady," he said, turning to me, "your life will be even more creative. For what else is there? We are all here, they and us. It is better to try and make the most of it. Life is beautiful. Don't waste it. Appreciate everything. Look at this room. Here you have love in abundance. Here we have the love of cooks, wine and perfume-makers, musicians, mural painters, designers of clothes, jewellers, hair-dressers. These once disenfranchised people have made it so. They have even invited me, an old man. It must be costing our many hosts and hostesses the earth. Five hundred guests! I am thankful to be here. The future we can do something about. Never forget the past, but don't let it prevent you from growing. I can see you have known pain. We wish you well."

"Rena is my bright, passionate, grandchild. She is deeply hurt and speaks from experience. Be understanding. She cannot bear injustices. But if you are inclined to Rena's thinking, if you are intent on searching for justice at all cost, you will become bitter, disillusioned, and will waste away. A life with its potential unfulfilled is a life lost. My mother would say, a whole world lost – she talked like that. I always talked too much, even when I was an assistant teacher, long before I became head-teacher. We have tired you, and you have to travel."

I turned the page and see that I have written:

The Country Mayans I have met here are becoming both skilled labour and capital assets. Here in Toronto, the system offers them an opportunity to think and rethink, to create and rebuild. They will find their way without maps and will create maps for others. They are resilient. It is the human way. The human spirit will soar and find new skies. We will become birds with a sky, Marguerite. And we will learn to understand purple, for the colours in our spectrum

*are too small to lose even one, especially one so rich in tone and light
and warmth.*

*   *   *

When she arrives at Heathrow airport, a chauffeur is there,
holding up her name on a card . She is pleased Arun is not there,
but has made these arrangements. He is not at home either.

It is too early for the daffodils. In another week, she thinks, as
she opens the gate, they will be there crowding the path to the front
door, announcing, "Spring is here once more." And so the earth
begins afresh, begins untiringly another orbit.

It is later when Arun returns. He removes his coat and walks to
the kitchen. "I could tell you were here," he says.

"How come?" She presents him with a spoon-taste of pumpkin
soup.

"Delicious. You have been busy. I see we are having chilled
Julie mangoes, and dhal puri and salmon, and prawns in garam
massala and what else is here... Yes, I see melongene choka, beans
and squash with those small tomatoes and spring onions. I'm very
hungry... Where is Nyasa?"

"In his cot, bathed and fed and fast asleep. Sylvia next door
brought him over as soon as she saw the taxi, and stayed back to
help me... Don't be long now. Everything is just right."

He knows then that this day marks the beginning of his
marriage. She radiates warmth, looking as beautiful as when he
first saw her with Vasu, and he is stirred. She is celebrating. So will
he. So will they today and tomorrow and the next day. It is how he
has always wanted to begin his marriage.

The following morning the daffodils are out.

PART FIVE: AN AWAKENING

50   I DREAMT THE LONE DRUMMER

Buoyed by the wind, sailing in the sky.

BOM! BOM! BOM! The lone drummer I hear.

Sly fox, he knows. I know not how he knows.

I am Marguerite, the kite in the sky.

I await the lone drummer. He knows my resolve. But why am I sailing, sailing in the sky?

At what is he looking? Ah! This medical bag? I must join the procession.

The procession is here.

Put away! Put away!

BOM! BOM! BOM! The lone drummer is near. Slow and sombre. Darkness surrounds.

Forward he beats. The lone drummer is here.

On he moves, the cortege with him.

That banner hovering above the Court of Appeal? What does it say?

THE PRESIDENT FOR LIFE OF THE REPUBLIC OF MAYA IS DEAD.
ROBERT AUGUSTUS DEVONISH IS DEAD.
ALL FLAGS AT HALF-MAST.

These sounds reverberating in Maya are hollow, signifying nothing to those long fled. The thousands of bystanders at the procession are confused, not knowing what it means. For too long they have left the meaning of things, the perception of things to the President for Life. The poverty they are immersed in, they left to him to interpret, as they did the crumbling of the sea-wall; the absence of bread and of light from their lives.

The procession is *moving to a place that befits a hero*. So repeats the state-run media again and again. 'Crucifixus et Resurrexit' from Bach's Mass in B minor is being played. The cortege avoids the depressing streets of abandoned shells, the rotting, crumbling, buildings that once sheltered men and women, that housed enterprise, the unfettered, the free.

BOM! BOM! BOM! The lone drummer beats. It is not a slaves' march, weary and wretched, says the voice of the state. It is not the sound of retreat, of withdrawal, but a celebration of a great Mayan's life, say the inheritors of the President's Constitution.

It is the funeral cortege of the President for Life. But where is that protective pharaonic cloak of the Constitution that was intended to preserve him for life? "I am judge and jury," he once said. Now he can say nothing. To those who sought to live outside his net he added, "When I fire you, you remain fired." They may now comfort themselves with the thought that when the President for Life dies he remains dead.

In death, the President is hoisted high on a gun carriage. It is fitting. His rapidly decomposing body is sealed within a steel, flag-draped casket. He is closely followed by a riderless horse, by family members – Aunt Maude and I are there – and the obliging Cabinet. Behind them are some of the oldest stalwarts of the Party, cobwebbed and dusted for the occasion. We are instinctively moving our heads in unison, low and bowed, up and down, up and down, echoing the movement of the riderless horse before us.

Aunt Maude hands me a black bag. It is her bag, the one that has become a part of her. The one that was with Shivnarine, and visits Vasu. It is the one that could do nothing for Gavin. I turn to her for I do not understand. Her head is moving up and down, up and down. I unzip the bag. There is an empty phial – potassium chloride is written in her hand on its label. There are other things in the bottom of the bag. I place my hand deep – a syringe and a piece of ruled paper. *To close a dark chapter*, is written on it. I look at her, but her head is bowing up and down, up and down.

"I will get rid of this," I whisper. And I too move in unison. She looks up at me, but the riderless horse is before me and I am taking my cue from it.

I look up for an instant and there is my brother's white mare, Abundance. She lifts her forelegs high in salutation as if she is at Rose Wood. She throws her rider backwards, and I do not see his face. "Who is now riding Abundance?" I whisper. But I only hear the sounds of tired marching feet and the lone drummer.

There I am again sailing in the sky.

The cortege is led by a finely decorated cavalry – thirty mounted escorts – reinforced by one hundred officers with drawn swords. The military does not only lead, it reinforces the procession at the rear. Behind the Cabinet mourners, come other Government functionaries and visiting dignitaries, many with insignia-bedecked chests and lapels. There are marching troops comprising the Defence Force, the National Service, the People's Militia, the Women's Socialist Movement and the Young Socialist Movement. A sea of purple faces, masqueraders in silent carnival, accompanying the Master Planner to another place.

Now come members of the Bon Aire proletariat, keeping in line, following the tempo. They are poor and though there is no bread, no light, no buses, and their government pensions this year or next will be worth nothing, they recall at length how their President repeatedly reminded them that his Government was for the poor man, for the little man. They have come to pay homage to the man who gave them these words, for these words, if nothing else, at least acknowledged their presence. And for this they come to give thanks.

But it is all he left them, and now they are ill at ease, not knowing whether this small string of words – 'the little man' – this hymn to their past and their present – will still be called from high rostrums by their President's successor.

We in Maya are magicians with words – we can resurrect the past, camouflage the present or bury whatever disturbs us. Hallelujah to the magic of sound! Behold thy God in the great magic of lifting sounds! In their shaping and directing, behold the spirit of man!

Masked Party functionaries hoist large banners on which are written the tributes from the Region and from Maya. It is as if his own wishful thinking has returned to accompany him to his end.

Wave after wave of purple banners rise above our heads like the masts of ghost ships emerging out of the mist. One by one they flap past and in turn disappear.

From subservience to self-reliance
He gave us dignity
The President's image and ours are one
He offered the true meaning of Independence
A David amongst Goliaths
He wrested the economy from foreign parasites
A political giant on the world stage

These banners move on; still others come:

An outstanding Trade Unionist
An intellectual of the highest order
There will never be anyone to match him

This last was too sad to see. What a low expectation of future generations!

Maya belongs to us. To no other. No other
He captured Maya for us! He fought tooth and nail for us!
Mourn, Mayans, mourn. Mourn, Mayans, mourn
Mourn. Mourn.

These words comfort the carriers and the onlookers. These words are an affirmation of what they ate and drank when there was nothing on the supermarket shelves.

As the cortege continues on its eight-mile march, the majority of Mayans look on impassively. They look through windows, from house tops and the branches of tall trees. This is an occasion. A chapter is closed. *Of historic significance*, the Government radio repeatedly declares.

"Authoritarian rule passes," Aunt Maude whispers. "Your AUL fraternity: are they present? Where is your nice Mr Carl Goodbody?"

What can I say? She nudges me.

"No one backs a dead horse."

No doubt in the university departments of the Region, they are voicing their concern that those without the requisite psychic inheritance may claim Maya. They fear that unknown ghosts, from Ica, from Hope Bridge, have already claimed the silk cotton trees, roof tops and cross roads. This, they fear, may signal the shape of things to come, the reclaiming by the dead, by the disinherited, of what was raped and stolen. They must act as swiftly as Robert Augustus did years ago to prevent Pottaro from forming the Government that led Mayans to Independence. They are gripped by deep uncertainty. No one ever envisaged this. The President for Life was not meant to leave before them. They fear retaliation from 'the enemy within'. Will it now be their turn to fear, to run, to be pushed, to emigrate in droves? Fear was the meat and drink the President offered. This monotonous diet has weakened them; they are now susceptible to every passing rumour, warm wind and shadows of wishful thinking. Who will take his place, they are asking.

Along with their masks, fear of 'the other' has become a part of themselves. The masks that once created fear in others they have, but the Government that distributed the masks, giving them validity, offering power without accountability, has crumbled. They were a passport to jobs, to security and a kind of dignity. Now they wonder what price they have paid.

For years the State ladled out sweet, cheap soups to government supporters in the many cages the President built. They have lived in the security of these cages for too long. There has been an unwritten understanding that once within the cage, they would be fed whenever the Government could muster buckets and ladles, water, electricity and ground provisions. Occasionally there were delicacies – fish when in season and sugar when it could be spared.

With my brother's death, something strange has happened. Aunt Maude points to it. The gates of the cages have been flung wide open and the inheritors of the President's Constitution are singing a new song. They would like the cage dwellers to leave the cages and go their own ways. They would like to have fewer cages and fewer people in them for they cannot muster buckets and ladles, still less ground provisions and electricity. The cupboard is bare, they say, and gently suggest, even on this day of the funeral, that the caged should go out and feed themselves. "Fending for yourselves is preferable," they say softly. "It means exercising your enterprising muscles. You will become fitter, more able to live in the new Maya."

But no one is listening to this shocking new understanding. It is an outrage! An error! No one is leaving the now uncovered cages; there is no movement towards their mouths though the gates are wide open.

What is it that keeps them in the dark recesses of their cages?

Is it the sudden glare of daylight? The piercing visibility of things that comes with perfect light?

The remaining Country Mayans are relieved. Perhaps their nightmare is coming to an end. Yet they must try and look sad too. The occasion requires it. Common sense and survival demand it.

Intense suspicion overwhelms the caged ones. Those they were taught to fear pass before the open gates and their shadows briefly enter the cages. The comings and goings of these shadows are confusing, even threatening, to those long caged. They don't know what it can mean and would take any meaning offered. But the President, the interpreter of shadows, of Maya's history, the giver of meanings, is not here to give them one. It has been too long. Too long on a poor diet to think for themselves. Give them time.

"Let us move on," I say to Aunt Maude. But she will not move, cradles her head in her hands. When she stirs she shakes her head. "The President's inheritors will offer them a meaning," she tells me.

"What will it be?" I ask.

She looks at me with disdain, as if I am too stupid for words and she is too tired to make the effort to enlighten me.

A group of Mayan Americans are visiting. They are among the many Americans touring the Maritime Region. This group must have heard about the end of an era, the funeral of a President for Life. They come to the mouths of the cages to see for themselves and ask about conditions inside. They are all prosperous tourists now, with soft leather handbags, binoculars and cameras, carrying foreign accents and foreign ways.

The caged despise these visitors who say in their prosperous American accents that this suffering was a result of poor management by their President. They do not wish to hear these visitors saying, "The collapse in value of your currency, and your houses and state pensions – is not something we have seen elsewhere in the Maritime Region. We have visited many, many islands, far too many," they say. "Prosperity is spreading everywhere," they add, in a matter-of-fact way. They suggest to the cage-dwellers that the flawed ideas that created this misery should be dispensed with immediately, that they are on a road to serfdom, that prosperity can be had if the strategy is right. They know many rags-to-riches stories. "America," they smile with pride, "is a land of opportunities." Their rings and bracelets, fine shoes and clothes make silent statements. They turn away, whispering amongst themselves, as they open their soft leather bags to hand out some generous charity, saying, "These poor poor things."

The caged ones gnash their teeth, pick up their banners, waving them before the visitors, stamping their feet to make their point. Their banners say:

> *The President is a political giant*
> *The President wrested the commanding heights*
> *He released the economy from grasping hands*
> *He fumigated foreign vampires*
> *We cannot replace him*

He single-handedly taught us the true meaning of independence

Aunt Maude shakes her head, for she can read from the banners the names of the men, within and without the Region, who strung these words together.

The caged ones laugh, amused. "Yes," they say, "these are all high-ranking men, highly educated men. Isn't education the light of the world?"

They can see that Aunt Maude is not impressed and is about to address them. They cover their ears and begin to shout at the visitors outside the mouth of the cages.

I try to pull Aunt Maude away. But she tugs herself from me and says she is not leaving.

From deep within a cage we hear a low moan, and then a woman emerges. She walks with dignity – and must have had great beauty in her youth, for even after a generation of service to Maya's Independence its remnants stir. She comes to the mouth of her cage, flanked on either side by other women. Together they chorus: "Lies, lies, intolerable lies. We warn you do not enter or we'll rip you apart with our bare hands like the Furies. We are the chosen, hand-picked by the President. Unlike you, we stood by him, this political giant. He warned us of the likes of you. And behold! It has come to pass. We were warned of your fabrications and distortions. Do you know what you are saying? That it has been a waste! That our very youth, our precious lives, our painful sacrifices, our deprivations, endured so long without complaining, that this life we lived was for nothing? That we've been taken advantage of? Our suffering was the indulgence of an unsound idea? That ours was an idea flawed from the start and so could not have worked in a rapidly changing world? If what you say is true, where are those upright, respectable men who allowed the ideas by which we lived to leave their mouths? Name them! Bring them here to stand before us to listen to what you are saying. No you can't. Of course you can't. Now take courage. Say it was a mistake, an error on your part. We will forget what you have just said. Now start afresh. Tell us the truth. We will be patient."

Mayan Americans look askance. A few walk away. Two women have tearful eyes. Another matronly visitor in a Salvation Army uniform comes closer to the mouth of the cage. She is warned to stay where she is, to come no nearer. Then she speaks: "We have been guided by the Light, to come here and speak these harsh truths. Leave this dark cave, my sisters, and I will show you the real world that our Heavenly Father created for us all to enjoy. In the real world, the spirit of good enterprise thrives, my daughters. You are young and you too will thrive. Come with us. Leave these cages of dependency. They are suitable for a public zoo. Leave them – a museum piece – that others may learn."

The caged ones smile and say, "We know you will sweeten your lies. The President spoke to us about all this. In his wisdom he foresaw this and told us in private that these views would be expressed when he was not here to defend himself. But we carry his torch, for he loved us in a way no one else ever has. We were always on his lips, he said; on every platform he stood upon, he thought of us, spoke of us, he said, though we were not there. The echo of his voice still vibrates within our heads. It will not die. It cannot die. We offered him our precious vitality, our youth that comes but once. It cannot, must not, be a waste. To say that is treason. High treason. We advise you to repeat it no more."

"We are suffering today. This grieving racks our spirits – and you say it need not have been. You speak of poor management, of a misunderstanding of the nature and conditions of growth of the human spirit, its imagination and creativity. You speak of a false foundation, of cheating and deception. Deny it, say it was not so, we beg you. In the name of sanity, deny it. Do you know better than the Prime Ministers of the Region? Better than our Assorted

University Luminaries? You are misled and don't know it. You are confused by grief. Again, we beg you, in the name of truth and compassion, to reconsider and admit your error of judgement. Deny what you have said. Deny it lest we lose our reason. We beg you. We promise to forgive you, to forget what has been said."

The caged ones, seeing more visitors approach, cover their ears and hear nothing. They huddle together deep in a dark corner of the cage, but after whispering among themselves they return smiling to the mouth of the cage and speak to the visitors. "If what you say is true, why could we not discern it? If what you say is true, why does the entire Region honour him so? Were they all blind? Are you the only ones with sight? May heaven forgive you for your obscene misrepresentations."

They bring out new banners, smiling confidently as they proudly hold them high.

LIES LIES COLONIAL LIES. WHEN WILL THEY CEASE?

DIVIDE AND RULE IS YOUR INTENT. WE ARE NOT FOOLED

Again more freshly made banners are brought to the mouth of the cages:

WE MOURN AN OUTSTANDING STATESMAN WHOSE CONTRIBUTION

WAS EXEMPLARY

HISTORY RECORDS HIS GREAT CONTRIBUTION

HE UNIFIED THE REGION

A MAN OF GREAT COURAGE

A MAN OF VISION

A SPIRITED DEFENDER OF THE NOBLE PRINCIPLES OF THE

UNITED NATIONS CHARTER

Again the young women point to the banners, for the names of the men they refer to as 'giants' (whom Aunt Maude calls 'political terrorists') are on the banners. These were the men who had strung those words together, men from the field of sports, regional institutions, and governments of the Maritime Region.

I was about to leave the mouth of the cage, when one of the women handed me an envelope. She smiled and waved as I found myself being lifted away, sailing in the sky. Inside the envelope I read: "If what you say is true, why was the President not charged? Why was he allowed to rule for so long? Why did the Region help him? If what you say is true, what did you do to stop him? What was it you did? We have been spectators at your game. You have had your fun. Now end it. You are not welcome here."

I allowed the paper to slip from my hand, and as it floated down I knew, given time, and provided new fear-creating lyrics were not composed, their curiosity would be aroused. They would move out from these state-owned cages; at first to stand at the mouths and stare to see the wide open spaces and receive the dawn and cool winds on their faces,and later to join in the activity of the living.

Those hewn down, sliced in two in daylight, blown to smithereens; those raped and murdered at Ica; the old man strangled at prayer; the nine year old shot in the back as he struggled with flour; the victims of jealousy, robbery, humiliation and torture, all still stalk the land seeking shelter in abandoned houses, cotton trees, unused dead-ends and unfrequented cemeteries. They walk the sugar-cane fields, jump the trenches and weep silently in the dead of night for the miracle of life denied them, for their children and their untimely deaths. They will not be comforted until they are recognised by the living. They have no mouths and yet must scream from their earth-covered silences. Do you not hear them too? Listen, they are with you. Listen, do not speak. Listen, it is their voices you hear.

Beware! There are those who will say, "We have no time for Ica, nor Hope Bridge, nor Gavin, nor Vasu, nor all the others without mouths. We have no time for all that. Rebuild! Build anew!" But if you ask them you will find that *their* wives and daughters do not sit on branches in Ica, walk its broken, rusty roof tops, nor do their mothers sit by the gates of Hope Bridge.

These ghosts without mouths are not part of official history's weave. Who will give memorial lectures in their honour? Who will honour their deaths with the dignity their lives were denied? Why have the truths of their ends been suffocated?

When I awoke I knew the time had come for me to act. I was resolved.

Aunt Maude's face was above mine. "You were asleep," she said. "The President is awake."

"I am ready," I said.

"I will go to him," she said. "It is better this way. I have told him

I will be giving him an injection in preparation for the operation tomorrow."

I followed her into the room. I held his hands.

"Good night, Maximus," I said. He handed me a note. I read:

Do not fret yourself, for even if the island sinks when I am in the hospital, the splash will not be large. Aunt Maude tells me the island is sinking fast. Mend the walls and all will be well. MEND THE WALLS. Keep the Devonish name raised high. You can do it. Do not fret. I am weary. Think not too harshly of me. I am of my time. I wanted the best, the cream of government for my people. Remember this. I am not ashamed to have used my Government to their advantage... Good night, Marguerite!

When Aunt Maude had filled her syringe, she lifted his arm gently. "This will not hurt," she said. "Jessica is here with us. This will put you to sleep, enable you to be at rest."

"Good night, Maude. I see I am in your hands again, when as a child you bathed me."

"Goodnight, Robert Augustus Devonish, President of Maya. Good night, dear boy. Rest. Be at peace. May you be at peace with your maker."

When she had injected the solution into his arm intravenously, she gave me the syringe and the empty phial to dispose of. The label read 30 millilitres potassium chloride. I removed the label.

*   *   *   *

The sinking sun came close to the horizon. I threw the syringe and phial over the sea-wall. As I walked along it, happier days with Vasu and Aasha came back to me. I stood before the wide expanse of ocean and waited for the sun to leave. When it did, it embraced the land, offering a softer shade of itself with each passing moment.

*   *   *   *

As Marguerite walked homewards, the lights of the lecture theatre came on and I was left with the sea-wall crumbling before the waves.

Again that familiar tune entered the room. *Where are the clowns, there ought to be clowns. Well... maybe next year.* I stood up when familiar Mayan faces appeared on the screen, masked, then unmasked, on colourfully painted toy horses – a merry-go-round. Round and round the horses galloped. Gradually they faded. Words unfolded, slowly moving as if on a rising escalator:

The President died in his sleep and was buried in pomp and splendour in keeping with his office and style of living. He was accompanied by his aunt, Nurse Maude and sister, Miss Marguerite Devonish; both ladies now live in Santa Maria.

Subah lives in London and is studying for a degree with the Open University. Dorothy emigrated to Santa Maria. These two women have kept up a correspondence. Dorothy has 'taken up' with a Chinese baker. With her energy and resourcefulness the business is expanding. Every now and then she comes up with ideas for a new bread. Above the bakery a sign board in her own hand says: FRESH HOMEMADE LOAVES BAKED DAILY ON THESE PREMISES.

Anil's and Carmen's marriage did survive Tara's assistance, but it was a close thing.

The eighty-five year old man at the *Palace Hotel* in Toronto has since died and his ashes were scattered over his family's rice field in Maya, by his granddaughters Utra and Rena, as he had requested.

Marguerite Devonish returned the sapphire to Meera Mistry. An enlarged colour photograph of it hangs in the exhibit room of the library.

No one knows for certain what became of Vasu Nath. Some think he went down with the island. Others believe he was helped by friendly dolphins, and picked up by a passing fisherman.

Before leaving Maya, Marguerite and Nurse Maude explained his past to him – that he had a son, Nyasa. They gave him the photograph that Aasha had wanted him to have, but overcome by what she saw of his loss of memory, thinking it kinder not to mesh his past with his present, decided not to give.

Marguerite and Nurse Maude took him to the house where Aasha danced and then to the sea-wall. They tried to persuade him to leave, explaining that the island was sinking. How much sense he made of what was said to him will never be known, but it appears that he did not wish to leave the sea-wall. It was from there that Nurse Maude and Marguerite waved to him for the last time as their helicopter lifted, and he, standing there, waved back, his clothes and hair flapping like a kite in an approaching whirlwind. Tears came as he became smaller and smaller to them, and they flew past him like migrating birds.

*   *   *   *

I left the room and entered the corridor. I heard the curator's voice. A group of visitors had gathered round him.

"Those of you who would like to see these purple masks, may do so for a small fee. Please enquire at the desk. You may wish to know that the bonded skin has been surgically removed and though the masks are safe to handle, please do not touch them, for they have become too fragile and can be easily broken. There are other exhibits in this adjoining room..."

As the group followed after him, I left the library and faced the street. A rush of cool, bracing wind refreshed me, yet as I walked away, that female voice overflowed from the hinterland and accompanied my steps.

Where are the clowns? Send in the clowns... Sure of my life. No one is there... But where are the clowns? Quick send in the clowns.... there ought to be clowns. Well... maybe next year.

The End

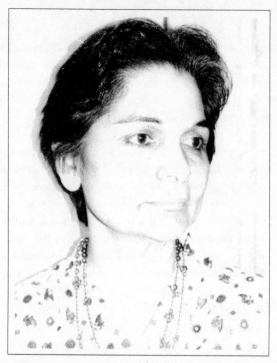

Lakshmi Persaud was born in the small village of Streatham Lodge, which was later called Pasea Village, in Tunapuna, Trinidad. She read Geography at Queen's University, Belfast and taught at Queen's College, Guyana, St. Augustine Girls High School in Trinidad and Harrison College and St. Michael's Girls School in Barbados. She now lives in London.

Her first book, *Butterfly in the Wind*, published in 1990, was praised by *The Sunday Times* as "a tremendous celebration of life" and by *The Observer* for writing of the "natural world with empathy and warmth".

Professor Kenneth Ramchand of the University of the West Indies wrote that to enter the world of her second novel, *Sastra*, published in 1993, "is like walking at night and knowing that there is no danger in the crowd, no evil in the air. And feeling that you are part of something very abstract and very physically there." Professor Mervyn Morris praised the "assurance with which *Sastra* registers inner turbulence", and *India Weekly* wrote, "There is poetry in this tale. Its delicate shadings of generational relationships gives its characters strength and durability".